I0672650

The Weaving

Part Two of

Changels Genesis

By Peter King

Peter King Publishing
Wellington, New Zealand

Edition 3
First Published 2013
ISBN-13: 978-1-927264-38-6
Fiction
Publisher and Distributor: Peter King Publishing
Wellington, New Zealand
For more information visit http://www.changels.info

ACKNOWLEDGEMENTS

My thanks to Najva Mirhashemi and Katayoun Hassall for their assistance with Farsi transliterations.

I must acknowledge the writing of Australian journalist Sharon Pincott who at the time of writing was a special guardian of the Zimbawean presidential herd of elephants. Her information about the language of Hwange game reserve was also very valuable. I commend her website sharonpincott.com and books to my readers.

I am indebted to the anonymous blogger Hadia whose Iraquigirl. blogspot provided an essential insight into Mosul during the period mentioned. Her blog (as she struggles with ISIS) continues.

I must also acknowledge a failing, and that is my rendering of Yat (as spoken by the Robinsons) is only approximate, based on Youtube videos and website guides.

SPECIAL NOTE TO READERS

A new convention is that dialogue that originates telepathically is rendered in *italics*. Telepathic exchanges do not include accents but may have some "flavouring" language to indicate who is communicating.

Changels Genesis is fact based fiction so there is a detailed fact and fiction section at the end of this book. There is also a detailed section on language at the end of this book.where a sentence in the story is factual it is marked with a dagger symbol†.

As in Initiation events in the present are told in the present tense and events in the past are told in the past or perfect tense). A boldface ellipsis seperates the narratives. e.g. ... Profanity has been included but with omitted letters.

Accents are rendered as recalled by the narrator. At first these will seem strong but this diminishes over time.

It was mine art, when I arrived and heard thee, that made gape the pine and let thee out

– **The Tempest, Act 1, scene 2**

CHAPTER FOURTEEN: IN THE BEGINNING

At eight twenty I wake up in the western side of Caz and Julia's house. Everything is in shadow, and the leaves give the place a greenish tinge. There's a lot of twittering from birds squabbling in the roof somewhere. It seems to be another fine Sunday, like the day before it.

For just a moment I panic, thinking I still have the Administration tag in my stomach. Then I remember. I'm clean. I've beaten them again and for the moment I'm safe.

I'm lying there just enjoying being safe and warm in bed when the door opens and Sue looks in. She's already dressed.

"I was just coming to wake you. Better get up if you want some breakfast."

She leaves me to get dressed which I do rather slowly. Then I go downstairs. After finding a large lounge and an office I discover the kitchen which is more or less under the room I'd been sleeping in.

The kitchen is quite a modern one. Obviously our hosts aren't lacking for money. But the main feature is the eating area which is all under a greenhouse that extends out from the house and is full of plants. It has a big, long table with benches running down it on both sides.

Sue is sitting with Julia, who has an apron on, and Caz at the far end where sun from the North beams down on them.

"You're up!" Julia remarks, getting up. "How do you like your eggs?"

Saying "Benedict" might be a tad rude, so I say "Um, scrambled thanks," instead.

Julia's a tallish, white woman with reddish-brown hair, tortoise-shell glasses and a nervous sort of smile. But I can tell at once she's not only very interested in others' problems, she also has a very stroppy streak if she needs one. Caz is Chinese, with long dark hair and high thin eyebrows and a far more relaxed smile. She seems the kind who you can rely on in a crisis. Somehow I know at once they're both lawyers.

Julia goes into the kitchen.

"I've been asking about temporary custody orders. You have to go before a judge this week and we need something concrete to propose or you'll have to go to Sir Michael or back to welfare," Sue says.

"Oh," I mumble. I hate all this adult stuff.

"I can't look after you Sam. I'm a single police officer. A judge won't like that. I can get called out anytime," she goes on.

"And you also have to get back to school ... so what I'm getting around to is that Julia and Caz have kindly offered to act as your temporary legal guardians."

"Oh ... OK," I say, pleasantly surprised.

"That means you can stay here with us for a few months. What do you think about that?" Caz asks. It's a genuine question.

"You mean until my Aunt and Grandpop come back?" I check.

"Of course," Caz smiles.

"Oh yeah ... I ... I dunno ... thanks," I say, a bit confused.

"That's OK, it's a bit much to expect you to be wildly enthusiastic about living somewhere when you've just woken up," Julia says as she comes over with some toast. There were jams and honey on the table.

"What would you like to drink?"

"Umm, apple juice please," I say, more aware of what she's thinking than what I want to drink. Julia smiles and goes back to the kitchen. I start putting some jam on some toast.

"I've been telling Julia and Caz about what you've had to overcome and how you look after people," Sue says.

"Who me?" I ask biting into the bread.

"Of course you."

"Who do I look after?" I swallow.

"Your sister, and me," Sue replies.

"Sue says you're psychic," Julia says from the kitchen.

"Ah ... yeah ... sorta," I say, not being too keen to commit myself. "It just means I feel stuff and know stuff."

"Do you see ghosts?" Julia asks.

"Sometimes. I feel them rather than see them, mostly."

"Have you felt any here?" Caz asks. She's checking something out. I could feel it.

"Uh-huh. There's a really nice one called Sarah."

Julia drops a plate. That's a shame because it had my breakfast on it. But she's staring at Sue.

Caz is looking rather shocked too, looking at me.

"Did you tell him?" Julia asks Sue.

"Tell him what?" Sue asks, a bit surprised by her reaction.

"About my ghost," Julia says.

"I didn't know you'd seen a ghost," Sue says.

"I told you about it!" Julia insists.

"When?" Sue wonders.

"Last year. Sue! You weren't really listening were you?"

"Um … well, I had a lot on my mind. Rach' was being such a bitch. I just thought you'd dreamt it."

"Dreamt it! I was wide awake," Julia insists.

Julia looks at me.

"I met Sarah last year. It was the room you're in. I found the door open and the bedside lamp on at one in the morning and found her in there sewing. I was a bit freaked out but she was very friendly. I went to the loo and when I came back there was no light and she was gone."

"Uh … yeah," I say, and then realising they expect more, "cool."

"That doesn't surprise you Sam?" Caz asks.

"No," I reply, honestly.

They seem a bit surprised by this, so I go on.

"Sarah's sweet. She likes you two too, although she's not so comfy with the lesbian thing."

Caz smiles at me like a cat.

"And what do you think of the lesbian thing."

I shrug, "nuthin' to do with me."

Julia has her back to me and is making more eggs, but calls out, "I think you might be right, Sue."

Sue smiles and looks at me.

I don't know what they're talking about and I don't really care. I'm far more interested in thinking about Sir Michael, how quickly they would catch up with me, and getting some breakfast.

"So what have you got planned for today Sue?" Caz asks.

"Umm, well, Sam and I have a lot of talking to do," she says, looking at me. "I've got a whole heap of questions after our visit to the island yesterday."

"Why don't you sit in the garden?" Caz suggests, "It looks like it'll be a great day for it."

Julia comes over with my eggs and juice for which I thank her. I'm really hungry.

"We're out this morning, but we should be back around two," Julia says.

"Unless we go to that movie," Caz reminds her.

"Unless we go to your movie," Julia agrees. "Anyway help yourself for lunch. There's a bit in the fridge, but there's a good deli just up the road. It's good if you want a change of scene."

"What about locking up?" Sue asks.

"There's a spare key on the key hook by the front door. If you're out for any time set the alarm. When you come back in you have a minute to disarm. The code is the street number, twice, backwards"

Sue and I look a bit bewildered.

"The street number is 31 so the code is 1313," Caz explains.

"It's a bit obscure …" Sue mutters.

"No it isn't," Caz disagrees with her grumpily.

"But it's as simple as we dare get. You were hungry," Julia remarks to me. "Do you want some more toast?"

"Yes please."

So I get more toast and they natter on about judges in the Youth Court, which doesn't interest me much. Mum is in the corner. She looks quite happy to see me here. Much happier than she had been when I was with Sue. But mum was always a bit easily impressed by money. I notice speckles of dust in the sunlight. Some seem to shine lilac and blue briefly, then the effect vanishes. Perhaps our friends have found me again.

I help with the dishes. It's no big deal, we always did at Renwick,

5

and then we wave as Julia and Caz drive off in their bright green Peugeot.

As they go they seem to take Sue's fake cheeriness with them.

"What are we going to do today?" I ask Sue, as we go back into the sunny kitchen.

"Relax," Sue says breathing out slowly, and sitting at the table.

"Relax?" I ask, sitting opposite.

"Yep. Relax," she nods seriously at me.

"Is that all?" I ask.

"No, you can tell me about how you got into all this shit you're in, as well."

"While you relax?" I check.

"Yep."

"And how is that going to help?" I ask doubtfully.

"Sam, you may be used to UFOs chasing after you but I'm really, really not. Seriously, I had nightmares about them all last night. I'm getting flashbacks, Sam. Just sitting here with Caz and Julia I was getting flashbacks of being in that cave with all the light and the sand pouring down in my face."

She sighs long and hard, controlling her breath, then goes on.

"I know I don't look it, Sam; you probably just see me as an adult who can help; but really, I don't know if I can cope with all this. I'm stressed to the max. I don't know what to do. I don't know what I can do. Because that's how they make me feel Sam. Totally and utterly powerless and it scares me rootless."

She stops and looks me in the eye.

"I've got post traumatic stress. I know it! I've got classic symptoms. So what I need is to relax while you talk me through this."

I can see it in her eyes too. Everything she knows and feels secure about is against her. The law, the police, her own skills, all of them seem pathetic against an alien power who can bend the laws of physics and ignore all human laws and institutions. I nod, understanding.

"So today I want to sit in the garden, smoke way too many cigarettes, and get up to speed with this whole damn thing."

I look up into her eyes again.

"You don't have to if you don't want to," I suggest.

"What do you mean?"

"I could just f___ off, out of here. I mean, I'm not doing you any damn good am I?" I admit.

Sue stares at me intensely for a second, then gets up and walks around the table behind me and puts her arms around me and hugs me tight. I love it, to be honest. It takes away my stress too. I turn on the bench and put my arms around her and I hold her for quite a while.

"Sam you saved my life. I owe it to you to at least try and help you. But you don't need to carry the whole world on your fourteen-year-old shoulders. I want to help you but I do need some time to catch up with you. I need to understand what is going on," Sue says softly.

I take a deep breath. We pull apart. She sits next to me on the bench. I'm thinking about what I can tell her.

"I know when you look at those UFOs it's like we can't touch them, but really we aren't totally powerless, Sue. That's why they haven't caught me, or any of us. They can be tricked. They can be beaten."

Sue looks at me.

"Sam, not many people are as tough as you are," she starts.

"Do I really look so tough to you?" I ask, disbelieving.

We're sitting close so I can see myself reflected in her blue eyes. I know I look young. Not a kid any more but not really an adult either. The fuzz on my face is no beard.

"You're tough on the inside," she says.

"I'm not tough," I disagree. "My dad was tough. All I do is make friends."

She smiles, then chuckles and ruffs my hair, nodding.

"You're right," she agrees. "And you're good at it."

She gets up.

"Let's just get ourselves nice and relaxed out in the sun. I'll get my fags and you tell me how you and your friends got into this."

So Sue and I get some shades, and some sun cream, and find a corner partly in the shadow of the big oak tree outside my room, with a couple of old sun chairs and take up very relaxed positions in the autumn sun. I'm pretty sure they can't see us here.

"So, so far we'd got to Renwick house, you'd got up in the night and met some of Dr Prosperov's people doing some astronomy and then you'd been chased by ghosts when you went back to bed again. Then what happened?" Sue asks.

"Well, to begin with we found out about each other," I reply.

"Yeah, OK, but what happened?"

"Uh...well, nothing really. Except ..."

"What?"

"Well, think about it. We were on the run. Just like here, say. And we suddenly find that there are five others just like us. So imagine we came here to Caz and Julia's and there were five other lesbian cops from all over the world with guys my age with them. That would be pretty weird wouldn't it?"

"Yeah, I guess it would," Sue says, rearranging the pillows

behind her back.

"And we just felt soo familiar to one another. Like we had always known each other but just never met. So when I say we got to know each other what I mean is we really wanted to know how it was that six of us, all psychic, had ended up under one roof on an island miles from anywhere. I guess we were looking for an explanation."

"Did you get one?"

I smile, "Ah, yeeah in the end. But we couldn't believe it at first. I mean what happened to us was a bit different to you. You got thrown in the deep end. We started off almost normally. What we didn't realise was that while everything looked sorta normal to begin with it was all tied together by something even bigger and weirder than a UFO chasing us."

"You aren't going to freak me out with it are you?" Sue asks, a bit worried.

"I don't think so. Just expand your horizons, so you can put that UFO experience in a bigger context.

"OK, but take it easy on me, alright?"

She settles back.

"I'll keep it relaxing. But Sue?"

She looks up at me, "Yeah?"

"This isn't small, OK? We're talking two years of this crazy, crazy stuff. You aren't going to get answers in half an hour."

"OK."

"You may not even get them all today, either. I reckon it's going to take at least a week for you to get your head around what's going on here."

"A week!?"

"Uh-huh. Most people don't have any idea what's going on on

Earth, quite apart from beyond it."

She sighs, then gets out, and lights a fag, draws heavily on it, then wriggles into her cushions.

"OK, so expand my horizons then," she says.

...

I was late up after my first night at Renwick. Aunty Liz thought I was just being lazy but when she found she couldn't rouse me she left me to sleep. When I did finally wake up I was almost surprised to discover where I was.

The previous day had been so full of change that I felt like it had been more of a dream than a reality. Thinking I might miss out on breakfast I was out of bed in no time, dressed and down the stairs. I was a bit scared of the corridor after meeting the ghost in the night and I didn't want to hang around there if I could avoid it.

I found everybody at breakfast talking loudly and generally having a good time. Aunty Liz and Rewa had kept a place for me so I went over to them.

"You're lucky there's still some left," Aunty Liz muttered.

She pointed to the counter where there was what was left of a large plate of pastries. I'd never had any before but I picked one of each of the four kinds and some orange juice from the almost empty jug and came back to the table. I'd just bitten into the long cylindrical one and been thrilled to discover it was full of chocolate when Mrs Jones stood up and clapped her hands.

"Well, when Dr Prosperov told me he'd hired a cook without tasting anything he'd made, I admit I was a bit ... surprised. But that was a very impressive bit of pastry making Mr Trân, so let's all show our appreciation in the usual way."

I would have preferred to show my appreciation by eating more, but joined in the clapping. Mr Trân was happy but a bit embarrassed and gave a nervous joke bow as if he were on a stage.

"Now we haven't got a lot of work today because we haven't any guests, but we need to start getting up to speed with our tasks. For the adults I realise that many of you are skilled people well beyond the kind of domestic skills you are initially being asked to use now, but Dr Prosperov wanted everyone to know that while we won't need your special skills in the short-term he is very sure that they will come into play later. My advice is to remember how long it took to get settled in your last job and just relax. The main thing to remember is that Dr Prosperov sees this as a collective in which everyone helps everyone else and uses their skills and training to best effect. This morning is your own time to get your households in order and make any arrangements you can make on a Sunday morning. We'll have a meeting after lunch to go through duties. Dr Prosperov will be available to talk through immigration issues."

"Children. As you'll be on holiday for the next two months now is a good time to get to know your duties. Remember we will pay you but only if you do the work. I've assigned you to teams of two and they are: Ashley and Scotty; Cam and Tarik; Tahira and Sam; Rewa and Asal. Ashley and Scotty are to help Gunter with maintenance; Cam and Tarik are to help Ken; Rewa and Asal are to help Mariko in her studio; Tahira and Sam are to help me with the house. We'll spend this morning sorting out a routine for you and this afternoon you can amuse yourselves. Any questions?"

There weren't any. I was busily scarfing my pastries because I
could tell I'd have to start working soon. I was just disappointed
I wasn't paired with Ashley or Scotty. Still Tahira was very pretty
and at least I wasn't paired with Tarik, who I was sure would get
on my nerves.

"Children? Find your supervisor. Parents do as you please. Dr
Prosperov has a business call at the moment but he'll be down
soon."

The two girls dashed to Mariko who led them away to her studio
making a huge fuss of them. I rather doubted they would be
doing much actual work. I went up to Mrs Jones and Tahira
joined us a moment later.

"Right, you two," she said, "follow me."

I had the strong feeling that this wasn't going to be a whole
lot of laughs. We cut through the kitchen and she led us to a
storeroom. Inside we found buckets, mops, cleaning liquids and
a couple of industrial-sized Dyson vacuum cleaners.

"Our first task is vacuuming. Start on level three and then work
down to level one. Do all the corridors and open areas. I'll show
you how to empty the machines and change the heads."

She made us open up the dust traps and empty them into the
waste units behind the kitchen. Then she got us to change heads.
She must have been a teacher once because she made sure we
understood every little thing. Then she stood over us as we
dragged the machines and a spare reel of power cable into the
service lift. Only when the door closed did I think she was off
our case.

Tahira, who was wearing a kind of tracksuit, said nothing in the
lift and seemed a bit shy. I wasn't sure what to say either. Then
the door opened and we dragged our gear out of the lift and on

to the floor.

"How do you want to do this?" I asked.

She smiled and shrugged, but didn't seem to want to look me in the eye.

"OK, well how about you start at this end and I start at the other end and we meet in the middle."

"OK," she said. She was very softly spoken.

I dragged my machine down the long corridor until I got to the main staircase. Luckily there was no-one, and nothing, around. I was a bit nervous about meeting the ghost I'd seen last night. Then I set about finding a power socket. A whine from the other end of the corridor told me Tahira had found one. I searched around and finally found a polished brass one, plugged in, and set to work.

Vacuuming is a pretty dull task and time seemed to drag. I decided to meet Tahira rather than go down the other corridor. It was a pretty loose partnership as she never looked up until we met in the middle. Then we went to the other corridor and did it all again. I hoped this would get easier because it was a real boring way to make ten bucks.

We finished the third floor and went down to the second. I wasn't keen to go to the stairwell by myself so I suggested we work down separate corridors. Tahira didn't have any view on that either, so two hallways were soon filled with the purr of busy vacuum cleaners rather than one. For some reason I preferred this way of working. It was sort of like an undeclared race to get to the other end. At least the competition made the time go quicker.

Suddenly Tahira screamed. It made my heart stop, and I knew at once what had happened. I was scared of it too, but I wasn't going to leave her there to face him alone. I ran along the corridor back around the old chapel, and found Tahira sitting on the floor covering her eyes. I ran up to her.

"Are you OK?" I asked.

She was cold and shaking, with tears under her hands. I crouched down next to her.

"What did you see?" I asked.

She just shook her head.

"Was it a man? a soldier? a ghost?" I asked.

She nodded and peaked out at me. Her eyes were wide with fear.

"I've seen him too," I told her, "it's awful."

There was a moment of understanding between us. We both realised we saw this sort of thing more often than most. But we were interrupted by Mrs Jones appearing in the corridor followed by Tahira's grandmother Soraya, and mother Mitra. They cried out for Tahira and Tahira cried out for them and there was a lot of tears and squawking in a language I had never heard before. Mrs Jones wasn't getting a word in edgewise. But it soon became clear that for all her begging for them to take her away Tahira's mother and grandmother's sympathy was rapidly drying up as she spoke.

Both women looked like they had once been quite glamorous but now, in addition to being a bit fatter, they had become worn down by years of tough menial work. I didn't need to speak Tahira's language to understand what was happening at all. Like Grandpop they didn't like mention of ghosts and regarded it as a way to try and get out of working. They seemed to be telling her to stop making waves and keep her fantasies to herself.

"No mind my daughter, Mrs Jones," said Mrs Khadem, "She's big actress. Big movie star."

And the two women went off talking loudly.

Tahira was looking hurt and sad in the direction of her mother and grandmother as they left. She had a very pretty pout. But Mrs Jones was studying her closely.

"I'm afraid I don't speak Farsi, Tahira," she said quietly. "What did you tell them?"

And then she spoke. Her voice was surprisingly clear with a French accent.

"I told zhem I 'av seen ghost Missers Jones. 'Orrible 'orrible ghost with no face."

"Really," Mrs Jones said evenly.

"Yes. And thees boy, ee says ee has seen 'im also," she said looking me in the eye for the first time.

I was pissed off to be called "this boy" but I was also struck that behind the Bambi act there was a will of iron.

"Did you Sam?" Mrs Jones asked.

"Well ... not just now," I conceded.

"When then?"

"Last night."

"When, last night?"

I explained about my midnight wandering. Tahira seemed to be more interested in me as I spoke. Mrs Jones showed no emotion. When I finished she looked from me to Tahira and back.

"Give me a minute," she said.

Then she walked down the hall a short way and stopped. She closed her eyes like someone about to sing. Both Tahira and I watched on in confusion. Then her eyes opened again but they were just white. We both flinched and glanced at each other, alarmed. Mrs Jones spoke loudly, but the voice was not hers, but

15

that of an old man we heard more in our heads than our ears.
"Gwirodydd, gadeal y plant hyn!"
And the force of it! It was like the old Maori ghosts I had met
back home. I was shocked.
Then she closed her eyes, and seemed to empty like a balloon,
almost as if something had seeped out of her. Her expression
relaxed and then she opened her eyes again. She seemed a bit
dizzy for a moment and then she focused on our two astonished
faces.
"There should be no more interruptions," she said in a businesslike tone. And then:
"Back to work!"
She stood there and watched me as I went down the corridor
back to my vacuum cleaner. Behind me I heard Tahira's vacuum
cleaner start up.
Mrs Jones had certainly done something, because there wasn't
even a hint of anything spooky in the whole house. In fact
the mood of the whole place seemed to have lifted. I realised
that Mrs Jones was obviously a lot more than just a bossy
housekeeper. It was kind of comforting to know she was around.
We did race each other down the corridor, into the lounge and
across to the gallery. Where before Tahira had seemed pretty,
but shy and aloof, now her eyes sparked with fun and energy
as we worked together. The competition to get power sockets
and disconnect each other in the lounge had us both giggling.
The reason was obvious. We now knew we were both the same.
We both knew the cold, skin-prickling tingle of spirits, the
knowledge they impart and the irritation it caused in others
without our sensitivity.
We raced down the stairs and competed furiously to finish our

sides of the house. Finally an hour and a half later we were finished. But Mrs Jones had other ideas and gave us bottles of brass polish and rags, showed us what to do with them, and we set off to do all the brass. We discovered there was heaps. We started on the now-empty ground floor and worked our way up to the top floor. Mrs Jones would sometimes show up for spot inspections so we couldn't afford to not polish properly or we had to go back and do it again.

But the good thing about polishing was it was quieter than vacuuming and gave us a chance to talk. We seemed to be in a comfortable little world with only the crunch of the sea on the beach to remind us where we were. I soon learned that Tahira had been quite shy about speaking English to me because she didn't think she was very good at it. I told she was fine and another barrier between us seemed to drop away.

I asked her where she was from. She told me she, and her sister Asal, were born in Tehran, the capital of Iran. But unlike most Iranians her family were not Muslims but Baha'i. She said the Baha'i were different to Muslims because they believed in equal rights for women and believed in a new prophet: Bahá ulláh. She said the mullahs and the police hated Baha'i in Iran, which was why they had to leave, although she missed it very much. She said the people were OK, it was just the Government that was bad.

I asked her where she had learned English. She said she had always learned English. Her mum had taught her and she had learned it at school in France, where they had been living last. I asked her if she spoke French as well. She said she spoke five languages: Persian; Arabic; French; English, and some German and Spanish she had learned at school. She asked me how many

I spoke. I was embarrassed to say I only spoke English and
hardly any Maori. So I asked her about ghosts.

"I have zeen zhem always."

"Since you were how old?"

"Since I can remember. And you?"

"Me too. Since I can remember," I told her. Then I thought of
something.

"Is your dad dead?"

"Yes. In Iran. Zey say ee was spy and 'ung him."

I got a very strong and very ugly impression of a man, his face
distorted in death, a knot tight about his neck, swinging on the
end of a motorised crane's long arm. The shadows of the barbed
wire on the wall behind him and big men with beards in pale
green uniforms standing around as if he were an exhibit in a
museum. I shook free of the vision and noticed Tahira looking
closely at me.

"You see him, yes?" she asked quietly.

I nodded. She looked at me with her big, beautiful, brown eyes
and then turned away to her polishing.

A tear appeared on her cheek, and she brushed it away with the
back of her hand. I pretended not to notice.

"And your fazzer?" she asked, not looking at me.

"Oh, he's alive," I said.

She nodded. I could see how much her heart ached for her dad
and I didn't want her to think she was alone in having bad things
happen to her.

"We're hiding from him," I admitted. I felt embarrassed saying
so.

"'iding from 'im? Why?" she asked. It was the last thing she
could imagine herself doing with her dad.

"He ... he just got out of prison for killing my mother," I said.

Tahira was shocked.

"'ow 'orrible!" she said, her eyes wide. She had even forgotten to polish.

Then she stared past me for a moment.

"I wondered 'oo zhat woman I saw near you was. I did not understand. Now iz clear. She iz your muzzer. So lady you are wiz?"

"She's my Aunt. My mother's older sister."

"But your fazzer. 'E seeks you, no?" she reasoned.

"Maybe. We're not sure yet."

We polished in silence for a little while.

"Do you zink we all 'av ghosts?" she asked as she finished one thing and moved on to the next.

"You mean everyone in the whole world?"

"No, ze people here. I feel many, many."

"Me too. I couldn't sleep last night."

"Me too!" she gasped. " I 'ad so many nightmares!"

We polished on for a while.

"Ashley is the same as us," I told Tahira.

"Same? I do not understand."

"She sees them too."

"Truly?" Tahira asked, surprised.

"She pointed them out to me."

Tahira thought about this but had nothing to add.

"And her dad is dead too," I added.

Tahira looked at me intently.

"Zis is no coincidence. Something strange iz happening. I know it."

I had to agree she must be right. I thought about the others.

Scotty was obviously not Bernard's son. He was white with freckles, and Bernard was dark black. Even though they were obviously close, they were not related. His father had gone over, and a woman close to Bernard had too. And Tarik. I felt his mother was definitely not on our side either.

"What do you think this is?" I asked. "I mean, it's pretty weird, eh? We all need somewhere to live at the same time, at the same place, and then this man appears and brings a bunch of strangers who have similar things in common together on this island, in his house. That is pretty strange isn't it?"

"Very strange. And zen zere is Mrs Jones. She iz no fishwife. You 'eard 'er talk to spirits and zey 'av gone."

Then I realised what was happening.

"Tahira. What if this is about us, not our parents at all! What if this Russian dude is just hiring our parents to get us all together!" I suggested.

"For what?" Tahira asked, her eyes wide.

The drama of the moment fell flat.

"I dunno," I admitted. "But think about it. Why hire my aunt or your mum? There must be dozens of others who could do their jobs. Remember Mrs Jones said 'your specialist skills won't be useful until later on'. But what skills do they have that nobody else does? My Aunt's nobody special. The only thing that really makes them all different is they all have kids with our ... ability ... who have lost a parent. It's us!"

"You zink thiz iz trap?" Tahira asked.

"It's only a trap if something bad happens I s'pose," I admitted. We swallowed that thought in silence.

"I zink we need to find out more about ozers," Tahira suggested.

I agreed. We chatted about the others for a short while, then Mrs

Jones came up and told us we were now off duty. We were about to run off but she made us carry all the cleaning stuff back down to the cupboard as well.

We went back down to the café where we found Ken, being helped by Ashley and Scotty to make coffee and tea for the adults and juices cocktails for us kids, while Mr Trân, Tarik and Cam were making pancakes with whipped butter and maple syrup for everyone.

Lunch was totally delicious. All the adults seemed to be a bit more relaxed as they had obviously been talking about their circumstances with Dr Prosperov and felt more confident. Dr Prosperov himself, however, was again not there, and Mrs Jones was chatting around like everyone else. Aunty Liz was joking with Pat Robinson and they seemed to be getting on very well. The weather was typical spring. Not quite warm enough to go swimming but not exactly cold either. After a whole morning cleaning I was keen to go outside and wondered if anyone else was too. It was Tarik who came up with the idea of exploring the old gun emplacements further around the bay. I wasn't too keen on Tarik. He was too in-your-face, but I had to admit it was an interesting idea and Scotty and Ashley wanted to go too. Mariko had to do an errand and was taking Cam, so Tahira had got roped into looking after Rewa and Asal who wanted to play girly stuff.

We set off from the kitchen back door, around the base of the pine forest behind Renwick House, following the bay. It was clear that a road had been built here once, just as one had connected Renwick with the lighthouse. The road curved around between the beach and the pine forest and then climbed up above the cliffs to the bluff on the other side of the bay. It was out of the sea breeze and the way was littered with interesting bits of driftwood, and pinecones.

I wanted to talk to Ashley about what me and Tahira had discovered about Mrs Jones but, as usual, Tarik had to be the centre of attention.

"Hey Sam, did they put landmines down around here?"

I had no idea but I didn't think so.

"Why?" I asked wondering if he'd seen one.

"Just in case. There's many on the borders where I come from, yeah?"

"I don't think they ever had landmines here," I said.

Then I added, "Those bunkers were never used. They built them to fight the Japs in World War Two, but the Yanks stopped them up north in the islands."

I suddenly realised that Ashley was a "Yank" and Mariko was a "Jap" but no-one seemed to be bothered. It was all, real old history. Ashley was looking at the sea.

We walked along for a while. Then Tarik took to whacking stones into the sea with his stick and we all started doing that for a while as we went along. The path gradually started to curve up the side of the hill. A lot of the hill's steep slopes were covered in gorse but the path, which wound through to the paddocks above, was all long grass with tall thistles here and there. Lacking any more stones we whacked the thistles which were easy to imagine being some sort of purple, alien plant.

The road passed above the small beach at the bottom of the bay. Looking down on the clear, brilliant, blue sea anyone could tell this was going to be a fantastic swimming beach come summer. The waves crashed through the narrow heads to enter the small bay Renwick House was in. This hill was much higher and much steeper than the headland on the opposite side which the lighthouse was on, so as we climbed we could see over the lighthouse (which jutted a bit further out to sea) and further north. There were more bays and an even bigger bluff with Australian blue gums on it a few bays to the north. The sea breeze that was driving the crashing waves through the heads hit us now, bracing us, but also adding slightly to the feeling of desolation that hung over this place. All you could see was coastline. Miles and miles of sea haze and rough coastline.

As we came over the crest of the hill the roof of the first concrete bunker came into sight. We ran up to explore them and found that the slope down to the ocean was quite steep with gorse everywhere. The bunkers were set into the hill, covering one another. Over to the right, where the hill climbed away, there was another building which no longer had a roof. We paused briefly by a sign which was so old and rusty you could barely read it. It warned that this was a defence area and that it could be dangerous. The only obvious danger were the odd bits of barbed wire which still stuck out of the ground from place to place. It was a sign doomed to be ignored.

We climbed down the hill and came around to the slit of the first bunker. Inside there was just a round concrete room with a rusted mount in the middle of the concrete floor. It might have held a gun once, it was impossible to tell. The floor was full of rust flakes, dirt and broken glass and it smelt damp. There was graffiti all over it.

"There's a door at the back," Scotty pointed out.

It was true. There was a rusty old metal door that was obviously built to give access into a tunnel behind the bunker. There was enough light inside to see it quite plainly. Tarik was the first in through the narrow slit to try it, but I was right behind him. He gave it a tug. Then he climbed up with his feet on the wall and pulled it with all his might.

"It's jammed," he announced.

"It's welded shut," I told him, showing the telltale welding marks on the hinges.

We climbed out of the bunker.

"Say whad if dere's an open tunnel 'round here someplace?" Ashley said.

We fanned out over the whole place searching. There were a lot of other bunkers, big and small, up and down the grassy hill. We ran uphill and down, looking inside, finding old rails embedded in the cement, smashed beer bottle glass, rusted metal things which we couldn't guess what they were for, and weeds. Altogether there were about a dozen small bunkers about four meters across, and eight medium ones about eight meters.

On top of the hill there was a large concrete slab which had no obvious purpose and two big, round, concrete holes about twenty meters across on either side, that looked like a giant cookie cutter had taken a bite out of the ground.

The holes were about three meters deep with concrete stairways on the island side. They had a circular rail and a large rusted metal bit in the middle. There were weeds growing through the concrete everywhere. These had obviously housed some big guns while the bunkers around them were to stop anyone landing to attack them. Both of the big gun emplacements had once had a tunnel that linked to the big concrete box in the middle, but both tunnels had been walled up with concrete.

"They must have kept the shells underground and fed them up to the guns through the tunnels," Scotty guessed.

We stared out to sea. There were a few islands to the north but nothing else to the horizon. It seemed mad to imagine anyone attacking this island. Why would anyone bother? There was nothing here. I was thinking back to my talk with Tahira. The words just slipped out of me, as they so often do.

"Why are we here?"

"Whaddya mean, man?" Tarik asked aggressively.

I noticed he became more annoying the less confident he was.

"Why us, and not anyone else?" I asked.

Ashley was looking at me thoughtfully through her glasses which had gone dark in the sun. So too was solemn, silent, Scotty. It was obvious they had talked about it too.

"It's cos we are the coolest," Tarik said, with fake confidence.

"He means da ghosts, Bra," said Ashley seriously, brushing her hair off her face.

Tarik looked around at us. We could see in his eyes how much fear he had been covering. He looked suddenly shocked, relieved, and a bit embarrassed all at the same time.

"You ... you guys see them also?" he asked softly.

"All of us," Scotty nodded.

"Tahira too," I added.

"We done always seen dem is mah guess," Ashley said.

"And we've all lost at least one parent," I added.

"From violence," Scotty guessed looking to the horizon. I could tell he was reading it.

"And suddenly all our guardians get jobs here. Why?" I repeated.

Tarik had been looking at us nervously in turn.

"Hey you guys are really freaky, you know that? Why not you all point at me and just say same thing like in horror movie and make me shit my pants," he suggested.

"So y'all don't think it's weird or nothing?" Ashley asked.

"Yeah, but we're here because it's better than being dead, right?" Tarik reasoned.

Ashley looked worried, and I noticed we all looked a bit haunted, and this time it wasn't by ghosts. I wondered if the others were being pursued like Rewa and me.

"So it's like we all got lucky and by whatever routes ended up here isn't it? Just coz we're alike doesn't make it a bad thing. Maybe if we weren't, we'd be dead. Like evolution, init. Survival of the bleedin' fittest. You know what I mean? Only those who can, get to make it to a place like this."

I realised then that Tarik was probably the smartest in our group. He was a smart arse, and a loud mouth, but he was quick with it too.

"So who is it you are hiding from?" Scotty asked quietly.

"Ergenekon," Tarik said quickly, as if saying the word, even on a windy hillside in the middle of nowhere, was enough to bring trouble.

And he was in huge trouble. I could tell.

"What's that?" I asked.

Tarik grinned.

"Why did I know you'd ask me that?" he said smartly.

"Dunno. Maybe you're just psychic," I replied, eyeing him.

He looked at the others. They had no more idea than I did.

"Oh OK. Let's sit down. This is going to take some time," he said.

We found a spot in an old bunker out of the wind and sat down letting the sun warm us.

As psychics we could tell so much about each other just by looking. Tarik had a huge hole where his sister and mother should be. But he was also being chased by an army of criminals who would kill him without even thinking about it.

Ashley was the same. She and her mother had fled their home, their country, and everything they knew, to escape vicious, gun toting gang members tattooed like demons. She half expected them to arrive at any moment. At the same time there was loss in her heart. Her heart ached for her father and for her destroyed home life in America.

Scotty wasn't so much looking over his shoulder as only half there. He got on with Bernard, the black man who was his guardian, but his heart was with his mother, who was still back in South Africa. She was having Bernard's baby and Scott wouldn't be happy until they were all together again.

There was something more about Scott, though. Although he was quiet he was also extremely confident. Way more than Tarik and me. He just seemed much older than the rest of us, though I didn't think he actually was.

We could tell so much about each other by reading you might think it meant we didn't need words. But strangely it meant the opposite. We could tell a lot, but it only made us hungry for the details. We felt this incredible bond between us even though we were complete strangers. We were more alike than any other group of kids I had ever met, even my family, and yet we didn't know anything about each other. So when Tarik started talking it was not the jokes and checking each other kids normally do at school. It was a hard out sesh to learn each other's stories as fast as possible so that this strong feeling we had – a feeling that we had known each other all our lives – could be matched by some real knowledge.

CHAP†ER FIF†EEN: TARIK'S S†ORY

"So you can tell I'm not English, right?" Tarik checked with us. We all shrugged and nodded.

"Well, I sort of am, coz I'm naturalised aren't I? But I was born in Turkey. But the funny fing is, I'm not Turkish neiver."

We all looked at each other, a bit confused.

"Coz what I really am is Kurdish," he announced.

That meant absolutely nothing to any of us. Tarik seemed to expect that.

"So Kurds is the biggest nation on Earth without actually having a country to call 'ome. There's about thirty to forty million of us Kurds but no Kurdistan†. Well, not officially anyway. And that's a large part of why we're on the run and 'iding out 'ere. It's pretty complicated."

He gave a bit of a sigh and looked around.

"So because we Kurds don't have official country our land is in four different countries. My dad was born in Adiyaman province in Southern Turkey, which would be Northern Kurdistan. Me mum tho', she was born in Kirkuk which is a city in Northern Iraq or what would be Southern Kurdistan. And there's Kurds in Syria and Iran which would be East and West Kurdistan."

"So because all these countries know the Kurds could rise up and make new country out of their territory they all try to keep

the Kurds down, don't they?"

He paused again to gather his thoughts.

"Course when I was li'le, growing up in Balgat in Ankara I 'ad no idea what being a Kurd was. Sure, me mum didn't speak Turkish very good, and I wasn't that good at it either, but all that meant to me was being picked on by teachers and other kids. Compared to what some Kurds go fru that was nuthin, init? I mean what's a teacher makin' you stand in the corner til you piss your pants compared to being bombed with poison gas? You know what I mean?"

That sounded pretty heavy. Tarik rubbed his nose.

"Anyway I don't remember much about livin' in Turkey anyway. I was five when we left and me li'le sister Layla was born. That was when we moved to Lunnin, weren't it?"

He stopped and looked around at the horizon.

"I hahted Lunnin at first. It seemed cold, grimy and awful, yeah? The people was all pale, stiff and arrogant and looked down at us. The ovver kids at school was rude and bullied me because I didn't speak any English jus' like Turks 'ad for not speakin' Turkish! Worse, me dad was away a lot because the company 'e worked for sent eem to different parts of the world yeah? So me mum was lonely and cried all the time."

"We wasn't poor, cos dad was making more money than he would back in Turkey, but we was pretty miserable for a few years, yeah?" he paused remembering it. Then he brightened. "But fings got betta didn't they? North Lunnin isn't such a bad place, init? And now the Turks who'd treated us badly back in Turkey treated us as friends yeah? Cos we was more alike than diff'rent. And Lunnin's got all sorts innit? So I was mixed in with kids from everywhere. A lot of me friends was black or Bangladeshi or Polish yeah? We all spoke English even if our parents wasn't so good? Even me mum got 'appier cos she found uvver Kurdish women to talk to. But she told dad never to talk politics wif 'em 'cause she needed 'em, yeah? She knew dad would always disagree with every Kurd 'e met about politics."

"From the time I was six til I was eight I lived a pretty ordinary sort of life, yeah? We wasn't poor, so we could have holidays back to Turkey to see my grandparents yeah? Me dad's muvver and farver, live in Adiyaman City in southern Turkey.

The English kids think England's old. And OK it's hundreds of years old. But Adiyaman? It's fousands of years old. I mean like dawn of bleedin' civilisation old. But there's also oil fields there, yeah? So it's got industry too. It's like weird mix of new and bloody ancient. You know what I mean? Me grandfather, Azam, and grandmother, Nesreen, spoiled us, whenever we went there, yeah? Sweets and toys an all sorts. They silversmiths and they ain't poor neivver."

"At night me dad would drink coffee and talk about politics wiv 'is dad and is uncles and cousins. I didn't understand nuffin they talked about. It was just lots of names, yeah? But those visits never lasted long. Often we flew back to Greece or Cyprus to make holiday yeah? And dad was always careful to use English passport, rather than Turkish one. Know what I mean?" he remembered happily. Then his face clouded.

"We could have stayed like that too if the Americans hadn't invaded Iraq."

"Some of us Americans would have been pretty damn happy about that too, bra" Ashley said forcefully.

Tarik looked seriously at her.

"Well, Kurds in general was very 'appy about that invasion. Americans done us a huge favour when they took out Saddam Hussein who'd done 'is best to kill my family in Iraq, so that was good. But unfortunately for my family it started a series of events which killed my muvver and li'le sister."

The hugeness of that loss hung over Tarik like the shadow of a mountain. It was so big he seemed to see it in front of him like something unbelievably big had crushed his footsteps.

"Sorry for your loss," Ashley muttered, embarrassed.

Tarik shrugged, and went on, remembering.

"Mum had told us about escaping over the border from Iraq into Turkey before she had met dad. Before that, her family had had to leave everything behind and just run. They had lived out in the cold, 'iding from Saddam Hussein's jets, yeah? She tole us about jets screaming in and blowing up families she knew. Mum 'ated Saddam Hussein because he had bombed and gassed Kurds all over Iraq. But in 2003 the Americans was bombing Iraq and sending armies in to destroy him, so mum was frilled, weren't she? She would cry and yell at TV set as Iraqi ministers pretended they would make Americans suffer. She wanted the Americans to make them to suffer like she 'ad. You know what I mean?"

"So when Bush 'ad finished and Bagdad 'ad fallen she was really

excited coz the border from Turkey into northern Iraq was
finally open yeah? It was mostly open to oil truck drivers and
supplying the Americans and Kurdish fighters, the Peshmerga,
but it was still open init? So mum really wanted to see 'er
parents, who had gone back to their 'ome in Iraq."

"Mum 'ad been so sad for so long about not being able to
go home so dad promised we go see them, right? He called
Mum's dad in Mosul and between them they fixed it with the
Talebanis."

"Say what? I thought the Taliban was in Afghanistan?"
interrupted Ashley.

"No! Not the Taliban! It's the Talebanis init? S' spelt different.
The Talebanis is a Kurdish noble family. They run northern I-
raqi Kurdistan. Anyway we flew to Ankara and bought cheap
car. We stayed a week in Adiyaman seeing dad's relatives and
making sure everyfing was alright, then we headed for Iraq."

"There's only one border crossing so we joined this 'U-mungous
queue. We waited in a line for three days, camping on side of the
road and sleepin' in the car. Then we finally drove across border
into Iraq."

"It was crazy, crazy over there. People was stealing fings from
Saddam's old Government. New Kurdish Government was
running around bossing everyone and stealin' too. But we
managed to get through to Mosul where me Grandparents – me
mother's parents this time – 'ad moved yeah? They moved after
Saddam Hussein 'ad chased them from Kirkuk."

"Mum couldn't stop crying because she was so 'appy to see them
an everyfing. Grandmother Amineh and Granddad Barham
cried and cried too when we arrived yeah? They was a bit hard
to understand at first. They speak Sorani Kurdish which is a bit

different to our Kumanji Kurdish and they mixed it with Arabic. But Sorani and Kumanji still use the same words which meant you could tell what they was talkin' about and they made a big fuss of us, didn't they? But we couldn't go out or nuffin cos it wasn't so safe. Me grandparents place was like most 'ouses there 'cause it 'ad walls 'round it with a garden at back. You know what I mean?"

"Mosul isn't some village. It's another ancient city about size of Auckland 'ere – 'bout a million people, 'cept it's flat, an' cut in 'alf by Tigris river, like London is by Thames, and of course, it's much older, yeah? The west side is mostly Arab. The east side mostly Kurd. Before Kurds was under Arab's thumb weren't they? Now it was the other way around."

"But the Americans 'ad invaded Mosul, an built a base at airport in west side. There was a funny sorta feelin' all around, yeah? Everyone was nervous, 'cause bombs had gone off near markets, yeah? Saddam himself had just been caught and nobody knew what was going to 'appen. Everyone wondered what the Americans would do and the Arabs was nervous of us Kurds and vice versa. You know what I mean? Still it made mum 'appy and that made all of us 'appy."

"For me and Layla though, life in Mosul was a bit strange, yeah? Everythin' kept runnin' out – 'cept for Americans. No end of Americans who 'ad everything, but didn't mix much with us locals, yeah? The 101st Airborne was based at airport† and they treated both Kurds and Arabs the same right? Cos all they knew was we wasn't American right? Both Arabs and Kurds was shit-scared of Americans cos they 'ad heaps of guns and seemed crazy to them. You know what I mean?"

"We kids played in the walled garden at the back and didn't go out much, yeah? But unlike the local kids we wasn't scared of the Americans, right? When we meet them we talked to them in English, and they was like, really pleased, and gave us chocolate an stuff, yeah? They laughed at my accent and I laughed at theirs but they was still real friendly like."

"All kids in area was still going to school so mum said we should too. It was 'ard coz all the lessons were in Arabic which I didn't understand at all, yeah? But the English teacher liked me an' I got to 'elp teach the other kids English while they teach me Arabic, right? That worked pretty good. Mum seemed real pleased wiv us settlin' in, yeah? She fort maybe we could stay in Iraq."

"Dad wasn't so sure. I could tell that he wondered if there was any future there. And Layla was scared and liked me to be around her, especially at night. She was only li'le. You could always 'ear the American 'elicopters and planes flyin' around, yeah? Sometimes there was explosions but they was usually a long way off."

"Mum asked us if we wanted to live in Mosul. Me and Layla didn't really, but to make her 'appy we said we did, yeah? Of course we was sure it couldn't last, and we was right init?"

"Dad was meant to be looking for contracts for 'is work but 'e found there wasn't a lot of work for 'is company in Mosul. The Iraqis, like grandfather Barham, who worked on the oilfields, knew 'ow to run their own country, yeah? But the Americans 'ad all the money and only gave it to other Americans who drove around in big new trucks pointin' and not talkin to anyone. You know what I mean? So jobs dad might 'ave got was given out in either Washington or Bagdad, right? After six weeks 'is bosses told 'im it was a good try but it was time to come 'ome, yeah?"

"So we loaded up car and drove back to Turkish border. The queue at border three kilometers long in both directions† init? Trucks was bringing supplies to Peshmerga for the Americans then returning full of fuel bought from oilfields in Iraq to sell in Turkey. It took us a day and a 'alf to get to the front of the queue. We was only car for miles."

"At border the Customs man he wants his bribe don't 'e? We was ready for that – but the Immigration man takes a look at dad's Turkish passport and goes to back office, yeah? Then 'e said something about "irregularities" an' told us to wait, didn't 'e?"

"Well, me dad didn't like that at all. He gets really nervous. He keeps sayin' there was nothing wrong wif 'is bloody passport. It 'ad got us from Britain to Turkey and into Iraq and nobody had questioned it then, you know what I mean? Then the man gets a phone call and 'is eyes turns to us. All 'e says is 'evet', 'evet', 'evet' which is 'yes', 'yes', 'yes' in Turkish right? Then he puts down the phone and says to us that everything is OK."

"I fort that was it didn't I? But dad? He didn't believe a bleedin' word of it. We was all quite 'appy to go through, wasn't we? But dad surprised us all by sayin' 'e didn't want to go to Turkey now, and that we 'ad changed our minds. This pissed this chappie right off and 'e shou'ed we was 'olding every f___ thing up and we better go through the f___ border right f___ now!"

"Dad still didn't want to go but mum couldn't see what the problem was. She wanted to stop travelling and get Layla settled, so she nagged, which she was good at. I tried to make mum agree with dad and go back to Mosul and 'er parents. I 'ad a bad feelin' in my stomach and I knew something really bad would 'appen if we went to Turkey. But my mum wasn't listening and she and the immigration man make dad go through."

"We drove for about an hour or two through city of Sirnak to highway with dad lookin' in the rear view mirror all the time. Know what I mean? He was sure we was being followed but nobody else could see anything and we reached Adiyaman a day later wivvout any problems. Mum had convinced us dad was jus' being crazy, didn't she? Dad even admitted he felt stupid, yeah?"

"So we arrive and everyone wants to hear the news and there's talking and laughing for hours. Grandma Amineh makes us loads of food and calls up 'alf the tribe to come see us, so people are coming and going all afternoon and into the evening. After dinner we kids is just goin' to bed when there's a big knock at door."

Grandad Azim answers happily, right? He's expectin 'is brother, and dad's uncle, Osman who lives in Mardin province about four hours away. But it's Turkish police."

"Uh-oh," said Scotty. Tarik nodded.

"They burst in wearing balaclavas, pointin' machine guns and waving clubs and say they is there to search the 'ouse. Then they just go mad smashing everyfing. Mum and grandma is screaming, dad and grandad is shouting. Then they shove us all down and point guns at us. They keep on searching and smashin' everything, taking away any papers they find. I was shit scared. We all was."

"After an hour they tell us they's taking Dad and Grandad. Mum and Grandma try to stop them but they hit them and march the men into cars and drive off in the night. I was so scared for dad. I already knew what happened to Kurds in Turkish police stations, didn't I? Me Mum and grandma was crying. We kids was crying. We was all bloody scared for dad and Grandad. You know what I mean?"

"Uncle Osman drives up an hour later and he calls up everyone to come and look after us. It was hours before we was all asleep. We was all together in the smashed up house, too tired to do anything and too scared to move. That night I 'ad this 'orrible dream about running fru the streets back 'ome in Lunnin. Runnin' to save me mum and Layla but everyfing was stuck in slow motion."

"The next day we spent worryin', waitin', and tidying up. Grandma was very sad that so many of her things 'ad been broken and she and mum kept chattering about everyfing. Uncle Osman organised a small army to come an 'elp cos, as they say, 'a Kurd is never alone' and Adiyaman is where our tribe is from, yeah? Many friends and neighbours came by to offer 'elp. Our tribe, the Hidisor, we got connections there, right? Some 'ad angry words for the Turkish police. These ones had connections to Kurdish resistance, the PKK who often attack Turkish police and soldiers. But others had pull wif the authorities, you know what I mean? Grandma begged the fighters not to do anything while Grandad was in a Turkish jail."

"Luckily that night Grandad came back. He looked very beaten and he even cried. Uncle Osman was very angry for his brother. Grandad told us they kept asking what he was hiding for dad and if he said nothing, they 'it 'im. His face and body was a mess of bruises and cuts. Me and Layla was scared, coz if they'd beaten old Grandad what would they do to our dad? You know what I mean? But Grandad said he had told truth, that he had nothing, and finally the police had believed it."

"It was a full week of fear before dad came back. We was so glad to see him we almost wet ourselves, didn't we? He was thinner, quieter and covered in bandages and bruises and missing a tooth, but he was alive, right? Not so many Kurds stay that way in Turkish police stations. The PKK 'ad been getting ready to do a revenge attack if dad 'ad gone missing. Mum was overjoyed. When we asked what happened to 'im he said 'e wanted to go 'ome to England. We all did didn't we? England 'as its problems but they's nothing compared to Turkey, init?"

"But me dad became different didn't he? Ee didn't laugh as much, and he seemed 'aunted by what they'd done to 'im. I could sense a rage and I didn't like what I saw in his mind. When I heard dad scream in 'is sleep I realised how bad it was for 'im in jail, right? It's not good hearing your dad scream like that. You know what I mean?"

"Back in Bri'ain he spent long hours on his compu'er, and going off on walks by himself, yeah? We didn't know what it was about. Not even me cos it was dark an cold an' 'e jus wasn't around much right? Then one evenin' in March he tol' us somefing big would be published in one of Turkey's leading papers. And sure enough he was right, wasn't he? The next day the paper named police chief of Adiyaman province as murderer of Kurdish leaders. The source of the information was a secret police report."

"The Turkish news was full of it for days. You know what I mean? One day the chief was sayin' it was lies, the next, he was suspended, then he was being questioned. The PKK was vowing vengeance. And dad? Dad seemed almost back to his old self again."

"A month later same reporter is in news again, yeah? This time it was politician who 'ad been receiving money from smuggling ring, right? A month later it was story sayin' Turkish spies was working with Israel's spies, against Syrians. And a month later again it was the news that the Turkish Kurdish Resistance, the PKK, had swindled Iraqi Kurdish group out of secret CIA money. Dad read all these stories out to us with a big smile, right? But 'e told us there was even more to come."

But a bit la'er dad comes home really worried, right? He spends ages on internet and it didn't look like 'e'd slept when we got up in the morning, yeah? It took us a few days to find out what 'ad happened init? The paper said the repor'er who 'ad written all the stories dad was so 'appy about 'ad disappeared. You know what I mean?"

"Oh no," said Scotty.

"Exactly mate," Tarik agreed.

A week la'er the phone rang late at night? Dad answered but the person on the other end said nuffink. Dad freaked out. Mum told us next day she was real worried, weren't she?"

"Immediately dad looked for work in the U.S and pretty soon had a number of offers. He was still frantic and real nervous. Mum wasn't so sure. She saw the U.S as a step up from Bri'ain, but she didn't want to be lonely again. She 'ad a good circle of Kurdish friends in Lunnin now and didn't want to lose 'em. You know what I mean?"

Tarik paused. I could tell this was a bit he found hard to talk about. He took a deep breath and went on, though his voice was higher now, as he tried not to break down.

"Then one day I was in school – I jus' knew mum and Layla was walking into danger, right? I jus' ran out of class, ignored the teacher yelling at me, out of school, and ran back 'ome. It was jus' like in me dream. I knew what was 'appening to them! The questions, the gun poin'ed at Layla. The shot. The screamin'. The shots. But I couldn't run fast enough, could I? I got to our street an' saw the car drivin' off. I got to the flat an found the door open and me mum and baby sister lying inside covered in black blood. I could see them an' they was dead."

"Oh my God! How awful!" exclaimed Ashley. She had tears in her eyes. Tarik stopped for a moment. He was on the verge of crying too. Ashley got up and went over to him and hugged him tight. We didn't really know him, but somehow everything we did know meant we knew him better than a group of strangers should. Tarik let Ashley go, and had to brush a tear or so aside, while he avoided lookin' at us guys. Then he took a deep breath and went on.

"The cops fought it was burglars didn't they? They said mum 'ad surprised 'em, and been shot. It happens a lot more in Lunnin now than it used to, yeah? They said there had been a flood of guns from Eastern Europe. But nobody had heard nuffink did they? So dad said they musta 'ad silencers, right? But burglars don't 'ave silencers, cos that's a special bit o kit, init? Only professional killers use silencers. Know what I mean? The coppers said if that was true we must be mixed up wiv the Kurdish drug gangs, so they was no 'elp at all."

"We moved outta our flat that day. Dad stopped me goin' to school. Some of me mum's friends offered to 'ide us, but dad said we 'ad to get away from anyfing to do wiv Turkey, right? He suspected informers. We had a small funeral. It was so rushed, we didn't 'av time to say goodbye or nuffin. We even 'ad to speed that up coz we noticed two men in a car watching us, didn't we? We always moved after that. Never stayed a week in the same place. Dad was always watchin' out window at night. He often fell asleep in a chair facing the door, or on the floor in my room. 'E cried a lot. So did I. I was scared an' 'ad no idea what was going on. He quit his job to keep me safe, 'e said. He took the first job he could to get out of Europe, which was in Melbourne, Australia."

"Dad wanted to be so far away. I was getting a bit scared. Know what I mean? I fought maybe me dad's crackin' up or somefing. I was missin' all me mates from school an me sister an mum too, right? Anyway we got on a plane and flew all day and all night to Australia.

"When we got a flat there dad started to tell me why we was on the run and what had been going on all my life. It took whole week to tell me so I'll try to keep it short, yeah?"

"OK, so as I said my dad grew up in Adiyaman in the 1960's, right? And back then it was pretty primitive. Lot's of goats, and donkeys; farming and not much money. But my dad was real good at school and he ended up going to the Mediterranean Institute of Technology in Ankara to study electrical engineering. He wanted to bring electricity to his parents old home, yeah?

"Now as it 'appened, the Turks were planning a huge dam project in Adiyaman. It was called the GAP scheme and it was a bunch of dams on the Euphrates river, way upstream in the mountains where it starts. It was one of the biggest hydroelectric schemes in the world and my dad worked on it, got trained for it, and spent most of his early life thinking about it. He even got to study in America and got his doctors in engineering designing somefing for that project."

"When 'e started, all 'e knew was that the big dams, like the Ataturk dam and power station he worked on, was going to make a heap more electricity for Turkey. To him that meant the lights would stay on and factories could open in the South where

41

lots of our people was really poor. Sure it would flood some of the old Kurdish lands, but goat pasture didn't pay a lot while electricity meant more industry and better payin' jobs? Know what I mean?"

"Anyway 'e thought, 'e was goin' to be a 'ero. He thought 'e would be the Kurd that brought electricity to the Kurds. Unfortunately 'e really didn't realise what a political shitstorm – that's what 'e called it – he was walking into."

"See the problem was, and still is, Turkey is run by the army. Sure there's elections and politicians but it's the army that 'as all the real power. The other problem was the army, and the whole government really, doesn't like it that most of the South is full of Kurds who'd rather 'ave their own country. So they tried to make Kurds into Turks by banning our language, customs and all that."

"We had that too, here," I told them. "When my Grandpop was a kid they used to cane anyone who spoke Maori at school."

"Yeah, well in Turkey, it wasn't just caning and it wasn't just school. The army drove people off their lands and killed anyone who resisted.

"They tried that here too," I argued. "We had wars with the British and the settlers two hundred years ago."

"What happened?" Tarik asked.

"Aw well everyone just sorta stopped, we didn't lose but we didn't exactly win either. They just stole our land using cheating laws. Now our old people argue in courts 'n stuff to get it back."

"Do they?"

"Do they what?"

"Get it back?"

"Yeah. Not all the land but there's a thing called the Waitang-i Tribunal which makes the government pay us heaps in compensation for stealin' it. It takes a long time though. It's been hundreds of years and they are still taking their sweet time paying us for what they took."

"In Turkey the courts is run by the army. Kurds never get any justice. That's why we've always fought. And that was why my dad was so different. He was a Kurd working with the Turks to build a dam on Kurdish land. That was 'ow he came to the attention of a special general called Cem Erkender."

"Cem Erkender was an army general who worked in intelligence. Dad didn't know anything about spies or nuffin cos he was an engineer, and a good one, but Cem Erkender wanted to use dad to try and get more Kurds to think more like him. He knew dad was important in the Hidisor tribe and was an elder in the Alevi religion so he tried to get him to spread the message."

"He told dad that the Kurdish resistance leader Abdullah Oculan, or Apo as everyone calls him, the leader of the PKK, had been put up to resistance by the Syrians. You see the Syrians didn't like the GAP scheme at all because it meant all the water in the Euphrates – their main river for farming – was controlled by Turkish dams. They wanted to use the Turkish Kurds to stop the dams even though they treated Syrian Kurds like shit."

"So dad tried to get the Kurds to listen to him, but they thought he was just a young fool who had been brainwashed by the Turks. They told dad about the Police attacks, and about JITEM and the Grey Wolves who murdered Kurds and never got arrested."

"What are JITEM and the Grey Wolves?" Scotty asked.

"JITEM are sort of like spies and the Grey Wolves are sort of like a gang run by the army. They aren't officially in the army but they do stuff for the army, like kill people. The police just look the other way and they never get in trouble."

"Just like the Green Bombers back in Zim," Scotty said, nodding.

"Dad says now he was a bit stupid to think all the Kurds rallied around Apo because they were being tricked. The Turks obviously weren't going to tell him about what they were really doing to the Kurds. But he got frustrated with Kurdish politicians in Ankara who had electricity but said how bad GAP was because it was destroying old Kurdish ways. He knew the young people hated living on hillsides in the old Kurdish ways. They liked the nightlife in big Turkish cities with all the electricity they wanted. Talking like grandfathers but living the young life dad calls it, yeah?"

Tarik's dad reminded me a bit of Grandpop and our Kau-ma-tua, or elders. When Grandpop was young all the young people went to Auckland to get away from the elders half the time. I found I could really relate to what Tarik was saying.

"So anyway my dad was a young Kurdish engineer who the Turks trusted, who could talk English and was friendly with General Cem Erkender. Then just as they began filling the Ataturk dam Saddam Hussein over in Iraq invaded Kuwait! So President Bush – that's old Bush, the current president's father, right? – he got the whole world to line up to fight Saddam in the first Iraq war, and that's how my dad ended up talking to the CIA."

"The CIA?" Ashley checked.

"Yeah, American spies, init?"

"What for?"

"Well they wanted the Kurds to attack Saddam from the north, while Saddam had 'is whole army ge'ing ready to fight the

Americans in the south."

"Did they?"

"Yeah, but fat lot of good it did the Kurds. After the Americans saved Kuwait, they jus' left, so Saddam stayed president of Iraq. He was so pissed off with the Kurds attacking him in the back for the Americans he sent what was left of his army to kill all the Kurds. They 'ad tanks, heavy artillery, jets, 'elicopter gunships and they used poisonous gas. The Peshmerga just had rifles†."

"What did the Americans do?" Ashley, who looked sick, wanted to know.

"Nothin'. Thousands died. Millions fled to Turkey."

"Sonovabitch f__n Bush family!" Ashley swore angrily. She looked fierce with hate. It surprised all of us. Tarik went on.

"Yeah, but there was a … whadoyacallit? A silver lining. That was how my dad met my mum."

"While it took ages for US airforce to stop Saddam's jets attacking the Kurdish refugees, at least the CIA was in Turkey helpin' the Kurds on the border. They found out grandfather Bahram was chief engineer in oilfields at Kirkuk. CIA want to know about the northern oilfields because the war in the South had left Iraq's southern oil fields on fire, right? Problem was Grandpa Bahram didn't trust Turks or the CIA, so he wouldn't talk to no-one right? To get around this Cem Erkender asked me dad to talk to him instead, yeah?"

"Dad says he got on with his future father-in-law immediately, yeah? They both understand each other's Kurdish, they both trained in America and both 'ave engineering in common. So Barham wants dad to meet 'is family. And that was how me dad met my mum init?"

"Me mum was younger than me dad and studying as best she

could in the refugee camp to be doctor. Dad says he loved the way she was tough and had big heart, yeah? She was always helping people in refugee camp. Because the Turks was not letting Iraqi Kurds out of the camps Dad brought his parents from Adiyaman to meet hers and they got on well."

"Me mum and dad took until 1992 to get married, yeah? Dad's patron Cem Erkender had to sign papers allowing mum into Turkey. So Dad in return got more and more involved in political work with the Turks and Kurds. But 'e said the deeper 'e got, the more 'e discovered just 'ow dodgy the whole Turkish government really was."

"What 'e discovered was some Turkish generals were against the CIA plan to support Kurds in Iraq. They was sure any weapons the CIA gave the Iraqi Peshmerga would end up back in the hands of PKK in Turkey to shoot Turks, right? But Cem Erkender was working with the CIA and Talebanis on other side of border. Slowly dad was learning about everything General Erkender was involved in, yeah?"

"It turned out that Erkender wasn't just a security chief, 'e was also drug and oil smuggler, working with some PKK groups and fighting others. Dad was discovering he was mixed up in a huge battle between these enormous gangs what included armed Kurds and Turks all the way to the top of the Turkish Government. It was a bit of a shock init?"

"As ordinary engineer he's trying to look the other way weren't he? But he can't escape the fact he was involved in an network which treated energy and drugs and people as a way to make money. Know what I mean?"

"People!" I asked, "how'd they sell people?"

"They smuggle people don't they? Fousands of them want to

go to Europe so Turkish smugglers take 'em. Mostly Iraqis and Iranians. I'll bet Tahira and 'er family paid a Turk to get them out of Iran into Europe didn't they?"

I realised Tahira hadn't exactly talked about that bit.

"Anyway me dad says he tried not to get involved in anything criminal yeah? But it was impossible, because General Erkender had become his friend and 'e was up to 'is neck in it. Dad says he used to ask all sorts of technical questions about selling stolen electricity to Iraqis and Syrians, yeah? He was just businessman who liked to make his own rules, yeah?"

"So then another police general like Erkender got killed in a small plane crash, didn't he? The plane was good before this general gets in but it suddenly broke up in mid-air and kills everyone†. Boom! Know what I mean? Turned out this police general had found a huge secret shipment of Turkish guns and stuff going to Iraqi Kurds so he was asking questions about it. Suspicion about who put bomb on plane got directed at the CIA or more likely, General Cem Erkender, right?"

"Then when I was like, two, 1996 right? there was a huge scandal. There was this car crash in the town of Sursuluk. Big Mercedes crashed into truck. In Mercedes was anuvver police general, a wanted criminal hitman, a famous beauty queen, and a member of parliament with several million American dollars and lots of guns in the trunk†! Fink about it. What was a politician and a police chief doing with wanted killer and his beauty queen girlfriend with so much weapons and money? 'Avin' a picnic were they? Know what I mean? The army tried to shut down the story but journalists just kept digging didn't they?"

"When the Turkish government tried to ban story from the news

47

millions of Turks protested by turning their lights out each night at set time didn't they†? Everyone wanted to know what the army, police and Government was hiding, right?"

"So it was payback yeah? The truck wasn't an accident, it was a hit. Coz Turkey's like the mafia, init? The friends of the police general killed in the air crash wanted to show up the faction Cem Erkender was in, right? And that's what Ergenekon is. They call it the government inside the government, or the deep state†. It's a bunch of politicians, generals, judges and police who run the drugs, the oil, the people smuggling, everything. They use the law to keep ordinary people in the dark, and if anyone asks too many questions, well they're dead ain't they?

"Sounds like the good 'ol U.S of A, if you ask me," Ashley said darkly.

I thought she was just being dramatic. Tarik went on.

"Anyway when I was five, you know when I started, back in 2000, Cem Erkender came to me dad one night and gives him a big box of papers, yeah? He told dad that if anyfing happened to 'im, Dad should leave country and take papers with him, yeah? The papers should be fed to journalists following up Sursulak scandal, right? Erkender said it would help bring light to Turkish politics and show who was really behind PKK."

"Me dad was surprised that he was trusted with this stuff but Erkender said dad was probably the only honest man he knew. Know what I mean? So he was only one he could trust to do as he was asked for the good of Turkey and the Kurds, if things got really bad, right?"

"Six months later Cem, his girlfriend and his bodyguard was all shot dead. Dad just knew we wasn't safe. Without protection from a General he was sure it was only a matter of time before someone would come after us, yeah? So we moved to London, England when I was five like I told you."

"But how'd all that get your mum and sister shot?" asked Ashley.

Tarik said nothing for a while. Then he sighed.

"Cem Erkender's enemies knew he had an archive and they chase down everyone who could 'ave it, right? That's why dad was on the watch list when he crosses border from Iraq, yeah? When they arrested dad after the trip to Iraq there was 'ardly anyone else left."

Tarik looked a bit troubled. I could feel he wasn't sure about what he thought of what came next. He still missed his mum so much. He looked down. His voice, normally quite loud was suddenly quiet.

"Dad said they did things to him, no man should 'ave to suffer. They threatened 'im, and us, 'is kids, but he convinced them 'e didn't 'ave archive so they let him go."

He sighed and looked out to sea again.

"He's told me so many times how he wished he hadn't started feeding information to that journalist. It cost three lives. The journalist, mum and Layla. If he hadn't wanted revenge, they would never have come looking in Lunnin. He says it's the biggest mistake of 'is life."

Tarik sniffed.

"Have to agree wiv that," he added.

Then he sighed and took a deep breath, wiped his eyes and went on in a louder voice.

"So I ... um ... we moved to Melbourne yeah? We lived there for a year – which was good right? I like it there – there weren't too many uvver Kurds so it was 'arder for them to sneak up on us, init?"

"But last week I noticed there was two guys in car following me to school. They called out in Kurmanji and when I looked up, they sped away, didn't they? I knew they was the same ones what killed mum, right? Then after school I saw them waitin' outside so I go through the back gate. When I got near home I saw them waiting outside again, yeah? Luckily my friend invited me to his place so I stayed there until they was gone, yeah?"

"When I told me dad, he got real scared again. He called the coppers who came pretty quick. I had to describe them, but what could I say? Guys our colour, wearin' leavver jackets driving old BMWs is pretty common in Melbourne, yeah? Cos it's got so many different people in it, right?"

"Next day me dad drove me to school. That was OK init? But after school dad was at work weren't 'e? So I stuck wiv the ovver kids out of the gate, yeah? But when I was walking 'ome I saw the same car again, didn't I? This time I ducked into a shop, and hid til dad got 'ome. When we got inside we found the flat was all messed up, right?"

"Dad was nervous as 'ell. He called the cops again. They came. They said they would put a special patrol in area if we was worried, yeah? Dad was worried, right? We slept in same room and dad had a bat with him, though what good that would be against a gun with a silencer I didn't know."

"Next morning we hid at home with nuffink to do but read. I found this ad in the Melbourne Age. It was looking for an electrical engineer to work in New Zealan' on a special project. Dad rang the man and they talked. The man said the job was his if he could fly to New Zealand that night. So yesterday night we packed our bags and flew here. Dad met Dr Prosperov in the morning and he gave him the job.

"What about that meeting at the hotel?" I asked

"That was for New Zealand Immigration. He had to be able to prove that there was't anyone from this country to do the job," Tarik said.

I was surprised and said that was the first time we'd met Prosperov. Ashley was the same.

"Well, maybe dat's your story, but in our case, dat was the first time we'd ever seen Dr Prosperov," she said speaking for herself and her mum. We all looked at Scotty.

"We're like Tarik. We weren't recruited here either," Scotty said.

"So what's your story then?" Tarik half challenged Scotty.

CHAPTER SIXTEEN: SCOTTY'S STORY

Well, moi father was a beet different to yours, bra. He didn't get into trouble by accident, hey? Agh, more loike he went looking for it on purpose! Of course, I deedn't know that when I was small either. I just thought he was some kind of bloody superhero."

"You see I grew up with my family miles from anywhere in the bush in a part of Zimbabwe called Tsho-lo-tsho, near the border with Botswana. It's a place of red dust, scrub and trees under this huge, blue sky. The nearest city, Bulawayo, which we call Skies, has a population of one and a half million – a bit like Auckland – but it was over three hours away on broken-down pot-holed roads."

He looked at us and read what we were thinking.

"You probably don't even know where Zimbabwe is, so I'll make it easy for you."

He picked up a bit of old broken concrete and began to scratch a kind of map in the dirt with it.

"South Africa is the upside-down triangle country at the bottom of the African continent. North of that on the left or Atlantic Ocean side is Namibia which is dry and full of deserts. On the right side is Mozambique on the Indian Ocean which is very green with lots of forests."

"In the middle, north of South Africa, is Botswana and Zimbabwe, here and here. Botswana is on the left side where the Kalihari desert is, and Zimbabwe is between Botswana and Mozambique."

"So at the bottom is South Africa. And going from left to right, dry to wet, is Namibia and Botswana, then Zimbabwe and Mozambique."

Then he scratched out more of Zimbabwe, talking as he did so. "Zimbabwe is sort of diamond-shaped, which come to think of it makes sense because there are lots of diamonds there. On the top, left side of Zim, over here, is Zambia. The Zambezi river, which is our border with Zambia, runs around the top half of the diamond. It goes over the big Victoria falls here, in the west or far left hand corner, then flows around the north eastern side into lake Karitiba which is another big hydro lake. Then it curls around the top corner and flows around our hills into Mozambique."

"Opposite on the bottom right side of the diamond is the border with South Africa where the Limpopo river is. You may remember the Elephant Child calls it 'great gray green and greasy'. That also flows into Mozambique. But the bottom left side is Tsholotsho where I was born. It has no rivers. This is our border with Botswana and it is long and dry where our game ranch was."

"What's a game ranch?" I asked.

"It's like a game reserve except you hunt the animals."

"You mean like real lions and tigers and stuff," I asked, amazed to think anyone would have animals like that outside their house.

"Lions, yes some, but tigers come from India, so no tigers. We had leopards though, the odd Cheetah family, hyenas, hunting dogs, elephants – no end of elephants – buffalo, giraffes, zebra. No hippos, but we did have rhinos."

"But people could shoot them?" Ashley asked.

"Yes, that was the whole point."

Ashley must have looked upset.

"Well, someone's got to hunt them. Because, I'll tell you what, if you don't, animals like elephants take over and they become a bloody nuisance."

His accent became more obvious as he put emphasis on words. I found that rather funny. Elephants, a nuisance! Like ants, or mice.

"Look at it this way, if your family totally depended on what they grew and a herd of elephants ate it all in one night, you'd be pretty browned off I can tell you," he told us.

I couldn't help it. There was just something funny about elephants.

"But couldn't they just fence them out or something," Ashley asked.

"No, not over hundreds of miles. Fences might stop sheep but stopping elephants is hard. You've probably never seen an angry elephant. They weigh five tonnes each† and a herd of a dozen or two can smash almost anything. I saw a family of eight smash up a car once and they flattened it. And when there's a drought on you can't expect them to ignore human crops and stand around waiting to starve to death either. They aren't stupid."

Scotty seemed a bit pissed off that we weren't taking his elephants seriously.

"But do you have to kill them?" Ashley persisted.

"Yes and better we hunt them selectively and shoot them quickly than let poachers shoot them indiscriminately and let them die slowly. Fairer for an animal to have a fighting chance than be killed in some slaughterhouse by a robot."

"But what sort of chance have they got against a man with a gun?" Ashley argued.

"More than anything we ate for lunch, that's for sure. It's not safe to hunt wild animals you know. They can still kill us."

I had to agree with him there. Grandpop hunted bush pigs and it was way fairer than when pigs went squealing on a truck to the slaughterhouse.

Scotty paused for a moment, trying to think of a way to make us understand, then began again.

"What you have to understand is that Africa is not tame. It's

55

a place where there's always violence because nature is really violent and you can't watch hyenas tearing an antelope apart and think otherwise. Killing isn't unnatural because it is completely natural. You know what kills what, and you also know a lot of animals can kill you pretty quick, too."

"So when you're small, like I was, you look up to your parents to protect you. Back then, my father, Alan Highborough, seemed like he was ten foot tall. He always carried a point three seven five hunting rifle and a holstered point forty five revolver on his hip and nobody messed him around. Everyone was scared of him because he was so tough. He had been a Selous Scout – the toughest soldiers in the world – back when Zimbabwe was Rhodesia, when the government and everything was run by us whites, and he wasn't scared of anyone."

"When I was five, he gave me my first gun and showed me how to use it. It was a BB and he was very proud of me when I used it to shoot a snake in the storehouse. It made the cook happy too. Of course the cook, Dingani, was his name, was Ndebele. There were some whites in our area but you could easily go for a week without seeing any. My best friends were Thabo, David, Melusi and Musa whose parents either worked for us or like Thabo, lived nearby."

"Of course to my dad all blacks, Ndebele or Shona, were staff. Even though Robert Mugabe, the president, and the rest of the government were mostly black. To him being white meant being privileged and anyone who didn't like it could talk to his fist. He used to tell me you had to show everyone who was the baas. That was what he had learned from his father – the great white hunter Grandpa Robert."

I could feel Ashley recoil, like she was listening to the enemy.

But Scotty just told it because it was a fact, not because he agreed with it.

"My dad was old fashioned like that. He was born in 1955 and as he told it to me, life then was one big, long, happy, boys' own adventure full of safaris, swimming and faithful black bearers with huge picnic lunches. It was what he tried to create for me I guess. But he was the only one who couldn't see it was all over. Even when I was five I could see the world my dad wanted for me lived in his mind, more than in the real world around me."

"My mum is very different. For a start Mum was seven years younger than dad. Her family, the Applebys, come from Harare where her dad Sir Geoffrey is a judge and her mum, Constance, a housewife. In the days of Rhodesia he was against white rule and wanted democracy. So the two families were very different. Mum was the spoiled daughter of a judge, who was a bit of a tomboy, while dad was raised to be a tough guy by his father, who was the ultimate tough guy."

"You might wonder how they met at all. It was all because my mother trained as a geologist. She was working for the Government Mineral Company which licences all mining in Zimbabwe† when she met dad in a bar in the bush. At that time my dad was working with his father as a hunter, stocking game ranches with rhinos."

"It was a business that was taking off in Zimbabwe at the time†. Cattle ranches weren't doing well, so people were hiring the old hunters to catch rhinos – which is not easy. You have a little dart gun but the drugs take a couple of minutes to take effect, plus rhino hide is so tough and the dart guns so weak that you have to get to within 15 yards to make the bloody things work. So if anything goes wrong at best the rhino hears you or smells you

– two things rhinos are very good at – they gap it, and you have to spend another couple of hours stalking them again. At worst, you get a two-tonne rhino charging you and that is not good for your health. "

"Anyway, it was during this time that dad and mum met. They said they couldn't help noticing each other because there were so few white people there. Mum was based in Tsholotsho which was a couple of hours drive from Hwange National Park where dad was working, but he drove over in his beaten-up landrover on a regular basis to woo her. Mum said she couldn't resist him because he was so good looking and so much more manly than any of the other guys."

"Maybe they should have spent longer getting to know each other. Mum told me she certainly had no idea of the bad things dad had gathered from his past as a mercenary."

"What's a mercenary then?" asked Tarik.

"A soldier who works for money instead of a country. My father left Rhodesia when it became Zimbabwe and went to South Africa. That was when he worked as a mercenary until he was wounded. Then he went back to hunting. He was working for Bernard who was a senior ranger at Hwange when he met my mum. Mum said she didn't see any of the warning signs because, as the daughter of a judge, she never thought anything bad could ever happen to her."

"The way mum tells it, there were no problems at first. They were in love and excited by the ranch they were creating. Within two years it was up and running, and making good money. They spent a lot of time in the bush together, dad stalking animals and guiding guests, and mum doing a geological survey of the ranch. But all the time around them the situation in Zim was getting more of a big hunna hunna."

"Hunna hunna?" I asked.

"A problem," he translated, then went on.

"I only remember the 2000 elections very vaguely, although they turned out to be very important later on. I was only six and there was a lot of excitement with mum and dad driving people to places to get their votes counted. All I knew was everyone hated President Mugabe and the election was about stopping him."

"I didn't really understand why everyone hated the president. All I knew was he was talking about taking our ranch away because we were white. But that didn't explain why all the black people in the area hated him too. I knew it had something to do with a new political party called the MDC, which stood for the Movement for Democratic Change, and because Mugabe always cheated in elections, but I didn't understand what was going on until much later. For me, my world was my friends, the ranch and my parents."

"But as I got older I slowly began to realise everything around me was falling apart. My parents spent days at a time not talking, or fighting. The school I went to was spending more time closed, and even when it was open things like chalk and paper were hard to get. Roads were never fixed. Everything that used to work, slowly stopped. And my mum said laws my grandfather had spent his lifetime arguing over were being replaced by the Government, who wanted to steal everything for themselves."

"Finally, when I was eight my parents were told the government was going to take over our house and it wasn't going to pay them anything because the British Government hadn't paid Zimbabwe compensation as agreed. A local politician named Jason

Takunda boasted to my father he was going to own our ranch in another year and there was nothing he could do about it. Mum called her father, who had a share in the ranch, but he said it was hard to know if the law meant anything anymore. My dad's drinking just got worse after that – and he went around drunk and armed, scaring everyone."

Scotty paused for a moment, weighing up what he was going to say. He felt both ashamed and uncertain what to say. Nobody interrupted. He decided he had to tell.

"I am ashamed to say that one of the things my mother had overlooked about my dad was that he drank too much. He would go out dopping and come back stupid quite often. Sometimes he was cheerful and fun but other times he was mean. He hit mum too. It was one of the things mum turned to her black friends for help with. Being beaten was something they all had experience with. It's something many Zimbabwean women know about."

"Bernard was one of the few people who could talk to him. He worked for the Wildlife Service at Hwange National Park then. He still hired my dad and his father Grandpa Robert because they were some of the best hunters. Bernard could talk sense to my dad when he went off to the local bush bars to doppo. Bernard tolerated it and would sometimes see dad safely home. But Bernard's visits were rare and sometimes dad was gone for days at a time – and not because he was guiding guests. It made me and mum feel sad. I sometimes felt more at home in the houses of my friends than I did in my own."

"At that time Bernard was married to Busani, although they had no children. I only met her later. They say opposites attract and Busani was definitely the opposite of Bernard. Where Bernard is patient, Busani isn't. Where Bernard cares more about balance and knowledge, Busani was ambitious and liked power. Bernard says it should have been obvious that beautiful Busani only saw him as a stepping-stone to greater things but he says love made him blind to her ambitions."

"About four years ago things started to get bad. Jason Takunda's gangs started to harass our workers as well as mum and dad. The police didn't want to hear when mum called them, and had clearly been told not to interfere. Even mum's dad couldn't get past all the lies, political influence and thuggery of Harare to get anything changed. Jason Takunda would show up and start telling workers that they worked for him, although they never saw any pay from him. Dad tried to see off the gangs and once or twice fired over their heads. But all that did was get him a visit from the police who told him to surrender his rifles. He complained bitterly and after a lot of negotiation he was allowed to keep a few."

"The gang, was headed by a one-eyed thug named Simbarachi Sibenda. They scared me because they drank a lot and carried big, sharp Pangas – which is a big machete. They set up a camp inside the ranch and stole things from the house and the workers. Anyone who crossed them was liable to be beaten-up. They liked to make gestures of cutting throats at me when they saw me. It gave me nightmares where I saw our house burning down. But if they scared mum and me, they didn't scare dad. They were still a bit scared of him because he was like a lion with a thorn in his paw."

"So instead of fighting my dad they started jeering and taunting him. It didn't seem to do much more than annoy him, but one of the things they taunted my mum with, hurt her more than any physical thing they could have done. They shouted out at her about Dad's girlfriends at 'The Sizwe' bar down the road."

"Those girls were already famous in the area for two things. They'd do anything for money and they had HIV. As you probably know HIV is a disease which causes Aids. There is no cure and is usually passed on when people have sex without a condom."

Me and Tarik snorted. I didn't really know what a condom was, although my cousin, Clive carried one in his wallet and he'd shown me the packet. I don't think he ever used it, though some girls in our class knew what to do with them.

"Oh grow up," Ashley told us angrily, "Aids ain't funny."

There was an awkward silence.

"No it isn't," Scotty said filling the pause gently. "If you've seen it, you don't forget it."

"You shure don't," Ashley agreed, and although Ashley had been looking at Scott like he had horns, this small point of agreement made her side with him. Scotty went on.

"Aids is everywhere in the world but nowhere like it is in Southern Africa†. In some places everyone has it. Even the babies are born with it. Some kids know they are going to die before they've even wondered what they might do when they grow up. And the disease is slow and cruel."

"You got that damn straight," Ashley said bitterly. Scotty went on.

"At first you don't know you are infected, only later does it open the door to other diseases we can usually resist like Karposi's Sarcoma which gives you sores and blotches on your skin. Then you grow slim, waste away and finally die. It's very slow."

I had to confess it didn't sound very funny at all – and I couldn't help but think of the injustice of kids having it.

"Back in the eighties when it started people in southern Africa didn't know what to do. Many thought it was caused by witchcraft. There's still a lot of witchcraft all over Africa. There are many Sangoma – they used to be called witch doctors – and they can do some pretty spooky things some of them. Others thought it was a plot by the West to wipe out black people. There was no treatment then and many people died, as much because they gave up the will to live. Aids isn't the reason for Zimbabwe's problems but with so many sick, so many widowed and orphaned, it doesn't help people stay hopeful for the future. Anyway in southern Africa Aids is no joke."

"Finally one day mum confronted dad. They argued bitterly and dad drove off in his truck. Mum cried and the gang jeered. Sibenda made various threats to mum which scared us both a lot. We spent a worried few hours until sundown with the gang outside the house drinking, throwing stones and breaking things. Then just as it looked like they had worked themselves up to break in, dad came back."

"He was furious, but just for once he wasn't drunk and they all were. He leapt out of his truck brandishing his hunting rifle and told the gang to clear off. One man waved a Panga swearing at dad. Dad brought the sight to his eye and shot the thing clear out of the guy's hand, breaking it. Now they were all shouting at him. Sibanda had a pistol and pointed it at dad, and dad aimed straight back at him with his point 375 hunting rifle. I remember dad yelling. 'I hope you're prepared to die taking this place because I'm prepared to die stopping you.'"

We all held our breath. I didn't want to look, but I couldn't stop myself. I knew what a point 375 H&H could do to a gazelle and I didn't want to see it happen to a man's head. Fortunately it didn't come to that. It wasn't a fair contest. If Sibanda was a war veteran like he said he certainly wasn't a front line soldier, while by comparison it was obvious dad could pick a fly off a rhino at a hundred yards. For a moment there was a stand-off then Sibanda made a comment to his gang and laughing and jeering they all retreated back to their camp."

"I knew things were bad because mum and dad didn't hug when the gang went away. Dad just told us to get some sleep while he kept watch. The sun set blood red that night. It felt like it was setting on our family and on our entire race. In the morning we knew there would be hell to pay."

"The police came the next day in two trucks and arrested dad. He couldn't fight them. They had automatic weapons and the whole army to back them up if he resisted. Dad argued he was protecting his family and property. They said he was drunk and a public menace and kicked and beat him. The gang jeered him and abused us. They moved into the house and took what they wanted, and smashed anything they felt like smashing. Mum and I ran down the road to Thabo's house where they took us in. Six hours later we came back to find the house a total mess with shit smeared around the kitchen."

"We went to Skies to find dad was in hospital. The police had given him a bad hiding. Mum talked quietly with the doctor for a while and he said he would do what he could. Back at home we had to put up with Sibenda's victory party which went on for two nights and three days. We managed to gather what we could when everyone was sleeping their nights off."

"We moved into a hut owned by my friend Thabo's dad. All the locals were furious with Sibenda. They may not have had much income when my dad ran things but now it looked like they'd

end up with nothing at all. Jason Takunda came around to the
house paying the men and then ordering them to clean up.
Of course the problem was that without any knowledge none
of these guys was going to make a cent out of a tourist ranch.
Takunda even visited us in an attempt to persuade mum to work
for him. Mum wasn't interested."

"A week later we went back to Bulawayo and discovered dad had
been told he had HIV/Aids. We all had to have tests. Mum to see
if she had caught it from dad, and me because I could have been
born with it. I wasn't, and mum was clear too."

"At that time it was hard to get around. The problem was there
was a bad shortage of petrol throughout the whole country and
the combination of big motors and bad roads meant we went
through a lot every time we went anywhere. Mum started going
off with a few trusted friends out for long walks through our
game ranch.

There wasn't much else to do. Takunda may have had possession
of the house but he had no papers because mum's dad said
his occupation was illegal. So there was a stand-off. Takunda
couldn't do anything and neither could we. That suited Sibanda
and his drunken crew who sat around drinking, fighting and
breaking things."

"The most unpleasant surprise was when Takunda showed up
with Bernard Khumalo. The two of them went for a long walk and
then parted with a handshake. Mum was appalled that Bernard
seemed ready to deal with the man who had kicked us out of
our home. They had known each other a long time and I think,
even then, liked each other. A few days later Bernard came to
visit mum, and they went for a long walk. Bernard looked very
uncomfortable and in the end mum came back in tears."

"A few weeks later Bernard and Bisani moved into our old house. Bisani was thrilled. Bernard was embarrassed. However he explained to me one day that whether you agreed with Takunda or not, someone had to manage the ranch, and it was better him than Sibanda."

"I liked Bernard. He's a patient and careful man. He was brought up by a Catholic nun named Patience Nkomo and he took her name to heart. He'd become a botanist because he knew there was more to Zimbabwe's plants than science knew and he had the same quiet, observant way of working as my mum, the rock hound geologist. So from Bernard taking over the ranch to take care of it, made sense."

"Unfortunately Bisani's view was that she had now become a Memsahib and should swan around ordering her staff to do menial tasks. She tried it on with my mum but Zoe had been raised a real Memsahib and simply told Bisani to stop making a fool of herself because that era was over."

"But as 2004 came it looked like mum was wrong. Now the economy was falling apart. People who worked for the Government – like our teachers or game wardens – weren't being paid†. Prices were insane. Even sweets were hundreds of dollars†. It was getting impossible for anyone to make ends meet. A lot of our money had been taken up getting dad out of jail. We'd had to pay court costs, lawyers, Government fees, and simple bribes. Dad's father Robert had spent a lot of money on him too."

"Dad had been sentenced to three months because they hadn't been able to find a charge which carried any more, but what with the delays he ended up spending six months in prison before he was released. When he came out, he was a wreck. The stress of

prison, the beatings and bad treatment combined with the lack
of food and light had weakened him badly and the virus had
taken advantage and struck hard. He was slim and weak, with
an ugly sore on his neck. He gave me a hug and told me he was
proud of me, but he had to turn away coughing."

"Grandpa Robert took dad home with him to South Africa.
Mum said we would stay to reclaim the ranch when her father
Geoffrey, finally got a hearing to get Takunda off our land. I
don't know if she believed her own words or not. I'd come to
believe that she had simply run out of other ideas and was
hanging around because we had nowhere else to go."

"It felt like all Zimbabwe was a wounded animal. It limped
along, hurt, but it refused to die. School was pointless. The
books were vanishing, there was no paper and the teachers were
always having stop-work meetings. Those of us who still went
spent our time playing games in the dust, but increasingly few
went. Families needed every available pair of hands to make
enough money to put food on the table."

"Mum was even forced to get work from Bernard. Bisani when
she was there, lay about and tried to make her act like her maid.
Mum did what was asked of her because it was Bisani's spite
that made her dangerous to us. She and Bernard argued about
the way Bisani treated mum. Bisani accused Bernard of wanting
mum the way white men had taken advantage of their black
maids in the days of Rhodesia, but that was to bring Bernard
down to her own level. Bernard liked my mum because they
were both careful observing people, but that was all."

"I'm a bit confused here because I'm not exactly sure what was
going on either. It all came down to the politics in Mugabe's
party ZANU-PF. You see the guy who was taking over our

ranch, Joseph Takunda, was part of a group in ZANU-PF that backed a powerful politician called Emmerson Mnangagwa. The important thing about him is he is not from the Zezeru clan like all Mugabe's other Ministers in ZANU-PF but he had become really high up in Mugabe's government[†]."

"Takunda was working hard for Mnangagwa in the ZANU-PF party in the Matabelelands where we lived. You see in Zimbabwe there are three peoples. The Shona, who come from the North around Harare. The Ndebele who come from the South in the Matabelelands who are related to the Zulus in South Africa, and all the rest: the whites, Chinese, Indians and others who came with the British."

"ZANU was the Shona party which had been the Zinla army in the war against the Rhodesian Army back before 1980. They were backed by the Chinese. The Ndebele party used to be ZAPU, which was originally headed by Joshua Nkomo and ran an army called Zipra which were backed by the Russians. Nkomo and Mugabe hated each other and even during the war with the Rhodesian Army Zipra and Zinla sometimes fought each other too. So when the Rhodesians stopped fighting in 1980 and asked the British to run elections ZANU won because Shona outnumbered Ndebele three to one."

"But instead of giving up their guns, like they were meant to, Zinla stayed in the bush. So the new President, Robert Mugabe, joined his army with what was left of the old Rhodesian Army, got some of his troops trained by the North Koreans, and sent them into the Matabelelands to hunt down Zinla. This was when Bernard became an orphan because Five Brigade didn't just fight Zipra soldiers and ZANU leaders. They also murdered thousands and thousands of Ndebele people as well as any whites that got in the way. They say 200,000 people died in the Matabelelands then†. ZAPU was effectively destroyed and its leader, Joshua Nkomo, ended up hiding in Britain. Then Mugabe tried to create a one party state like China by merging ZANU and ZAPU into ZANU-PF."

"This was what the 2000 elections were really about. Mugabe wanted Zimbabwe to have only one political party– his: ZANU-PF, and make him president for life. Luckily after twenty years of lies and bad government enough people didn't believe Zimbabwe's problems were all because of us whites. Ndebele and Shona and Whites and others all joined the Movement for Democratic Change to stop Mugabe, the way the MDC in Zambia, just over the border, had kicked out their old dictator, Kenneth Kaunda†."

"So Jason Takunda belonged to ZANU-PF in a part of Zim where everyone always voted MDC. But that didn't matter because when it came to votes for vice president in the ZANU-PF Party what counted was party branches, not the number of members they had in them. A branch in the South where we lived might only have two members but it counted the same as one in the North with thousands. If Mnangagwa gathered the support of enough branches he could topple the current vice-President!"

"So Takunda was playing the bigshot and Bisani was impressed. The result was he hired her as his secretary which meant that she had to travel around the district on ZANU-PF business. Sometimes she had to stay in Skies overnight. Nobody was surprised when Bernard discovered she had not bothered to get a separate room to Takunda."

"So during that hot, rainy season (which is November to April) we would sometimes have what mum called 'Bisani Storms'

69

when she would sweep in, flash lightning threats and pour resolutions down on empty meetings in old halls which would do nothing for the people living there who were just trying to find something to eat."

"Because while this was going on there was no rain. Waterholes dried, rivers ran low. Farms were failing and food was getting hard to come by. Everyone would talk about, or pray for, or sing for, rain. Everyone would gather around lonely Bernard to take his mind off Bisani. There were rain parties at our old house and the last ones to leave was always me and mum."

"Through June and July, which is the cooler time, Bisani was working like a mad thing. Then in August she won! Takunda had delivered Mnangagwa victory. Under party rules Mnangagwa was a shoo-in for vice president! Should Mugabe die – which given Mugabe was over eighty was not impossible – Mnangagwa would be President and Takunda would be his right hand man. There was a big party I heard about where Bisani got drunk and was kissing Takunda like Bernard didn't exist."

"Then came the big shock. At a crucial ZANU Party meeting in Skies Solomon Mujuru the Army commander took aim at Mnangagwa. Quick as a wink Mugabe changed the ZANU-PFs rules so that a woman must be vice president. Before Mnangagwa even knew what was happening Joyce Mujuru, Solomon's wife and a very tough customer herself, was being sworn in for the job†. Mnangagwa's faction fell apart as the Mujurus and their friends went around making life tough for anyone opposed to them."

"And this is where it all came to a head. Ditching Mnangagwa like the back stabber he was, Takunda offered to let some Chinese "friends" of Joyce Mujuru take as much rhino horn as "his man" Bernard Khumalo could find for them. Bernard was outraged. His whole reason for taking on the job had been to stop rhino poaching and now to save his political skin Takunda had cashed that promise in. Bernard refused."

"Bisani screamed at him for most of a day. Then Takunda showed up with his Chinese guest and half a dozen bodyguards in mirror sunglasses armed with AK47s. Bernard was told to find rhinos or he'd find himself buried alive in an ant's nest. That wasn't a joke either. They meant he'd be eaten alive. I saw Bernard on that truck as they went out. I have never seen a person look so miserable."

"They shot thirty rhinos that day. You know an AK-47 was designed to kill people. It doesn't kill big animals cleanly like a point 375. They take hours to die. The guest however was in a hurry and didn't want to wait so they sawed the horns out of the rhinos while they were still alive. They didn't bother with the calves because they didn't have horns. Bisani hoped to go with Takunda and sneered at Bernard but Takunda's jeep drove straight past her. She chased after Takunda on foot but he left her in the dust. Then she went inside and drank and screamed at Bernard until she fell asleep."

"Bernard came to our place that night. When he came to the door he was shaking. He fell into mum's arms and just cried. Our neighbours came to visit and took me away for the night. In the morning when I came back they looked a bit embarrassed but I knew what had happened. Their friendship had become love."

"We're moving back to the house," Mum told me when she hugged me that morning.

"Bernard threw Bisani and all her belongings out in the dusty

road. She'd hardened his heart with the insults she'd poured
on him and he took no nonsense. He literally carried her out
kicking and screaming. Lying in the dust she screamed the worst
swearwords at him and called him many names. She even threw
her shoes at us, but in the end she collapsed in tears in the road,
and nobody came to comfort her. She hobbled off looking for a
lift."

"The rest of Zimbabwe was falling apart. New money was being
printed in Harare every day with extra zeros on the end. We had
billion dollar notes that couldn't buy you anything†. Prices were
getting ridiculous and wages couldn't keep up with them. The
drought was terrible†. The farms which had been taken over by
veterans were failing, and there was a serious food shortage†.
People were crossing the borders into Botswana, Zambia and
South Africa in enormous numbers†. But mum and Bernard
were an oasis of calm and happiness."

"I had never seen mum so happy. Bernard seemed to glow with
happiness. We went on walks to see what we could do for the
wildlife who were suffering both from lack of water and from the
increase in poaching. Of course our neighbours made no secret
that they were taking wild meat – nyama – from the ranch. We
couldn't stop them and given the price of food we didn't blame
them either. But it was during these walks Mum revealed to us
her special secret. She had found a diamond deposit."

"Mum had always suspected diamonds because it was the same
geologically as the area where diamonds were found across the
border in Botswana. But the problem with diamonds is that raw
ones are difficult to sell these days unless you can certify their
origin. And trading in something so valuable with people who
don't mind bending the rules can not only be dangerous but

deadly. The chance of a murder investigation is pretty slim. So we were sitting on top of enormous wealth but we were terrified to do anything about it in case it brought us trouble."

"Unfortunately our peace couldn't last. Six weeks later Bisani was back and she had Simbarachi Sibenda and an even bigger gang than before. They arrived at night in a couple of stukkend old trucks and lit torches and sang before they attacked. Fortunately I had dreamt of this night many times before. I'd warned mum and Bernard and convinced them to keep packs ready in case we had to leave suddenly. We were out of the house and heading into the bush before they even started pouring in, waving their Pangas and torching the house."

"I couldn't help turning to watch my first and only home burn and I was spotted. I hadn't imagined the depths of Bisani's anger or Sibenda's bitterness. They had their men mount up their trucks and chase us. Now we were running for our lives through the dark with most dangerous animals on Earth – men – roaring and screaming after us. I've never been so scared."

"But we had one enormous advantage. We knew the land and they didn't. We ended up hiding in a hollow tree where they stood no chance of finding us. They drove around for an hour doing us the huge favour of scaring away all the dangerous animals for miles around before they returned to watch the house burn to the ground."

"The loss of the house shocked me more than the loss of my father. Even when it had been occupied by Bisani the knowledge the house was there had always been my anchor. I felt more alone even than Bernard or mum – who had known other houses and at least had each other. But we had to gap it now because in the morning the trucks would make it easy for them to catch us. We decided to make for mum's diamond deposit for one last shot at gathering some valuables before we escaped to South Africa."

"We set off moving carefully through the bush. We covered about eight kilometers which in the dark is pretty good going. It was a cold night too so the best way to keep warm was to keep moving. I was exhausted when we finally reached Mum's secret spot just before dawn."

"Mum's diamond mine was in a crevice in the ground near what had probably once been a stream but was now at best a damp bit of ground. We holed up in a semi-cave that was out of sight and rested there. It was a good place. It was hard for leopards or lions to get at and out of sight of wildebeest."

"We slept curled up together as the sun came up and warmed the day. At ten we were woken up by gunfire and engines. Bernard snuck out for a recky and came back to say the veterans were driving around shooting things. They had to be drunk because nobody would waste valuable petrol like that if they weren't. Once again the amount of noise they were making told us exactly where they were so we didn't need to worry about them. For breakfast we ate some fruit loaf mum had packed."

"After a while there was a loud bang in the distance and the sound of the truck stopped. Then there was a lot of distant shouting followed by a blast of machine gun fire. I knew they'd shot the driver. I was glad I didn't have to see that. Then there was quiet so we settled down to work our diamond mine."

"Mum had brought a couple of rock hammers and we started work on a layer she showed us. At first it seemed like boring hard work chipping away rocks and dust. Raw diamonds look a bit like splashes of glass in the hard rock. Most of them are yellow but clear ones are the best. She had already got all the easy ones so we had to do a lot of digging as the sun warmed the air around us. Every now and again one of us would take a look around either because our arms were sore or we had to use the bush toilet."

"There was a troop of baboons not too far away but apart from that the forest was mostly quiet and dusty. After three hours we had smashed out our first diamonds. Most of them were pretty small and dirty so they were hard to tell from other rocks but when you hit them with the hammer you could feel the strength in them."

"We worked for the rest of the day digging up the precious rocks. They looked like a handful of broken glass. Bernard slipped away with the rifle leaving us with the revolver. He was out looking for something we could eat or drink."

"While he was out mum told me the reason she was sick in the morning. She was going to have a baby. Bernard's baby. I was going to have a brother or sister. I couldn't help thinking then that being stuck in the bush running for your life was not a good place for mum to be pregnant. But she was less worried. She had spent a lot of time around Ndebele women and she was pretty sure she could carry the baby into South Africa."

When Bernard came back he only had bad news. There was no game and no water either. Worse it looked like the veterans had set up camp and were planning to stay in the area for some time."

"We dug all day living on the small amount of food we'd brought with us. By sundown mum estimated we had about 500,000 American dollars worth of raw diamonds. It was more money than we would make any other way but that didn't make it any easier. More to the point we'd need a lot more than that to get set up in South Africa. From all we'd heard it was not a fun place to be poor in. But Bernard was worried about mum now. She hadn't had much to eat or drink and he decided that if we didn't move soon we would be less able to move later. So we camped a second night in the open without a fire."

"Unfortunately this time there was no veterans to scare the animals away. The night was made busy by a family of Hyenas and a lion who were fighting over something – probably the dead driver."

"The next day we set off for Hwange Game Reserve where Bernard used to work. The Park HQ was a long way. We knew the vague direction but had no compass. It would be easy to end up in Botswana and not even know it. As we walked we couldn't help noticing how dry it was and how few animals there were. I found I had a pretty good sense of direction and just seemed to know my way to Hwange. So after a days walk we had put about twenty kilometers between ourselves and the house and were closing with the southern borders of the national park."

"At about four in the afternoon we had the good luck to find a small herd of Duiker deer. Bernard went out alone and twenty minutes later the sound of the rifle put birds to flight. Five minutes later Bernard was back with a little deer over his shoulders dripping blood where he'd got it in the chest."

"The deer weighed about sixteen kilos which doubled the load Bernard was carrying. He didn't want to butcher it while there was still good daylight to walk in so he gave me the rifle to carry seeing mum was already carrying a lot and I wasn't and we walked on.'

"Our order of march was Bernard first, me next and mum at the back. We hadn't been walking more than fifteen minutes when something made me look around. A lion was sniffing the blood, stalking us no more than thirty meters away. Our eyes locked. I think I made a noise."

"You shouldn't ever look into the eyes of a lion. They go from being pretty much like lazy cats to ruthless killers in an instant. His eyes held mine and then he silently charged.

"It must have been my father. I don't know what it was but I suddenly felt like something was guiding me. I had handled a rifle before. I knew where the safety catch was and how to work the bolt. There was no time to do anything but aim the thing as this huge golden shape ran at us."

"It was all in slow motion. My mother screamed and fell to the side. Bernard turned behind me. The lion roared this stunning roar and leapt at me. I fired and fell over partly from the recoil and partly from being off balance. The lion fell sideways with a strange gasp."

"But he wasn't finished yet. Bernard bent for the rifle and the lion gathered for a desperate last leap when there was another bang and he recoiled back, stricken. Mum had shot him with the revolver. Now Bernard quickly picked up the rifle and shot him one last time through the head. He was definitely dead."

"I got up. My heart was pounding madly. We slowly went forward to look at him. The first thing we noticed was that he had already been wounded before. He had a wound on his side which had gone bad. My shot had hit him in the chest, probably the lung. It would have killed him pretty soon anyway. Mum's had hit him in the back behind the neck. Bernard's had gone into his brain."

"We felt sad about killing a lion but he would have eaten us and

we had no choice. Bernard said I had done well and I deserved
to carry the rifle. We all knew killing a lion is a traditional
test for young Africans entering manhood. Technically I was
a man, now. But it made me feel strange. Like somehow the
Highborough part of me had come out even though I had kind of
let go of him. We all felt haunted by my father, even though he
wasn't dead then."

"Bernard decided to butcher the deer on the same spot so we
could leave the leftovers to the scavengers in the same place as
the dead lion. We gutted and beheaded the deer, which wasn't
easy with only bush knives, but kept the carcass intact because
it was easier for Bernard to carry that way. Then we walked on
until almost sunset and found a place to make a camp."

'The only way we humans can survive in the wild is because of
fire. But of course a fire, while it keeps you warm, cooks your
meat and keeps predators away, also makes a plume of smoke
that tells anyone in the area where you are. The veterans might
see it and find us. On the other hand Bernard didn't want to
sneak onto the game reserve because he didn't want us to look
like poachers. So we made a fire and slowly cooked the deer on
sticks."

"It was another two days before we got picked up in the park.
Then we had to wait again. It was interesting to see the park at
work and I noticed Bernard obviously regretted leaving it. At the
same time the staff complained that they were being paid at old
civil service rates while the cost of everything was ten times what
it used to be. They were only there because they loved what they
did. The boss, Mr Mbeke, told Bernard he couldn't hire him back
and even if he was allowed to, he couldn't pay him. They had a
long talk about the political situation especially as it related to

the rhinos and the elephants which were a special worry because of the poaching."

"We decided to leave the rifle at the park because we wouldn't need it in Harare at the Appleby's house but we kept the revolver which mum had in her pack. We all agreed that if anyone might need it most it was mum. Eventually we got a ride in a truck to Skies."

"Skies was a mess. There was almost nothing to buy in the shops and people didn't know what to do. Mum went to the bank and came back very depressed because all her savings weren't worth a can of beans. And I mean a can of beans was millions of dollars. That was if there had been a can of beans to buy – which there wasn't."

"The next day we paid a ridiculous amount of money to get on a Kombi to Harare. It was an unpleasant ride because it was crowded. Some were rude about us being white and it was worse when they realised mum and Bernard were together. Bernard tried to calm things down but mum was just rude back. It was a long day."

"In Harare we were met by Grandad who took us home. Grandma Constance had done her best to look after us but it was obvious that even with their lekker house in Avondale the shortages and the collapse of the Zimbabwean dollar was hurting them too. I was surprised how well Bernard and Sir Geoffrey got on. I think he could see Bernard was everything my dad wasn't."

"It turned out there was a black market for raw diamonds which were being smuggled into South Africa. They paid in American dollars which was the only money anyone trusted anymore. My Grandad was not hopeful in his outlook for Zim. He said people were pouring across the borders especially into South Africa and he advised mum to get out completely. He was the one who said that New Zealand was taking Zimbabweans until the end of the year and if he were young and not so attached to the place that would be where he would go. He said South Africans were getting antsy about Zimbabweans – especially the poor ones."

"Neither mum nor Bernard were sure about New Zealand. It seemed a long way away and as they were a qualified game warden and geologist they felt sure that they had a better chance of finding work in South Africa than in some far off islands halfway around the world."

"But the first trick was to get out. Bernard learned from some friends that it was possible to get South African passports for a few hundred Rand from the South African embassy†. Sir Geoffrey kept on about New Zealand and finally convinced mum and Bernard to at least fill in the forms. He said having a back-up plan never hurt."

"During this time we lived on mum's diamonds. There was a black market for nearly everything and diamonds of course always get a good price because the South African diamond corporation, De Beers, make sure they do. Thanks to Grandad mum had actually prospected the diamonds completely legally as they had obtained prospecting rights for the ranch when they bought it. But the law was becoming a slippery thing now as various ministers changed it to make themselves rich. Although officially Bisani and Sarawachi were squatters or trespassers, the ranch itself was a concession, still officially part of the Park, and the government wasn't going to let mum get the land back."

"But news travels and although the Government Minerals Company was meant to be stamping out the back market in diamonds the collapse in the Zimbabwean dollar meant that the pay that the officials got for a year wouldn't cover a week's groceries. So the officials were as much a part of the black market as the street dealers. It wasn't too long before some of mum's former colleagues had started to make the connection between mum and the diamonds Bernard was bringing to the market."

"Now I should probably explain something about diamonds. Diamonds have been at behind a number of wars in Africa. Namibia – where my father was a mercenary – is full of diamonds. In some places they're just lying around on the ground with the landmines. So in the days when the Russians were helping various black liberation movements, wars of liberation were being fought between South Africa and various rebel leaders. But underneath it all was control of the diamonds. Whoever had control of the diamonds could buy weapons and soldiers and set themselves up as 'president for life'."

"This didn't stop just because the whites were driven out of Government. There have been civil wars in various countries funded by these so-called blood diamonds. Now don't get me wrong, wars over rocks are stupid, but De Beers realised they could cash in by branding these stones "blood" or "conflict diamonds" and convincing the South African government to set up the Kimberly process to certify diamonds so that they had to be proved not to come from war zones. This meant their South African diamonds had more value and made all other African diamonds suspect."

"The problem is Zimbabwe's government is making a joke of the whole thing. Zimbabwe has always had diamonds just like South Africa. And Zimbabwean diamonds are not conflict diamonds.

But Solomon Mujuru, Robert Mugabe's right hand man and husband of the vice president Joyce Mujuru, has been running the Zimbabwean army as a mercenary force in the civil war up north in the Democratic Republic of Congo. His payment was access to rain forest timber and of course the diamonds from the DRC†. These diamonds are as bloody as they get but Mujuru brought them into Zimbabwe and had them classed as Zimbabwe diamonds. "

"So while our plan had simply been to try and get out of the country with what little we could salvage from having our ranch stolen by ZANU-PF thugs we were accidentally finding our way into one of the ugliest businesses in Africa."

"It wasn't too long before Bernard began to get nervous about the diamonds. Men in mirror sunglasses followed him and he had to be quick to give them the slip. Then cars started parking outside the house and we began to get the clear idea that we were being sized up for some kind of raid. Technically they needed a search warrant and to get a warrant from a judge to search the house of another judge was never going to be easy. However it wasn't long before Grandad began to hear through the grapevine that he was being fitted up for some kind of charge of plotting against the President. This would be an excuse to pressure mum and Bernard into giving away the location of the diamond deposits."

"Then in August Mum and Bernard made a decision that I had long expected. We were leaving for South Africa. We didn't pack anything much. We didn't have much to pack. It was a surprise trip. We crowded into a Kombi minivan with ten seats and sixteen passengers and rode for ten hours back to Bulawayo. There we stayed with an old orphanage friend of Bernard's named Patrick, his wife Grace, and his family. They were very kind and even though food was becoming quite scarce shared what they had with us. They wouldn't hear of payment but mum left them a diamond anyway."

"The next day it was another stuffed Kombi ride to Breitbridge."

"There were tens of thousands of people there all trying to get out. Many had already got to South Africa but been kicked out again. The queue was miles long and the South African officials were working in slow motion even though they would collect a handsome bribe from anyone who realistically expected to cross. Without a bribe passports were examined closely for 'irregularities' which vanished if the right sort of 'visa' – meaning Rand or US dollars – were tucked inside. "

"But waiting wasn't much of an option either. Conditions on the Zimbabwean side were bad. It was hot. There was hardly any food, little water, and of course no sewerage system so it stunk and people were getting sick. Babies cried and so did some adults. People were sick, hungry, tired, and desperate. The going rate for a guide to get you across the border was 200 Rand† and the soldiers on the other side wanted 100 Rand each and a patrol could have five or six each and there was no guarantee you mightn't meet more than one patrol. Most people simply didn't have that kind of money."

"Mum and Bernard were better equipped to deal with these situations than most and they didn't look that happy either. It didn't help that mum felt so sick all the time. We took two days to organise a crossing."

"The crossing guide was a bent old woman. She was reputed to be the best and cost extra. She knew the river bank better than anyone and only took small groups of ten or so and guaranteed to only meet one patrol who she had a deal with. The Limpopo was very low but there had been cases of flatties getting people as they blundered about in the dark.

"Flat tyres?" I asked.

"Crocodiles. We call them flatties. One man had been killed by a lion. And of course the South Africans were not to be trusted. Some would take your money, and then rob you, or hand you over so they sent you back to Zim as well."

"The old woman, whose name was Melusi, had seven with her the night we crossed. Other guides took dozens at a time but she said they were stupid and greedy. A small group always had a better chance of getting through. Bernard had to talk her out of charging more for us being white. She said white people at night were too easy to see. My dad who'd spent years sneaking up on black fighters in the bush obviously hadn't had that problem. She probably just wanted extra because she thought we had it. I think Bernard talked a lot but paid more as well. "

"I thought the main problem with the crossing was being eaten alive by flies as we snuck through the long grass. We all joked they were the real border guards and they took their bribes in blood. But they really were painful."

"The patrol that was waiting seemed a bit nervous. Their eyes flicked over me and mum and you could tell they wanted extra for whites as well. The guide went off with the patrol leader. She came back. First you must pay extra and second we must get moving they are going to start a sweep soon."

"We were in the bush illegally at the mercy of nervous men with guns. Of course we paid. Then, with surprising speed for someone so old, the guide led us away from the area. A bit later they fired flares that cast a red light over the whole place. We heard helicopters and motors as a line of Cassipirs – the big armoured trucks the South Africans have – with lines of soldiers behind them began moving forward. There were shouts and even shots in the distance. We were glad we were not in that roundup."

"Our guide took us to a hotel where our lack of baggage and our fresh South African passports were not questioned. The only thing that surprised them was Bernard and mum being together. And of course we had to pay again."

"The next day we woke up in South Africa. We didn't feel safe yet however and along with some of our fellow refugees got a Kombi South, heading for Johannesburg. I guess it was only then that I started to realise how backward Zim was. South Africa has its problems, believe me, but when you've lived most of your life in a country where nothing works and everyone is trying to rip everyone else off, seeing a country that works at all is a bit of an eye-opener."

"South Africa is a big country and it took us a couple of days to get to Jo-burg. And when we got there we damn near decided to come home again. It's a big city and agh, it's a tough place! The crime is bad and nobody likes Zimbaweans, black or white. Everyone's armed and the houses have every kind of security on them."

"Mum called Grandpa Robert and went to see my dad. She was pretty upset when he dropped her back. Dad was almost dead but he'd become bitter and mean rather than accepting fate. He said she'd driven him to the girls he'd caught Aids from and hadn't tried to help him when he was in jail. Grandpa Robert had been polite enough with Bernard when Bernard had been paying him but now he'd retreated into the past and called him a 'bloody useless munt'. Grandpa was bitter with his own wife for leaving him and detested his youngest son Ted who he called 'an english faggot'."

"Mum and Bernard decided to cash in the diamonds. At least in South Africa their money wasn't losing its value with each passing minute. Still, it was tricky to find a buyer who wouldn't rob them or try and rip them off. They met a few unpleasant people. Finally they settled on a guy named LeCreu who was a diamond trader who dealt in diamonds from Botswana but wasn't too fussy about stones that came from neighbouring Zimbabwe or Namibia. Like everyone else he wanted to know exactly where they came from but all mum would give him was the prospecting authority number she and dad had got when they first set up the ranch."

"The money from the diamonds was enough to set us up in a part of Jo-burg called Spring, which is well off but not really expensive. It was the first time I'd lived in a suburb and it felt really weird. There were houses all around us and no animals. I felt kind of hemmed in and I wasn't sure if I liked city life. We rented a house because we didn't know where mum or Bernard would find work. While they looked for work I had to go to school."

"I hadn't done any school work for years. Mum had kept me reading and doing basic maths so I wasn't too bad with that. But I hadn't ever written anything and I hated it. It didn't help that the teachers were grumpy and saw me as white trash."

I noticed Ashley's face had softened a lot as Scotty told his story and now she even seemed quite sympathetic. But Scotty had more to say.

"It turned out that neither Bernard nor mum could find any

work they were qualified to do. Bernard could have his pick of junior jobs on game reserves but the senior ones were locked up in a bit of a clique he wasn't part of. It probably didn't help that he would get no support from Grandpa Robert. He ended up having to compete with thousands of other Zimbabweans and South Africans for jobs like gardening which paid poorly."

"Mum got a little bit of work mostly as a secretary but she wasn't enjoying herself either. They stuck at it for a few months but it was obvious neither of them was doing what they were good at or wanted to do. They started to fight a bit. Mum was worried Bernard would desert her like Alan had, but he never showed any sign of that, and when they weren't worrying about the future we had a lot of fun together."

"In October I spotted an ad in the paper which seemed weird. It read as if it was written for Bernard and mum. They wanted a game warden and a geologist. It was a live-in job. The only problem it was in New Zealand. We called Dr Prosperov and he said the job was theirs if they could get to New Zealand."

"Mum rang the Embassy and discovered that the entry visas her father had pressed them to get in their Zimbabwean passports would expire at the end of the year and after that the special entry conditions were over and we'd be locked out. The big problem was mum was now too pregnant to fly. No airline would take her. The only way they would let us in was if her family moved over and she came to join us. The next problem was that mum was still technically married to dad. He would have to agree to a divorce and the last time she'd seen him it was clear she was in no mood to do her any favours."

"Then we had some luck. Dad died. That probably sounds pretty harsh but to be honest I'd lost any special feelings I might have had for him long before."

"I must be one of the few kids who went to his mum's wedding in the morning and his dad's funeral in the afternoon. Neither event was very grand. The funeral was sad and depressing with hardly anyone else there and Grandpa Robert looking angry and bitter. The wedding was a queue in a registry office where a clerk chewed bubble gum and waited for them to sign things."

"But none of that mattered. Now Mum, me and Bernard were officially a family and Dr Prosperov was still keen. Bernard wasn't keen to leave mum in South Africa by herself but my grandmother, Constance, crossed the border to come and stay with her until the baby was born."

So a few days ago Bernard and I got on a plane and flew to Argentina. We spent one night there then flew to Auckland. Like Tarik we had a fairly good idea we would get the job before we got here but Bernard was a bit disappointed the job didn't really need a geologist and a game warden at all. But having come so far and given all the other things we were looking for were right – well, we signed up like everyone else," he finished.

"Mate!" said Tarik, who sat up having been lying on his back with his arm over his eyes for the last fifteen minutes. "I gotta say that's a pretty crazy story too. So what about you dude?" he said to me.

"Mine's nothing special," I told them. And after their stories I meant it.

"Bra, this ain't no competition," Ashley said. "We's jus' chewin' the fat an learnin' about each other. So Sam, what brung you here?"

It was really strange to have three psychics just like me, looking at me. You just couldn't hide. Every thought, every feeling they picked up almost as you had them. I started to realise why the others had talked so much. You couldn't help it. You just wanted to tell them everything clearly and in your own words so you could keep control of your story and keep it your own.

So I started to tell my story, pretty much as it was. I didn't add much in and just kept to the main points so I was a bit surprised about all the questions they asked. I suppose a lot of stuff that they didn't know about I took for granted. They were interested in the stuff about the history of our tribe – some of which I didn't know, about the gangs – especially, and just about the country generally.

Halfway through there was a sound of a helicopter taking off behind us. A minute later Dr Prosperov's chopper was clattering over us and heading along the Eastern beaches. We wondered where Ken was going and whether Dr Prosperov was aboard. As the machine headed away we returned to my story and five minutes later it was all over.

We all turned to Ashley who bit her lip.

CHAPTER SEVENTEEN: ASHLEY'S STORY

Well dis is kinda weird 'cause my story is like a mix of y'alls? Ah got gangs an' drugs like Sam an' Tarik, and ah got a war like Tarik an' Scott. But me an' my mom, we're also like Sam an' his folks, coz we only heard about dis place today, so ah gotta say it's all real strange," she said.

We had no idea of where she was going so we just let her talk. I was just glad I wasn't the centre of attention any more.

"So I 'spose ah gotta back up some and start wid why we ended up on a plane to New Zealan'? Widdout no luggage and no idea of what we was gonna do when we got here. And dat goes way back! Back a'fore Katrina to when my momma was a girl like me in the 70s," she said thinking it out.

"So ah grew up in da same neighbourhood as my mom, which is Bywater in da nineth ward o' New Orlins."

"Where's New Orleans?" Scott asked.

Ashley looked at him like he was joking, but then she looked at me and Tarik, and realised we didn't know either.

"OK, y'all know where Louisiana is?" she checked.

We looked at each other. Nope.

"But you know where the United States is, right?" she asked gently, wondering if we were truly ignorant.

That we did.

"OK, so Louisiana? It's like in da South? So you got like da Gulf of Mexico an' da Caribbean Sea?" she said drawing it in the air," an it's like between Texas here, an' Florida which is da hanging down bit dere. Y'all know where Cape Canaveral is where Nasa launch da rockets?"

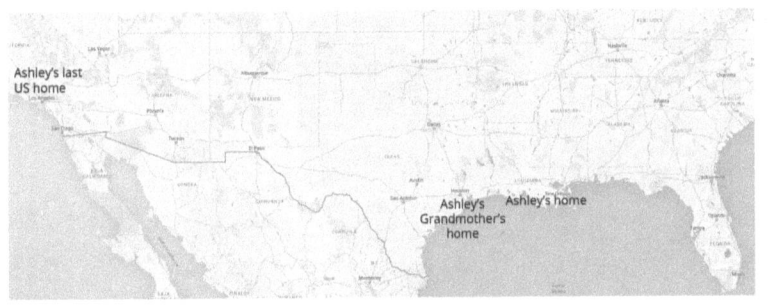

map data © Google 2016

"What's the population?" Tarik asked.

"Of Louisiana? Oh 'bout four million. New Orlins 450 thousand a'fore Hurricane Katrina anyhow. Now, ah dunno? But ah guess a whole lot less."

"Is it!" said Scott surprised.

"Whaat?" Ashley asked.

"New Orleans is even smaller than Skies!" Scott said,

"And Louisiana's the same size as New Zealand!" I added.

"That's less people than Ankara where I was born, init?" Tarik said, surprised.

It was a strange turning point in Ashley's story for us. Before I think we had all thought because she was American she must be used to everything being much, much bigger and shinier than we could imagine. Now it seemed smaller, more human-sized and somehow more real.

"Yeah, you right! Louisiana's not a real big state," Ashley agreed. "But o' course it's just one state in da United States. It's not like crossing the state line into Texas is dat bigga deal, an' Texas is ...

well … it's as big as Texas!"

There was a pause as she collected her thoughts.

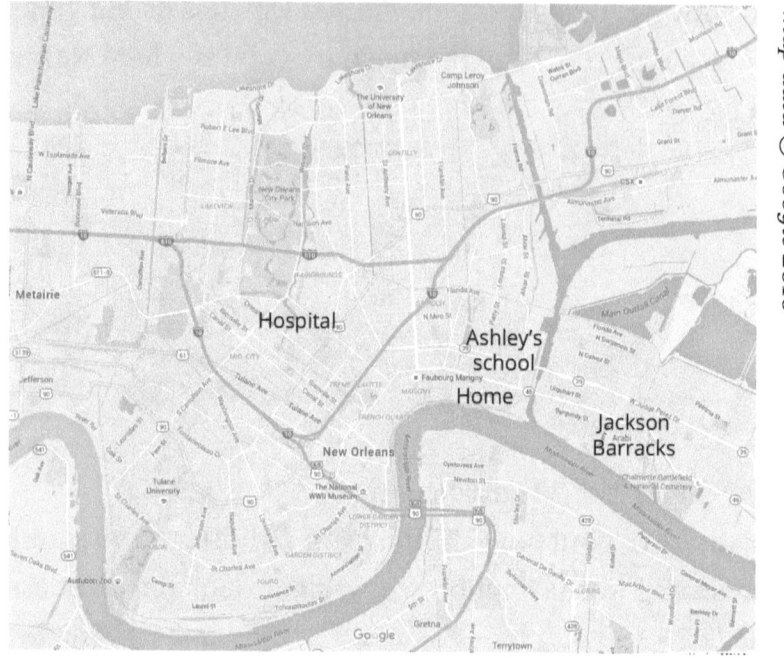

map data © Google 2016

"Anyways … where was ah? Oh yeah, da Bywater! So Bywater is on da river – dat's da Mississippi River – an' it has a big ol canal out to da sea. It's a mixed-up sorta place? Mosta da houses are made outta wood, jus' like here, an' cheap. So dere's a whole lot a workers, but dere's also artists an' musicians, an' da Navy has a place nearby too. Dere's always somethin' happenin'. People sat out on their porches at night cos it's usually warm but it wasn't a rich place or nothin. Dere was always crime an' you gotta watch your back."

"Why do you say 'was'?" Tarik asked scratching his nose.

"Ah'll come to dat later."

"Was it mostly a black area?" Scott asked.

Ashley looked at him, and I think she read that Scott asked

because he felt more at home in what he imagined a black area was, than because he had any bad ideas of what it might be like. It was a surprise because she hadn't expected it. She smiled.

"Dere's plenty o' white folks dere dawlin, o' course, but mostly, yeah, it's black," she said.

She looked at him for a moment wondering and then realised she was meant to be talking.

"Yeah, so Bywater is very New Orlins, and dat means it's pretty wit' some oh dem ol' French style buildings; an' ugly wit' some shotgun shacks, an' concrete and heavy industry from da oil industry. It's fun coz dere's always somethin' interestin' going down somewheres; and dangerous coz dere's muggings an' drug killings all 'round ya too."

"Ah went to da Dr Charles R Drew Elementary school, just like my momma did. It's a big school an' its pretty poor. You gotta watch yourself so you didn't get mugged. Dere was always drug dealin' going down in da neighbourhood and where dere's drugs there's guns and where there's guns there's killins."

"Drugs is real big in Louisiana. You got all sorts of gangs. The meanest one is MS13 which nobody wants to mess with. Dey get their shit from the Mexican cartels who ship it in over the border either by sea or via Texas. Dey's corruption but people are used to it. The FBI caught one politician with $90,000 in drug money in his freezer and guess what? Dey voted him back[†]!"

"That's pretty crazy," Tarik admitted.

"So my mom? She's an ER nurse and my dad was a mechanic."

"What's an ER nurse?" I asked.

"Emergency Room? Triage? She had to deal with da gunshots, da overdoses, drunks, the car crashes, all dat. My daddy specialised in heavy machines like bulldozers."

There was a pause. None of us wanted to ask the obvious question about what had happened to him. Ashley looked a bit upset thinking about him.

"So my mom had a brother, Ray, and a sister, Camille?" she said changing the unspoken subject.

"Her daddy, my Grandpa Willlams? He was a legal secretary to da great civil rights attorney A.P. Turaud. He woiked for Mr Turaud throughout da foifties an' sixties an' ran a number of co-mmittees of da National Association for da Advancement of Coloured People in Louisiana advancing the rights of people of colour through da law."

"But if the law gave them roights what did he have to work for, hey?" Scotty asked." In Rhodesia the coloureds had no roights. That's why we had a war."

"Well bra, we haid a war too. Da American Civil War back in da 1860s. But even though da South lost and freed da slaves, we still had our own kinda apartheid like in South Africa back in my grandpa's day. White and black folks just weren't allowed to mix, even on da street. If'n anyone did anything to make it different da Klan – dat's da klu klux klan – would be up an' along at night to take em out, burn 'em with blowtorches and hang 'em from a tree."

"But wasn't it against the law?" Scott asked, surprised.

"Well sure it was dawlin, da murders were, but half da time da people investigating were da same people who'd used da blowtorches. Jus' like you an' Tarik was sayin'. When da Po-lice are against you, you got problems."

"But ... well what was the point of the law at all?" asked Scott, not understanding.

"Well some folks aisked dat. But ah guess you gotta start

somewhere? Anyways that's what kept A P Tureaud and my grandpa busy."

I had a question.

"How many black people are there in America?"

"Ah don't know? But more'n some places dan others, dat is for sure. I think ah hoid maybe fifteen percent for da entire United States ... Where was I?" she asked, confused.

"Your grandfather was working for coloured rights in the courts," Scotty summarised.

"Oh yeah. An' dat weren't so easy neither. Da legal world was full of racist whites who made life hard for him in da courts, in government, an' even legal libraries. He sometimes had to take documents to white people who really didn't care to receive dem, so he was often seen off by thugs or doigs. However mom told me he always said "Da high walls of racial segregation had been built up over decades and had to be taken down patiently brick by brick."

"So anyways dat was my Grandpa Williams 'though ah never knew him, cause he died when mom was a bit older 'an me. My Grandma Williams was, and sometimes still is, a midwife.

"A what?" asked Tarik.

"Someone helps other women deliver babies? Anyways dey had three children. Uncle Raymond who was the oldest by a few years, my mom, an' Aunty Camille who was youngest by three years."

"Mom says it was da generation gayp dat separated Uncle Raymond from his dad. He grew up in a house devoted to da law – even if it was devoted to changing da law it was devoted to changing da law by legal means. But it was da sixties? Young men was being drafted off to fight in Vietnam, dere was flower-power, long hair, Jimmie Hendrix, Dr Martin Luther King and Mohammed Ali. Everywhere young people black and white was challenging authority. Uncle Raymond fell in with da Black Panthers. Dey was a radical black liberation movement which was inspired to armed revolution by da loikes of Nelson Mandela and Robert Mugabe," she said nodding to Scotty.

"Mom says Uncle Raymond and Grandpa argued bitterly all through da sixties. Uncle Ray said Grandpa was a slave to da system who spent all evening at da NAACP making speeches about freedom and all day kissing white butt."

We couldn't help laughing a bit over that. Ashley seemed pleased to make us laugh.

"O' course Grandpa was really angry at being dissed by a teen who knew nothing of da history of da civil rights movement and who cay-ed even less. But it offended him too, dat young people knew all about the Baptist Martin Luther King and Moslem Malcolm X but nuttin' of dose a'fore dem who he believed had done all da woik."

"So dere was a bitter split in da family. Mom said her parents refused to talk to Uncle Ray, and even pretended dey had no son! Mom was torn between her brother who had always taken care of her an' Camille, an' her parents who gave her lots of attention to make sure she didn't turn out like Uncle Ray."

"Mom did well at school and went on to qualify as a noirse. She started work at Mercy Hospital in New Orlins which would have to have been da toughest place to learn about nursing in da country. So Mom was definitely da good goirl of da family and Ray was da bad boy. But Camille was'n somewhere in da middle. She was prettier than mom an' maybe not as smart. She used to see a bit more of her brother than mom and as a trainee hairdresser she used to party harder too.

"Mom says she lost track of her lil sister after she moved to Alabama. She only saw her at Christmas and Thanksgiving but she was too busy to worry about her much. Then mom moved to Washington DC and they lost touch altogether."

"It woin't 'til da 90's dat mom loirned her little sister had Aids. Mom got a job back at Mercy (which she still called 'Mercy' tho' it was now Lindy Boggs Medical Center) so she could be dere to help her mother look after Camille. Camille lived 'til 2002 so ah remember her. She was always lovely to me? Ah liked her a whole lot. But slowly an' surely she got weaker an' weaker. Even Uncle Ray tried to help but Grandma blamed him for not setting a better example an' driving her husband into an early grave. Finally Camille was little more'n a sad-eyed skeleton an' she died. It was real sad."

"Dat was da first funeral ah ever bin to. It was strange to know da loss while ah could see Camille standing roight there, lookin' at everyone a'fore she went on. She seemed ... what's da word ... wistful? Like she was pissed at herself for wasting her life? A'fore she went on, she made me promise ah wouldn't be like dat."

"After Camille died Grandma moved to Houston, Texas. She wanted to leave NewOrlins 'cause she just associated it with too much saydness and pain. She'd lost her husband, her son, an' her daughter dere. She moved to da neighbourhood where'n her sisters live and had a much better time."

"Anyways ah guess ah have to introduce my daddy. My dad came from up north in Detroit. It's all industrial, cold an' hard up dere. He hated da ploice an' always sayed he spent his whole, entire life trying ta git as far away as he could from it. He was the fourth of four sons so he was always da smallest and had to put up with a lot from his brothers."

"He joined da army as soon as he could, which was da early eighties. Dey trained him as a mechanic and shipped him out to Frankfurt, Germany where he looked after tanks for a few years."

"He was different to most soldiers cause he was always interested in different people an' places? When he got furlough he travelled around Europe. He especially loved Paris? He loved da nightlife and dere whole way of life dere. He even loirned to get by in French."

"Den he was transferred to Alabama to da big army support base. He was dere for Desert Storm an' was sent out to da desert to provide field maintenance to da tanks as they rounded up da Iraqi army. He said he saw some shit dere dat made him decide to git a discharge. He never talked about it, but he had da nightmares."

"After dat he drifted a bit around da States. He could always find work on agricultural machinery or earthmovers, but he woin't really sure what he wanted."

"One of his big adventures was when he got a job on da South Pole at McMurdo base for da summer season. He worked on da tracked tractors in the base's heavy shop but sometimes he had to go out and recover a ve-hicle. He said what was amazing was when ya got away from da base? And dere was dis huge silence. He always said dat was da closest he ever felt to God. Dat was when he caught a glimpse of NooZealan' on his way back through Christchurch and always wanted to come back here. And weirdly maybe dat's why we came here, though it had nothing to do wid it."

"Daddy went back to da States and travelled more. He managed

to injure hisself passing through New Orlins. Dat was where
he met mom. Mom said she knew he was different when he
wooed her with French and talked about far away places. So dey
fell for each other, and he fell for New Orlins and a few years
later I came along. Mom took some time off from da hospital
while my dad worked at Advantage selling parts for agricultural
machinery not far from home."

"Ah guess 9/11 affected everyone somehow. It certainly affected
my dad. Maybe he had itchy feet anyway, he was always
talking about travelling, and we was one of da few families
with passports because Dad liked having one, so we vacationed
in Haiti, Mexico and even Venezuela. We all learned a bit of
Spanish. But da day after 9/11 Dad volunteered for da National
Guard."

"What's that?" I asked.

"Well, it's sort of part of da reglar Army but it belongs to da
State rather than da Federal Government. It's only part-time:
one weekend a month an' two weeks a year like dey say, but
in a national or State emergency da president can coyll up the
National Guard as a part of da Army. With a good Army service
record and da knowledge to repair tracked ve-hicles dey signed
him up for da 141st field Artlllery Regiment based nearby us at
Jackson Barracks."

"I don't think my dad really thought that joining the National
Guard would mean being sent to I-raq. I mean all the 911
terrorists were Saudis, and Al Qaeda was based in Afghanistan.
What did they have to do with I-raq? But he hadn't figured on
that M__f__ George W Bush."

We were all a bit stunned by Ashley's language. Not just using
a word that we didn't even use when swearing at school back

home in Northland but also the deep hatred in it. Even Tarik
was impressed.

"So after he bombs Afghanistan he decides to invade I-raq to
make their oil safe for his Texan buddies down the country club.
And of course he doesn't have enough Army units so of all the
National Guard units which one gets called up? The 141st Field
artillery. My dad gets told he's shipping out to I-raq!"

Ashley stopped and just smouldered about that for a while.

"He was blown up by a roadside bomb riding in a Humvee in
Bagdad. It killed everyone in it and some Iraqis as well."

She seemed on the verge of tears. She looked away for a while
and then when she spoke again it was like a kind of sigh.

"Dere was two guys in uniform who came to see mom? She
was so angry. She threw dem out! Den we cried for about three
days."

Ashley looked around at us.

"I always been visited by da spirits. My mom never believed me,
and ma dad got freaked out by it. But now dad came to see me!
He's been wid me ever since. My mom couldn't cope with dat
at first, but I tink it helped her when I gave her messages from
dad."

"Anyways after daddy died my maw-maw came to stay because
mom had to woirk.

"Your what?" Tarik asked.

"My what? What?" Ashley asked.

"What's your maw-maw?" I asked.

"Oh dat's mah grandma! We call her 'maw-maw'? Anyway's she
was real strict and old fashioned. She tol' mum ah needed more
discipline. Ah didn't think so. Ah said ah cayn look afta myself,
but momma? She was too tired too argue. She was woirking

nights, sometimes even double shifts? Da hospital was ... well ...
it coulda been better run."

"In New Orlins we'd had some big storms 'fore Katrina.
Everyone remembered Ivan? Dat's when they tol' everyone to
e-vacuate the city, an we-all did, an' spent da whole entire day in
traffic jams, an nuthin' happened. Dem guys on da weather said
Katrina would be real bad and people should e-vacuate."

"We'd done saw da TV reports about what she was doing to da
Caribbean. But we'd seen dat a'fore too. Some people did leave,
but most folks wanted to stay and protect dere homes, best dey
could. Da freeways was jammed again anyways. Mom, o' course,
wasn't going nowhere but woirk."

"Mom worked the graveyard shift so she was usually not home
nights, but around for me in da aftanoon. At fiorst Katrina was
jus another bad storm? Ah slept through the start of it. But ah
woke up about five, and it was getting real bad out there. Then
sometime about six the floodin' started. Dat was a real surprise.
We was lucky coz it wasn't deep or nothin' where we were but
it was in da house. We had no power, so no news. Nobody
in da neighbourhood seemed to know what to do. So Maw-
maw decided we oughta get out while we could and walk to da
hospital, where Mom had da car.

Da sky was kinda pale gray? And it was rainin like dere was a
firehose, or somethin, in the sky. Dere was wind and broken
trees and poles and stuff. People was like in a daze. Dere weren't
so many people out-doors but everyone wanted news. One
time someone waved a gun at us, but we had no money and he
seemed to be as confused as everyone else! He ran off.

"When we finally got ourselves to da hospital; it was a madhouse
in dere. Dere was people everywhere. Dey was fighting, an'

crying. Some was badly huirt, others just in shock. Da doctors was swamped. When Maw Maw'n me we finally found mom she was so busy n'all, she hardly recognised us! We tol' her da house was aflooding. She just put us in the corner and tol' us to wait! What else could she do?

Ashley stopped and looked around at us.

"Ah think what shocked everyone dere was dat we was waiting for help to come? And it didn't. It didn't come all night or all da next day, neither. Everybody kept sayin', 'hold on, dis is da U-nited States of America. It's da richest country in da woild, not some third-world nation! Help will come.' But it didn't, and it didn't, and it didn't. Everyone could see da whole damn hospital was falling apart a-round us, but it was like the only place left. Whole rest of the city was under woita! Where else could we go? The shock of not being rescued still hurt. She frowned like a kid whose mother had left her behind instead of taking her.

"About day three – its all a blur now cause'n you could hardly sleep or nuthin, people kept coming and going, and dere was no food – somethin' strange happened. Someone brought in a gunshot victim who was in a bad way? Ah wasn't dere, ah only got tol this by mom. And dere was so much chaos? Dere was toilk of closing da hospital and dis guy wasn't making no fuss – he was just quietly dyin' in da corner. Mom went to take a quick look at him to give him morphine, when she discovered it was her own big brother Raymond!"

"He didn't say much, but he was pleased to see her. It looked like he had been beaten, as well as shot. Wid a lot of pain, he pulled a leather cardholder out from his pants, and gave it to mom, holding her hands. He gasped not to let them, have it. He couldn't say who. He just choked and died in her arms."

"Dat was sorta like da final straw for mom. She got Maw-maw who cried and cried over her son. It was soo saaad?"

And now Ashley was crying, which didn't surprise me at all, but she went on, sniffing and brushing away the tears. I was a bit embarrassed, like Tarik, but Scott suddenly put his arms around her. He hugged her for quite a while. I told you Scott seemed older somehow, and he did right then too. There was no question it made Ashley feel better. She hung on for quite a while and her glasses fogged up. Then she let Scott go and polished them on her shirt while she thought about the flood.

"Da hospital was starting to be 'vacuated but da bodies woin't being looked after! An Maw-maw wouldn't leave? It just seemed to go on and on like a nightmare you can't wake up from."

"Dey finally got us out after a week! We found ourselves on a bus for Houston. All we had in the whole world was da clothes we was wearin'. When she weren't sleepin, from being exhausted Mom had a loong kind of stare. She kept say'in everyting her daddy ever worked for had come down to a moment of truth at Mercy hospital in the middle of a hurricane, and you could dress it up anyways you liked, but when it came down to it, America had deserted poor folks in dey hour of need."

"Da reason dose twin towers mattered was da people in dem were rich and white. The reason Mercy didn't, was we was poor and mostly black. Momma had been bitter when my daddy died. She was ten times woirse now! And you know, I couldn't see a damn thing wrong with her thinking!"

"It weren't for four weeks when we was in Houston at Maw-maw's house dat we realised what Uncle Ray had given mom. Dey was charge cards. Simple gift credit cards. Ya'all know da kind wid a chip? Dere was of six of dem. When my mom put da first one in da ATM she thought there mus be somethin' wrong with the machine? Dere was a million dollars on it! She took da cards to another machine. Dey all had a million dollars on them! She only tol me cause she knew ah always know her secrets, anyways."

"We both knew at once dis was drug money. Uncle Ray had been a drug dealer who lived with a gun under his pillow. Mom said we gotta keep damn quiet about this if'n we didn't want a visit from da people who killed Uncle Ray."

But same time we was homeless. Our house in New Orlins was condemned. Who knew when insurance would pay out if'n dey ever gonna pay out at all. We was broke. Mom had no job and hardly any savings but we had six million in cash cards. As far as we knew nobody had any idea of a link between Uncle Ray and my mom."

"Mom didn't like doin' it, but by asking aroun', she found out how she could transfer money ten thousand a day into a new bank account. Suddenly we gone from being penniless refugees to millionaires over night! My mom didn't tell her own momma about it. Dey'd been fighten an Maw-maw wanted her peace an quietness back. She said she loved us but she was tired after Katrina. We moved out of Maw-maw's and into an apartment dat was nice, but not too nice. Y'know what I'm sayin?"

"Momma didn't want to live off no drug money. She wanted a real job! Problem was, dere weren't none. She was either too qualified, or not qualified enough, too young, or too ol'. Seemed in Texas da stories about Mercy during da hurricane had begun to go 'roun' and she felt it was almost like people thought she was jinxed or some damn thing."

"We bought ourselves a nice new Honda Accord! Nothing fancy

but just a new car, which had dat new smell in it? I went to a
new school in Houston which I gotta say was way better'n Dr
Charles Drew Elementary in New Orlins. But for all we was
richer, we was lonely. An' Houston jus' didn't feel like home."
"It was da Texas thing. It's just so different to Louisiana. Bigger,
harder, richer and I gotta say it feels like the gayp between black
and white is just so much bigger."
"But we weren't da only refugees from Katrina in town.
Dere were thousands and thousands of folks like us who'd
fled Katrina, in Houston. And jus' like Scott was sayin 'bout
Zimbaweans in South Africa, we weren't too damn popular
neither. An it's true, lotta dem had brought dey drug habits
and dey guns to Texas. Folks dere saw us Louisianians as trash,
though what dey thought a whole bunch of homeless people
widdout jobs was goin to do? Ah don't know."
"Mom couldn't get no job neidder so she started volunteering
and ended up woirkin' a few days at a drug rehab clinic? She'd
been real bored stayin' home or shoppin' and she shure liked to
be 'ppreciated by someone. Maybe it weren't so clever given so
many Lousianians were in da city, an' her brother's bein' wanted
an all. Or maybe dat had somethin' to do with it — guilt or
somethin'. Anyways mom couldn't just sit around the house and
old people drove her crazy, so drug rehab it was."
"Dere she met Ray's ol' friend Martin. He hadn't seen Ray in
years. Martin said last he'd heard Ray had been working with
the Sinaloa drug cartel and working with MS-13. He was sorta
like a transportation manager, runnin da drug and money
shipments in and out of da city. He paid big bribes and ran a
tight crew of truckers who walked a tightrope between making a
fortune and being killed in really horrible ways."

"Martin was 'n addict, not a dealer. He was kinda soft an acted like a big baby hopin' someone would look after him? Cos he knew Ray, Mom told him Ray was dead, and somethin' of da way he died. Course she didn't mention da money. She didn't mention Maw-maw movin' to Houston neidder. But cos we didn't know no-one in Houston she invited Martin back to our apartment for dinner."

"Dat tuirned out to be a big mistake. Martin started turnin' up all the time! Ah hated him! He was jus' da woirld's biggest loser! Full of sad-arse stories 'bout how dumb he was! An' he gave me da creeps, way he looked at me. Ah knew he looked at a whole lot of dirty stuff online an' he had some real strange ideas about goirls. Ah don't know what happened coz I went to bed but I was woken up by mom an Martin in my room and she was yellin' an' telling Martin to leave an' not come back! Mom's real scary when she's like dat. Comes of years o' dealin' with gangstas in da hospital, and Martin was basically a wimp."

"But, turned out, he was a dangerous wimp! I saw him hangin' outside my school a few times so I told mom when she picked me up? She made shure the school security was warned about him."

"School security?"I asked.

"Yeah, dey had a couple of security guys at the gate when school finished."

I had never head of that before. Scotty looked pretty amazed at the idea too.

"Anyway, turned out dat Martin was da least of our worries. Bein' a prize asshole we tink he decided to get back at us by telling his dealer 'bout Ray, an how we had money an no job? He had put two and two together and along with what he heard on da grapevine realised we must have got some money from somewheres."

"Dey nearly got us! Dey broke into our apartment when mom came to pick me up after school. Seein it was friday we had already decided to go see a movie and eat out, so we didn't come home until eight. Ah had one o my feelins an luckily ah noticed suddenly a light went off in our apartment from a couple of blocks up da street. We jus' drove 'round da block and waited. A bit later a car jus' sped off. We called da cops an told dem we thought dere was a burglar in our place?

"Turned out da apartment had been ripped apart in a search for the cards. Da cops said dey would send a fingerprint technician in da next day or so. Mom filled in a few forms, and she asked the cops to hang around, while we packed a few things. She didn't want to stay dere overnight any more than ah did."

"We drove outta town an' stayed in a hotel. We'd never done that a'fore. We only had two small bags o' clothes, our bathroom kits, our passports, a car and five and a half million dollars in stolen drugs money. But da problem was whoever was afta us knew who we was."

"Mom decided Houston wasn't safe, an da best place for us was somewhere where no-one knew us, and where we knew no-one. It really was totally random dat we picked L.A."

"We sold da Honda and got a PT Cruiser convertible. We got ourselves a camera and headed out on our very own road movie! Dat was fun! It was fall now? But in da desert it's drah, 'though at night it got damn cold! We talked and talked and talked all the way! We had ourselves a great time an' really got to know each other again! We went where we liked and stayed at all these funny places on the way. It was great!"

"Finally we got to L.A. Ah was a bit surprised and disappointed. Ah don't know what ah expected really. Hollywood and beaches everywhere? Maybe it was because it was almost winter now and dey don't show a lot of California in the winter on TV. But of course L.A is a big city which does more'n make movies an TV. We ditched the Cruiser and got an Acura then rented ourselves a house. It was only temporary cos mom seriously wanted to find another job."

"Mom had much more luck in L.A. Dere were all sorts of clinics and mom had a choice of offers in the fiorst week! We settled in Willowbrook? It's a black suburb where it was easier for us to blend in. Dere was also some medical centres which needed better management. It was jus' in time for Christmas!"

"After all da 'citement of leavin' Houston las' Christmas shure seemed lonely. We bought furniture and new clothes but we still didn't know no-one. So our New Years resolution was to make some new friends. An we sorta did."

"Course all da time, at the back of ahh minds, we was askin: are dey still looking for us? What do we do if dey find us again? We thought about different plans for 'scaping in case dey caught up wid us. We even practised them. Y'know what I'm sayin? And den – well, ah guess we fergot all about 'em coz we was too busy havin fun!"

"We had a lot of fun in L.A. We went to the original Disneyland a few times, visited Universal Studios, and of course we could just cruise to Beverley Hills, or Venice Beach or Hollywood. It all felt a bit unreal really? O'course mom had to get back to woirk and ah had school which was borin."

"It wasn't a baad school? Way better than the ones in Houston and it left New Orlins fer dead. But ah felt bad 'cause ah was so way behind for my age so they done put me in a class with kids a year younger'n me. Being small for my age nobody really noticed nothin, but ah felt kinda dumb, 'cause even though ah was older, ah still had problems.

"We was there for nearly a ye-ar. We watched out for anyone after us, but there was no-one. We looked it up on de net and we thought we had done got away with one o' da biggest robberies of all time. So ah don't rightly know what gave us away. It coulda been mom needin' a letter from Mercy in New Orlins for her new woirk. Who knows? But two days ago dey nearly caught us again."

"For some reason ah noticed an ol white BMW following us after mom picked me up from school? It was about two or three cars back, not doing anythin' special, but ah noticed it. Ah tol Mom so she took a left where she would normally take a right and da BMW followed us. Den we drove through a whole bunch o' intersections until we was headin' back home again but da BMW stopped following. Ah was still nervous so we decided to act like we was headed home, but drive on past and see what happened."

"What happened was a car chase like straight out of a movie! We slowed down some, then mom floored it, and we drove off. Suddenly two cars pulled out and started chasing us! At fiorst mom tried to look natural but this big merc tried to overtake and swerve into us! Mom braked, let 'em go ahead but swerved right down a side street. It felt good at da time but now da other car, a red Lexus, was on our tail and we was racing side by side down this backstreet wid all these little kids playin? Another car appeared on da other end of the road but the Lexus took no notice! They had to swerve off da road to avoid a collision. Dat was when ah saw da Mac ten."

"The what?" I asked.

"Mac ten, S'a machine gun. Gangsters use 'em."

"Oh, shit!"

"Fortunately a truck suddenly appeared from da left and da Lexus had to stop suddenly to avoid hitting it. Da Merc was still behind us so mom took another side street and another and another. Luckily we knew dese roads real well. We thought we'd lost 'em when turning on to West 120th we passed the white beamer coming the other way! Dey turned around and were on our tails."

"Da road was gettin' slower and busier. What we was really scared of was gettin' caught at lights an gettin' shot up. So Mom took the turn-off onto da freeway. Mom drove quick as she could. If we attracted the CHIPs all da better. But for some reason da California Highway Patrol didn't seem to be about dat day. Da white beamer was gainin' and we knew da others couldn't be far behind. But mom tricked em by suddenly swerving to take da airport exit. Our plan now was to ditch da Acura and rent something else. We figured we had about five minutes to lose da Acura and disappear into da airport."

"Well, it was a good try. Unfortunately da queues was huge. We saw da Merc and Lexus arrive as we was runnin' to get a bus. Dey found da Acura and chased us. We would be dead meat waitin for a bus so we went inside Los Angeles International Airport."

"Some of dem musta had good eyes cause we was spotted. We dodged dem all over using airport security as much as possible. Dey weren't runnin' no more but we knew if dey got close we was dead. So it was like slo-mo football. Somehow we found ourselves at a ticket counter. Everything was international.

I dunno why New Zealin' popped into mom's head, maybe it was dad or somethin. Da guy said there was a plane at 9.45pm which was full, when up popped two late cancellations on NZ1 to Auckland! Mom bought those tickets at once. We checked in with no baggage, showed our passports and went through security leavin' dem outside. It was only when we was lift'n off dat we stopped worrying about who was chasing us and realised what we'd done."

"So how did you find out about the interview in the hotel?" I asked.

"We booked into a hotel when we arrived. We only found out when we read the paper at reception."

The clattering of the helicopter in the distance woke us up. We had been talking for ages, up there on the hill above the sea, amongst all the dead old concrete battlements. The sun lower now over the high hills behind us, and its rays seemed yellower hinting at the end of the day. And now the chopper was back and landing over by the house behind us.Behind the house was a plume of smoke which had been rising for an hour or two now. It was weird how still it was until the chopper came down and blew it around.

After all that talking there was a bond between us. We knew where we came from. We knew that we were all escaping someone and we knew we were more alike than any other people we had ever met. We got up, as if there was now nothing more to be said and went back to the track up the hill. There was something good about the old sheep pellets, the thistles and the smell of grass. We felt as if we had all been pushed to the edge of the world but that somehow this was the limit. Together somehow we would not only elude our pursuers but ultimately defeat them. That, anyway, was the sense of promise we felt as we headed back down the track.

111

CHAPTER EIGHTEEN: DOCTOR PROSPEROV'S STORY

Wow," Sue says. "Those friends of yours weren't just your average bunch of twelve-year-olds were they?"

I've stopped because I need to go to the toilet. I get up.

"No, 'though you shouldn't dis' twelve-year-olds. We found plenty of kids around the world who coped with a lot more than adults let twelve-year-olds do in this country," I say.

I go inside leaving Sue to the sun and the birds. Talking to Sue might not be the most exciting thing I could be doing right now. But the more I tell Sue the more I remember what had happened, too. And now I was thinking there had to be something in our past that could help explain how we had been caught out so badly.

But talking to Sue isn't risk free. Have I made her a security risk too? On the other hand if everyone from Renwick came back it wouldn't hurt to have a friendly cop who knew enough of the real story to help us out. She can't start blabbing about psychics and flying saucers if she wants to keep her career, but a cop who can bridge the gap between the official world and our world could be useful.

That is if everyone comes back.

I know Aunty Liz and Grandpop will do whatever they can to bring me home but I also know there might be political complications with our friends at the other end which could over-rule them. Our friends have more than just a few families to worry about. They have to think of the security of their entire planet. That might mean delays for who knew how long? Days? Weeks? Months?

Then there was the question of Ashley. Who could have tagged her? I hadn't paid any attention to her visit at the time. She was doing her thing, I was doing mine. If she had been attacked I would have heard. But there was no sign that she was in trouble or that she'd met anyone sus' at all. And yet, as soon as she'd arrived back at base, the sensors had gone bananas warning us we had twenty minutes before they would be all over Renwick House. How could she have been tagged? Who could have done that?

There was also this Antonio Rossi dude working for Sir Michael. He'd sent Leonora to New Zealand two days before Ashley was tagged. They must have been onto us before Ashley even left. But Sir Michael had shown yesterday, talking to me, he had no idea about the full extent of what we were doing. So was this Rossi an infiltrator or what? And when I was with Sir Michael, where was he?

I check in on Ka-rea-rea in my room on the way back out. He's still sitting there, all folded up, as I'd left him. He's an important part of my escape plan. They will still be looking for us and if they find Caz and Julia's I will have no choice but to leave the country. I didn't want to run because I know as a fourteen-year-old alone in the world, even with money, I would still have problems with adults no matter where I go. I want to try to stay in the system because I don't want to have to live the rest of my life on the run. I grab a couple of drinks and come out again to join Sue.

"You know, the more I think about your story the more I
realise that you still haven't told me anything much about 'your
friends'," Sue says taking the drink.

"I know."

"Why's that?"

"To be honest, because they're even stranger than everything
I've told you about so far."

"OK, that has to be pre-tty strange."

"Well, it's not so much strange. When you think about it, they
make perfect sense. It's just they are a bit of a shocking surprise.
They certainly were for us."

"Why are they shocking?"

 "You'll see why when I get there."

"OK, go on."

 So I do.

•••

As we came down the hill we could see figures down on the
beach. They seemed to be making a house of driftwood. It looked
like everyone was busy with it. We wondered what that would be
for. But as we went down the track the driftwood house vanished
from view.

"Do you think anyone's after Tahira?" Scotty asked as we walked
down the hill again.

"She didn't say so," I said.

"What about Cam?" Tarik asked.

"I dunno about her," I answered, looking around.

The others shrugged. We still didn't know Cam's story, but we
felt sure it would be as involved as our own. Tarik stopped and
looked around.

"This is emptiest place I ever been, you know what I mean?"
Tarik said. "It's like the world has gone away or somefing?"
"Yeah, it's so," Ashley searched for a word," bleak," she
concluded.
"Doesn't look so empty to me," Scotty said," and at least it's not
hot."
"Hey Sam, how 'ot does it get 'ere in summer?" Tarik asked as
we walked down the gravel path.
"I dunno, 'bout 25, maybe 30 on a hot day."
"What's dat in Fahrenheit?" Ashley asked.
"About 70 I'd guess," Tarik estimated.
"Twenty five is nice. Forty in the shade isn't is it?" Scotty said
contentedly.
"What's 40?" Ashley wanted to know.
"About 120," Tarik put in.
"It's warmer up North where I come from. It's usually about 32
over summer. That's nice," I said.
"90ish," Tarik answered before Ashley could even ask.
"When is summer?" Ashley asked.
"Soon. It gets hottest toward the end of January," I said.
"What about Christmas?" she wanted to know.
"It's warm but not hot."
"A warm Christmas? Dat's weird," Ashley said. "It's cold back
home."
But Scotty, didn't think so because he was from the Southern
hemisphere too, and Tarik, had lived in Melbourne and as an
Alevi in London hadn't celebrated it, anyway. I supposed Tahira
and Cam probably weren't into Christmas much either.
"I wonder if Prosperov has Christmas," Tarik said hatching a
plot.

"Y'all mean will he give you presents as well as money?
Ain'tshoo a Muslim?" Ashley accused him.

"Worf a try, init?" Tarik grinned.

We walked on past the thistles we'd whacked down on the way up.

"Mrs Jones will celebrate Christmas," Scotty said firmly.

"Gunter probably," Tarik added.

"Betcha Mariko will – if'n it's fun," Ashley added.

"Ken might," I suggested, "he lived in America a long time."

So we talked about how to convince Dr Prosperov to have a Christmas party for us all the way back down the track.

When we got back to Renwick House, the sun was almost behind the hill. Everyone was out on the beach where trestle tables had been set up. There was a barbecue being overseen by Ken. Mr Trân was helping with salads, breads and nibbles which were beginning to go out on the tables. The breeze which had been noticable up on the ridge was not present in the bay, protected as it was by the ridges and the curve of the inlet.

As we came up to see what was happening Mariko, Rewa, Asal and Tahira came up with some animal hats made of paper coloured with crayon they had made, which everyone else was wearing.

"No choosing!" Mariko yelled, "you gotta wear what we give you!"

She herself had a Peacock hat which looked fabulous, while Rewa had a dolphin and Asal a deer.

I got a bright blue fish from Rewa, Tarik got a goat, Ashley got a horse, and Scotty got a Lion. I wondered if they were trying to tell us something. It was funny seeing all these adults talking, walking around or carrying things wearing children's hats on their heads.

Aunty Liz told us to go inside and get warmer clothes on because it would get colder later. I caught Ashley's eye. We were still worried about the ghosts. I tried to say we would all be OK but then Ashley's mum, Pat, came up and said the same thing to Ashley. So we went back to the House, with Scotty and Tarik coming too. We felt better in a group.

There was something about Renwick House in the sunset. It looked and felt happier. Perhaps it was the yellow light. We walked in through the big front doors and started up the stairs. There was nobody on the first floor. We passed through the lounge and down the long corridors. They seemed deserted but also waiting for something.

I went into our apartment, found myself a jumper, and came out again. It felt strange, as if the ghosts were busy somewhere else. When we met up in the corridor again, we all were aware they simply weren't there. Tarik wasn't sure if he wanted to wear his animal head but the rest of us convinced him, so wearing our hats we went back outside again.

The shadows were lengthening over the beach but it was still early and the sky was light. The fire was hot with huge chunks of white wood glowing brilliant scarlet, and sending up dancing flames of yellow, red and sometimes even green. Ken, and Mr Trân were roasting legs and cuts of lamb which had been covered in something that made the meat dark brown on the outside. Gunter and Bernard were chainsawing up large chunks of driftwood. The smell of the petrol mixed with the fire and the meat, while the whining of the small two-stroke seemed to be shushed by the crump of waves coming ashore.

Mariko was gathering all of us kids together. She had made

up this game of simultaneous tag. Everyone got a card with an animal on it. You had to tag the animal that you had a card for. If you caught someone they had to give you their card. But if you got your own card you were out. So if you caught someone straight away and they had your own card you were out. But if you caught someone with another card you had to chase that animal. You could tell who had your card cos they were chasing you. The last person out was the winner.

It was kind of a random game. You knew who you had to get but you didn't always know who had to get you. Rewa got me because I was so fixated on getting Ashley, who was very fast, that I forgot I was being chased as well. It worked best when nobody knew who you were trying to get. For a bunch of psychics that was hard. We had to practise not thinking about anything because all of us could read one-another. Cam and Tahira proved to be the best at that. You could never guess who they were chasing.

Then, we had another game with the adults. This time the adults had the cards and we had to ask them questions about what animal they had without seeing it. The adults could only answer 'yes' or 'no'. The first person to get their own card was the winner. We were all very fast at this and we realised we could read each other's parents quite easily.

To keep us from starving the adults carried out a table and set out some Vietnamese dumplings, and juice. They were great and we wolfed them down fairly quick. We played around randomly for half an hour while the adults chatted, drank and ate snacks. They seemed to be getting to know each other quite quickly. Mrs Jones seemed to be fairly friendly with Tahira's mother Mitra and grandmother Soraya; Aunty Liz and Pat Robinson were chatting with Bernard, while Gunter and Dr Gursoy were discussing something about the House. Ken and Mr Trân were mostly talking about the food, while Mariko had Rewa and Asal following her around like ducklings.

Even though we now knew that most of us had been driven together from all over the world more by desperation than anything else, it was surprising how well everyone seemed to get on.

Slowly the sky changed colour, the warm yellow followed by pink, by dark blue and then finally the dark night. We had to wait ages for the food to cook and in the meantime Dr Prosperov joined us and to our surprise he had a woman on his arm.

She was very thin, but tall and grand. She had long gray hair tied up, and the palest skin. She wore a gray-green wool outfit that looked a little like a uniform. Her eyes swept over us and you felt her cool penetrating glare slide through you. Dr Prosperov was wearing polarfleece, jeans and his usual cunning smile. He seemed to be in a good mood and had brought a violin. He went among us introducing, "my wife, Dr Ekaterina Morozov," to the adults. She looked briefly at us kids but neither smiled nor said anything. Each of us must have known at once that she could not have children and it cut her like glass.

The adults drank wine and talked for an hour and then Dr Prosperov took out his violin and played slippery tunes he said he had learned from the gypsies. Then Mariko appeared with a flute and they jammed together. Finally Dr Prosperov stopped playing, put away his instrument and started to speak to us.

"Friends," he began, "is my belief that we are not gathered here, in this place, by accident."

"No shit, Sherlock," I heard Ashley mutter, next to me.

I noticed his wife's eyes, almost nervous, shift from the crowd before her, to her husband in front of her.

It was a statement that seemed to be the answer to a question that had hung over all of us ever since we had arrived at Renwick House, and instantly had everyone's attention. He smiled and shrugged.

"Trivial reason, of course, is I hired you."

There was a polite laugh at that.

"But is deeper question: how is it that you came to seek job at this place and this time, and that I, former Soviet scientist, am also here and able to hire you? This is itself strange. Is plenty of former Soviet scientists still in Russia, literally starving, and yet I am rich."

"My explanation will be big shock. But goes to heart of all my plans for this place and without your help and understanding these plans, is impossible. I must therefore ask for you to listen to story of how I have decided to make this place. Is best to be comfortable as story is long so please to sit down."

We sat down. The air was cool but the fire was hot so we had to roast ourselves carefully – moving around to cool the hot side and warm the cold side.

"I begin at beginning," Dr Prosperov said his face flickering in the firelight.

"Was born in city of Krasnoyarsk, Siberia in middle of Great Patriotic War – is what we Russians call World War Two. Should explain for children – at time Russia was Union of Soviet Socialist Republics. USSR was fighting Nazi German-led invaders for its life. Twenty million Russians, Ukrainians and other Soviet citizens die. My father was one. Was not unusual. Every family lost someone in Great Patriotic War – even leader,

Josef Stalin."

"Father's name is all left of him. Is not even real Russian name. He was Italian communist, second son of Count from Milan, who went to Russia to join revolution. He made his name, Achille Prospero, more Russian, so Prosperov," he shrugged. "My mother, Raisa, was Jewish. Her mother already dead. She is daughter of Rabbi, Mikhail Timofeyovich Stavisky who worked for railways. He is like father to me, and brilliant man who taught me very, very much including mathematics, Torah and Kabbal."

I realised Dr Prosprov, like me, was raised by his grandfather. For some reason as I thought this he nodded at me, but he went on. "War very bad for Soviet people but very good for Krasnoyarsk. To escape Nazis much industry moved to Siberia. Krasnoyarsk grew, and after war kept growing. So I grow in growing industrial city. In winter, very cold. In summer, very hot. Even with pollution is beautiful place. With help of teachings from Grandfather I am good at school: Pass exams; go to Krasnoyarsk Polytechnic Institute and pass with top degree in electrical engineering, special interest in electromagnetic fields. Such good degree, and so young I am recommended for Leningrad State University for post-graduate study."

Map Data © Google 2016

"At Leningrad State I am mentored by Professor Aleksandr Dubrov at Vasil'yev Laboratory.

"Dubrov completely revolutionised my life and thinking. His research programme is unusual phenomena. In West called paranormal."

There was a kind of embarrassed shuffling by the adults. It was like he'd said he believed in fairies or something. Dr Prosperov coughed, and went on.

"Must explain in Soviet Union then, is no religion. Religion banned. In United States many people believe paranormal connected with religion. Not so in Soviet Union. Is strictly science. Dubrov gathered unusual people from Soviet Union. People with powers to move objects in test conditions using mind alone. Personally observed many cases of subjects levitating objects. Some very light, like cigarette packet, others heavy. One woman moved piano. Unusual numbers of such people live in Siberia. Dubrov's interest in identifying, and if possible amplifying any radiation of this form. My doctoral thesis is 'Field measurement of human telekinetic energy'."

As I listened I was amazed. All my life I had imagined that my … well, curse, as I had believed it, was something that only affected me and my ancestors. Until I had met the others yesterday it had never occurred to me that anyone else might have it. Now I was learning that I was not even very good compared to someone who could move a piano.

"Naturally am already member of Communist Party. Brings many benefits but thesis brings attention of KGB. To explain to younger ones. In Soviet Union is bureau of intelligence which spies on both citizens and foreign nations for Government. KGB is above law. Can do anything to anybody. Very ruthless, very intelligent and very merciless. Many millions sent to die in hard labour prisons in freezing Siberia for minor things such as suggesting our Government might need improvement."

"In 1970 Soviet airforce reports large numbers of encounters with unidentified aerial phenomena resembling craft under intelligent direction. Foreign bureau suggests USA is encountering similar craft. There they are called 'flying saucers' or 'UFOs'."

"Because of thesis am recruited to KGB by General Vladimir Segeyev. I am to observe investigation. KGB investigating commander believes pilots in conspiracy to defect to West. Is many complaints by Air Force over KGB interrogations hurting pilots and no evidence found. Conspiracy theory rejected, investigating commander sent to prison and I am promoted to command. I begin new, open investigation."

•••

"Hang on!" Sue interrupts.

"Yeah?"

"Dr Prosperov investigated UFOs for the KGB in the Soviet Union?"

"Yeah."

"Like, he was the guy in charge?"

"Yeah. You can find his report on the web now. It's been declassified."

"Wow."

"Shall I go on?"

"Yeah, yeah."

•••

"All pilot evidence is checked again and calibrated. Evidence from radar shows hard returns: means unidentified flying object reflects electromagnetic waves. Is solid object, not illusion. Refining of evidence results in reduction to 23 cases of unidentified aerial craft with multiple witnesses and hard radar returns. General Segeyev accepts report that craft are real and possible security risk." "Intelligence from USA suggests Americans secretly have similar view. General Segeyev issues orders I am to assess threat and find potential counter-measures."

•••

"What?!" Sue interrupts again. "The Soviet Union and the Pentagon knew that flying saucers were a real threat way back in the 70s?"

"Yeah."

"Shit!"

I shrug. It seems the experience of having been chased by one has changed Sue's skepticism a bit.

"Go on, go on!"

•••

"But is unnerving technical component of problem. Evidence of unknown craft behaviour is impossible under known physical science. This suggests that any counter-measures we can devise based on inadequate understanding of physics. To have any chance of devising counter measures new physical theory is needed to understand potential weaknesses of alien craft threat."

"So in 1972 I begin private exploration of physical theory with Grandfather to account for phenomena. In 1973 I am principle author with Professor Dubrov of first cosmic theory "Extra-Dimensional Phenomena: Theory and Measurement" which was classified "Special File" – is second highest secrecy classification.

In this I anticipated what physicists now call String Theory. Predicts ten dimensional universe and gravity particle[†]."

"What means Universe has ten dimensions? Dimensions often confusing for non-mathematical people. They imagine dimension as some kind of imaginary space like normal space but somewhere else. This incorrect. Dimension is not a new space, is new property of space we already know. Right here and now we see three simple dimensions: up-down, left-right, and forward-back. These dimensions contain everything we can see around us," he said, and waved his arm around.

"Additional dimensions we cannot see. Or perhaps do not recognise. Is good analogy by English writer Abbott Abbott in book called Flatland[†]. In book, world is two dimensional. Is no up-down. All characters are shapes, like cartoon drawings on piece of paper. One character meets stranger who is circle but claims to be three dimensional. Character grows then shrinks again. Seems like circle changing size to two dimensional character, but is actually three dimensional ball passing through thin two dimensional world."

As he said this I noticed Dr Prosperov looked at all six of us kids in turn, making sure we were listening. I was listening all right! I got it easily. He thought our powers meant we could sense other dimensions! I looked around at the others and found they were looking at each other too. We all got it. Now we all knew we were the reason we were here!

Dr Prosperov was smiling, ironically.

"While impressed by ten dimensions theory General points out theoretical work of no practical use. Suggests no countermeasures to aliens or superior weapons technology to defeat USA follows from my first cosmic theory. Also General

Segeyev's superiors place no priority on potential extraterrestrial threat. I am disappointed but comrade General points out position is justified because extraterrestrials have no obvious warlike intent while USA has 12,000 nuclear warheads aimed at annihilating our cities."

"I see reason, so to address nuclear threat I suggest to Comrade General that psychics from Dubrov's studies could be employed for defence against American nuclear threat at minimal cost, assuming right individuals selected for psychic operations."

"This project is approved with modest budget. For this I join civilian anthropological project headed by Dr Lana Vilenskaya to study Siberian Shamans in natural habitat. Involves six month's field study in the far north-east of Soviet Union."

Prosperov paused, and examined his feet for a moment. For a man who always seemed confident it seemed strange to see him look quite uneasy.

"Can now say experience very, very, unusual. I am young and perhaps arrogant. Had believed first cosmic theory step toward explanation of much unexplained phenomena but Siberian experience forced me to reconsider many assumptions. Is very strange experiences in Siberia. Can admit now I entered state of profound inner turmoil. At time such turmoil not considered productive. To avoid losing position I denounce comrade Vilenskaya as Western liberal social deviant. Is her idea and a decade later allows her to escape Soviet Union for United States at height of Cold War."

"Siberian encounter, however, forces me to rethink first cosmic theory and after six months of intensive work results in second cosmic theory. General Segeyev not interested in cosmic theories but believes in real possibility of psychic spies and approves recruitment of agents."

"Recruitment test procedure of conscripts entering Red Army introduced in early 1973 results in selection of twenty psychics. Through further refinement unit reduced to twelve under my command. Operations begin in summer of 1974."

"In first six months our unit identifies sixty three US spies inside Soviet Union, of whom forty-four confess under interrogation, and a further sixteen are found to have incriminating evidence. A year later, in 1975, we begin remote viewing operations where psychic sees features of remote locations by mind alone."

"Initial tests find five subjects – including myself – proficient at accurate remote viewing of Russian secret installations from map references. KGB now convinced and programme extended. Next is to locate American targets including people, laboratories, submarines and aircraft. Unit identifies 53 targets of which 21 are independently corroborated."

"But in 1976 our unit encounters Americans psychics attempting remote viewing of Soviet bases. In response we begin offensive operations. Operations involve remote hypnosis, second-sight, forecasting and even assassination. Assassinations prove highly dangerous for our operatives and abandoned after two enemy agents killed but which lead our own assassins to suicide."

•••

"Assassinations!" Sue interrupts again. "Are you saying Prosperov's KGB unit killed people with mind powers?"

"That's what he said," I nod.

"How is that even possible?" she asks doubtfully.

"Oh, it's possible, alright."

"How do you know?" Sue wants to know.

"Because I've been attacked, and nearly wasted," I tell her.

"What? By Russians?"

I shake my head slowly and just point up.

Her eyes get wider.

"Holy shit!" she gulps, realising what she could be up against.

I pause, looking at her. She nods and adds, "go on."

•••

I was creeped out when he said that. People killing others using psychic powers! It was way too heavy for me. And I got the strong impression something very, very creepy had happened to those assassins. Something I knew I didn't want to be near. So it made me nervous of Dr Prosperov. But then he changed the subject.

"My interest, not on mind battles. Consume much energy and produce no benefit. Is very hard to make Comrade General believe that straining and sweating Russian psychic operative is fighting enemy agent and not just making stupid joke. So interest turns to time dimension of remote viewing in order to provide better warning of possible nuclear attack. In English is called 'prescience' or 'precognition'."

Dr Prosperov paused to have a drink of water.

"How is even possible? How is possible to know future? Future not like book where reader can just peak ahead. How is possible to foresee anything? How is it possible to predict seemingly random event such as this talk on beach here and now?"

For a moment Dr Prosperov said nothing, letting the question hang in the air as the fire crackled and the sea crumped onto the beach.

"Is accurate forecast even possible? Every day weather forecast tells us probable weather for next day. Is usually right – except here on Aotea, where is usually wrong – but is usually right. But weather forecast for week ahead?" He shook his head from side to side, "not so reliable. Month ahead? Useless. Ten years ahead, just guess."

"Accuracy of every forecast depends on resolution. Low resolution forecast predicts summer is hot and winter is cold. Is correct, but not interesting. Many ancient peoples built astronomical sites able to predict movements of stars and planets for centuries because large bodies do not need high resolution. But small bodies very different. How can they be predicted?"

"To understand ability to predict is necessary to understand causation. Classical theory of causation says if you have perfect information perfect prediction of everything is possible for all time. Theoretically if you have information on every tiny bit of information you can make perfect weather forecast for tomorrow, next week, next year, next century. So since ancient times is argued if all future things caused by events now, then all things now have been determined by events in past. Therefore like billiard balls released from frame all events determined when universe began."

He looked around at us, letting us catch up.

"If is true means probability of me talking on this beach was certain not just yesterday, or last year but at beginning of time! Also means everything that can happen tomorrow, or next year is already determined right at the start of universe."

I could understand that but the idea annoyed me. It meant Ax was always going to kill mum, I was always going to end up here, and whatever happened was going to happen because that was the way it was, and there was nothing I could really do about it. It was frustrating, but Dr Prosperov wasn't finished.

"This is deterministic theory of causation. Deterministic theory is good logic but bad science because universe has real physical limits. For instance in logic a universe is infinite in all its dimensions. But looking up at sky now, we see is obvious Universe not infinite. If infinite would mean infinite energy and infinite energy would mean no darkness at night. Infinite stars in all directions would fill all space with light from all directions. This is difference between infinite and very big. Universe very, very big, compared to us, but compared to infinity is very small."

"Another problem with logic instead of physics is entropy. Entropy means all energy, all information, all organisation, breaks down. If probability of this talk is certain at beginning of time this means infinite resolution of information for all time at beginning of time. All information is contained at start of universe and no entropy exists. Is simply not possible! Infinite combinations of events are possible at start which again implies infinite energy."

"Reality is universe has limits and entropy. This means that is limit to information in universe. So weather tomorrow was not fixed at beginning of universe. Here on Aotea might not be even fixed now! Simply not enough information in universe to fix such unstable event so far ahead. So what I am saying is universe makes up future as it goes along. Many things in future may or may not happen. Is not only not known by us, but is not possible to know future with any certainty.

He turned to look out over the darkening sea.

"I imagine moment of 'now' in time as like a surface of sea or black hole in space. Below surface of black hole is past. Things falling into past cannot be recovered or changed. Everything is falling to surface at speed of light or time. Above surface possible events condense like clouds. Some fall in large certain drops, others are a mist that either become events that fall like rain to the surface or blow away."

"To change perspective time is wave of certainty passing through sea of chaotic possibilities. At present moment everything is certain. But into future are multiple alternate universes. A continuum of potential multiverses of varying degrees of probability collapsing as wave of certainty of now moment rolls through."

"Past events are certain but have less effect on future events further from present they are. Large scale events fixed centuries ahead but smaller events, like beach party are not. In other words future is not fixed at beginning of time so future can change. This is why prediction is difficult. Is not simply that huge quantity of information unknown. Is because necessary information does not exist."

I was a bit surprised I got this. But it made sense when you thought about it. It just meant that you could change the future because it didn't exist yet. That made me feel better. It meant we could change things. How could it be any other way?

"But if information may not exist how to make long term predictions for KGB or anyone else? This is where my cosmic theory departs from mainstream science. Remembering am proposing seven unseen dimensions? Answer is in nature of dimensions of our existence. I am suggesting in addition to dimensions of time and space we see, also exists dimensions of information most people cannot see."

Again his gaze deliberately moved around us kids.

"Am suggesting universe is like television picture. Spatial dimensions like TV picture and sound we know well. But in addition to spatial dimensions is information dimensions. Is like subtitles or programme schedule. Events occur in spatial dimensions but also information dimensions and all dimensions are connected."

"But what is important about information is not simply how much, but also, how meaningful information is. For example DNA code for pine tree bigger than for human but what can pine tree do? Pine tree cannot move from place to place or think. Pine trees do not make great music or poetry or scientific ideas. Proves quantity of information not important. Some great ideas, like Euler's identity, or Einstein's energy equation can be written in only five or six characters. Very small in terms of information but very great in terms of meaning."

"So what is important when we discuss information content of universe, is not how much information there is, but how meaningful information is."

"Now let us consider again problem of predicting party on beach. What is meaningful information to predict beach party? Information about your atoms meaningless to predict party. Information about your molecules equally useless. Information about physiology no explanation why you listen to me rather than eat – and we eat soon. But to predict party requires information about none of those things. Requires information about consciousness."

"Proves consciousness cannot be left out of any predictive model of universe. My discovery is more simple and yet more astonishing. Information about consciousness is also included in information dimensions of universe. Is to say consciousness part of fabric of universe itself. Is not certain that universe itself is conscious – though that is possibility – but means consciousness not just generated by human brain. Consciousness permeates entire universe."

"After experience in Siberia is my belief that some individuals receive conscious dimension information into minds directly. What old people call 'second sight'. Returning to metaphor of universe as TV set is like they see programme schedule on TV set rather than have to wait and see what happens in picture and sound."

He paused and looked around at us, his eyes sparkling with excitement.

"What use? Allows prediction beyond normal powers of logic or intelligence. So in this way is possible to predict this talk. This, I did, ten years ago today and here is description on sheet of paper. Of course, obviously I have worked to make happen also. But story is long and food is ready, so let us eat now."

Dr Prosperov passed around a piece of paper in a plastic sheet. Me? I was glad he stopped there. My brain was getting a bit tired and my stomach was pacing back and forth growling to be let at the barbecue.

For a while there was just quiet as people ate, drank and chatted. When the paper came to me I was amazed to see my name and most of the others' too, though some were misspelled. If he hadn't cheated and just written it all before coming out I wondered what else he might have seen.

•••

"How detailed was it?" Sue asks

"The prediction?"

"Yeah."

"It was a map of where we were all standing," I say.

"And was it right?"

"Yeah, I didn't get it until after we'd moved to get food but yeah, it looked mostly right."

"And you don't think he cheated or anything? I mean stage magicians do that sort of thing all the time."

I nod, "Yeah, he could have easily cheated. No trouble at all."

"But you don't think he did, do you?" she checks.

"No."

"But if what he said is right then the chances of getting it right, were almost non-existent weren't they."

"Yeah, pretty much."

"So how did he do it?"

"He really can forecast the future. It's how he makes all his money. His theory of the universe helps."

"He's a pretty interesting man, your Dr Prosperov."

"Keep listening it gets even more interesting."

•••

After half an hour we were full and Dr Prosperov played some more on his violin. It was a friendly upbeat sound and you couldn't help but like it. Then he put his violin away and went back to his story without any introduction.

"My KGB unit already had techniques of remote viewing of places at present time. Needed was to learn remote viewing of places in future. Such technique would provide essential early warning of nuclear strike, or provide planners with information to plan operations."

"First task to establish the credibility of our predictions. So we start small. We start with decks of cards. Once shuffled is two and a half million possible five card combinations that can be dealt from 52 card pack. After year of practice had a correlation rate over 80% which meant statistically accurate in predicting card draws. After Soviet Union collapsed twelve years later one of our number, Uri Karalov, used skills to be professional poker player in USA. But then, our next stage was to begin work on strategic forecasting."

"In late 1970s focus of Soviet strategic planning on defending northern, western and eastern frontiers. Main threat American and NATO forces, particularly American nuclear threat over North Pole. My unit identified southern threat in 1977. Predicted fall of Iranian Shah in 1979, and threat to southern flank from strengthening Islam. We foresaw war and disaster."

"Report caused concern in Kremlin. Unfortunate that in effect report caused invasion of Afghanistan in 1979. In predicting disaster we caused disaster. This is problem with all forms of precognition. Is like Shakespeare's play 'Macbeth'. Witches predict Macbeth will be king and will be disaster. Macbeth makes himself king by murder and brings about disaster witches predict. Is called recursion effect."

"Afghan war disaster for Soviet Union and psy-ops unit. General Segeyev retired and unit moved to tactical operations support near Afghan border. Initially unit provided excellent results but horror of war destroyed morale of psychic operatives. Soviet Army and Afghan fighters extremely brutal. As psychics were repeatedly brought face-to-face with bloody consequences of own actions. Were suicides in unit which haunted us. Command considered unit soft so moved us to combat zone. Result was nervous collapse of entire unit, including myself as commander."

"In 1982 KGB psyops unit disbanded. I am sent to Moscow sanatorium. Here that I renew relationship with brilliant student of Professor Kolyagin – Dr eKaterina Morozov, and we were married that year."

He smiled at Dr Morozov, who smiled back. Although she seemed very aloof and cool she clearly loved Dr Prosperov very much.

"My wife, Katya, is electronics intelligence expert in KGB working on system to crack new London Stock Exchange electronic system due to go live in 1987. I became aware that my forecasting technique could be readily employed against capitalist system directly. I learned from Katya about capitalist banking system and financial instruments such as swaps, futures and hedge funds. The more I learned the more I realised it would be relatively simple for Soviet Union to operate in market and greatly improve financial fortune. I wrote a paper co-authored with my wife. The proposal was endorsed by General Arkady Yemenov who sent us to London in 1985 to work for the Moscow Narodny Bank."

"I am nervous about General Yemenov. His interest did not seem to be in enriching and securing Soviet Union, but more enriching and securing himself. He was not alone. In London it seemed many parties were enriching themselves at expense of others. I studied at London School of Economics as well as developed my system for financial forecasting."

"Futures contracts are simple. In effect they are promise by one party to buy, and another to sell, a certain thing at a certain price at a certain time in the future†. Things that can be bought and sold range from soy beans to oil to money. My interest was in long range future contracts. Reason is most future contract prices usually simple extension of price today. If future price range is much different, whether higher or lower, is possible to make largest profits."

"My abilities to predict led me to foresee two important future events. First was Western market collapse in October 1987. Second was collapse of Soviet Union in 1992. I set up fund and traded on own account in addition to work for Moscow Narodny Bank. Unfortunate however that prediction involving self is least accurate for reason of recursion. Like Macbeth we act on own predictions and leads us on a path which we think leads one way but in fact leads another."

"In May 1987 I was called to Moscow for routine meeting. Katya, having sudden health problem, stayed in Britain. At meeting General Yemenov – now one of Russia's richest men – confronts me with evidence of trade on own account. He merely angry I did not help him make fortune but as great hypocrite he has me arrested to betraying Soviet Union. I am interrogated and finally convicted and sentenced to five years hard labour in Gulag labour camp in Northern Siberia. Am fortunate Katya escapes KGB, and October 1987 crash occurs as predicted. This makes our fund worth fortune."

"Soviet prison camp very, very, hard place. Is beatings, is starvation, is colder than hell. I meet many good, and many bad, men in prison. Is very hard education."

He paused for a moment lost in thought. And then he sighed deeply and said as if from far away.

"In 1990 is Perestroika. Transparency. New General Secretary Gorbachev offers general amnesty and I am released. I am penniless, my mother is dead, have nothing but mind. So I travel in Siberia to meet shamans I met when travelled with Dr Vilenskaya ten years before. I travel to Mongolia."

"There I meet great old man named Nergui. He tells me of his son who has gone to United States after losing fortune for

Mongolian State Bank. He tells me I will meet son and we will work together. The son's name is Khenbish."

Prosperov indicated Ken, who nodded to him.

"I meet many great seers in Siberia and Mongolia. They helped me find my wife."

"Dr Morozov waiting for me in Chicago, in America. Worked for computer security firm. She helped me get to United States, and residency there. I find work as trader with Lewenstein Goldberg Partners. Using old system add to fortune made in '87 crash. Make even bigger fortune in Asian financial crisis. Then I leave Lewenstein Goldberg and establish Khronus Fidelity Fund in 1994."

"But this is not story of making money. Money is useful benefit of theory. Theory is life's work."

He stopped for a minute and then looked around at us again. I noticed he looked carefully at the six of us kids in turn.

"To pursue theory I assisted migration of six great seers from Siberia to Chicago to work with me at Khronus. These were two Mongols, two Tungus, and two Buryats. Three men and three women. They came to live with us and we learned much from them."

"Now I must reveal for the first time that success not due to innate psychic ability. My ability is due to psychic amplifier I have built, extended and modified based on cosmic theory. Was started with first doctorate and continued over years. Amplifier assists to open channel to consciousness dimension. Amplifier increases mental access to information extending from time past to time future independent of current place or time. I alone have designed this machine and I alone understand its construction."

"Use of this machine is unusual in that it extends own insight capability, creating self-fulfilling prophecy. It helps to perfect itself! I began by making copies of machine for visiting shamans. It took some months to explain what I was doing in terms that made sense to them but in the process I gained valuable insights."

"Construction very demanding and am producing only one every two months. However am noticing peculiar effect. Presence of second amplifier, amplifies first amplifier and vice versa. Two amplifiers not only need more than twice the power of one amplifier but also create more than twice the effect."

"Leaving aside financial affairs I use amplifiers to help understand amplification effect. We add third amplifier, then fourth and then fifth. I start to feel understanding of abstract dimension deep structure. Let me explain it to you."

"In information science one of simplest structures of information storage where one item of information references many other items of information. Each in turn each references more items of information. Is a repeating pattern."

He held up his hand.

"Main index, like a hand, subordinate references like fingers. Except that fingers are hands also and so on. This pattern is called a 'tree' because pattern of branches and sub-branches looks like a tree if drawn."

"I begin to realise I am navigating tree of universal meaning from topmost 'leaves' into uppermost twigs. The world tree is an ancient concept common to both Eurasia and North America. In Mongolian it is called Modun but it has many, many names. I become obsessed with delving deeper and deeper into mysterious tree structure. At root is potential discovery of vast consequence. The meaning of universe."

"So I add new amplifier. Information now flooding us. Resolution into certainty wave becoming excellent. I could make short-term predictions on tiny changes in oil prices, exchange rates and stocks and take profits on transactions over weeks rather than months. Our deals were making us millions a day."

"I finished seventh amplifier on June 11th 1994. That day I tested it by itself as I had done all the others. Was no different. On Wednesday June 12th Eastern Standard Time I joined the others as we powered on all amplifiers. I was to be last to join with seventh amplifier. At 11.14 exactly I powered on my amplifier to join others. There was massive surge in power. When I awoke at 2.21pm from being knocked unconscious the others were all dead."

Dr P stopped and indicated he needed a drink. He was obviously still quite shaken by this twelve years later. I couldn't help but notice that my birthday was June 13th, the next day. But something weird was happening. All the others were thinking the same thing! We were all born the day after Dr Prosperov's accident! Now we were all looking at each other with that creepy feeling again. Dr Prosperov took the glass passed to him by Gunter and drank it in one gulp. Then he seemed to collect his thoughts and took a deep breath.

"There was no mark on bodies. All dead with eyes open, quite relaxed. Very disturbing. All amplifiers destroyed. Confess I am very scared for three reasons. First, because I can still see dead friends and they as surprised as me. Second, because I have no understanding why they dead and I not. Third, because I am not wanting to go to jail again."

He let out a long breath and went on.

"Gradually ghosts of comrades fade. Leave me shocked and alone. Fortunately my wife helps me to recover and disassemble amplifiers. Then police come. Police investigate scene and find nothing suspicious except for six unmarked dead bodies. I am interrogated for days. I tell police we are carrying out deep meditation. Pathologist report finds no cause for deaths. Story leaks to tabloid press. Must face many terrible questions and terrible insults about my lost friends."

Dr Prosperov paused.

"This is darkest moment. Experimenting beyond limits of knowledge has caused death of six friends. Naturally I question everything. Then fresh disaster. Security and Exchange Commission investigators launch investigation of trades. Are convinced I am simply insider trader. Am exhausted and depressed. Investigation takes six months while trading licence suspended. But am luckily granted leave to return friend's bodies to Siberian homes."

"Is summer in Siberia and am able to travel to far North and white nights when sun never sets. Here among the funeral fires, the tears and feasts I meet very unusual man. This man is named Tsuygen. He is dwarf, 1.2 meters tall, with brown skin and black eyes. He says he is five hundred years old although he looks only forty. He says he has come to warn me I have released a great and terrible spirit from the World Tree and that although the spirit is bound to me it will seek its release so that it might re-start its mission to destroy the gods."

"Naturally we spoke at length. The man utterly convinced of what he is saying. I am convinced he is lunatic. He says I will find friends again, and I must continue investigations. He says I need to reopen the World Tree and enlist the aid of the shining ones. When I ask what he means, he tells me to stop being lazy and look up on Google! Then he drives off in old GAZ."

"I return to USA. For months I am forced into idleness by investigation. I start new company in Britain to continue trading. Also seem to have many chance encounters with more unusual people in similar vein to Tsuygen. Is time of much strangeness. I am assisted by meeting Mrs Jones who helps me through confusing time. Question my sanity many times but test myself constantly. Am slowly convinced that paranormal activity less unusual than generally thought."

"Past ten years very complicated, so to summarise. Have developed new company to handle business aspects of work. Better understand now abstraction interaction theory through practical experiment. Am now ready to begin new research phase to explore informational dimension. That is purpose of work here."

"Am recruiting psychic individuals from around world to reside with us here. Work to involve further refining theory of abstract informational dimension and connections between dimensions. Tests will include free and assisted visualisation of present, future and past."

"Laboratory to be constructed in lighthouse. Have received planning approval for refurbishment and now await delivery of equipment. Engineers begin work next week and construction follows early January. Facility to be operational early February."

"I hope can count on your assistance. We are on beginning of great journey of discovery which I believe will completely transform our understanding of the Universe and our place in it. Am thinking will be fun."

There was polite applause led by Mariko. A lot of people wanted to eat more. It was quiet because nobody quite knew what to say. It was like Dr Prosperov had farted long and loud and nobody wanted to point it out. After a while people started talking about the sky, or the food, or where they'd come from. Dr Prosperov's epic struggle seemed to be something too weird to talk about. Perhaps he realised he had frightened everyone because he and Dr Morozov soon went to bed. Mariko got everyone dancing and it seemed everyone wanted to put as much distance between Dr Prosperov's brain and themselves as they could.

I was still thinking about the six dead shamans and wondering if Prosperov was a bit crazed. I don't think I was the only one either. Still, even if the guy paying the bills was slightly mad, it wasn't going to put anyone off having fun. So we played with luminous frisbees, glow-sticks and bits of fiery wood in the dark until it was time to go in to bed.

We all went in together talking loudly in the hope it would make the ghosts clear out of the way. It seemed like it did. That was until I was brushing my teeth in our bathroom while Aunty Liz got sleepy Rewa into bed and into her pyjamas. I'd just spat out some toothpaste when I looked back in the mirror to see a man behind me dressed in army green. I flinched as he sneered at me.

"Bloody disgusting I call it," he said in my head. And then vanished.

I hate it when they do that sort of thing. It just leaves you all nervous and buzzy. I took a couple of deep breaths and then went to bed. Aunty Liz came in to say goodnight. She seemed quite cheerful.

"Are you OK Sam?" she asked, noticing I was a bit shaky.

"Yeah ... it's just it's an old house eh?" I told her.

"So ... do ... you see things here Sam?" she asked.

"Yeah. It's not just me either. All other kids here can too."

"Really?" Aunty Liz asked, surprised.

"Yeah, we talked about it today. We can all see them."

There was a pause.

"Aunty Liz?"

"Hmm?"

"What did you think about what Dr Prosperov told us tonight?"

"Not much. Most of it sounded crazy. But if he's paying I'm not complaining. It's better than I thought we'd end up with if you'd asked me on Friday night, that is for sure."

"What about those people that died?"

"I dunno Sam. He's playing with fire, but so long as we keep out of his way there's no reason any of us needs to get burned."

I liked the way she was still looking after us. It made me think we needn't worry after all.

•••

"OK, that was pretty weird," Sue comments.

"Uh-huh."

"So Prosperov built a prediction machine?"

"Using his theory."

"And it blew up and killed everyone but him?"

"No, it didn't blow up. It just killed the six shamans."

"OK.

"What?"

"OK."

"You think I'm talking crap again."

"No, it's just we're trained not to assume everyone's telling the truth,"

I sigh. It's so hard to tell anyone this story because it sounds insane.

"Well, Prosperov does have a lot of money. Nobody doubts that."

"Yeah, but he could have been an insider trader and he's made up this story to fool you all."

"Yeah, he could have."

"But you don't think so."

"Well, not now. Back then I was as suspicious as you are now. But the problem with Dr P is he has this annoying way of sounding crazy and being completely right."

"How do you know?"

"He proves it right in front of your eyes!"

"Well, I guess I'm no different than you then," Sue points out. She's right.

"Fair enough. But I proved UFOs to you, didn't I?"

"Yeah, you sure did."

"So if I tell you about what I've seen, at least you'll be warned a bit more in advance."

"Yeah, that would help."

I stop and think for a second, assessing her.

"What?"

"I wanna tell you how it was for us. OK? I mean the strange stuff didn't just all leap out of no-where. We kind of built up to it over months. Most of it was all quite normal."

"Just as long as it doesn't take months for you to tell me about it."

"Nah, it's just about how we all sorta came together as a group."

"Good. Sounds useful. Go on."

•••

The week or so after the barbecue seemed weird for most of us. Every day we woke up wondering where we were and how we'd got there. I missed my neighbours and friends. I missed everyone back home. I even missed my cousin Clive.

All of us kids looked a bit wigged out. The others were always talking about where they had just come from. And I had to admit that compared to Melbourne, Paris, LA, or Johannesburg a little island miles from Auckland seemed pretty dull. Even Cam, who had been living in Auckland, found it isolated.

Cam's story took some time to come out. Like Tahira she was a bit shy and didn't like to talk about herself. She's a very quiet, watchful person, but she's a lot more into listening and doing than talking. I think she learned that from her father as a way to survive. But her looks and determination she got from her mother.

It turned out that her mum had been kidnapped by Thai pirates in the South China Sea when the boat they escaped Vietnam on was attacked. She didn't talk about it much but we all got the reading of a terrified little girl of about four watching her mummy being dragged away screaming by cruel looking men with knives and guns. She never saw her again, although Cam knew she wasn't dead. But when Cam heard our stories she, like Tahira, opened up much more.

They had lived for years in a refugee camp in the Philippines on the skills her father had learned from his father who had served as a chef in a French household in Saigon. When he'd been our age Mr Trân had been a house boy for an American officer during the Vietnam war. His whole family had risked death by spying on the Americans for the communists. I couldn't help imagining Grandpop maybe grabbing Mr Trân as a boy as he ran through the jungle with a message for the Vietcong. Unfortunately Mr Trân's parents were killed by one of the last acts of the doomed South Vietnamese police before Saigon fell, and he spent his teenage life as an orphan. After the war he'd trained as a chef. Shy and never confident, he loved cooking and baking, and was trained well.

He was unmarried for a long time. But then to his surprise a pretty younger woman made time for the shy cook. She was also an orphan but she had grown to hate the communist system.

So not long after Cam was born they began planning to escape
Vietnam and start a new life in Australia or Canada.

They never made it as far. After the pirates they were hit by
a typhoon which nearly sank the boat and drowned them all.
But the wreck which was left drifted into a shipping lane and
they were finally picked up by a container ship and taken to the
Philippines.

They were put in a holding camp to be returned to Vietnam. But
the process was slow and everyone ended up working for the
camp boss. People who annoyed him were sent back to Vietnam
to prison. Mr Trân had been doing quite well in the camp but
with the chance of being sent back hanging over them, it was
no fun. Then a fellow Vietnamese visited the camp looking for
skilled people. He offered to say Mr Trân was a nephew in return
for cooking in his bakery in Auckland.

It sounded good but when they got to New Zealand they
effectively became slaves, working for almost nothing under the
threat of their 'Uncle' telling the Immigration Department they
weren't relatives after all. Luckily their 'Uncle' couldn't stop Cam
going to school.

At first Cam suffered badly. Small, quiet, and barely able to
understand what was going on around her, she was picked on
by other kids and ignored by the teachers. But slowly she made
friends with older girls and got the help she needed. Although
she, just like her father, had learned to keep her head down and
keep out of trouble to survive, she picked up more and more
English becoming more confident and more like any other kiwi
kid. Being clever, she began to realise that their 'Uncle' was the
one breaking the law more than she and her father.

Then suddenly one day after work their 'Uncle' kicked them

out without warning telling them that their replacements were arriving and they were lazy and ungrateful. They'd spent the night before the meeting with Dr Prosperov at the Sheraton sleeping in a park under a tree. Cam had found the ad in a scrap of morning paper that had blown over them.

Like Tahira, the only good bit about Cam's story was that nobody had a reason to chase them any more. Unlike Ashley, Tarik and me, they didn't have to worry about anyone suddenly appearing at Renwick.

But while none of the others sounded like they had had easy lives at least they had been somewhere. I was pretty vague when they asked me about New Zealand because I'd hardly seen any of it. I just felt like a dumb Maori hick who knew nothing, and had been nowhere.

On the other hand I had less difficulty adapting to Renwick House. Apart from the Khumalos, none of them had ever really lived in a village before. The adults didn't adapt any better than us kids. Patricia complained when anything was different to the States – which was a lot. The Baha'is grumbled about a lack of contact with the Baha'i community. Bernard complained that managing a garden was a bit of a come down from managing one of the largest game reserves in the world. But Mr Trân never complained about anything. He was happiest in his kitchen cooking and baking. Dr Gursoy was also having a great time having long serious chats with Dr Prosperov and Dr Morozov which always ended with him saying "of course" and then rushing back to the computer screen in his room.

Aunty Liz wrote a long letter quitting her old job and cried all over it. She had really enjoyed it and wrote she had been forced to leave to ensure our safety. She said she wished she could say where she had gone but did not want to be traced. She even took the ferry back to the city to post it.

The person me and Rewa really missed was Grandpop. From his messages it seemed Grandpop had switched from fishing to hunting for a living, so he only came into the village to check his house and trade bushmeat. I asked Aunty Liz how she would be able to find him again. She said we would keep in touch via Ed, the next door neighbour, who would take messages for him. She said as soon as she was paid she would buy a pair of prepaid cell phones so we could call him again.

Of course we weren't the only ones with problems from the past either. The Robinson's had the same problem as us but their home in the States was further away. Patricia called her mum in Houston to let her know they were safe. She didn't tell her where she was.

Bernard was getting worried about Zoe (his wife and Scotty's mother) in Johannesburg. The baby was due to be born soon and he felt bad about not being there with her. Although they spoke on the phone every night, and she said that her mum, Constance, and midwife thought everything was looking fine, he couldn't help worrying.

A common worry of all the migrants was the Immigration Department. They were always bothering Mrs Jones about it, but all she would say was that there was still plenty of time to think about that later. When they got to talk to Dr Prosperov he seemed very unconcerned and said there was at least three months of temporary visa before they were doing anything illegal. His casual attitude didn't help much.

To try and help everyone relax Mariko, Gunter and Khenbish organised "orientation" picnics on "Betty" the big yellow school bus. They were really great fun. We went all over the island: we visited the town and surf beaches in the South, where it was still a bit too cold to swim; we went to Port Hobson, the harbour in the North, where the expensive yachts anchored; we walked the bush trails through the centre of the island; we went to the hot pools, and we rode the horses. It was like this weird kind of holiday where the more us kids relaxed the more the adults thought about what they had left behind and got uptight.

Things got better as the adults got more to do. We kids were still cleaning the spotless house but we were still being paid and that felt pretty good. Each week Mrs Jones handed out giftcards she got in town from the Post Shop. It seemed like money for nothing – which it sort of was, because none of us could work out what to spend it on, or find any local shops with things we wanted.

The women weren't 'specially busy. Aunty Liz, Pat Robinson, Mitra and Soraya ended up spending part of the day in the kitchen helping Mr Trân, and the rest with Bernard and Gunter who were reconstructing the original formal rose garden, hedge maze, and shrubbery. This had started with the slow job of building a network of drainage ditches with a small tracked digger rented for a month.

If the women went from job to job gossiping, the men had lots to do. Mr Trân was usually up before dawn baking and was in bed by nine at night. Cam said he was used to it. Bernard was also up early and was usually pretty tired by the end of the day. Gunter seemed to be everywhere helping everyone while Khenbish stuck close to Dr Prosperov.

Dr Prosperov and Dr Gursoy were very busy organising a gang of electrical contractors, Gunter and Khenbish, to wire up the lighthouse. Every day four vans with two to three tradesmen each took the 8 a.m. ferry over from Auckland and spent the day at the lighthouse, returning home on the last 7 p.m. Auckland ferry. Often they were joined by a truck, either mounting a huge roll of cable, or some electrical doohicky like a heavy square lump of metal covered in cooling fins. These would all disappear inside the lighthouse.

Another person who was very busy was Dr Morozov. She spent all day in the library upstairs, working in the semi darkness on her computers and only emerged to consult with the Dr Prosperov, or read through a huge pile of paper full of strange words. She complained the internet connection was too slow so Mrs Jones had contractors in. A number of times vans came to the house and a week later they put up a big dome on the roof which housed our new satellite link.

As we got to know each other we kids found more to do when we weren't working. The weather was settling, just as we were. The cool breeze that had followed us about for the first week was warmer now. Cicadas had begun to sing, and while it was still too cold to swim, we were ranging ever further to explore the area around Renwick House.

We walked for miles up and down the coast, finding paths, lookouts, bays, beaches and caves. There seemed to be caves everywhere. The ridge of the island that rose high up above us seemed to be cut through with underground streams which would suddenly appear gushing out of a crevice in the rock. The water was cold, clear and delicious.

The hill behind Renwick was a pine forest but full of banks cut with cave entrances. Some had collapsed but others went in far further than we dared go. Khenbish warned us that some may have holes which would be impossible to rescue us from, so we didn't push our luck.

At the top of the hill was a small chapel and a graveyard. It was a pretty little chapel – it would barely be big enough for a class at school. It wasn't an active church and had a padlock on the door. A sign said it belonged to the Department of Conservation. But the overgrown graveyard was large and interesting. There were some early graves – the original Renwicks from when the house was first built, and some names from the twenties and thirties when it was an asylum. But most were from the first World War, either of soldiers who died of their wounds, or of Spanish flu. There was also a mass grave of Spanish flu victims. It was here in the long grass with the cicadas singing their heads off we found the graves of some of the Renwick ghosts.

You'd think you'd get used to ghosts. You know, get casual and chatty with them like in stories. On TV, ghosts are sort of like transparent people who wouldn't scare anyone. Half the time they're cracking dumb jokes. Real ghosts aren't so funny. I'd already met enough of them to know that. Real ghosts are always scary because they are unnatural echoes of the dead. And death is lonely and scary. Lots of people talk tough about it, but the reality is nobody wants to go there.

Most ghosts don't last long. They want something unfinished done for them. Then they fade away. A few remain. They are attached to a place by people left behind and wait for them. Others are attached by something else. A sense of injustice or anger. They can remain for a long time clinging to one idea as they slowly go completely mad.

When we were together the ghosts didn't bother us. For some reason they didn't like to be around all of us at once. But they liked catching us alone and it became a constant worry. They always stayed around the gallery. So much so that we didn't like going into it, day or night, which was a pity because it had a nice view. Bathrooms were a favourite because they could catch you alone. They didn't jump out at you. They'd just be behind the door or in the mirror unexpectedly. They didn't hang around. They just wanted to make sure you'd seen them. Then they'd vanish. You never get used to it. It always creeps you out.

The adults, Rewa and Asal rarely saw them. They noticed the cold when they were around and didn't go into the gallery at night. They became quite casual about them really, and just say something was a ghost. I guess that was easy to do when you couldn't see them.

They sometimes did annoying things too. They liked to flick switches, so sometimes you knew your vacuum cleaner had been turned off by one. They'd wait for you to come turn it on again. We hated that. They sometimes made things move – nothing large but it was always alarming to see footprints appear or curtains move or wastebaskets get knocked over when there was no-one there. Not too often they made awful stinks too that no amount of air freshener could cover up.

If the ghosts seemed to enjoy getting us kids they never went near Mrs Jones. And if Mrs Jones told them not to do anything they didn't dare cross her either. It was obvious they were really scared of her – which was both comforting and a bit worrying because it suggested Mrs Jones was dangerous in ways we didn't know about.

The graveyard by the chapel was a busy place for us psychics. You'd get flashes from all sorts of people and places. Presences come to you when you think about them. Others just leave impressions like flavours. One might seem cool and sad, another funny and random.

Corporal Bertie Higgins MC felt like the Renwick ghost who liked sneering at us. According to the headstone he had died in 1919. It felt to us that he died sick. Private Archibald Brown had also died in 1919. We had the strong impression he had killed himself. He was the mangled one. We wondered what held them to Renwick. It was strange thinking about something so cold on a hot summers day as we lounged among the stones.

"Unfinished business?" Ashley suggested.

"Bit'erness," said Tarik.

"Fear," said Scotty.

"Do you think Prosperov knows about them?" I asked.

"Ee must!" Tahira said. "Mrs Jones would not keep it secret, and 'e hired 'er for a reason."

"Tahira is right. It must be part of his plan." Cam agreed.

And then we fell to arguing about that again.

In the evenings we either hung around the upstairs lounge watching something on the big screens, playing board games or pool. I was definitely the best at pool although Tarik and Ashley were good too. I could even beat Khenbish and Gunter but Mariko wiped me out every time. Scotty, Cam and Tarik played chess. Tarik was the best, but Scotty and Cam could beat him on a good day. Tarik could beat most of the adults except his father but he was so badly wasted in ten moves by Dr Morovov when she ran out of excuses not to verse him that he never challenged her again.

So life at Renwick seemed sort of random. We were settled, but not. Working but not. Safe but not. And then suddenly it was just a fortnight before Christmas.

We had wondered about whether Dr Prosperov was into
Christmas. Tarik, who liked the idea of Christmas, but was
himself a Muslim, pointed out that as a Jew Dr Prosperov would
not have had Christmas as a kid but Hanukkah and as a young
communist he wouldn't have believed in it. However Tarik
turned out to be completely wrong, mostly because he forgot to
take all the others into account.

First there was Mrs Jones, the Welsh woman. She handed out
Advent calendars and announced that Sunday at breakfast that
as there were only fifteen sleeps until Christmas we had better
get organised. Gunter volunteered to do the Tannenbaum or
Christmas tree and traditional German baking while Mariko said
she would make the decorations. To our surprise Dr Prosperov,
who had been working hard on the lighthouse said he would
do the lights. Then he had a real treat for us. He told us if there
were special people we wanted to invite for Christmas he would
be happy to sort it.

Of course the first person me and Rewa thought of was
Grandpop. We wanted Grandpop to spend Christmas with us
as we had always done. The trick would be to get a message to
him and not have him followed. Mrs Robinson called her mother
to see if she wanted to come overseas to see them a couple of
times but her mother didn't even apply for a passport or take
it serious. Ashley said her maw-maw was very comfortable
with her sisters in Houston and probably wasn't interested in
travelling anyway.

Bernard had a special request. He wanted to go back to
Johannesburg to be at the birth of his first child. To everyone's
surprise Dr Prosperov agreed but pointed out that while he
was away someone would have to have formal responsibility

for Scotty. Bernard was torn. He wanted to go back for his wife and he also wanted to look after Scott but if they both went it might be hard to get back into the country again. They sorted out a deal with Mrs Jones as Scotty's temporary caregiver. Dr Prosperov also said that he would be inviting a number of people for Christmas and New Year as well. There were a number of names who at the time meant nothing to me.

Obviously though the main thing we kids were looking forward to about Christmas was presents. The first problem was there was nobody in a position to buy any presents because the credit cards Dr Prosperov had promised to pay the parents with had not yet arrived. The other problem was even when they did nobody was really in a position to buy presents for *everyone* else. It was an embarrassing little thing that nobody wanted to exactly say anything about – even the non-Christians.

But Dr Prosperov (probably pushed by Mrs Jones) saw the problem. That evening he announced that as his scheme for paying everyone was behind schedule he would pay for gifts for everyone to a maximum value of two hundred dollars kiwi which would chosen by sub-committees of friends and relatives for each person. He then gave the job of sorting out each committee to Mrs Jones.

It wasn't exactly a lot of money as those from the richer countries pointed out. But to me $200 was heaps. No-one had ever spent that much on me ever before. We made a big trip into Sylvia Park, Auckland's largest mall, in Betty the school bus, which Mariko made lots of fun.

I was on the committee for Rewa, Aunty Liz, Scotty and for some reason Tahira. It was odd having little Asal on the committee for Rewa too, because I was used to just me and Aunty Liz planning her presents, but having a girl about the same age to check things out with – especially clothes – turned out to be really handy.

I was a bit unsure about Scotty too. Bernard left behind a list of suggestions, but a couple – like trainers – were too expensive, while we simply didn't know what some of the others actually were. So me Cam, and Ashley went on instinct and got him some pocket binoculars. That used up nearly all the money so we got him yo-yos and stuff like that with the rest.

Mrs Jones had organised the whole trip so we got four shops of one hour each for each person, then we were back on the bus picking up pizza from town on the way home, because it was Mr Trân's day off.

In some ways the present shopping seemed a bit of a let-down. We had got some good presents: binoculars for Scotty; an MP3 player for Tarik; perfume and makeup for Tahira; a shiny red jacket for Ashley; and a camera for Cam. But somehow you wished you could do better. Get a fancier version rather than the basic one, or get more.

I mentioned it to Aunty Liz, when she came in that night to say good night. She said she was glad Dr Prosperov had been generous, but not over-generous. She said it made her trust him more because it was always possible to want more, but more was never enough and everyone had to learn to be happy with what they had. I thought about that and realised she was right but I went to sleep wondering what I'd do if I ever became rich.

The next day we kids went out to explore some more. We came upon a family having a picnic a the top of a small hill overlooking a bay, a few bays north of Renwick. The dad was a medium-sized, lean, Maori dude with a trimmed beard, curly hair, wearing pale green polarfleece, jeans and a jade tiki around his neck. His wife was European, small, pretty, but a bit big around the waist and thighs, with round glasses and red cheeks. She also wore polarfleece and jeans.

There were two kids. A girl who was about our age, and her little brother who was about Rewa's age. The girl was pretty and confident. Not as pretty as Tahira perhaps, but she had a kind of cheeky and cheerful spark where Tahira was moody and shy. The boy was very cute, with dark eyes and skin and gave the impression of being used to everyone adoring him.

The father asked us if we were from the Renwick House Refugee Centre. It was news to us that it was a refugee centre but we said we were. He asked us where we were from, and then told us he was Tama Reeves, the Department of Conservation ranger responsible for most of the land on the north-eastern side of the island – including Renwick. He introduced his wife Fiona and children Emma and Andrew. He suggested Emma could show us around. Emma smiled but didn't seem that keen. She told me later she felt a bit dumb with her dad there. He told us the bay below was great for swimming in summer with good waves, a long gentle slope, and no rips. He also offered to take us caving. Ashley, Scotty and Tahira weren't keen. Ashley said she got claustrophobia and Scotty was the same. Tahira just hated the idea of dirty places. But me, Tarik, and Cam were interested so Tama said he would call our parents and sort it out with them.

Tama seemed like a good father who obviously felt sorry for us and wanted us to appreciate where we were. He also wanted a bigger social world for Emma who he thought would appreciate what she had more by mixing with us. They showed us around the hill and beach, and everything was sweet when we said goodbye.

When we got home that night we discovered we had a guest. It was kind of surprising because it was an old Maori woman who was called Nea Te Kahukura but who we were to call Aunty Nea. I knew at once Aunty Nea had to be really old and really high born. It wasn't just because she was bent and wrinkly, but because she had a moko, the traditional chin tattoo Maori women had in the olden days. Not too many Maori women have those any more. She had a wheelchair but could also walk with the help of a beautifully carved old stick. Aunty Liz told me Aunty Nea was ninety-four.

She just had this amazing strength about her, even as she coughed and wheezed. She smiled at all of us children with a twinkle in her old black eyes. She laughed easily too, and she and Mrs Jones seemed to really enjoy each other's company. At one point Corporal Higgins was looking in at us in the lounge as she told us one of her stories and I noticed her notice him, and then notice me and Ashley had noticed Corporal Higgins as well. This seemed to make her very happy and she smiled at Mrs Jones in a way that suggested she approved of us.

Me and Aunty Liz had to show her up to her apartment. Aunty Liz would sleep in one of the rooms in her apartment in case she needed help in the night. I was a bit bothered by this because the ghosts didn't scare me so much when Aunty Liz was there. Somehow Aunty Nea seemed to know this and as Aunty Liz was about to wheel her into the American apartment she stopped her and spoke to me.

"Thank you for lending me your Aunt, boy."

I mumbled something because I didn't know what to say. I looked at the dimly lit passage wondering whether the ghosts were waiting. I was sure the presences were waiting to give me a hard time.

"Don't worry about them child. The living are far more dangerous," she said quietly.

I think she realised this was no real reassurance because she added:

"Confidence boy. Confidence. Cowards can't stand it because they have none. And they are cowards, most of them, because they fear moving on."

I mumbled a vague, if unconvinced agreement. She smiled and patted my hand.

"Here, boy ..." she said and reached stiffly around her neck and took off a small pale jade hei-tiki.

"Put this on. A swap for your Aunty Liz while I'm here. This is my protector Te Ma-tu-a. He's hundreds of years old and should be in a museum – of course I say I am a museum." she laughed.

Aunty Liz objected.

"Oh Aunty, he's too young to look after valuables."

"Nonsense, girl. You're a careful boy, aren't you Samuel?"

I looked from Aunty Liz's worried look to Aunty Nea's dark bright eyes shining from her brown wrinkled face.

"I'll be very careful, Aunty, I won't take him off!"

She put Te Matua in my hand. I could feel what she was talking about. Small though this little piece of jade (or as we call it "pou-na-mu") was, it was like a presence in its own right, and a powerful one too. With this around my neck the ghosts could get stuffed.

"Good boy. Now off you go, and don't stay up late. You also have that pretty sister of yours to look after."

"Thank you, Aunty Nea," I said putting Te Matua around my neck, and meant it.

"Look after him well and he will look after you," she told me. It didn't turn out that way though. That night the Maori gods bothered me more than the ghosts ever did. The dreams I'd had on the Ma-rae back home were even stronger than before. Ta-whiri-ma-te-a, the god of storms. showed me the black seas raging and the moon being erased from the sky. Tau-ma-tau-enga, the god of war, showed me a volcano lighting up the sky and shadows chasing a terrified black girl dressed like a soldier through the jungle. And blackest of all Whiro, god of evil showed me a white girl dressed in red, carrying a candle walking through a grove of bare trees in the fog to be murdered by adults in a sick ritual. Then Mahuika the fire goddess made fire pour onto men in red hoods. I could see them burning and screaming and I woke up, to the sound of my own whimpering. I look off Te Matua and put him in my bedside drawer which felt much better.

I didn't tell Aunty Nea how badly I'd slept when she asked. I just lied and she seemed happy enough. Over the next few days I learned though, that while Aunty Nea looked small and frail, her mind was sharp and she was almost as charming as she was tough. We found out from Mrs Jones that it had been Aunty Nea who had suggested Renwick House to Dr Prosperov when he and Khenbish first visited the country six years ago. It was Nea Te Kahukura who had lobbied the Minister of Conservation in some quiet moment on a visit to one of her trusts and got approval – despite the Department's opposition. So although she acted the kindly old nana, she was obviously very important and close to Dr Prosperov and whatever it was that he was up to. That got more mysterious on the morning of Friday 15th December when a white helicopter appeared out of a gray, overcast sky over Renwick House. While we were used to Khenbish landing on the helipad this helicopter was newer and smaller. Ken and Dr Prosperov went out to greet the visitor who was a tall, good-looking, blond man of about forty wearing expensive-looking clothes. We were on the beach at the time, although it was too cold to go swimming, so we watched through the screen of grasses as Dr Prosperov and the man chatted together in Russian.

The man pointed out to sea and just on the edge of the horizon you could see a small ship. Dr Prosperov invited his guest, who he treated with clear respect, inside while Ken chatted with the pilot.

Dr Prosperov and Dr Morozov and his visitor talked in his study for most of the morning over a pot of coffee and pastries and at lunchtime we were roused from our lunch of Laksa by the whine of the rotors. The white helicopter took off and flew back to the distant ship.

Dr Prosperov said nothing about his visitor but that night Ken let us know that the visitor was Edvard Shulyagin a business associate of Russian mega-billionaire Kolyga Adamovich. The next day the Auckland Star had a picture of Le Monde Bleu one of the world's largest superyachts owned by Adamovich arriving in Auckland.

The next Monday another Russian Christmas guest arrived – Professor Lana Vilenskaya. Ken picked her up straight from the airport and flew her to Renwick. She was one of the most beautiful women I had ever seen, even though her skin was the palest white – almost blue – and her blonde hair was greying noticeably. Her eyes seemed to be slightly bigger than normal, but a dazzling kaleidoscopic blue, like two stunning gems that hypnotised you with their intensity.

She was small and had obviously once been thin, but now she was carrying a little more weight. Her choice of clothes was odd. She wore long hippy dresses complete with beads and little mirrors in them but with jeans underneath. She wore big hats with feathers. And then for shoes she wore Ugg boots. She looked like a beggar.

Tahira immediately concluded she must have been a model who fried her brains with too many drugs. That was until Tarik pointed out Dr Prosperov had already told us she had known Dr Prosperov in Russia where she was the anthropologist in Mongolia he'd helped get out of the Soviet Union.

And it turned out she was far from crazy. She was a professor of anthropology at a big Californian University with a special interest in clothes and adornments. She said she wore her odd combination of clothes because it made her feel safe, relaxed and happy and she didn't care what anyone else thought about it.

She and Mariko got on very well. But there was an odd undercurrent between her and Mrs Jones – almost like they had history together which wasn't fully resolved. She was initially fascinated by Aunty Nea – something that seemed to be mutual, although they tired of each quickly. I didn't know what that was about. She also got on with Gunter, and with Khenbish who she spoke to in Mongolian.

Her relationship with Dr Morozov was friendly but not familiar. I wondered if there was some jealousy over Dr P (as we were starting to call him) there. As for everyone else she was friendly and inquisitive and chatted away in her Californian-Russian accent. I asked her if she had any family, either in America or back in Russia.

"I used to. But my American husband has remarried and my Russian family are all dead."

I asked her why she had no children one morning at breakfast – a question Aunty Liz told me off at once for.

"No, it's OK Liz. I had a little boy a long time ago in Russia but he died when he was very little. It was disease in my family which has no cure and I decided after that I wouldn't have children and risk them suffering as little Dmitri did."

For some reason all us kids felt something from her then. A sadness so big and deep it was hard to imagine. It rolled through the cafe like some huge wave of suffering, even though only we could feel it. It made the ghosts seem quite weak. And for all her smiles we could see Lana was almost ready to cry.

It was Cam who started it. She had been on the same table, listening in. Maybe it was because she had lost her mother, I don't know, but she jumped up and walked around and put her arms around Lana's neck and hugged her. They made a strangely good pair. Cam with her neat Asian features and her bright brown eyes, and Lana, blonde with her bright blue ones. Then Ashley joined in, then Tahira, then me – and there wasn't any room for anyone else.

Lana was laughing and crying a little at the same time. The wave of suffering had turned into sunlight and a happiness lit the room you could almost see. It was strange how we all felt it so strongly from this strange, older white woman. Her spirit was so much stronger than anyone else's I'd ever met, except maybe

165

Mrs Jones.

"This is my best Christmas present!" Lana kept saying.

The only face in the room not smiling was Dr Morozov. She looked sad and thoughtful. I caught her eye but she ignored me and retreated back into her cold and technical world. I felt sorry for her, not only because her pain from being childless was so clear but because she refused to allow herself any vulnerability as Lana had.

The next arrival at Renwick was Genghis Khan.

Well, he seriously looked like him anyway. In fact his name was Nergui and he was Ken's father. Dr Prosperov had already mentioned him at the barbecue and here he was in real life! He wasn't as big as Ken but he still looked in good physical shape. His hands were very rough and his skin dark and deeply lined from the sun. All his clothes were traditional and had been made by Ken's mother who had died ten years before, so he wore them in her memory. He looked like he was missing a pony and a hunting eagle, which it turned out he was, having both back in Mongolia.

He had a few missing teeth but his hair was still only gray which was surprising because (Ken said) he was ninety-two. I didn't have much to do with him. It wasn't that I didn't like him. It was really that I couldn't talk to him because he spoke no English. But even Lana and Dr Prosperov who spoke some Mongolian didn't get much out of him either. Nor could Aunty Nea who tried her girlish charms on him. He laughed and smiled pleasantly enough, but even with Ken there to translate, he still had little to say. He seemed very content just to watch everyone with his warm but penetrating slanted eyes.

Sometimes he would go outside and sit on the beach looking out to sea. He would laugh at our games, sniff the wind, but mostly he'd just think about home or doze off in the sun. He didn't like being indoors much. Sometimes he'd go to Gunter's workshop get some tools and carve driftwood. He made horses mostly but there were also eagles, bears and deer. Then he'd go to Mariko's studio and paint and decorate them. He gave them as presents to Rewa and Asal who made up games with them. He seemed to like the two little girls a lot. Ken said it was because he had six sons and never a daughter.

The strange thing was I never saw a presence when Nergui was around. Not one. It was as if they were scared of him and he seemed so strong and certain of himself I could feel why. He stayed upstairs in Ken's apartment.

The week before Christmas was quite busy. The whole house was transformed with decorations made by us all under Mariko's guidance. Gunter had installed an enormous Christmas fir tree in the ballroom and all the presents had been wrapped in huge boxes in bright paper with huge ribbons. Even Scotty's pocket binoculars were in a blue silk wrapped box big enough for a soccer ball. I spotted my present in a slightly larger red box and hoped that meant it was bigger.

Dr Prosperov had promised to put in decorative lights, and if anything he over-delivered. The front of Renwick house was lit up with sparkling lights of white, red and green as were the Pouhutakawa trees along by the beach which, as normal for this time of year were covered in crimson flowers. Even the dark pine wood that surrounded the driveway had white and blue lights in it.

Tarik was the first to notice that although the house and grounds were decorated there was no religious symbolism: no crosses, no

Marys, nor even a Santa or reindeer to be seen. The only symbol at all was Gunter's Tannenbaum.

As the countdown to Christmas entered its final week the weather finally settled. While there was still a sea breeze from the north, it was warm and lazy. The bay in which Renwick nestled was heating up so that the air over the beach swam in a haze. When we weren't working – which now just broke up the days – we were lying in the sun covered in SPF-30 sunblock; playing soccer, volleyball, or beach cricket (a game I had to teach everyone); or taking brief swims to cool down.

The air was warm but the water was still chilly. You ran in and dived under the waves, which seemed to be magnified by the narrow passage into the bay and then swam around and body surfed for about ten minutes until the cold started to bite. Then you came out and lay in the sun like a lizard until you were too hot and ran back into the water again. We were going through the sunblock like crazy.

On Thursday December 21st we were in the sea body surfing when Mrs Jones came running out of the house calling for Scotty. We all splashed out onto the beach and watched while she gave him the phone. He listened for a bit answering in a low mumble. Then he rang off. He smiled to himself and then noticed we were all standing around him expecting him to say something.

"It's a girl. Her name is Patience. Everyone's fine," he announced.

Ashley gave him a huge hug, followed by Cam and Tahira. Us guys just gave him a punch on the shoulder. He seemed quite distracted by becoming a brother all day.

The contractors worked like crazy the next day, crawling over the lighthouse installing cables at Dr Gursoy's direction. There seemed to be doohickeys arriving by truck every hour which were loaded in by a big mobile crane. At six Dr Prosperov presented each of the men with a hamper of beer, wine, ham and pudding and they drove off, leaving the place a good deal quieter than we had known it.

There was a weekend before Christmas Day on the Monday that year†. Mr Trân was happily baking all Saturday with Mitra and Soraya helping because of his day off the next day. But the others were slowly finding themselves without much to do so that afternoon we had a six-a-side soccer game with the adults. Gunter and Scotty played goal. Tarik, Cam and Ashley were our forwards. Ken, Mariko and Ali Gursoy were theirs. Tahira and I were backs and Lana and Dr Morozov were theirs. Dr Prosperov was ref and it was a role that was needed because both sides cheated like crazy. Mariko was the worst and gaily grabbed us and laughed about it. It was a surprising game because while only Tarik and Gunter had any skills we played surprisingly well. Tahira showed herself to be much tougher than I had expected and Tarik was far better at teamwork than I had expected too. I had expected Ken and Mariko to be tough, but the surprise was the two Russian women who were dogged defenders despite not being as fit as us kids. Everyone agreed it had been great fun and we should have more games with adults versus kids.

But after the game the big news for me and Rewa was that Ken was going to fly north to pick up Grandpop. Apparently Aunty Liz had organised the pick up with Ed who was going to drop Grandpop off on a secluded beach by boat. Grandpop and Ed didn't even know about the helicopter. They thought Grandpop was being met by another boat.

At about four they took off heading north. Rewa and me felt a bit nervous about Grandpop. We wondered whether he would like Renwick or whether he'd say something embarrassing. We were eating dinner – a Persian pilaf this time – when we heard the steady beat of rotor blades coming down the island.

We were so excited Mariko came out with us to make sure we didn't run out before the chopper had landed. As soon as the chopper was down Grandpop swung open the door and ran doubled over out of it like he'd been around helicopters for years – which I guess he had. He ran up to us and gave us both the biggest hug. It almost squashed us! Then Aunty Liz came out to join us and we went into the house with Rewa on Grandpop's shoulders.

Grandpop was very polite to everyone. He seemed very pleased to meet them and surprised me and Rewa with a few words in Russian and Vietnamese when he met Lana and Mr Trân. Mr Trân was very impressed and they seemed to get on surprisingly well. That in turn seemed to make Cam more friendly toward me than she had been.

Surprisingly, for everyone else, Grandpop seemed most remote with Aunty Nea. They touched noses, as is traditional, but they didn't spend much time talking. The others didn't know how Grandpop hated traditional Maori stuff. Grandpop was very impressed by Gunter's craftsmanship and seemed to find Mariko very funny. Dr Prosperov came down to talk to Dr Gursoy and Grandpop came over to thank him.

"No problem, is no problem. Am pleased you here," Dr Prosperov told him. And he really seemed to mean it too.

He was put up in a single room apartment, down the hall from Lana. These were similar to the ones we were in, but smaller.

That evening in the lounge upstairs I felt a warm sense of happiness that my family was now around me. I slept far easier that night than I ever had previously.

Christmas Eve was a great day for me. I spent nearly all of it showing Grandpop around. After the previous day's cook-a-thon Mr Trân was having his day off and so he and Cam joined us on our walk around Renwick. Mr Trân still understands more English than he speaks but because the same was also true of Grandpop's Vietnamese he was less selfconscious about speaking. The result was Mr Trân spoke Vietnamese, Grandpop spoke English and they understood each other most of the time with Cam interpreting when they got lost. Rewa and me just got by in English.

We used Grandpop's old car (the one he gave Aunty Liz) to drive around the island and check out all the places we'd visited in Betty. Grandpop couldn't help noticing there was no end of potential for hunting and fishing on the island. He was interested by the caves and wished he had the money for a new boat.

We didn't like to ask, but we could tell that Grandpop was barely making any money at all. He was scarcely more than a wild man. We also overheard him telling Aunty Liz that things back in the village were worse than ever. Ax had set himself up with two huge henchmen Wiri Curtis and John Tami-ha-né and they were demanding protection money from everyone. Sergeant Rahiri had practically given up and nobody did anything without Ax's say-so.

"If I thought shooting the bastard would help, I would," Grandpop told her. "But it's not just him. It's an organisation. It's like a machine which is taking over the whole place, sucking

171

people in, chewing them up and spitting them out."

I wondered what Clive was doing.

When we arrived back at Renwick I couldn't help thinking I was incredibly lucky to be celebrating Christmas where I was safe and relatively well off. I had put Aunty Nea's tiki away in a drawer ages ago because it seemed to work better when I wasn't wearing it. But that night I suffered for it with a terrible dream.

CHAPTER TWENTY: PATIENCE

In my dream we were at school, playing soccer, but everywhere there were explosions on the field that could blow us to bits. We had this horrible knowledge we were going to have to go up the hill where the explosions were non-stop. We had to walk up this deep ditch full of stinking piss, mud, crap and blood lined with millions and millions of crawling flies past the bodies of other kids who had gone ahead, knowing we were next.

We were all incredibly dirty and thirsty, but there was no clean water, just stinking sewerage, and if we stood up we knew we would be killed like the others. If we ran away the teachers would shoot us. Then I saw Clive slumped beside the ditch wall among the flies, sobbing, his face in his hands. I ran up to him but for a while he wouldn't look at me, and then slowly he uncovered his face. It was like meat that had gone off, all green and putrid, and crawling with maggots. He only had one eye left. The other was sunken with maggots in the corner.

"Help me. Sam, help me," he croaked, tears in his remaining good eye. I backed away, full of horror and guilt. I wanted to run but I could hardly breathe. "Help me Sam," he repeated.

And then I woke up. And the first thing I saw was the horrific ghost of Archibald Brown. I wanted to scream but I couldn't. And then he vanished.

I gasped for air and lay there panting for breath, like I'd been trapped underwater, trying to get Clive's face out of my memory. But eyes open, or closed, I couldn't. Nor could I forget what he'd said. He needed help.

I got up and looked out the window. It was 6:23 a.m. on Christmas morning 2006. The sky was a mass of pink and gray cloud. It looked quite cold outside. Whenever I closed my eyes Clive was waiting, so I got dressed and slipped out into the hallway. Then out the front, past the gallery. The presences were there, but they left me alone. Finally I escaped outside into the cool morning air.

The smells of the sea and the wind made me feel much better. The cool air was bracing and the pale light seemed to help make the nightmare fade. The birds were twittering a lot and their company seemed more of the here-and-now and less of the awful combination of past and future in my dream. I sat on a driftwood tree trunk and threw stones at the waves.

Up north Christmases had been fun. Rewa and me would get up early and inspect all the parcels. Grandpop would make a big fry up. Then we'd exchange gifts and about ten seconds later we'd be next door with the Barrys. I missed that casualness now. With everyone involved it was going to be more slower and more formal.

But I was surprised when I heard the door bang and looked around to see Scotty come out of the big house, along the beach toward me. He looked around at the view, which was quite lovely as the morning glowed apricot and orange, and came over to where I was sitting. I raised my eyebrows in greeting. He sat down, without talking, with his back to the log I was sitting on, and let his head fall back on to it with his eyes closed.

He looked a complete wreck.

"Merry Christmas," he groaned.

"Sup with you?" I asked.

"Ghosts, the whole night long. Ag, it's lekker to be out in the sun."

There was a pause.

"You had them too, hey?" he suddenly guessed looking over at me.

I sniffed and nodded.

"About their war mixed up with your own stuff?" he checked.

"Yeah," I admitted and threw another stone.

He let his head slump back and closed his eyes.

"They must really hate Christmas," he muttered.

I thought about that for a while.

"They had a shit of a time," I reflected, searching for stones.

It was funny, but as I said that it was if a spell was broken. This sense of cold anger that had been keeping me awake lifted.

"Bloody awful," Scotty agreed with his eyes closed. He yawned.

"Maybe they're just pissed off that they suffered so much and we show them no respect," I suggested.

There was a silence between us filled only by the sea as we each pursued our own thoughts.

"How much respect do you want to give them?" Scotty asked, opening one eye.

I thought about what a dick Corporal Higgins seemed to be.

"Not much," I admitted.

"They had it bad but now they're just bitter. Even if you set up a shrine to them they'd still complain it wasn't big enough," Scotty said.

"Hey, that's not a bad idea you know," I said seizing on his idea.

175

"Haw! A shrine? Serious?" Scotty asked looking up at me.

"Well, a statue or something. Just to make them feel remembered."

The door went again. Ashley and Tahira came out shielding their eyes from the low morning sun.

"I bet they've had the treatment too," Scotty suggested.

The girls walked over toward us. The sun glinted on Ashley's glasses. They had their arms crossed and looked distracted.

"How come you guys are up so early?" asked Ashley.

"Ghosts. What's your excuse?" Scotty explained.

"Same," said Ashley. She shuddered at the memory of it and sat down.

"Sam thinks if we build them a statue they'll leave us alone," Scotty told.

"Why?" Tahira asked huffily. Her eyes were puffy with lack of sleep. "Zhey are common peeping-toms," she complained.

"Was that what kept you awake? Not the war?" Scotty quizzed her.

"No," Tahira admitted looking back on the horror of her memories. "It was zer war."

"It was the eyes that got me. That was the worst," Scott said.

"Yeah," Ashley agreed.

"And the mag ..." he was about to continue but Ashley interrupted him.

"Djou mind? We came out here to git away from all dat!"

Scotty checked our faces.

"Sorry guys."

The girls sat down with us and we threw stones for a while at a particular rock.

"When do you think the others will be up?" I asked.

"Mr Trân, and Cam are in da kitchen already. I ain't seen Tarik. Everyone else is still in bed," Ashley said.

"What's the time?" I followed up.

"'bout seven. When d'you think we should go in?"

The door opened and Mrs Jones came out.

"Uhh nooo! She'll be afta us to woik," Ashley groaned.

Mrs Jones stalked towards us. She was dressed in black and looked like a grumpy shadow coming towards us. It was too late to run, so we waited knowing we could only delay the worst. Finally she was close enough.

"How many of you had nightmares?" she asked.

We all put our hands up.

"Right!" she said grumpily and turned back to the house.

We all looked at each other. We weren't going to miss this! We all got up and ran after her. We caught up with her and walked along beside her for a bit.

"Whatcha goin' to do Mrs Jones?" Ashley asked.

"I'm going to have a talk to someone," she said.

We thought about that for a moment.

"A ghost?" I asked.

"A spirit dear, we deal with spirit."

"You goin' to kick dey butts, Mrs Jones?" Ashley asked what we all wanted to know.

"I will demand an explanation. And if that isn't good enough, an apology and a promise there will not be any repetition of this interference."

We were impressed. We were scared of the ghosts and Mrs Jones was acting like they were cats that had been howling all night. We followed after Mrs Jones like a bunch of ducklings into the house.

177

"Wait in the dining room," she told us. "I just need to get a few things," and she went upstairs.

The dining room was busy. Gunter, Mariko, Mr Trân, Tarik and Cam were decorating and getting ready for breakfast so we joined in. When Mrs Jones came back we all followed her to the hall.

When we opened the doors to the hall we all gasped. The decorations on the tree had been pulled off, scattered and smashed. The tree itself was on an angle, which can't have been easy given it was fixed top and bottom. The presents in their beautiful wrapping torn open and strewn everywhere.

We walked into the middle of the room astonished at the destruction. Mrs Jones looked furious.

"I'll not put up with this," she muttered. Then in a voice so loud it startled us ordered, "All of you, out!"

We protested we wanted to see.

"Out!" she demanded and her voice had a ring of command you don't argue with.

We backed out the doorway but didn't close it, while Mrs Jones remained standing in the middle of the hall looking around at the top of the ceiling. Then she noticed us peeking, and I swear all she did was glance and the door slammed shut all by itself. We could feel something electrical tingling up and down our spines.

Then came a voice. It wasn't a female voice either. It was chanting a prayer or a spell but you couldn't tell whether you could hear it or you were just imagining you could.

> "O 'S tus a Chriosd a cheannaich an t-anam
> Ri linn dioladh na beatha,
> Ri linn bruchdadh na falluis,

178

Ri linn iobar na creadha,
Ri linn dortadh na fala,
Ri linn cothrom na meidhe,
Ri linn sgathadh na h-anal,
Ri linn tabhar na breithe..."

"It's Gaelic init," Tarik said wide-eyed, "I 'eard it on TV when I lived in the UK."

And his voice startled us because it was both louder but less pressing than the voice in the hall.

Presences were being drawn past us. They seemed nervous as if they were being summoned to an execution. Then a woman's voice joined the man's. I knew the high clear notes and the dying fall which always makes my hair stand on end, only too well. It was Aunty Nea with the Maori kara-kia (prayer) for the spirits of the dead. I wondered how I thought I could hear her even though she wasn't there.

"Aunty Nea," I only breathed, and Ashley who was next to me nodded, the light reflecting on her glasses.

Now even more presences were being drawn through the walls into the hall where Mrs Jones waited for them. And if that wasn't enough now we heard another voice. It was a strange very deep half-strangled voice combined with another that seemed to tweet like a birds and never seemed to stop to draw breath but just droned on and on.

"That's Ken's dad, Nergui," Scott whispered. "I've 'eard him sing like that before."

For a minute all three sang, a sound that was not a sound, in a strange mixture that still managed to work together. It was electrifying. And then it stopped.

All that was left was a cold feeling of terror in the air. But the peculiar thing was, it wasn't human terror that polluted the hall but that of ghosts. We didn't hear anything. It was so quiet that if it hadn't been for the wash of the sea you could have sworn time had stopped.

Slowly like ice melting, the terror slowly relaxed. The cold in the hall which seemed to numb all thought warmed as if it was a frosty patch of grass that had been in shadow. The tension eased and then after five minutes it was gone.

The tap of a woman's shoes approached behind the door and quietly, almost gently, Mrs Jones opened the door and stepped through it, closing it after herself.

"We won't have any more of those disturbances again," she said quietly. She walked on and then paused.

"Oh ... don't go in yet. I think Mariko may want to repair the damage to the boxes. You can all help later with the tree. Christmas will be delayed until dinner time. I'll just let the others know."

We desperately wanted to know what had happened in the hall but didn't dare disobey Mrs Jones. We were now completely in awe of her and we felt damn sure that if six psychic kids were going to learn anything we were probably in the best place in the world to do it.

We were just returning to the stairs when Mariko appeared from the kitchen. She had been so busy I don't think she had any idea what had happened in the hall. She just bounced over to us grinning happily.

"Merly Chlistmas you rot," she began playfully. "Now we having breakfast! Wake up everlyone! Then we eat!"

We were still thinking about what we had just witnessed in the hall and turned to walk up the stairs when Mariko, who watched

180

us with astonished disbelief, called us back.

"Stop! Stop! Stop!" she shouted and waved us back looking at us angrily.

"What are you? Kids or mice?" she shouted aggressively. We looked at each other and wondered what we had done wrong.

"This is Chlistmas right? Plresents? Santa? Too much eating? Are we happy about that?" she shouted.

"Yeah," we agreed, smiling and nodding mildly.

"What?" she screamed like a mad banshee putting her hand to her ear.

"Yeah!" we yelled a bit, catching on.

"You sad bunch of ooooold peepul," she sneered.

"WHAT?" she yelled louder than ever.

"YEEHAH!" we screamed madly.

"Muuuuch better! OK! Go wake everyone up!"

We ran up the stairs.

"Roudly as possibul!" she yelled after us.

We began whooping and soon woke the whole house. They were only slightly grumpy about it too. Dr Prosperov and Dr Morozov came down and we all wore silly hats and drank eggnog which hardly anyone had had before. Mariko had organised a whole bunch of silly presents which we had to wear until dinnertime. Mine was a tall hat with the Stars and Stripes on it. Rewa's was a feather, Aunty Liz had a cheap crown to be Queen Elizabeth with. Grandpop got a microphone. Scotty got a kilt, Tahira got a tiara. Ashley got a Cinderella hair-scarf, Cam got a giant rubber band for a belt and Tarik got a Tarik teabag. She was cheeky as well. Her beloved Gunter got a pig mask (which she snorted about, laughing like a pig herself), Mrs Jones got a witches hat, Dr Prosperov got a red nose (not sure what that was about),

181

Aunty Nea got a pair of plastic binoculars. Only Dr Morozov escaped, she got a white mask on a stick.

Breakfast was humungous. There were four courses Mrs Jones warned us. First we had our usual pastries with chocolate and custard. Then we had a choice of pancakes, waffles with every kind of jam, syrup or topping. With all of this we had teas of different kinds including liquorice, juices, hot chocolate and coffee. The coffee machine had been moved out of the kitchen next to the big samovar and by now we had all learned the art of frothing milk and making hot chocolates, café lattes and chai. Then there was the main course. Eggs done all sorts of ways with ham, bacon or salmon or herrings or dried fishy things or … well … to be honest I don't know what they were, on toast or rolls with potatoes every possible way and salads, and cooked vegetables. When Mr Trân came out last with his plate Mariko interrupted the talking and joking to lead a round of applause which he found really embarrassing – as always. The final course was plates and plates of small sweets. Turkish delight, Halva, tartlets, baklava and stuff like that.

We were stuffed! We were groaning around when Mrs Jones came back into the room carrying a phone. I hadn't noticed it ring but now she handed it to Scotty and went over to Ken. Everyone slowly realised what was happening as Scotty hung up. He looked around suddenly aware everyone was looking at him. "They landed late last night and they only just woke up. They wondered if they could be picked up at the airport."

Dr Prosperov nodded at Ken who drained his coffee cup and stood up.

"C'mon Scotty let's do this in style."

Ken and Scotty went out. Then we kids looked at each other and followed them like a bunch of overstuffed penguins.

"We call you back for dishes," Mariko yelled at us as we left. Outside the day was still, but cool, with a slight breeze. Ken went over to the hangar, opened the doors and started the ATV which was the chopper tractor. Then he drove the low trailer and the machine out into the daylight and onto the helipad. We didn't have much to do as he checked the Squirrel over and then got in and switched on the electrics so he could check its systems. Finally he called out to Scotty and told us to stand back. The motor began to whine and slowly the blades began to turn. We were still fairly unused to it and kept an eye on the blades as they turned faster and faster with Ken looking at instruments, talking on the radio and looking around. The sand whirled around so we had to get way back out of the way. Scotty, inside the bubble with earphones on, looked fascinated. We were all jealous-as. Finally the engine got louder and the machine lifted itself up, steadied and then roared off into the distance.

We turned in time to find Rewa and Asal handing out tea towels and telling us we were on kitchen duty. We went in feeling a bit bloated and bored. Still, it wasn't so bad. Mr Trân and Grandpop supervised and when we were finished they led us out for a walk while they smoked and talked. We skipped stones, threw things at targets and beachcombed. We actually walked all the way out to the lighthouse. We looked inside. I had never seen so many cables and wires in all my life. It was like a building of still plastic snakes. We had no idea what it was for.

We walked slowly back to the house and got sent upstairs while Grandpop helped the others arranging the ballroom. Nobody felt all that pushed to do anything much and I dragged myself back to my room and lay down on my bed. The combo of a full tummy and lack of sleep made it hard to keep my eyes open.

I drifted into a strange dream. I was outside looking at the lighthouse. Then the wires inside began to snake out the windows and grow up to the sky. Then they began to twist and turn very fast like a kind of twister or something. And as the wire twister turned, the whole thing began to sound like a helicopter loudly roaring outside.

"Wake up Sam. Scotty's back," Rewa yelled in my ear. I was about to explain that it was actually the lighthouse when I realised I was asleep and woke up.

I staggered out, head pounding, and found my way downstairs to join everyone else gathered around the chopper which Ken had landed back on its trailer. The blades were still turning as I ran down the stairs to join in.

Scotty was in the front again, trying hard not to act like this was the best day of his life, taking off his headphones, and talking to Ken. Then the side doors opened and Bernard got out on one side with a baby capsule in his hand, and Scotty's mum, Zoe, got out the other side. The crowd wasn't sure who to pounce on first and then made up its mind and surged forward.

Zoe was a pretty blonde woman about the same age as Aunty Liz. She was thin too, except for her tummy, and tanned, but looked really fit as well. Everyone was really friendly but, of course, they all couldn't wait to meet baby Patience.

The impression I got, as she went by, was a small, very peaceful, little black bundle dressed in pink. Ashley seemed to be magnetically attracted to her. Bernard looked really pleased but also really tired. He explained the jetlag and the baby – who was not usually this peaceful – had got the better of him. Ken, Grandpop and Gunter grabbed the bags out of the chopper and

184

carried them to the Khumalo apartment.

Scotty had to introduce his mum to everyone and it seemed that Bernard had already told Zoe our stories. She smiled as she recognised us all. I also realised I had never seen Scotty look so completely relaxed before. He liked and trusted Bernard but with his mum around he became much funnier and way less serious.

When he discovered Bernard and Zoe hadn't had breakfast yet Mr Trân immediately repeated brunch as lunch for them. While they ate they told about their trip, which was mostly a story of Patience not being patient at all, not sleeping, and screaming a lot. They said she was only sleeping now because of jetlag and exhaustion. They had arrived at 11 p.m. and then been kept up half the night by her complaining.

We spent Christmas afternoon helping Mariko and Gunter get the ballroom ready again. The Khumalos, except Scotty, had a nap. We did too. Mariko re-wrapped the presents and the men set the Tannenbaum back in place. The presences had gone, although you knew they were around somewhere keeping out of sight. We were all a bit grumpy that they had ruined Christmas morning and kept us from our presents but now the house was coming together again.

Mariko's design for the Christmas decorations was based on the story of the three Kings. She had painted a series of pictures of the Kings travelling apart and together on large sheets of plywood. The pictures were not very good but were brightly coloured with lots of gold. Gunter said they were based on icons which were pictures drawn by, and of, ugly old monks in their monasteries pretending to be Mary or Joseph. But Mariko had drawn the Kings a bit like Dr Prosperov, Dr Gursoy and Ken.

Other people in the crowds looked like us.

The centre was the tree but she had got some straw and a crib and mounted a powerful light in it to so that it shone up at the ceiling and put it in front of the tree which had the presents all around it.

On the ceiling Gunter had rigged up a curtain rail and taken apart a couple of toys to make a monorail with a slow clockwork motor and a white halogen bicycle light. On the rest of the ceiling they rigged up a big net of white tree lights. There was no question it was going to look quite lovely.

Mr Trân had already gone back to work and the dinner would be ready in advance. He was being helped by Mrs Jones, the two Mrs Khadems, Aunty Liz and Mrs Robinson. He and Cam would bring each course out on a cart and each table would have a turn clearing away and loading the dishwashers. The only table that didn't have a job was Dr Prosperov's – which was fair enough because he was paying for it all. He picked Nergui, Aunty Nea and Ken as well as Bernard, Zoe and Scotty to join him and Dr Morozov. Nobody felt too bad about that because Bernard and Zoe looked so tired and the old people deserved to be waited on anyway.

We sort of got dressed up for dinner. I mean we weren't in our best but we weren't raggy either. We gathered in the downstairs lounge where Mariko and Ken were making cocktails out of fruit juices, berries and mint leaves with umbrellas and other things in it. The adults had alcohol from all sorts of bottles of clear, wood coloured, or green, yellow or blue drinks. We had strange mixtures of soft drinks, juices and food colouring. Tarik invented a pineapple, lemonade and mint which I liked. Cam's ginger ale, ice cream and banana wasn't bad either. But Scotty's

tomato juice and cola was a bit too weird. I tried to make
something blue but Rewa told me it just tasted like lemonade
with blue food colouring in it which wasn't really what I wanted.
After drinks we all went into the ballroom.

It looked magical. The tables were all lit with candles. The lights
on the tree danced. The ceiling was lit with millions of stars and
the flashing guiding star swam through this slowly and silently
above. All the wall panels Mariko had painted shimmered with
dull gold and the presents gleamed in their shiny boxes.

We found the tables all set with Christmas crackers, bread and
oil on them. The middle table for Dr Prosperov was the biggest
and it had a Jewish candlestick thing on it. I sat with Rewa,
Aunty Liz, Grandpop, Ashley, and Patricia. Tahira and Tarik's
family sat together. Cam sat with her dad, Mariko, Gunter, and
Mrs Jones. Baby Patience was with her mum and dad. Zoe fed
her at the table with her portable bed by her. It was kind of nice
seeing her little black hands clasped around her mother's white
breast. Only Dr Morozov didn't smile at them.

Mr Trân came in with the cart and Cam came over to join him.
He looked embarrassed, awkward but very determined to say
something so we all fell quiet.

"This meal very special. Is both Christmas and late for
Hannukah. So meal has Middle East theme. First course is
mezze including Hanukkah latke, falafel, kibbeh, kofta Jewish
cheese knishes, bread with hummus, baba ghanoosh, and
tabboleh. Second course is roast lamb with rosemary and
lemon and assorted regional vegetable dishes, dessert course is
assorted sweets including baklava, Turkish delight, halva. Hope
you like. Bon Appetit."

We all clapped. Then Mr Trân and Cam started bringing out

plates to the tables. They were very quick and you knew they had done this a million times before. Each plate had six things on it and there was one of each thing for us so we couldn't get too full. He also put down a big clear bottle of Apple juice and a white wine.

We munched our way through these snacks fairly quickly because by now brunch had worn off and we were getting hungry again. That didn't stop me enjoying the food though because the different flavours were all interesting.

When we finished eating and the first table cleared away there was a bit of a break for chatting which seemed to go on for longer than expected. Then Mr Trân came back into the room and Dr Prosperov stood up.

"Friends, guests and colleagues. Before next course wish to say words about occasion," he paused.

"I am not Christian. Was Jewish as child but am becoming communist later. Now? Hard to say. In Russia was no Christmas and Hanukkah forgotten. But discover Christmas in London. Seemed to my Soviet self is festival for masses inspired by bourgeois shopkeepers, manufacturers and bankers. But later in Chicago visit friends homes and start to see something more. Is celebration of children and wonder and hope a child brings."

I noticed Dr Morozov glance up at her husband. She had not looked at Patience much, but when she did it was sad to see so much pain in her eyes.

"I now think is reason so many countries adopt Christmas even if not Christian. Buddhists, Muslims everyone can see special festival for children a good thing. Is celebration of hope for peace and hope for future together," he paused for a moment and took a cap from the table and placed it on his head.

"Hanukkah was officially over day before yesterday. Is old Jewish celebration. Story is of triumph, of survival of faith and hope, in face of adversity. Is special to Jews and makes Jews special. To me story is special, not because I raised a Jew and not because Jews special but because is about keeping faith and spreading faith to those who have become lost in darkness and forgotten specialness we all have as children."

"I am not religious man. I am scientist. I believe in evidence, experiment and theory. To me much religion about priests controlling masses with stupid stories. But I am not blind. I see importance of symbol to all people. I see importance of hope to all people. I see importance of faith and tradition to all people. So is not logical to say these things untrue and unimportant. These things very true and very important to being human."

"I see lessons in all people and all religions. I believe no-one has monopoly on truth. So I shall ask all of you to join with me to celebrate all festivals important to us here. We will celebrate Newroz, Muharram, Bon, Ridvan, Matariki and Tet in their turn also. For in all of these celebrations we celebrate something basic, good and true in all of us."

He had all our attention now. It was nice that he was acknowledging how many of us were not Christians.

"So returning to Christmas and to Hanukkah. Tonight we celebrate a child and our faith in ourselves and in children. We celebrate the preciousness of every little life such as little Patience just here, just born. We celebrate our hope for peace and goodwill for without these things how will we here, and we as a species, survive?"

"My friends you are microcosm of world. We are white, black, yellow, brown. We are Christian, Jewish, Muslim, Buddhist.

189

Our hope is world's hope, our faith is world's faith, our light
is world's light. So please to excuse and indulge if I say small
Jewish prayer taught by Grandfather."

He closed his eyes for a moment. Then he began to sing this
prayer.

"Baruch Atah Adonai, Barucha At Shekhinah,

Eloheinu Melech Ha-Olam;

Baruch Atah Elohim,

Eloheinu Melech Ha-Olam –

asher kidishanu b'mitz'votav v'tzivanu l'had'lik neir shel Chanukah.

Amein."

I had never heard Hebrew before and it sounded ancient and
wonderful. As he spoke he lit the lamp in front of him and each
of the nine candles shone brightly in the dark. Then he switched
back to English.

"This is our light for the world. It will shine in the dark places
and the dark times through our faith in each other and despite
adversities we shall overcome."

Something suddenly seemed slightly different about Dr
Prosperov. His English was better, his voice faster and clearer,
and he was standing straighter. His eyes seemed locked, lost in
the flames of the candle. It was a touch spooky.

"Let it shine for the children and for the smallest voice who has
faith left in hope, in mercy and kindness. Let it shine for the
past and for the future. Let it shine in our hearts as a beacon for
ourselves and for others who have lost their way. Let it shine
until the end of days when all shall learn their place in God."

Suddenly Patience cried out. Zoe picked her up and cuddled
her but she kept wailing so she took her outside. Dr Prosperov
suddenly looked around, as if seeing us for the first time as we

watched him. Then he faltered, seemed to look a bit faint and
then steadied himself. He looked slightly lost for a second, then
saw Mr Trân in the corner.

"Ah, second course is ready," he said lamely and sat down
looking a bit pale. Dr Morozov looked a bit worried and he
patted her hand and asked for some water. Mr Trân came in
with his cart but I noticed Dr Prosperov wiping the sweat from
his forehead – and it wasn't that hot. But I was easily distracted.
The food was brilliant again. Lamb which melted in your mouth
with gravy, chicken as well with lemon, stuffed vine leaves
(which took a bit of getting into), roast pepper salads with
squares of soft white cheese, fat olives (tho' I hate olives) in this
grainy stuff called couscous, the tastiest carrots I'd ever had, and
of course roast potato, roast pumpkin, sweet potato and parsnip.
Where the starters had been carefully doled out this course was
a pig-out and we stuffed ourselves to oinking.

We were all pleasantly full again and talking loudly when Mariko
stood up.

"Hey! Hey! Shut up everyone!" she yelled bossily. There was
quiet.

Then in a reminding sort of voice. Her eyes turning to the tree.

"Kiiiiiiddss? There's some preeeeseeeents! Go get em!"

We ran to the tree. There was a huge stack of boxes. I found
Rewa's first and gave it to her. Finally I swapped the box I was
holding which was Ashley's, for the one she was holding that
was mine.

"Merry Christmas," she said.

"Yeah, Merry Christmas!" I agreed. Because it was.

We sat at our tables and opened our boxes.

Rewa got her's open first. She squeaked with delight. We'd got her a pair of shiny red boots and a matching handbag. Ashley was rapt with her jacket too. I opened my box and pulled out a wetsuit. I was stoked. I had wanted to do more swimming but it had been too cold. Now I was into it.

While we were talking to our adults Ken appeared at the table and put a shiny card in front of Aunty Liz. It was the credit card Dr Prosperov had promised. Dr Prosperov stood up.

"For information. Cards arrived four days ago. Have added small bonus for Christmas," Dr Prosperov said and sat down.

Then Zoe Khumalo stood up.

"Hey everyone. Uhh … I'm pretty new here. We only arrived five hours ago. But I would like to thank everyone for making me feel so welcome. I've never seen such a mixed group of people who seem so happy together before. And you know I think that's partly because we have to get on because … well, we haven't got a lot of choices. But I think it's also because of Dr Prosperov and Dr Morozov. They have invited us into their home and their lives on terms so generous that when Bernard told me about it I couldn't believe what he was telling me."

"So at the risk of being a bit of a new chum overstepping the mark could I ask everyone to fill their glasses, and stand while I propose a toast."

The adults filled each other's glasses with wine and stood. We kids did the same thing with Apple juice.

"Dr Prosperov, Dr Morozov. We thank you for this very Merry Christmas. We thank you for your hospitality and your generosity. And we wish you both the best of health, prosperity and happiness for the New Year. Happy New Year."

"Happy New Year," we echoed.

Both Dr Prosperov and Dr Morozov looked both pleased and

surprised. We all sat down. Then Dr Prosperov stood up. His
eyes were beaming.

"Is very, very bad idea to toast Russian! Toasting is Russian
national sport. Russians toast to win!"

All the adults laughed.

"Though, of course, Russians toast with vodka," he added.

"Thank you Mrs Khumalo for kind words. We," he looked at Dr
Morozov and back at us, "very happy to receive good wishes for
new year. Of course your presence is not charity. You are here
because you are valuable. But must say we have no control over
how this community relates to itself. When started worst case
was six families in constant dispute. In actuality very pleased
at way everyone tries to make community work. So to toast. If
everyone would stand."

We filled our glasses and stood up.

"To our community!" Dr Prosperov said.

"To our community," we echoed and all sat down.

It looked like that was it, as everyone went back to chatting.
All us kids got together and admired each other's new stuff.
Ashley looked pretty fantastic in her jacket and Cam took her
first picture of her pouting like a model. Tahira was rapt with
her makeup and at once was making up Ashley while Scotty and
Tarik seemed pretty pleased with their presents too.

It was our turn to clear so I had to help the others gather up all
the plates and things and take them into the kitchen. It didn't
take long to load them in the dishwashers and get rid of the
bones and leftovers. Mr Trân came in and loaded the cart with
the desserts and a whole heap of plates and just left them out for
people to help themselves.

I tried Gunter's Stollen, which I liked, as well as the Hanukkah suf-gani-yot, the English Christmas pud' and a bit of Baklava. But I couldn't finish it. Once again I had overstuffed myself. By ten most of us kids were falling asleep. We staggered upstairs in our family groups saying goodnight, went through our bathroom routines and feeling fat and happy, fell into a deep and untroubled sleep. It was definitely the best Christmas I ever had.

...

H ang on," Sue says, sitting up.
I open my eyes on the deck chair, and sit up too. It's good
to have another break. I wonder if my voice will last.

"So Doctor Prosprov could suddenly speak better English? How
come? Did he have multiple personalities or something?"

"Sort ... of," I agree carefully.

"Sort of?"

"Well, we didn't find out exactly until a bit later when a whole
bunch of totally weird stuff happened, and then it sort of made
sense."

"Sort of?" she challenges me gently.

"There is no way you aren't going to find this weird Sue."

"I already find it weird. Having your Christmas wrecked by
ghosts is already weird."

"But you believe me?"

"Well, I have to admit it's pretty hard to relate to. It's not the
usual Christmas domestic we get called to."

"It wasn't anything I'd ever heard of either. None of us had
realised what they were capable of when they were upset. But
Mrs Jones said it was actually partially our fault."

"Your fault!"

"Well not our fault but we made it possible. She said Spirit used

our fears, our dreams and our powers to wreck the room. She
said Poltergeists are a combination of powers. Undeveloped
psychics plus inspiring Spirit. Dr Prosperov said later most
of the poltergeist activity he had investigated with Professor
Dubrov involved people our age. That was one of the side-effects
he'd expected."

"Expected? So you weren't there at random?"

"No, but we didn't find that out until later."

"How much later?"

"Just a few months further on. It's coming up pretty soon."

"OK," Sue says and lies back down.

She sighs. She actually seems quite happy. Almost like she's
having a holiday from her old life with Rachel. I think she's
forgetting the UFO danger a bit too. That's part of my plan.
If I'd gone straight into more scary stuff she wouldn't have
coped. She'd needed a rest to distract her so she could process
everything that had happened to her so far. I'd told her the
stories of the others to open her mind and stretch her horizons
because like most people her experience of the world and its
problems was pretty limited. All of that was still relatively easy,
though. None of it challenged her the way the UFO and the light
in the tunnel had. Now that she's relaxed I can slowly introduce
the truly weird world we had been introduced to.

"OK, keep going," she says, closing her eyes, not knowing what's
coming.

•••

The days after Christmas were pretty relaxed. The only person
who looked busier was Bernard who now had to help look after

little Patience. Of course he wasn't alone. Everyone wanted a cuddle with Patience, especially Ashley.

Patience herself was a cute little black bundle with the beginnings of curly hair and big dark eyes. She was a happy baby and didn't mind being passed around. Scotty was very proud of her and to see Ashley and Scotty together with Patience, you'd think she was theirs from the fuss they made.

Zoe was obviously just hugely relieved to be with her family again. She was good at getting on with people and made friends with Mitra and Soraya immediately. Mrs Jones too made her feel welcome and Gunter and Mariko couldn't do enough to help. The only obvious exception was Dr Morozov who would hardly glance at Patience and buried herself in her work in her room.

For Rewa and me, however the main attraction was not Patience, but Grandpop. He took it upon himself to find good bush and seafood for Mr Trân and was soon leading expeditions with Mariko in Betty the Bus. Scotty and Cam were also regulars on these expeditions looking for shellfish, crabs, berries and greens and the strange sea creature we call Kina.

Cam and Scotty became good at digging up shellfish from the beach or off the rocks. Grandpop was also very happy to discover that Mariko was descended from a long line of Amai pearl divers from Okinawa so she joined us diving for Paua. But where we kids all found Kina – a shelled creature that floats free rather burrowing or attaching itself to rocks – totally disgusting, Mariko quite liked them. Grandpop said that made her an honorary Maori.

Mariko organised the New Year's Party. She got all the big flat screen TVs moved into the Ballroom and nagged Dr Morozov

197

into setting them up so they showed pictures from web cameras all over the world. Then, she set up some big speakers while Ken set up another bar. Of course Mariko couldn't have a party without a theme so she picked a magical creatures theme. Everybody had a great time making stuff in her studio or Gunter's workshop. Then at six we all came down.

I was dressed as the demi-god Maui – which was pretty easy because all I needed was my ka-pa ha-ka Maori cultural clothes and to paint a mo-ko or face tattoo with luminous paint. Rewa dressed as a pa-tu-pai-a-re-he or Maori fairy. Aunty Liz was ma-hui-ka, the Maori goddess of fire with shiny paper fire in Maori spirals, while Grandpop came as Ta-né, the god of the forest, dressed like a tree.

Ashley and Pat Robinson came as some of Michael Jackson's zombies. The Trâns came as two of the Tao Quan, the kitchen gods in their best silk. Bernard came as a Ndebele Sangoma or witchdoctor while Scott and Zoe were Amadhlozi or ancestral spirits dressed as ghosts. The Khadems came as Peri, or Persian fairies, Tahira and Asal looking very pretty. Tarik dressed like some kind of warrior called Sah Ismail, who I'd never heard of. His dad just wore his Alevi religious outfit and called himself a genii. Mariko put on a kimono and fur, with ears, to become a Kitsune or fox-fairy; Gunter was a dwarf; Mrs Jones wore gray and said she was a Gwyllion, though nobody knew what that meant. Ken wore some Mongolian clothes of Nergui's (who didn't come) and came as a Zaarin or chief shaman. Dr Prosperov and Dr Morozov came as Vila, or Russian wood fairies.

Anyway it was all kind of fun. Tarik tried to show-off dancing, but Ashley and Scott had much better dance moves. Tahira and

Asal danced with Rewa, and I tried to avoid dancing coz it made me feel dumb. I noticed Dr Gursoy and Mitra chatting, while Ken was dancing with Patricia Robinson. Mariko and Cam were a team running around getting redder in the face, pulling Mr Trân up to dance and making Aunty Liz dance with Gunter. I stuck it out but after midnight most of us went to bed.

A few days after New Year Tama came by with Emma and her friend Charli to see if anyone was interested in learning caving. Tahira and Ashley definitely weren't. They were doing girly stuff with Rewa and Asal. Scotty hated the whole idea of being enclosed, but Cam and Tarik were curious about it so we agreed to go. Grandpop insisted in coming too in his old car because he thought another adult was necessary in case there was trouble. Tama took us to the cave system we hid in – but of course it was new to me then. When we got out Grandpop was not impressed to discover that Tama had no overalls, no helmets, no ropes and only two working torches. Tama didn't help matters by telling Grandpop to chill and not to worry so much.

Our introduction to caving was the U-bend. Being a big man Grandpop found it much tighter than the rest of us. I found it a bit scary to stick your head into the dark not knowing what was on the other side but Emma was leading the way and I didn't want to look like a pussy in front of her.

The caves are very dark and take a bit of getting used to. Although Tama and Grandpop had torches, we were always tripping or sliding because we weren't used to the rocks or the slimy mud that seemed to hide in shadows.

Tama led us on a winding path past the slide we went down. As the way got tighter, things got harder for Grandpop who was bigger than any of us. For us kids it was still easy and Tama seemed to be a wiry twisty type who could go anywhere. It didn't help that he was leaving Grandpop behind. The path began to turn into a waterway and twist and turn downward. It was getting more and more slippery. We all slipped, even Tama, although now Grandpop had an advantage because he could brace his path using the cave walls and roof. Finally we emerged into the cavern at the bottom of the slide and took the route out you did out. We came out all wet and muddy to find a cold wind with a light rain had come up. The walk up the hill to the car park was an uncomfortable trudge but when we got back up Tama seemed pleased.

"See, it's pretty easy really," he enthused "if you want to do it again we can do some of the other routes."

The weather had been a bit cool lately so with swimming ruled out it seemed like something interesting to do. In the car home Grandpop admitted the route hadn't been all that dangerous but he still thought Tama was under-prepared and insisted that I take a few more things with me next time.

It turned out to be good that I did. We went back a couple of times over the next few days because the weather had got crappy. I enjoyed it, as did Cam, although Tarik was only so-so. We started exploring some of the trickier formations and seeing I had one, I started wearing my wetsuit. It was a bit hot sometimes, but I'd rather be hot than cold, and as the others were getting wet and cold, I was pretty sure I was doing the right thing, even if Tama thought I was listening too much to Grandpop.

Anyhow, to cut a long story short, on our fifth trip we were walking a narrow path above a fast underground stream when Emma, in her tight jeans, slipped, and fell about three meters into the water. Suddenly everyone was shouting in the echoing cave where before the only noise had been the rushing water. The stream was only about a meter deep but it was very cold and very fast. Tama called out for his daughter frantically looking for a way he could safely get down to her. He ordered us not to jump down because he couldn't be sure he could get us out again too. Well, there I was with a wetsuit, a rope and a cycle helmet with a light on it. In no time at all I had given one end of the rope to Tama and with the other already tied around my waist, was climbing down to Emma, who had got her head out of the water, clutching her arm and screaming loudly. She had a big cut in her head and the blood was trickling down her face. She tried to stand up but fell over again, and struggled to get her head above water coming up coughing and screaming.

Tama was sitting with the rope looped around him, and the others were doing their best to hold him on the path. There was no bank to the stream and as I got down I had no choice but to lower myself into the freezing current. Emma was forcing her way toward me. She launched herself at me and I ended up with my free arm around her. It would have felt a lot better not in a cave of freezing water.

The problem was Emma's left wrist. She'd hurt it when she'd put her arm out to break her fall, so she couldn't climb up the rope. At this point I missed Grandpop. He would have been able to haul us both out because he was so strong. Instead I realised I had to put my loop over Emma. Tama was worried for us both, but Emma was his daughter.

I put the loop over Emma and Tama managed to haul her out to the path. The others took her back the way we'd come while Tama hauled me out.

"Good work mate," he told me and then we went back to join the others.

Emma was in a pretty bad way. She was cold and shaking. Her wrist was useless and there was still blood on her face. I was cold but not too bad. We were about twenty minutes from the entrance and there was nothing for it but to walk it.

It took ages to get out. Tama drove us back to Renwick, dropped us off and hurried home. I spent ages warming up in the shower but then joined the others for hot chocolate in the lounge for a game of pool. Grandpop was out but when he came back and heard the story he smiled.

"Told you that idiot wasn't prepared. You did good, Sam. But imagine you hadn't had all that stuff with you. That girl could have been in serious trouble."

The next day Emma called me. She had sprained her wrist which was now in plaster and her head had needed stitches. She was a bit shy but she thanked me for helping her. I said I hoped she hadn't been put off caving, partly because I wanted to keep doing it, and partly because she was hot and I liked her.

"Not if you're around," she blurted out.

And then she seemed to be a bit embarrassed about what she had just said and babbled on for a while backtracking. I asked her what she was doing with her hand in a cast. She admitted not much, so I invited her to come over to Renwick sometime. She was interested, but a bit shy, and made no promises.

With caving out, Grandpop came up with a new toy for us. The marshy bay that Renwick had been built in was ringed by fairly steep hillside with plenty of tall trees. On one steep clay bank Grandpop made a huge Tarzan swing which carried you from the hillside high up into the trees' other branches. It was awesome.

We spent hours swinging and climbing and playing games getting up to ten to twelve meters up. It was a bit dangerous, but nobody fell. Grandpop added a few more ropes so we could climb and swing in other places and we soon had a chasing game through the tree worked out.

After a week off Dr Prosperov and Dr Gursoy went back to work on the lighthouse and the contractors' vans and trucks reappeared. The highlight was the delivery of a copper coated superconducting mast for extracting electricity from lightning strikes. The mast was worth over three hundred thousand dollars and Ken used the chopper as a flying crane to lower it into the top of the lighthouse.

Somehow, someone at the Auckland Star heard about the project and started bugging Dr Prosperov for an interview. Dr Prosperov wasn't very keen and Aunty Liz, Patricia and Dr Gursoy were even less interested in having our whereabouts revealed. But as Dr Prosperov said, if we tried to be secretive the Star would get even more curious, so it was essential that the Star was given something misleading.

The result was that one Thursday we packed up Betty and went for a picnic further up the island on the beach in the national park area. Just for once it was fine day and we even met up with Emma, Charli and her cousin Joshua who was visiting. We had the best time so we completely forgot why we were out for the day.

The story, when it appeared on Saturday, was headlined "Russian financier redevelops Renwick House for UFO research." The picture showed Drs Prosperov and Morozov wearing these weird hippy outfits which looked so strange we didn't recognise them. There were a whole bunch of hippy characters in the background that Ken had hired from a talent agency. The story portrayed Dr Prosperov and Dr Morozov as a couple of loonies who talked rubbish and giggled a lot.

When Dr P came down to breakfast, as usual wearing a suit, he said, "was very amusing to play fool". Dr Morozov looked very severe, and it was hard to believe she had acted the way the reporter had said she had. But as Dr Prosperov said the idea was that the newspaper had put on record a picture of Renwick which should mean we would be left alone.

While it probably meant Ax, Ergenekon, or Mexican drug gangsters wouldn't have connected us, the Gursoys or the Robinsons with UFO hippys in a million years, it didn't mean we were left alone. The problem was when real UFO hippies started showing up.

A man and a woman who seemed a bit vague and dirty showed up a few days later telling Mrs Jones they were already part of a network of UFO researchers and wanted to talk to Dr Prosperov about our work. When Dr Prosperov seemed like a severe businessman in a suit with shiny shoes who icily claimed to have been misquoted the hippies looked uncomfortable and left pretty fast. A few other callers rang up but had short, cold conversations with Dr Morozov who was ruder than any adult I had ever overheard talking on the phone. She always seemed very happy after those conversations too.

But for us kids that wasn't the real problem. The real problem was the local kids and teenagers. We now had a rep' for being a bunch of loonies. Older kids would shout out insults at us as they drove past us when we went to town. Everyone looked strangely at us. And cars started coming down our road and burning out to the lighthouse and back in the middle of the night. They had no lights on their number plates either.

The first night there was one. The second night there were three and the fifth night there were five. Dr Prosperov was annoyed and called the local cop. The cop – Sergeant Gavin Smith (there was only one on the island) – said that technically the road was a private one, owned by the Department, and he could only enforce a trespass order against specific individuals. He needed to know who was trespassing. He showed up once or twice but never when the guys in the cars came by. He didn't seem to like Dr Prosperov so much, and it was obviously mutual.

But Dr Prosperov had had enough of the late night racers. First he had Gunter and Mariko put up an official looking "private road" sign and further on another sign that said "trespassers will be prosecuted". That achieved nothing.

Next he sent Ken shopping, and he came back with a large coil of razor wire. It was vicious looking stuff. Ken and Gunter then cut the wire into three meter wide segments and welded it together into a kind of loose net. Then, after dark, they placed the net on the gravel road at the bottom of the hill and partially covered it. At about midnight we all heard the now familiar roar and rattle of the old white Mazda that had been driving by the most. Then there was a slide of gravel, a crunch, and an engine sounding like it was tearing itself to pieces. Then shouts, the slamming of a lot of doors, more shouts. I wondered what was going on, but Aunty Liz was awake too, and told us to go back to bed.

The next day we found the Mazda towed over by the garage. Its front wheels were snared in the net Ken and Gunter had made and all the tyres were flat. Later that day the cop came over and told Dr Prosperov off for using a dangerous trap. Dr Prosperov looked at him with a mercilessly cold stare and told him the identity of at least one of the trespassers should now be obvious. It turned out the car belonged to a guy named Mitchell McLachlan – a 21-year-old who lived several bays back towards Port Carlyle. His dad, Mike, owned the hardware store on the island. He called Dr Prosperov and said he wanted his son's car returned. Dr Prosperov told him it was abandoned on his property, and it was evidence to be used in seeking a trespass order against Mitchell.

The whole thing dragged on for weeks. I wasn't involved but I could see Dr Prosperov's stance wasn't making him any friends with the local community. The problem was only Aunty Liz cared what the community thought. Nobody else at Renwick really worried that much.

So while nobody on the island thought the Star had been even remotely right in portraying Dr Prosperov as a hippy, they liked the tough businessman that he actually was, even less. The result was the drivers stopped coming down the drive but everyone regarded us as weird and hostile, instead of weird and harmless, and that wasn't necessarily that great either.

The only local kids who would talk to us were Emma and her friends. With the so-called summer turning out to be colder and wetter than normal we spent more time indoors. Tama would drop Emma and Charli, or Emma and Melissa, or Emma, Melissa and Charli, over about ten and pick them up again about four. Charli was an active girl and got on well with Ashley and Cam, while Melissa was more girly and got on better with Tahira. Tarik thought Melissa, who had short, white-blonde hair quite cute. Cam didn't like her. Charli was fascinated with Scotty, but Scotty seemed completely unaware of it. She came by with Emma and some horses one time and took Scotty and

Ashley off riding. I wanted to go, and Emma offered to take me behind her on her horse, but I felt a bit shy about holding Emma close the whole time because I knew I would get turned on and I just knew I would end up being shamed, so I stayed home instead – kicking myself the whole time.

Luckily two weeks later Emma's cast came off just in time for summer to finally start acting like one. Now we were all in the sea the whole time. The water was fresh and the surf brilliant. We had bonfires on the beach, beach soccer and touch rugby and other times we just explored the creeks and shore.

It was during this time that me and Emma started diving together with Grandpop and Mariko. Mariko was an amazing diver who could hold her breath for minutes at a time. Grandpop was just big and powerful. It was Mariko who first discovered the sea caves and we spent nearly a whole week carefully exploring them with lines and buoys. The caves almost always had air pockets but we were always careful not to go anywhere we couldn't get out of. Everything was buddy-buddy with either Grandpop, or Mariko, with one of us.

But after a while Emma and I paired up because we had learned how to work with, and signal to, each other. It was Emma who found the big sea cave complete with glowworms.

The entrance was half-submerged down three meters at the bottom of a cliff. We dove a couple of times just to check it out but it was three meters high and about as wide so it didn't look too bad. We could see a light shaft about ten meters in suggesting there was a hole up in the cliff somewhere. The sea was calm and the only current we could feel flowed out of the cave so that meant we could get out of trouble faster than we got in. We anchored a buoy at the bottom of the cliff by the entrance and went to the entrance with a torch. About ten meters in we could see the water in the light shaft had a surface. I swam in first with the torch to the shaft. It was about a meter round and there was about a meter of headroom before the shaft narrowed into a chimney about ten meters tall and no more than a head-width wide. So I took a breath and went back out. Emma and I had a quick conversation on the buoy, hyperventilated for a minute, then dove down and swam to the shaft.

We surfaced together which was a bit tight and decided Emma would go on first while I would feed the line which was looped about her waist. We went under and I watched her strike out. There was still a fair amount of light in the cave and I could see her swimming deeper into the tunnel even without the torch that she shone around, as the water was very clear.

She seemed to be working hard against the current. Then, suddenly, when she was only another ten meters in where the cave had narrowed to about two meters around, she looked at me and struck out upwards vanishing from view. I watched the light from her torch on the floor of the cave and fed the line to her as long as I could, but then I had to return to the shaft for air.

I was a bit worried and quickly dove back only to find Emma coming back out. We both pushed up for the shaft again.

"You gotta see this Sam!" she squealed excitedly. "There's an underwater entrance to the caves!"

We hyperventilated for a short while and dove again. The current was a bit stronger at the back of the cave but when we got to the second, bigger, chimney there was no mistaking the surface, like a mirror, a few meters over our heads. We pushed up and found ourselves in this big cave with a waterfall feeding the pool.

Emma shone the torch around. It was really cold compared to the warm air outside, but surprisingly dry.

"Woohoo!" Emma whooped excitedly and we high-fived each other. We were stoked. We had our very own secret lair. How cool was that? It was cold and gave us goosebumps but we were excited and explored it thoroughly. There were cracks with air blowing in but no obvious exits. After a while of course it just felt a bit like a dark, cold hole in the ground.

"Maybe we should get back," I said.

"Yeah, they might worry when we've been so long," she agreed. We slipped into the water.

"Do you think we should tell them?" Emma asked.

A big black shape suddenly loomed from below up between us. We both panicked and Emma dropped the torch. But before we could do anything Mariko surfaced.

"You kids are pletty dumb, you know that?" Mariko said as she watched the torch fall beneath us.

We both gasped with surprise and shock.

"If you find cave you tell us before you going in," she growled.

"Sorry," we mumbled.

"OK, I go tell Mike you OK. Follow soon or he come to get you," she warned. I knew from her tone that that would not be a good thing. She dropped down and swam off like a fish. She picked up the torch effortlessly and disappeared with the light. We stayed on the surface in the cold hyperventilating, and then noticed something. The roof of the cave had magical little green lights all over it.

"Glow worms!" Emma whispered.

They were incredibly pretty, like stars in the sky.

"We'd better go," I replied.

And wishing it was warmer and we could stay we swam back to the light to face Grandpop.

Grandpop was pretty mad with us. But after bawling me out for not telling them what we were doing he demanded we explain, "step by step", how we had gone in. The only thing he could fault us for was not having our line signals clear. Still our only punishment was to be taken home early and miss out on a fantastic days swimming.

Slowly January was running out, and with it our summer holidays. We only had two more weeks of holiday left. After four weeks of holidays and a total change of home, the idea I wasn't going back to our old school seemed kinda weird. It seemed we would all be going to the school at Port Carlyle.

Dr Prosperov had made good on his promises to help everyone with immigration and announced that his British lawyer was coming to help the adults stay in the country, or in our case make sure Ax couldn't legally come anywhere near us. Dr Prosperov said this lawyer was one of the best in the British system that New Zealand bases its laws on, but that his real interest was to go down south to see an old plane show and add another old airplane to his collection. Apparently this guy had spent most of his fortune collecting airplanes.

In the meantime Dr Prosperov had also brought out a couple of Russian professors to help him with the lighthouse project. The professors were pretty old and their clothes were pretty rough. Professor Dubrov, the oldest of the pair seemed more thrilled about the clothes Dr Prosperov bought him than anything else. The other professor, Svintov. seemed to have a very low opinion of Dr Prosperov and spent most of his time eating Mr Trân's baking. The pair returned to Russia after only a week. Tarik said his dad thought neither understood what Dr Prosperov was doing but didn't want to admit it.

Of course they weren't alone. Nobody really had any idea what Dr Prosperov was trying to do with the lighthouse. The weirdest moment had come when, on the same day, he had delivered a huge solid copper bowl made by a company in Auckland that normally exports parts for precision high energy medical and scientific equipment, together with a truckload of old TVs. Ken, Gunter, Bernard and Grandpop had put on protective gloves and glasses and gone around pulling the TVs to pieces, smashing the glass tubes into a big, glass recycling bin, and tossing away the circuit boards and cases in another big bin, so they were left with the coils of copper wire which they took inside the lighthouse. It was all very mysterious.

Rewa and me weren't sure what was happening with Ax. The adults were all talking about their cases using words we didn't understand. One night I asked Aunty Liz what was happening. She said they were applying for an order from the court to stop Ax ever coming near us. She said we would have to go to Whangarei one day soon to talk to the judge but we didn't need to worry about it. The judge would always make sure we didn't need to talk to Ax.

More important to us was going to our new school. We were all a bit anxious about that, partly because school was never our favourite place anyway, and partly because we had heard that the school in Port Carlyle was very small and everyone knew one another. We knew we were going to stick out a lot.

Emma said our year was going to be a quarter bigger just because we were in it. Normally different years shared rooms but six new twelve-year-olds meant that we would have a classroom just for our year. She said there were only about 120 kids at the school over thirteen years of schooling. Rewa and Asal would make less of an impact.

According to Emma, Miss Greene usually took our year and she was a great teacher. We asked who we should look out for. Emma said the head teacher Mrs MacLean was old, a bit crabby, and smoked too much, but the worst was Mr Wakefield.

"He is such a jerk," she said. "He thinks he's something special because he's the only man on staff but he's just up-himself. He's managed to get himself made deputy head even though some of the other teachers like Mrs Morris who takes the new entrants have been there much longer. Everyone says he has this thing going on with Mrs MacLean who's divorced but nobody's ever proved it," she said.

The prospect of school made us all feel down. Tahira said she was really nervous about writing in English. She said she hadn't been so good at writing in French and changing languages again didn't help.

Ashley was nervous because she was going to be the only black kid in the school so everyone would notice her, and she had never done well at school. In all the schools she had been in, being black was normal so she had never stood out, and now everyone would notice her for being black and American and think her dumb.

Scotty was nervous because he had barely been to school for years. The school in Zimbabwe had been so run down because there was no money that they hadn't done much at all. He knew from South Africa he was way behind.

I was nervous because I never liked school anyway, plus I was used to a lot more Maoris around. Emma helped, because she was Maori too, so I knew I wasn't going to be completely obvious like Ashley. But I knew that the Maori culture which was such a big part of my old school wasn't going to be a lot more than for show in this white bread community.

Cam had mixed feelings. Her last school had given her a lot of help and she had drawn strength from it. At the same time it had been a big school with plenty of help for those who needed it. Cam knew she was still behind in English although her maths was very good. But she wasn't sure such a small school could give her the same level of help.

That left Tarik. He didn't like written English much because he wasn't very good at it, but he was very relaxed about his maths which he told us was always the best in every school he'd ever been to. Although he was usually a bit of a bluffer I think he really was the most confident of us all when it came to this new school.

Dr Prosperov had New Zealand lawyers but we found out the big shot British lawyer had arrived in the country right at the end of January. He scared us a bit because apparently he had flown his own jet out from Britain and, at the time, the idea of anyone being that rich was simply beyond our imaginations. But rather than waste time on a bunch of sad arses like us, he flew down South to the big vintage aircraft airshow they have down there. Aunty Liz told me that she was amazed that Dr Prosperov had hired a lawyer as expensive as Sir Michael to act for us. She hoped that we would soon be able to stop worrying about Ax and put all that behind us.

I asked, when she came in to see me one night, if that meant we could go back home. She seemed surprised by that and asked if I wanted to go back home. I eventually had to 'fess up and admit I was just nervous about this new school.

"Don't you think you should try it before you decide you don't like it? It might be better than your old one!" she said.

"Yeah," I admitted.

Pity it wasn't.

•••

CHAP†ER TWEN†Y TW⊕: LUNCHBREAK

It's just after midday when I stop. I've talked for almost three hours and my throat's dry. The sun's stronger now too but there's still something restful about sitting here in the garden with the birds flitting about us doing nothing.

Sue hasn't interrupted me much at all. Except for our bathroom breaks she's just lain there in her deck chair taking in the rays and my story. I'd thought she was asleep but whenever I pause she looks up at me to see what I'm doing.

"I need a drink," I tell her.

"Yeah, and I need to sort out my car," she agrees.

We go inside where I get some more apple juice while she finds the yellow pages. She calls a tow company and tells them her garage's details, her address and cell phone number and schedules them to tow the car in on Monday.

"So what do you think?" I ask her warily.

"I reckon we should go up the road. There's a couple of good places there."

"No, I mean about Renwick."

"Oh, I thought you meant for lunch. Umm well ... I can't see how it connects with what happened yesterday. I mean where do the UFOs come in? And Sir Michael has only just appeared."

Of course, I didn't want to talk strange stuff first and my plan

215

seemed to be working. She was looking very happy and relaxed. "Well, there's still a lot to come. And it's important you understand about all the families and why they were being chased because last year a lot went down on Aotea that Sergeant Smith didn't know about. That's when the gangs finally tracked us down."

I pause. I had been so busy remembering and working out what to distract her with that I haven't been reading Sue at all.

"So you aren't drifting off to think about Rachel or anything?" I ask.

Sue actually smiles.

"No! In fact, until you just mentioned her, I had forgotten all about her — which is a blessed relief actually."

She tousled my hair.

"From that point of view, being chased down a hole by a flying saucer and listening to you rabbit on about your old home is probably one of the best ways I could spend this weekend. Sure beats moping at home, crying and wishing the little bitch would call me, which is what I probably would have done," she says heartily. "Anyway let's go up the road and eat something. Do you remember what that code was with that amazing memory of yours?"

"1313, but I need to do something first."

"OK, I'll wait here."

My worry is that they have located us and might try to swipe Ka-rea-rea while I'm out, completely disarming me. I run upstairs and open him up. Then, with Qi translating, I set up a password and cell phone simulator based on my phone. It's important that he didn't talk to the phone network unless he was in trouble. Otherwise they might find us. Ka-rea-rea can easily emulate a cell phone if he needs to call, or receive calls. I tell him if he is moved by anyone who is not validated, he should call me, or attempt to get networked, so I can call him. I tell him not to start any conversations unless addressed by name. I also tell him not to evade unless he's threatened with opening, but that if he does have to evade, he can use any means to do so.

At the back of my mind is the worry that Antonio Rossi or some operative of theirs might try and smash him open. This might expose the vortex which could result in a Hiroshima-sized explosion as the antimatter interface collapsed. That would not do downtown Auckland any good at all.

I rejoin Sue who seems to have sorted out the security system and we stroll out into the street. Sue picks up the thread of her previous thoughts.

"So when you talked about a Russian connection when I first met you, you weren't just messing with me were you?" she asks as we walk up the narrow leafy lane past old houses and parked cars.

"No. Prosperov really does have business links back with Russia. He's in with one faction of oil and gas oligarchs and out with some others. The idea that a big Russian yacht came and took everyone away isn't beyond possibility. Adamovitch did visit a few times."

Sue looks thoughtful, striding up the road, head lowered, arms wrapped around herself.

"Hmm, there's a lot here I need to check out. It will look like I'm making progress anyway."

"Just don't put anyone's names in that computer, please Sue? It's really important."

"Yeah, OK. Still, I have to admit it is hard to keep in mind that a bunch of little green space men are after you Sam."

"Just remember the scout from yesterday."

There was a pause as we walked.

"I have to admit, I'm trying not to," she says.

I look at her. I'd expected this. She's trying to cover over the memory because it scared her so much. Lying in a safe house garden is helping her deal with her fright, but it was also giving her a false sense of security.

"Sue, I know it's hard, but you have to believe me when I say, they are after us."

"Hmm, I'm not sure because I'm not sure what 'us' means really," she says.

"What do you mean?"

"Well, I can't deny they are after you. And don't get me wrong Sam, I want to help protect you. But I'm only of interest to them as a way to get to you. Long term I'm out of this. So, in the end I'm not sure we want the same things," she points out.

That is true.

"You obviously want your family to come back safely," she says.

"Yeah, OK. But what do you want?" I ask uncertainly.

"Um I dunno really. I suppose I'd like to be recognised as a good detective. I mean I'm ... well I haven't exactly helped my career much lately" (she was talking about the pills) "... and this is actually a big case and though Kevin's in charge he knows I'll get further with it than he will."

"Sounds fair enough. What about this place?"

We stop outside an open air café set in a kind of walled garden. Everyone looks very Leonora-like. For a moment I worry she might even be there, but she isn't."

"Looks a bit pricey to me," Sue says.

"Don't sweat it, I'll pay," I offer.

"With what?"

"I still have the gift card Sir Michael gave me."

I didn't want to show her the Omnicard yet.

"What if Sir Michael's reported it stolen? Wouldn't I look a turkey – a police officer – accepting lunch from some dodgy kid with a stolen credit card?"

She's got a point. He might do that too, just to make me more vulnerable.

"I have my own cards – nothing to do with Sir Michael," I confess.

"Sam, I don't care. It just looks sus. Let's just go over there. That's more my style of place anyway."

She points to an organic looking cafe over the road.

"Oh, OK," I give in, and follow her across the wide road.

The cafe is in an old store which has been painted brown and decorated with white tendrils. The inside has been painted orange and with lots of chrome and lava lamps. Sue gets herself a salad full of mung beans and pumpkin seeds, with a bottle of locally made lemonade, and I get a panini and a chai latte. We find a table by the window away from everyone else.

"You know, ultimately you will only get your old life back if the others come back," Sue begins conversationally.

"When they come back."

"But if they have all this technology why haven't they been in touch? I suppose you've been asking yourself that too?" Sue asks.

"Yeah," I admit, biting into the Panini.

"And what do you think?" Sue probes, playing with her salad.

"I dunno. A lot of things could have happened ... or be

219

happening."

"Like?"

"Well the people they've gone to …"

"You mean 'our friends'," she says fingering the quotes in the air.

"Yeah … They are totally paranoid about security. It's all because they escaped being wiped out by the Center and they don't want to be found."

"So why are they working with you?"

"Because what happens on Earth is actually important. It ripples back through the Galaxy."

"How?" Sue asks, astonished.

"I don't know exactly. It's about the infiltrators. That is for certain. There's something special about them being here."

"What?"

"I'll get to that later. Anyway, there could be all sorts of reasons why they haven't contacted me. Some of them good, others not so good."

"You really are sure they will come back?" Sue says after a short pause, gauging my reaction.

"If my sister, Aunt or Grandpop are alive. They will come back for me — somehow," I tell her, confidently. "If they were dead I'd know, and they aren't. Look, it's been a week. I won't start worrying for another week or two. They might be setting up a new identity for me and that will take a while. I don't think they'll come back for me until they are ready. I can cope."

"Maybe you can, but if I were your Aunt I'd be worried sick."

"You're assuming she can't check up on me," I say, swallowing some Chai.

Sue looks shocked. All her salad fell off her fork.

"What do you mean?" she asks, voice slightly raised.

"Aunty Liz would only worry if she couldn't be sure I was OK," I say, biting my Panini.

"Can she?" Sue wants to know.

"Yes," I reply, simply.

"How," she challenges me.

"She can watch me."

"From another dimension?"

"No, you can't be in other dimensions any more than a circle can be a ball. You either extend into more dimensions or you don't. She's with 'our friends' in the same dimensions as we are, but she could look through another dimension. It's called a wormhole."

"A wormhole?"

"Yeah, so you remember the tag I told you about?"

"The one in your stomach?"

"Yeah."

"Yeah. How is it by the way?"

"Still, a bit sore. But the big deal about that tag is that it uses a dimensional gateway. It's called 'entanglement' and when a stream of electrons is split you can send a signal between them by changing the spin on the electrons on one side of the downstream end and it instantly changes the spin on the other downstream end no matter how far apart they are. That's because the electrons are entangled together in a dimension we can't see."

"OK."

"All aliens can send signals like this using two split radioactive materials so you can't intercept their communications. That's why searching space for radio signals from aliens is kinda pointless."

"Yeah, but what about these wormholes?"

"Well, a wormhole is where space is bent through these dimensions to bring two places together at the same time. It's like making a tiny pinhole in the wall between one place and another one in another place thousands of kilometers or even light years apart. Then you can see through the pinhole."

"So could she be watching us now?" Sue asks, half looking around.

"She could be," I shrug.

"So let me get this straight she can spy on you, but you can't see her?"

"Yes, although sometimes I have a good idea they're watching."

"Because you're psychic?"

"No, because you get a little harmonic disturbance when a channel is opened. It looks like tiny spots of violet light in the sunlight. I've noticed it a few times."

"So they can see anywhere?"

"Yeah."

"Anywhere at all?"

"Yeah, pretty much. Except anywhere *they* control because it's not secure. They can grab the other end of the pinhole and reverse it. Then they know where you are, they can make the channel larger, and send stuff back through the wormhole."

"Wow, wish we had that sometimes when we're searching ... but, hang-on ... they might be able to look anywhere, but looking isn't finding. You have to know where to look. How do they find you?"

"They can sort of find me through my family."

"How?"

"Well people who are related can kind of be entangled too? So

Rewa and me are entangled in a way too. If I meditate I can always find her."

"Anywhere?"

"Not exactly. It means I know how they are, and how they feel about where they are."

"But ... sorry, but that sounds a bit wishy-washy to me. If they have only an emotional connection to go on how does that help them find you physically?"

"Like I found you, remember? Animals do it. We can do it. It's just we don't have a science that explains this sort of stuff."

"And they do?"

"Yeah. I mean what do you think our technology would be like ten thousand years in the future?"

Sue stopped to think for a moment, then gave up.

"Cripes Sam, I dunno. It makes my head hurt."

"Exactly. Ten thousand years in our past is before civilisation! Before the Pyramids! It's before anything built in stone. No horses. No machines. Only the simplest tools. Like some of the tribes still living in the jungle today. Then think how fast our technology is changing now. We had new PCs in all our rooms at Renwick. Two years later they were just old. Just imagine ten thousand years into the future of that!"

"So what's your point Sam?"

"Well some of the stuff our friends and the Administration can do is going to seem like magic. I mean 'magic' like a helicopter is magic to a guy from the Amazon. So you may find some of the stuff I'm going to tell you next a bit unbelievable."

She starts to laugh.

"What?" I want to know.

"Sam," she laughs. "It's all bloody unbelievable. If I hadn't experienced what I did yesterday I'd be sizing you up to replace me in the pink ward."

I force a smile.

"So what you're telling me is it gets weirder?" she asks getting serious again.

"Are your" and she made quote marks in the air, "friends, are some sort of science fiction creature with tentacles that you think I'll find crazy?"

I smile, "actually the funny thing is all the aliens look a lot like us."

"All of them?" she complains good humouredly, "that's a bit dull isn't it?"

"Well, it might be dull, but when you think about it, it kind of makes sense."

"Why then?"

"Well it's because chemistry is the same everywhere in the galaxy. So DNA is the simplest self-reproducing molecule. Life can happen without DNA, but DNA is the easiest way to get life and DNA needs liquid water. Liquid water means it can't be colder than zero or hotter than a hundred and that means the planet has to be in the right place and be the right size. The moon, for example, is in the right place but its gravity is too small to create a pressure heavy enough to support liquid water. Mars might have been in the right place once, but now it's too small and too far from the sun so all the water would boil away. If the planet's too large the gravity is too strong. The age of the star is important too. A young star or an old star will produce way too much heavy radiation which will nuke DNA to bits. So that pretty much means life has to come from a planet in the same orbit as Earth, be roughly about the same size as Earth, and obviously be solid."

"It also helps to have the same day as Earth and the same tilt as Earth. What that means is nearly all the civilisations in the galaxy have the same year, with the same seasons as we do."

"Wow. All because of one molecule?"

"Yeah all because of DNA. So that gives you life, but the important thing about life is that it changes the exterior of a planet. You can have pockets of plant life, but for animals life has to dominate the whole planet. That's because animals need to burn oxygen, and free oxygen normally combines with iron on planets like earth. So getting oxygen in the atmosphere only happens when plants keep splitting carbon and oxygen to make food. That means you can't naturally have animals on desert planets or ice planets or city planets because without plants there simply wouldn't be any oxygen for them to breathe. It also means you can spot a planet with animals on it from literally light-years away because they have to be the colour of oxygen – blue."

"OK, but what's wrong with coming from water or gas?"

"Gas blows around. Water or ammonia even is too good at dissolving stuff. Plus you can't make fire underwater and fire is the first most important tool for cooking and making things out of clay or metal. Don't forget there's plenty of water animals on this planet with bigger brains than us. All of them live in the sea but none of them have created a civilisation. For that you need to live on land."

"OK," Sue grinned, "Why not on land, but with tentacles?"

"Nature tried that. Check out any book on dinosaurs. There've been animals with any number of legs but only a few actually work. Weirder arrangements just trip over themselves. Spiders, for example, don't get much bigger than your plate because they just can't fight against faster four legged animals. Mammals just eat them up – literally. I've seen kids eat 'em too."

"Aww yuk! Sam! I'm eating!"

"They do! They cook 'em on a fire and they eat 'em. Four legs beats eight or six. With nature less is always better."

"Oh alright, so forget the tentacles. But why do they have to be humanoid. It's just so boring."

"Because the most important thing is to be a really crap predator. So crap you are easy prey. You can't have fangs or claws because then you don't need tools. You have to have hands, like us, for fine work to make tools with. You have to have binocular vision for the same reason. You have to have no fur which probably means living partially in water at some point and you also can't be big like a gorilla or an elephant or a whale because then you don't need fire to defend yourself."

"As an animal we have nothing. Nothing but a brain and the ability for language and teamwork. Individually we are prey. Together we are the world's best predators by miles."

"Hmm … yeah when you think about it you do end up with pretty limited options."

"Even with all that you still don't get civilisation. There are still people living in the Amazon or Papua who don't need civilisation. Civilisation starts in river valleys when populations get large and start fighting each other. So what civilisation really means is being capable of war. Civilisation and evolution really starts when a creature at the top of the food chain starts evolving to fight for resources with itself."

"God! what a completely depressing idea," Sue says munching her mung beans.

"Yeah … well, it gets worse. At a certain stage civilisation gets so big it takes over the whole planet's environment. It's built on war but now it starts to consume the environment which made it. When it reaches that stage the civilisation consumes everything until the danger of a final war becomes almost impossible to avoid. And if the creatures can't avoid that war, they wipe themselves out. They told us it's already happened on other planets. That's what we are working to stop. The last war which will destroy our world."

"Sam, that's … uh … seriously heavy."

I shrug and went back to eat my Panini which was getting cold. Sue's frowning.

"And Sir Michael thinks there will be a war too?"

"Sure. He thinks there will be a war, and is planning to win it. We think there might be a war, and are planning to stop it before it starts."

"And what about them?"

"Which them?"

"Both of them?"

"They are watching."

"What, both of them?"

"Yeah."

"But won't they do anything if we have a final war?"

"No. It's a stage of civilisation we have to get through before they will officially talk to us. If we can't save ourselves we aren't deemed safe in the galaxy. I mean think about it – a civilisation that can't not kill itself? Who would want to share anything with them?"

Sue sighs. "That's really depressing. Our future as a species depends on a bunch of idiot politicians. We're doomed!"

"Well, we will be if we keep doing the same thing. Out future depends on choosing the right leaders. That depends on people making better choices. Lots and lots of them, and the right leaders being there. And it's not completely true *they* are doing nothing. *They* are trying to guide us there but they aren't allowed to be explicit about it."

"Why not?"

"Well, they tried that before ten thousand years ago, and pitted early human against early human. That started a war between the aliens who set us up against each other. That's why there is a treaty against intervention and fighting wars by proxy. Because of what happened here before."

"You mean like they were gods when they came here before?"

"Exactly. We have all sorts of stories about gods which turn out to be based on the aliens that visited us ten thousand years ago." We munch for a moment when Sue's forehead wrinkles.

"But why should they care?"

"About us?" I check.

"Yeah. I mean why get involved with a bunch of primitive creatures from another world?"

"Because it comes back on them. And because there aren't that many civilisations in the Galaxy. There are heaps of planets with life – like Earth was for billions of years, full of dinosaurs or whatever – but actual intelligent life with civilisations aren't that common."

"How many?"

"Nine."

"Nine! Out of how many?"

"About a hundred eighty billion star systems."

"In the universe?"

"No, just the galaxy. The universe is … way too huge to think about. Even 'our friends' don't know how to travel the whole universe."

"Nine!"

"Uh-huh."

"And they're at war?"

"Sort of. I mean the galaxy is dominated by the Center. The Center was started by two races who fought the ancestors of 'our friends'. When peace finally came some created the Center, but others – 'our friends' – didn't want anything to do with it. For a long time the Galactic Center worked OK but they developed the biobots who gradually took over. The ones that wanted to be independent had to go into hiding."

"Why?"

"Because Center wiped out anyone who wouldn't comply. It's the biobots. They were built as servants but they became servants of an idea of unity at all costs, and when others didn't agree they couldn't tolerate those who wouldn't conform."

"What if we don't conform?"

"Well, that's the thing. So they've been quietly working here to make sure when the time comes we do conform."

"On Earth?"

"Of course."

"How?"

"All sorts of ways. They study us. They do experiments in social control. It's not all Discovery Channel. But of course not all those living under the Center agree with it. Some live among us secretly plotting to restore their control over the biobots. Remember the infiltrators? Some of them are pretty evil. Others are … well, almost friendly."

"But what about your friends?"

"They won't risk an open fight with the Center for us. That's why they just help us. It was actually Dr Prosperov who convinced them it was in their interest to help. Otherwise they would do nothing too. Well, Lucky actually."

"Oh yes Lucky. You never did explain about him."

"Well, now I will."

"Now?"

"When we get back. He's um ... a bit weird too."

Sue shrugs.

"Well Sam, while your weirdness is all very interesting, back on Earth I need to have something to tell the judge on Friday."

"What do we have to tell him?"

"It's a her actually, Justice McMasters, Kathryn to her friends."

"Are you her friend?"

"No, in fact she's not got a lot of friends in youth circles. She's a bit of a tough love and discipline nut. She'd probably put you in the army if she had her way."

"Oh," I say, a bit worried.

"'Oh', is right," Sue agrees.

"But what about Kaz and Julia?"

"Well, they can apply for custody but first she'll make you a ward of the court. That means she takes over responsibility for your welfare. Then she'll hear arguments as to who can offer you the best options. Normally she'd expect your relatives to show up but your Aunt Rebecca wasn't interested."

"No surprises there," I mutter, and add, "just as well too."

"So on one side there's a lesbian couple offering to take care of you until your Aunt comes back — and we have to tell her there's no sign of that, because if I start talking about flying saucers I'll be back in the psych ward. On the other side is a rich lawyer who has your Aunt's statement that he should act in her place, with an account for your education with good money in it, and a place at Queens. So what do you think a conservative, straight judge is going to do?"

"Hand me over to Sir Michael," I guessed, gloomily.

"Now the fact that you don't like Sir Michael, but like Julia and Caz might be taken into account, but she will probably seek some sort of joint arrangement. She's going to ask if I think your Aunt is alive and I'm going to have to say there is no evidence that she is..."

"But..." I object.

"Psychics have no standing in law Sam, there's no evidence," she warns." Then Geraldine will give her recommendation that you should have a psychiatric assessment."

"Whaaaat!?" I demand.

"She thinks you're traumatised," Sue explains. "And the judge will probably agree."

"Oh great, so then I have to talk about my feelings for hours or something do I?"

"Yes. But if I were you I wouldn't say anything about the stuff you've told me."

"But I haven't even told you the really weird shit yet!"

"Well don't, for God's sake, tell them anything like that. Make up anything or they'll think you're crazy. Then the judge will talk to everyone — including you, and then she'll make a decision."

"And then what?"

"Then you go with whoever she picks, though my pick is she'll back Sir Michael, possibly with Caz and Julia for holidays."

"Yeah, well the other option is I piss off overseas in Ka-rea-rea and your judge can stick her judgement where the sun don't shine."

Sue laughs.

"Where would you go, Sam?" she asks.

"I dunno, and that's been the problem from the start hasn't it?" I grouse. "Everyone I know is worse off than me. I don't want to live in a slum. They're really awful. I could live in hotels but people don't trust anyone my age to pay for hotel rooms by themselves. Besides it might make it hard for the others to find me again? So that leaves some of the people we've worked with but I would attract *their* attention and that would ruin everything we've worked for."

"What about the Reeves?" Sue suggests.

"Nah! Tama knows Emma and me like each other a lot and he won't trust us in the same house together. He's pretty protective."

"He seemed to think you Renwick house people were a bit demented."

"Yeah I know. He somehow always ended up seeing half the story and that's why he didn't get us."

"So flying off isn't really an option then?"

"Well, it sort of is. I mean if I thought I was going to end up in *their* control through Sir Michael, it definitely would. Anyway I'd hope Aunty Liz will make 'our friends' act soon to find me. They can't expect me to escape the Administration forever."

Sue looks at me sympathetically.

"It seems a lot to put a young guy like you through."

"Yeah, I would have thought that once too. We all would, but like I've just been telling you, all of us had seen some bad stuff. But the more we travelled the more kids we met who were dealing with things that were even worse! So you ended up thinking. If that kid can cope with being kidnapped, and this one with being enslaved, I can just harden up and help them, rather than sit around crying about how hard the world is on me. The more you think about others' problems, the better you can cope with your own."

Sue smiles thoughtfully.

"I think that's what I like about you," she tells me straight.

"What?" I ask, feeling a bit shy.

"Well, most of the kids I deal with are self-centred little shits. They don't care about their parents, or their friends, or anyone but themselves. But you think about everyone else."

I shrug.

"I can't help it to be honest Sue. That's one of the ways it's tough being psychic. Everyone else always crowds in on my mind all the time anyway. You can't not think about how everyone else feels."

We get up and leave, walking down the busy road with the traffic zooming by. I decide to ask her what has really been bothering me.

"Am I wasting my time telling you all this stuff? I mean does it really make a difference?"

"No you aren't wasting your time. I think you're doing the right thing. I can't help you if I don't know what I'm dealing with. It certainly helps me."

"Does it? How?"

"Gives me something to think about."

"You mean to take your mind off Rachel?"

"No ... well yes, but it gives me something to work with. I mean now I know how the people at Renwick met and got to know each other. That tells me a lot about the social dynamic which is important in cases like this."

We walk a bit further when I had a thought.

"Bet this is the weirdest case you ever had."

"By a country mile, Sam."

"Problem is even if you do solve it you'll never be able to tell anyone," I point out.

"No, that's not true, I'll be able to tell 'em something," Sue says looking thoughtful. "It will just sound better than the true story. It's part of the secret art of detective work. Tell a good story."

"Sounds a bit sus to me."

"It is," she whispers behind her hand, and winks.

We walk along for a while, then Sue has a new question.

"Most of the people at Renwick had families overseas right?"

"Yeah."

"Whereabouts were they again?"

"Scotty's grandparents are in Harare, his uncle is in England and Bernard has no family, there were all murdered. Ashley has family in Detroit, Washington DC and Houston. Tahira has family in Iran and Paris. Tarik has family in Turkey and Iraq. And Cam might have family in Vietnam, but I'm not really sure, her dad never mentioned anyone. Mrs Jones has no family left. Mariko's family is back in Okinawa. Gunter's family is in Germany and Ken's extended family is in Mongolia."

Sue snorted, "They couldn't be harder to find if Prosperov had organised it that way."

"Why do you want to find them?"

"It's just one of the things we have to do Sam."

"But what would you tell them even if you had their phone numbers? Your relative is missing in a fire, should they

mysteriously turn up again, please call the New Zealand Police?
Like that's going to happen."

"You have a point."

We get back to the house. I remember the code and we wonder if
we've disarmed the alarm, and then, accidently, I re-arm it again
and have to disarm it. I go upstairs to check on Ka-rea-rea and
Sue goes to the loo. Ka-rea-rea is fast asleep. I go down into the
garden and find my chair. Then Sue comes out with some fruit
and some sunscreen. We do the sunscreen thing, because it's
really hot and then get comfy.

"OK," she asks, "where were we?"

"We'd had Christmas and the holidays and were just about to
start school."

"OK, but I don't really need to know about everything you did at
school."

"Well, what do you want to hear about?"

Sue thinks for a moment.

"Stuff that mattered later on."

"Well, we found out how much the locals didn't like us, and that
mattered later on."

"OK."

"And then we went to court and I saw Ax for the first time since
he killed mum."

"Yeah, tell me about that. What else?"

"And then Dr Prosperov started his lighthouse experiment
and that's when things got seriously weird and everything got
started."

"Fine. Well, tell me about that too, then."

So I do.

•••

235

CHAP+ER TWEN+Y THREE: NERVES

My first day at Port Carlyle School dawned beautiful and clear. The sky was a gentle satin blue lit by a big yellow sun that you just knew was going to heat up like a blowtorch. The sea was still and calm, with just the merest ripple along the beach outside Renwick. The lighthouse glowed a fantastic orange in the distance, and a lone seagull that was gliding the currents between the headlands of the bay seemed to be content to squawk once or twice only as if to say how pleased he was that he wasn't going to school today.

It was the kind of perfect day that only comes once the holidays are over. I looked out my window at the bay and fiddled with Te Matua, the tiki, around my neck Aunty Nea had given me for protection hoping it would bring me luck. The clock on my screen said 6:12 a.m. I wasn't sure whether I wanted breakfast yet or not.

I got dressed and went into our apartment's lounge. There was a shuffling behind me and Rewa came out yawning and stretching. "You're keen," she observed, in mid-yawn.

"No, I'm not," I disagreed. "It's just a great day and I wanted to go outside before we had to go to school."

Rewa yawned again blankly. She glanced out the window and then turned back to me.

"Wait up! I'll come too."

She went back into her room to get dressed. I went into the bathroom and brushed my teeth. Rewa reappeared wearing her pink jacket and gray pants. She brushed her hair while I did my teeth and then we swapped over. Then we went out into the corridor. There was a ghost in it. A nervous soldier named Patrick who Rewa couldn't see. He went past us like a chill in the passage. We went through the lounge. Rewa wanted to go into the gallery but there were ghosts in it and I said I wanted to go outside directly, so we went out through the main doors.

The sun was warm and low so we had to shield our eyes but the air was still cool. We ran out the front and down to the beach. The sea was barely rippling at the shore and reflected the hills around it like a mirror.

"It feels funny going to a new school," Rewa said. "It's been like this was a big summer holiday but that we should go home now."

"Yeah, except Ax is home now."

We walked along the beach. Rewa was barefooted and walking right at the water edge.

"You know, I don't remember him at all," she said after a while.

"I only have nightmares with him in them," I replied.

"That and mum. But he doesn't have a face. He's sort of like this zombie thing who's just after me," I admitted.

"I don't remember mum," Rewa said sadly.

"She watches over you," I told her.

She was walking next to us on my left in her jeans and a long black shirt with a jacket. Over the years as I'd grown I had been surprised to discover she was not actually that big. Probably why I'm so small.

"You told me that before. You really can see her can't you Sam? You're not just making it up like Santa Claus or something," Rewa said walking carefully along the line of salt the sea left behind on the sand. Mum laughed.

"Mum thinks you're funny. She says she's not Santa Claus."

"I wish I could see her."

"Then you'd have to see all the others too."

"Asal says Tahira gets quite scared back at the house. She says she sees men looking at her."

"I know. So do I. All six of us do, Rewa. But it's harder on the girls," I admitted. "Mrs Jones tells them off though. They're scared of her."

"I'm glad I don't see them, though it is creepy there sometimes."

"Would you rather be back home?" I asked.

Rewa thought about that for a while.

"No. Apart from the creepy stuff it's much better here. Everyone is so friendly and I feel safer than I did back home. I feel like we're part of a big family. I like Asal and Soraya and Mitra. They're teaching me Persian and I'm teaching them some Maori. Well, a little bit anyway. And Mariko's great and I call Gunter Uncle now because he feels like an Uncle."

"But is it home?"

"No," she admitted. She thought about that for a while.

"Home is Grandpop's house, but it could become home ... maybe."

"It'll be different when we start school again."

"Emma said the classes are much smaller. It could be good, Sam."

"Yeah, I hope so," I said not believing it.

We skipped stones on the beach for a while. Then Grandpop

came out to us.

"Everyone's having breakfast," he told us. "Pancakes," he added. So we followed him in. On the way he told us he had to go back home. I was a bit upset about that. I always felt much safer whenever Grandpop was around.

"I've stayed way too long. I'm amazed Gennady hasn't told me to go," he said.

Actually if anything Dr Prosperov seemed very happy to have Grandpop around. When I saw them talking, Dr Prosperov seemed to be interested in whatever Grandpop had to say.

"And I've got things to do on the house before winter comes. So I'm off home today. But don't worry, Liz and I have a pair of phones so we can talk to each other now. Gennady says I'm welcome to stay any time so I'll be back."

We had known this moment was coming. But it still seemed sad. Rewa threw her arms around Grandpop and he knelt to cuddle her.

"Be a good girl for Liz and listen to your teacher. I'll see you when you come up in a few weeks for the hearing."

Rewa didn't want to let go.

"You'd better go get yourself a feed of pancakes or the others will eat all your breakfast," Grandpop murmured to her.

Rewa hates missing out on food. She ran in and Grandpop turned to me.

"Don't worry about school Sam," he advised me. "There's harder things to survive. You should see your cousin Clive. That poor kid is a mess. You're so much better off here. Even if you don't like the school."

I could tell Aunty Liz had been talking to him. At the same time I was curious about Clive.

239

"What's the matter with Clive?" I wanted to know.

"He's worse. He's thin and losing teeth. It's the drugs they let him have. He's addicted and they're killing him."

Grandpop was right. I was better off here.

"Look after your sister for me," Grandpop said.

"And help your Aunt. They're good people here Sam. You can learn a lot from them."

"When are you coming back?"

"In a couple of months. I need to sort some stuff out back at home."

"You won't attack Ax will you?" I asked, worried.

"Sam there's nothing I'd like better than to slit his throat like a pig and watch him die for what he did to your mother but there's nothing to be gained and too much to be lost for that. So don't worry, I won't attack him."

The unsaid word was "yet".

He ruffled my hair.

"Don't worry boy, you'll be alright and you'll see me again in a while."

I wasn't sure what to do. Luckily Grandpop was, and gave me a hug.

"Now go get some breakfast or you'll have a bad day."

I left him outside rolling a smoke and went in to join the others. A little bit of my heart ached.

Breakfast was great. Pancakes, maple syrup, whipped butter and bacon. I ate a stack of five. Tarik had eaten ten just to beat Scotty's seven but he didn't look so well. Then it was time to go. We grabbed our lunches from the counter, stuffed them in our bags and ran out the front where Mariko was waiting with Betty. Mariko explained that she expected to see some solid air guitar performances tonight and the music for the trip in was for practice. So we headed off up the hill with the speakers blaring out "I love rock and roll," with a lot of yahooing around in the back of the bus.

The ride had our spirits sky high. Mariko ended up racing the official school bus in a slow motion contest because neither bus could go very fast. We were all wildly excited though the other bus driver looked pretty sour about it.

We arrived at school feeling ten feet tall. There were a lot of kids about but, of course most of them were smaller than us, and we formed our own little group waiting outside the school hall for the first assembly.

We noticed a bunch of kids about our own age giving us the evils across the playground. There were a group of about five boys gathered around a tall freckly looking kid with red hair and brown eyes. I had no idea who they were but they obviously didn't like us for some reason.

We were just hanging around when a pale tallish man with black hair and a pudgy face came up to us.

"You must be the Renwick children," he said. His high voice had a smarmy superior quality to it that made you want to kick him immediately.

"I'm Mr Wakefield, deputy principal, you older ones are in my class in room seven."

My heart sank. Exactly what Emma had warned about.

" ... and you two girls are in room five with Miss Green. Do you know where the classrooms are?"

We mumbled a general "no" just as Emma came up to say "hi".

"Well perhaps Emma, could show you where everything is. Assembly is in ten minutes don't be late."

Emma was annoyed to learn we were in Mr Wakefield's class. "It's probably because it's gonna be the biggest in the school and he wants to justify being deputy," she said.

The classroom was a typical prefab block of two rooms numbered seven and eight. Some of the older kids would be in with us too. There weren't very many of them. A lot of older kids went to boarding school in Auckland. The youngest were in room one. So there were two double blocks of classrooms, another double block for the office and library, a separate staff room, a toilet block and the assembly hall and that was it.

The school's motto "learning to be our best" was on a sign outside the office. And that plus a playground and a field, with rugby goalposts on it, was the whole school. There wasn't even a swimming pool.

The bell went so we went back to the assembly hall. There were no benches, we had to just sit on the floor. The teachers were up the front. You could tell who they were just by looking at them. Mrs Maclean was thin and grumpy looking with the lined face which suggested a heavy smoker. Miss Green was young and active looking in a tracksuit, Mrs Morris was round and kindly with big hair and glasses. There were two other teachers who we learned were Mrs Davidson, and Mrs Roberts. They were part-time, being mothers whose kids had grown up.

Mrs Maclean started by welcoming everyone and made a special point of mentioning the Renwick 'refugees'. That made us feel weird because we didn't think we were refugees – especially me because the teachers were all white and my people were here first. I realised as I thought about it, though, that we were refugees in that all of us had needed a refuge from bad things and Dr Prosperov had given us one. But after that first mention of us Mrs Maclean ignored us and talked about a lot of stuff everyone else laughed about because they had history at the school. That made us feel all the more different because we could only get hints of what everyone else was laughing about. After Mrs Maclean had spoken Mr Wakefield came up to tell us all what classes we were in. He tried to seem very in-charge but he looked to me like a loser who liked being the big fish in a puddle. Still for some reason all the other teachers seemed to think he was wonderful and it made him all the more swollen headed and pitiful.

Finally after we mumbled our way through the school song we were made to line up and walk to our classroom. That was when I realised the boys giving us the evils in the playground were all in our class.

When we got to the classroom we were all given a shelf for our textbooks and a hook for our coats along the back of the classroom. We then had to find somewhere to sit.

There were four groups of desks with six places. We just grabbed the one at the back. The boys who didn't like us sat at the front. Emma sat with Charli and a bunch of girls she had been chatting with also at the front.

Mr Wakefield called the roll and I realised why the kid up the front had been giving us the evils. His name was Marshall McLauchlan and it was obviously his brother's car that Ken and Gunter had wrecked with their razor wire net. I was a bit annoyed that we were taking the rap for Dr Prosperov.

Our experience with Mr Wakefield was not as bad as Emma had said. We all had to introduce ourselves and where we were from. I don't think Mr Wakefield was so much listening, as looking at ways of showing off, but he didn't have time to make a complete fool of himself. We talked about it at morning break.

"Oh, he's just on his best behaviour because he's a bit nervous about you lot," Emma said.

"Nervous about us?" I asked.

"Everyone's nervous about Renwick. They think your Dr Prosperov is dangerous. A lot of people are angry with my dad because the department let him have the place."

"What does your dad say?"

"It wasn't his decision. Your Dr P fixed it with the Minister. But he also says you guys are just like everyone else when you get to know you."

"Of course we are. I just realised that Marshall kid's brother was the one who's car Dr Prosperov caught."

"The McLauchlan boys have all been idiots. They're vandals and bullies. Their dad just thinks it's high spirits and he convinces Sergeant Smith they're harmless. See, Ian McLauchlan owns the only hardware store. He also owns the main liquor store. Dad says he charges a fortune but there's no competition so he gets away with it. He's not the only one. Stan Gee's got the only petrol station and Joan Perkins has the only supermarket. That's why they worry about Prosperov. They're scared he'll upset things."

"Why would he bother?" I wondered aloud.

"It's what they're frightened of," she shrugged.

I remembered Mariko's comment about "velly small brains" on the bus on the first day. But then I thought back to home in Northland.

"It was the same back home."

It wasn't until lunchtime that any open hostility showed itself. We had all split up. Tahira, Cam and Ashley were talking to

Emma and some of her friends. Scotty was off somewhere. I
think he was amazed a school could actually have a library. Tarik
and me were just mooching around when a soccer ball powered
into the wall next to Tarik's head. The ball bounced back onto
the field where a bunch of boys were playing. I recognised
Marshall as the kicker by the fact he was yelling, "No throw-ins!"
The game continued when another shot smashed into the
wall next to us. Tarik winked at me. I had no idea what he was
planning to do. To my mind staying here was stupid.
"They done this in Lunnin too," he said quietly.
"So what did you do?" I asked.
"Watch."
We didn't have to wait for long. The ball was booted at us again
but this time Tarik was ready and he punched it high up and
over the building behind us.
If he'd been in goal and playing, it would have been an excellent
save. But he was already roaring at them like one of the
professionals on TV. He was like a completely different person.
"Oi! Watch where you put that next time son, or I'll kick it out of
the school!"
The kicker was a big kid named Paul Smith. He was so shocked
that the ball had gone flying who-knew-where, that he didn't
seem to know how to respond. They all looked to Marshall. All
the kids in the area were watching.
"Better go get it Turk!" Marshall threatened Tarik.
Boy, that was a dumb thing to say!
"Get it yourself, asshole," was Tarik's response.
I was impressed Tarik wasn't backing down at all.
"What did you call me?" Marshall demanded, closing.
Tarik just stood there. He had a lot more guts than I had. He

245

was asking for a hiding. The others gathered around us to look menacing. I found myself having to back up Tarik against five bigger kids.

"I called you what you are. What did you call me?"

"Turk."

"Us Kurds kill Turks who pick on us."

He said it in a way that caused a few of the bigger kids to look at one another.

"Save us some time and kill yourself then," snickered Roland Soper.

"He's not a Turk," I told them.

"Who asked you Hori?" challenged Randall Johns.

These guys were starting to piss me off too.

Suddenly the girls were joining in.

"Hey! Sup' Tarik?" Ashley wanted to know.

"These lit'le boys 'ere, 'ave only got one ball between 'em. And they need my help to find it!" Tarik sneered.

Suddenly Marshall kicked Tarik in the groin. There was an explosion of outrage from the girls. The five were driven back as the girls yelled insults at them. I bent next to Tarik.

"Are you OK."

He was bent over gasping. I led him over to the bench. At this moment Mr Wakefield appeared. The girls now berated him with their accounts of Marshall kicking Tarik. Mr Wakefield went over to Tarik and told me to help him to the sick bay.

I helped him over. Cam came to help too.

"You know, they always do that," he groaned. "You'd think I'd block them just once."

"Have you done this before?" Cam asked.

"Ankara, London, Melbourne. I tour the world getting kicked in the balls. One day I'll do it professionally," he grunted.

"But how did you clear that ball?"

"Coz I'm a bloody good keeper. Aren't I?"

The woman in the office, Mrs Jenkins, showed us to the sick bay which was about the size of a closet. Tarik lay down curled up. He looked pale. Cam left us. Mrs Maclean appeared shortly after and called me into her office.

She asked me to tell her what happened. I explained about the balls being kicked at us, Tarik's save, and how annoyed he would have been at being called a Turk. She looked a bit guilty at that. I think she thought he was.

When I went back to the sick bay I found Tarik sitting up looking better. Then Marshall was led into Mrs McLean's office by Mr Wakefield. Tarik smiled at me and I realised immediately this was all part of his scheme.

"You ..."

He held up his hand. I high-fived him. Uncomfortably he got to his feet. We walked out and joined the others. The news was that Marshall was up for a week of detentions and having to apologise. Tarik was our hero. When the bell rang at the end of school we felt we were on top until a girl named Jasmine Wheeler, who was one of Marshall's supporters, yelled out in our direction as we went to get on the bus.

"What do you get if you cross a Turk and a Kurd? A turd!"

More people laughed than we would have guessed. We looked back. Mariko was standing by the door, arms folded, foot leaning on Betty, looking sour.

"Move it peepul," she ordered.

We got on the bus fuming. It was funny having Mariko waiting at the bottom because although she was an adult she wasn't bigger than most of the kids.

"It's a big, yellow turdmobile!" someone called out.

Mariko climbed up the stairs swearing in Japanese and held her thumb and forefinger up for us to see just as she had on our first day. Betty roared to life and so did the Rolling Stones. It was like something from a movie as we drove off back to Renwick.

Tarik got to tell his story a number of times that night and he obviously liked the attention. I noticed though, that his dad, who had been busy all day with the lighthouse, seemed less enthusiastic than everyone else. Rewa and me were also a bit depressed because Grandpop had gone. It was strange that such a quiet man left such a gap.

The next day at school set the scene for the rest of the year. We had to write a story about our holidays. Grimly we set to work but most of us were still writing when time was up an hour later. Mr Wakefield looked a bit unhappy about our handwriting, which except for Tahira's, was pretty awful. Then we had a maths test. It was a nightmare for me and Scotty but Tarik and Cam raced each other and finished in half the time. Ashley was looking uncomfortable too, as was Tahira. At break there was more discussion about the qualities of turds than was really necessary and Tarik was looking like he wanted to kill someone. But there were also a group of kids who were quietly on our side. They obviously found Marshall's group as boring as we did. Unfortunately Mr Wakefield showed his stripes by making Tarik explain about the Kurdish struggle for nationhood to the class. Tarik had to put up with muttered talk about turds and doodles of poo while he was asked questions by Mr Wakefield. He tried to emphasise Kurdish children were also fighters but he just got rude and stupid questions from Marshall's table. Mr Wakefield seemed to regard his racist needling as high spirits and told them to "calm down". We were all pretty pissed off by the end of the day.

Fortunately the first week ended with New Zealand's national holiday so we only had four days of school instead of five. The weather was much better than it had been through the holidays so we kids had a fantastic three days of swimming and playing. The adults on the other hand were getting ready for their various hearings while Dr Prosperov was working on the lighthouse. Ken flew Sir Michael out on Sunday so he could meet everyone. Sir Michael seemed … well "breezy" was the word that came to mind – and quite funny too. He showed us pictures of his daughter, Sian, who was at school in Switzerland. She was about seventeen and very pretty with big brown eyes and long, curly, honey coloured hair. He was very proud of her because she had won a design competition in France for her clothes. He made sure he talked to all of us kids about our parents' cases to make sure we understood what was going on. I was impressed that he didn't talk down to us or use big words either. He didn't take notes but I could tell he was listening very closely. He also asked questions which showed he had remembered everything. The parents seemed to like him.

I started to get a bit nervous now because Sir Michael was here to keep Ax away from us. On the island it was easy to forget Ax had even been let out of prison but now we had to face the fact he was free, and the only reason he wasn't anywhere near us was he didn't know where we were. I started to have more dreams where Ax had taken over Renwick. Sometimes I felt like I had when we had gone to live with Aunty Liz and Grandpop. All shaky and nervous.

We went back to school the next week with a whole bunch of
absence notes from our parents. There was not a day when one
of us was not going to be away. Monday it was Scotty. Tuesday,
Tahira and Asal. Wednesday, Tarik. Thursday, Cam. Friday
it was Ashley. None of the hearings came to a quick result
although our New Zealand lawyer said the judges were very
impressed by Sir Michael. The other kids noticed our absences
but we were still too strong for the others to try and bully any of
us.

Both of the Middle Eastern families were entering a fasting
period. The Alevi Gursoy family had a three day fast in mid-
February called Hizir Orucu that required them not to eat food
or drink while the sun was up. Tarik pointed out that where they
came from it was winter and the days were shorter, but over
here in New Zealand the days were long, with the sun rising
at five and setting at eight thirty. That meant a very long day.
To help them out Mr Trân made a huge breakfast with three
courses for them every day. Even so by home time Tarik was
pretty worn down and grumpy.

Tahira's Baha'i fast didn't start until March but it was nineteen
days and she wasn't looking forward much to that. Meanwhile,
just make things awkward, Cam and Mr Trân were celebrating
Tet, the Vietnamese New Year, at almost exactly the same time.
It meant that they had to hand out their traditional Tet foods
after the sun went down. I could tell Tarik really liked the way
Cam didn't give him a hard time or tease him about fasting but
just patiently worked with him until sunset.

When Marshall found out about the fast he tried to tease Tarik
as much as possible. Tarik said he was used to it from Britain
and was glad that at least Alevi didn't observe Ramadan which

was a whole month.

Meanwhile Dr Prosperov and the others had begun testing the lighthouse at low power checking their instruments. They were checking the system to make sure it could handle lightning. Dr Prosperov explained to us that he had developed a system to stimulate lightning strikes in order to milk clouds of their energy into high power capacitors like big batteries normally used by the national grid to store energy for short periods of time. The power would then be used in his experiments.

Of course this meant he needed a lightning storm. The heights of the island's main ridge helped improve the chances of lightning but the glorious weather we were having pretty much meant there was nothing he could do but fiddle with his instruments and wait.

Sir Michael and his pilot Anton and his secretary Debra spent the weekend at Renwick. They were curious to learn about Edvard Shulyagin's visit two months before and very curious about the lighthouse. Dr Prosperov said very little about the lighthouse but talked a lot about rich Russians Sir Michael knew of, telling gossipy stories. Sir Michael laughed at all the right places but I knew he had noticed how Dr Prosperov had avoided saying very much about the lighthouse.

The deal was that on Monday we were going to be flown by Ken to Auckland airport in the helicopter and then by Anton to Whangarei in Sir Michael's jet. Then Grandpop would take us back down south and Ken would pick us up again. So we would arrive in millionaire style and leave in the same old bomb we left the first time in.

Rewa and me were very excited about going in the helicopter and Aunty Liz was nervous about the case. Monday was another fabulous day. We had to lay out our best clothes but not get into them until after breakfast. The other kids were jealous-as, first because we weren't going to school, and second because we got to ride in Ken's helicopter. So far only Scotty had done that.

Ken took Sir Michael's crew to Auckland first because they had to get their jet ready for their flight home. We were just a stop-off on their long flight to Singapore. We watched the chopper kick up dust and leap into the air heading north around the island. Unusually Dr Prosperov had come down to breakfast to see Sir Michael off but as soon as he was safely out of sight he got his lighthouse crew together and they took off back to work. We watched the others go off on Betty the bus. It was kind of strange to be at Renwick without the other kids. The adults started work in a very relaxed fashion doing a lot of talking at the same time. It didn't look much like work at all to me.

Aunty Liz made an enormous fuss of getting us dressed. We had to have clean shoes, clean faces and clean everything. I was in a white shirt with black pants and shoes. She said I looked lovely. I thought I looked like a Mormon. I drew the line at wearing a clip-on black tie. I said no judge would ever believe I wore a tie except to a wedding. We had a bit of an argument about it and she said I should take it with me "just in case". Rewa wore her favourite pink dress and she looked great in it. She wanted to wear makeup the way Tahira had taught her but Aunty Liz said it was best if Rewa looked young to the judge, not grown-up. Rewa was annoyed about that.

Finally at about nine Ken was back with the helicopter. He didn't even stop the engines completely because we needed to hurry, so after all our fussing we all got windblown and sandy scurrying under the blades. I was totally stoked because he wanted an adult to watch the child in the back so I got to ride up front next to Ken, wearing the headphones.

He made sure everyone was strapped in, flipped some switches, and then looking around, adjusted the controls and the engine cranked up sending sand in all directions. Then suddenly the front was lifting away from the ground and we were gaining height over the beach. It was totally awesome.

We flew out past the lighthouse gradually gaining height. I could see all the bays and beaches we had been playing in all summer to my left as we climbed.

"Like flying Sam?" Ken's voice crackled in my ears. My grin must have told him everything.

"How's Liz?"

I looked back. She was looking calm and collected out at the scenery. I remembered that as a young nurse she had flown in helicopters before. Rewa was fascinated.

We climbed up to the end of the long ridge of Aotea Island and over towards Auckland. The sea was flat and there were a lot of yachts, ships and other boats on the teal blue sea. We were gaining height steadily when I heard a voice in my ears. I couldn't understand a thing they said. They were talking to someone else.

Ken pulled out his cellphone, flipped it open and made a call. "Sir Michael? I'll have them on the ground in fifteen minutes." Then he listened for a bit and replied "Roger," and hung up. "No point telling every plane in Auckland our plans," he commented to me.

We had started heading north around the island, but now we were heading back south again. After ten minutes Ken called the Auckland air traffic control and they talked a lot of numbers and letters. Ken made a slight change of course and soon we were belting along over the eastern beaches where the ferry terminal is. This sure beat an hour on the sea any day.

There was one more radio chat and then we were coming up on the airport. It was kind of strange because we could see the jet we were going to be flying in before we even landed. It looked pretty small with its engines back on its tail.

I was amazed how close Ken landed next to it. Once again he didn't stop the rotors and we had to run out underneath them. Now I knew why the people on TV ducked. Those blades sure were scary even if they were two meters above my head standing up.

We scurried over to the steep steps that extended from the jet. Debra was waiting at the bottom and ushered us on board. I led the way up the steps.

"Sam, welcome aboard," Sir Michael said.

He was seated at a wooden desk with a screen in front of him wearing a stunning blue suit and tie.

"Have a seat. We need to get going pretty quickly I'm afraid." In front of the desk was pair of huge seats facing opposite each other with a table between them. The sound of Ken flying off was noticeable even in here. On the other side of the aisle from the desk was a little kitchen area. The aisle led to a door which probably took up most of the cabin but was closed now. I jumped into the seat facing forward on the opposite side to Sir Michael. Rewa sat on the other side of the aisle and Aunty Liz sat facing Sir Michael. Debra closed the door behind us and came and sat opposite me. The engines started almost at once. "Excuse me. I'm also officially co-pilot," Sir Michael said and went through the door to the cockpit.

The engines increased in pitch and we started rolling away from the hangar. I was checking everything out, totally buzzing.

"Is this your first flight?" Debra asked me. She was pretty with short, brown hair, bright red lipstick and an English accent.

"In a plane. First time in helicopter too just now."

"Well Sam, start as you mean to go on. Flying doesn't get any better than this, believe me. My first flight was when I was your age – a holiday to Majorca with my family. There were endless queues, millions of tired, angry people, a sea of baggage, and the smell of disinfectant everywhere. It was simply horrid."

It sounded it.

"Oh, here we go," she said as a huge plane landed, charging down the runway to our right with a thunderous roar. Almost at once our plane was moving forward and turning on to the runway. We waited for a moment and then there was a change of pitch in the engines and we began to roll forward. The acceleration threw me back into my seat with amazing power. We were off the ground in no time and heading into the sky. It was totally righteous as Auckland dropped away below us. The view from the helicopter was much better but the speed of this plane was kick-arse. We climbed rapidly and were soon too high to see much. Of course my side was on the right so my view was just sea with the morning sun making it hard to see anything anyway.

Sir Michael re-emerged from the front.

"We'll be landing again in twenty minutes so if the children would like to look at the flight deck now's the best time."

I was keen but a bit uncertain and looked at Aunty Liz. She just nodded.

We got up and Sir Michael ushered us forward. I'd never seen so many screens and controls in my life. Anton looked back at us.

"Hi kids," he said lazily.

The view out the front was amazing. The whole world seemed laid out below in stunning detail.

"We're not flying that high today because we will be landing so soon after taking off. This aeroplane can actually fly five times higher than this and half as fast again."

"Is that the radar?" I asked pointing at a screen.

"Yes Sam, that's right. It's actually a collision detection system which is to make sure we don't bump into any smaller aeroplanes. It sees where other planes and helicopters are headed and warns us if our paths cross. This aeroplane can land at quite small airfields which don't have towers and some local pilots get a bit casual about flight rules so we have to compensate by acting as a sort of air traffic controller as well."

"How much money is an airplane?" Rewa asked.

Anton chuckled. Sir Michael paused.

"Ahh well this one cost rather a lot actually. At a guess I think I could buy ten houses like the lovely house you live in for the price of this plane."

"Wow," I said.

"I'm afraid we'll have to start thinking about landing soon and I'd like to talk to you about the hearing so could we go back and sit down please."

Sir Michael ushered us back to our chairs. Debra swapped seats with him so she could sit at the desk. He sat opposite me looking very relaxed.

"Now children this hearing is for what's called a protection order. That means that the Government tells your father to keep away from you because you are scared of him and they think there is good reason to think he might hurt you or Aunty Liz."

"What if he doesn't take any notice," I asked.

"Ah, well, you see normally a person can go anywhere they like so long as they don't go onto private property, and the police can't do anything about it. But if a protection order exists you can call the police just because your father is hanging around outside your school for instance."

"Now the Judge can only give you a protection order if she thinks your right to safety is more important than your father's right to freedom. But what is important is not you just being safe, but you *feeling* safe as well. So does your father make you feel safe?"

"No," I answered immediately.

"I don't know," said Rewa.

We all looked at her.

"He killed mum!" I yelled at her.

"But Sam, I don't remember him or mum."

I was appalled.

"Sam. It's alright," Sir Michael broke in, "It's perfectly understandable. Rewa was only two at the time and that has to be understood. But it's just as well we have this talk now," he told me

"Now Rewa when the judge asks you how your father makes you feel it's important that you answer with your first feelings. So if for example I said your father is right behind you now. How would feel then?"

"Scared."

"That is what the judge wants to know. It doesn't matter that a little part of your mind says 'I've never met him' or 'I don't know why I'm scared of him'. It doesn't even matter that you think the reason you are scared of him is because everyone else is. What matters is that first feeling of fear that you associate with Alan Xavier John Stephens, your father. Does that help Rewa?"

She nodded and said "yes."

"Excellent! Well, there isn't really much more to it than that. Just remember the judge is trying to look after you and be fair. Now we have a lady judge today called Judge McGeehan and she has grandchildren your age, Rewa, so I think she will be especially interested in making sure you are looked after."

"Now do you have any questions?"

"Will Ax be there?" I wanted to know.

"No Sam, only the judge and us lawyers. I'll be working with a New Zealand lawyer named Geoff. You will be in a separate room and Aunty Liz will be allowed to be with you. Your father's lawyer may insist that you come in separately however."

"Will Ax be in the waiting room?" I checked.

"He may be somewhere, but we have an interim injunction Sam. That means that at the moment it's as if the protection order already applies. Your father is not allowed to approach either of you until after the judge makes her decision."

"When is that likely, Sir Michael?" Aunty Liz asked.

"I see no reason why she would not rule today. It's a fairly straightforward case," he said.

He looked around at us. I think we were all feeling a bit nervous although Sir Michael was very relaxed.

"Well, I think Anton is getting ready to land and because I need the practice I think I'll just take over. So if you'll excuse me I'll talk to you when we've landed. Debra the car will be waiting for us?" he asked getting up.

"Yes, Sir Michael," she replied.

"Thank you," he nodded and went forward to the flight deck.

"Don't tell the judge you want to meet him Rewa," I warned.

"I don't want to," she said hotly, but I knew she was a little curious about him, and I had to admit I wondered if I saw him whether he would stop giving me nightmares. Mum was not keen on us seeing him.

When we landed at the airport we were met by a big taxi. Debra and Anton stayed with the plane so they could organise the rest of their journey. It was funny riding through Whangarei all dressed up with a fancy car. I felt a bit try-hard.

Grandpop was waiting at the courtroom. He was in his old suit which always looked a bit funny on him. He gave us a big hug each, then we went in to the court.

We had to wait for ages before our hearing started. When it did a man in a green uniform led us to a waiting room. It had a few crappy old toys in it and some magazines. Rewa found a book and Aunty Liz pretended to read a magazine about Hollywood stars getting fat or drunk or divorced or whatever. Grandpop read a magazine about fishing. I was just bored.

Then Grandpop and Aunty Liz were called in. We waited and waited. I had to go to the bathroom. I went out into the corridor. The guy in the green uniform was outside and I asked him where I should go. He pointed down to the end of the corridor. I followed his directions and went.

The corridor was the way we had come in. It was an L-shaped intersection with the toilets opposite the corner. I glanced right up the corridor back toward the entrance and my blood turned to ice. Ax was standing there talking to some smaller men in suits. He looked over them right at me.

He looked like a big, evil Jesus. His black, fine hair was shoulder length, and his beard short. He was wearing a long, white shirt with a black leather waistcoat and a huge cross around his neck. But the holyman effect was ruined by the black wrap-around sunnies, the gang face tattoos and the missing tooth in the smile he turned on me. I felt as if the Devil himself was waiting for me. I ran into the toilet and hid in a cubicle locking the door. I felt sick. Then I was sick. I flushed that away and then had to deal with fact I was about ready to go at the other end as well. I sat there terrified he was going to come in. I listened straining my ears at every sound. There was no question about it I heard footsteps approaching. A man's steady tread into the toilet. I sat there with my pants around my legs, shaking.

The man stood on the urinal, which you could hear creak under his weight. I could hear everything, smell everything. I knew it was him. I heard him zip up and step off the urinal and the tap of his shoes over to the basins. The water. Then it stopped. Then silence. The rattle of the towel in the roller was so loud I cried out in spite of myself. Then more silence.

"Sam?" his voice was low and surprisingly soft but so close I gasped again.

"Sam you look just like I did at your age."

There was a silence.

"One day when you are a man you will see me in the mirror. Maybe then you will be ready to listen."

And then he walked out.

About a minute later I remembered I needed to breathe. I finished in the cubicle and came out to wash my hands. There was a mirror in front of me. I looked into it.

What he said was truer than I liked. I felt a horror at my own reflection I had never experienced. And then mum was there

in the mirror looking right at me. It was far stronger than I had
ever seen her before. Not like a memory or an impression like
she normally seemed, but sharp and detailed so I could see the
weave of her blouse. She just looked sorry for me. Sorry and
helpless. I looked to where she should be standing but she had
gone.

I washed my face. I went back to where Rewa was waiting. She
looked up at me.

"What's the matter Sam?" she asked.

"I ... I ... just saw Ax," I confessed.

Rewa's eyes widened.

"What happened?" she asked, frightened.

"Nothing Rewa. He ... um ... didn't see me."

And I couldn't help noticing how much Rewa looked like mum.
It chilled me even more. I couldn't help wondering if some
time in the past two kids looking like me and Rewa had played
innocently next to each other not knowing that twelve years later
one would murder the other. I was still thinking like this when
they called us in.

The courtroom was a bit like a classroom except the judge was
in the middle rather than to the side. There were two rows of
desks. Sir Michael, Geoff, Grandpop and Aunty Liz were on
the right and one of the men I'd seen talking to Ax was on the
left. He was fat and white with curly red hair. He wore a black
suit and a blue and white striped shirt with a red tie. He would
normally have worried me because he had mean little eyes and
the look of someone who was good at what they do but today I
could see we were winning already. Sir Michael not only looked
a million times better dressed he also was smiling and relaxed.
Geoff was young and friendly with curly brown hair. The other

lawyer looked sour and angry. I guessed we were quite a few points ahead.

The judge was old, with short gray hair and a look that showed she was both strict and motherly. She wore round black and white earrings which attracted my eye for some reason. She smiled at us as we came in. There were a couple of chairs in front of her desk.

"Sam and Rewa. Come over here please," she smiled at us.

We came over.

"Please sit down,"

It was like being at the principal's office but to the max. We sat. She asked us a lot of questions about our family life. Why we had moved and how we felt about our father. I felt slightly weird. I kept thinking about little Alan Stephens. But then she asked how our father made us feel. I answered with some feeling. I noticed her frown.

"Sam you're being a lot more exact than Rewa. Have you thought about it more?"

I answered that I had had nightmares about him for years and I'd just seen Ax in the toilets, so I knew exactly how I felt.

Well, that got things going! The judge said she was very sorry that had happened and looked very angry at the fat man. The fat man looked whiter than ever and Sir Michael had a bit to say which sounded both friendly and sharp at the same time. The judge called the man in the green uniform and he was given a ticking off and then we were sent back out again.

Ten minutes later everyone came into the waiting room looking very pleased with themselves. We'd been given our protection order and Ax was going to be arrested for something. We walked together out of the courtroom in time to see Ax being put in a police car. Rewa looked at him with big eyes and he was clearly shocked at the sight of her. Although she was only ten she looked so like a little girl version of my mum, Joy, he couldn't take his eyes off her.

Grandpop and Sir Michael shook hands and Aunty Liz gave him a hug and thanked him and then he took off in a big car back to the airport while we found Grandpop's old heap in the carpark. It felt so much more real to drive off to Whangarei McDonald's for a celebration lunch than to ride in a fancy jet plane. It was just a shame Aunty Liz wouldn't let us play in the playground in our best clothes.

The ride back to Auckland was long and warm. Rewa fell asleep on my shoulder towards the end. It felt nice having her there against me and I felt the part of my soul that Ax had chilled with his words warming up again.

We met Ken on the beach at Waiwera, north of Auckland. It was funny going past the big swimming pool and just driving down the ramp onto the beach. We gave Grandpop a big hug goodbye and then he drove off leaving us there on the sand looking all dressed up with nowhere to go. There was a family collecting shellfish in the shallows watching us. We waited for about twenty minutes. I'm sure we looked a bit like spies in a movie. Then we heard the buzz of the chopper and saw the small dark shape of Ken and the chopper heading towards us low over the sea against the background of the distant peninsular.

He landed covering us in sand, we jumped aboard and left the folks on the beach staring as we lifted into the sky and headed back to Renwick. Dinner was a lime chicken salad. The others wanted to know all about the plane and I have to say I went to bed early that night without giving any thought to the ghost of a soldier named Parker who I passed on the stairs.

The next morning it was back to school again. It felt great to be with the others and we had a rubber band fight on the bus all the way there. I was even pleased to see Mr Wakefield again. Unfortunately it started raining at lunchtime and by the end of school it was dark slate gray over the whole sky. But we came home to find Renwick in a huge state of excitement. Lightning was forecast and Dr Prosperov's machine was ready. Dr Prosperov and Dr Gursoy were at the lighthouse getting their systems set up to extract power from the clouds. Dr Morozov was working from their suite and organising Mrs Jones to get everyone running around to help them.

Dinner was borscht soup with dark bread which Mr Trân said was "for luck". It must have worked. During dinner we watched a fantastic display of lightning dancing brilliant blue on a stone gray sky and sea. The air got colder and the clouds got deeper and darker all evening, then the wind and rain hit us and the thunder began to shake the windows as lightning started along the high points on the ridge of the island.

By ten it was hard to sleep. The thunder was right overhead and there was almost no time to count between the flash and the loud roll of enormous drums above us. Once or twice I was sure the lightning hit the lighthouse standing alone at the end of the bay but it was so fast you couldn't be sure. As the storm began to move on I fell asleep.

That night I dreamt I was flying around Renwick with Ken in the helicopter. All the others were on the ground and for some reason Tahira and me had to clean the helicopter while Ken flew it. Although we were sitting on the skids we weren't worried even though there were dull booms coming from the machine.

Then there were all these bright flashing lights dancing around me and I noticed it wasn't Ken flying the helicopter but Ax. Ax was flying lower, and below was Rewa. She was lying on the ground and started crying out for mum. Louder and louder.

CHAPTER TWENTY FOUR: A STRANGE DISCOVERY

The cry woke me up. It was pitch black in my room and I wondered why the LEDs from my screen weren't on. I got out of bed and blindly stepped towards it. I bumped into my desk – which hurt – but which at least told me where the screen ought to be. I leaned over and found the mouse to shake it. But the familiar red glow from it too was out. Now I felt my way around the desk to the door and found the switch. Nothing happened. I flicked it on or off a couple of times before I convinced myself that we simply had no power.

By now my eyes were becoming more accustomed to the dark. I shuffled over to the window and looked outside. Although the moon was full and very bright everything was completely dark. Even the lighthouse was dark, and that was unusual because I knew they had been busy on it tonight. I had no idea what the time was. Perhaps they had simply finished for the night. Being a country kid I was used to occasional power cuts at night. It seemed to be a time when the electricity companies thought they could cut power without anyone noticing. I was just about to go back to bed when I heard it again.

Or did I? Come to think of it. I hadn't heard anything. It sure wasn't Rewa. It seemed as if I'd heard something but now that I thought about it, it was more like the memory of a sound rather than a sound itself. That would normally mean the ghosts except that the sound I'd heard was not a man's cry, it was quite definitely a girl's.

I peered out the window looking for anything that might make a sound, but it was hopeless. It was simply too dark. But I did feel something. I felt quite sure I was not the only one looking outside just then. It was as if the whole house was listening – straining to hear that memory of a sound. I knew the others were awake, and even the ghosts were listening. I was wide awake now and there was no way I was going back to sleep, so I quickly got dressed, pulled on my jacket and trainers and slipped out of my door. It was funny to be in the apartment lounge with no LEDs from the screen, no sound from the fridge, knowing Aunty Liz and Rewa were dead to the world. Then I heard the cry again. So sad. Like a howl of despair. I resisted the temptation to go back to my window and went out into the corridor instead, quietly pulling the door closed behind me. I started out along the passage in the dark when there was a rustle and clunk behind me.

"Ashley?" I whispered.

"Shit!" she swore suddenly, trying to muffle her voice.

There was a pause.

"Ah didn't know you was out here," she explained tensely out of the darkness. I could just see the glint of her glasses.

Another door opened

"Tahira, it's me Ashley," Ashley whispered.

"You 'eard it also?" Tahira asked.

"We all did, Sam's just up the corridor."

"C'mon," I called

And we all padded softly up the passage through the lounge,

where the glow from the fire was down to the last few embers. Suddenly there were footsteps and Scotty, Tarik and Cam appeared from their corridor. Scotty took one look at us and simply asked, "what do you think it was?"

We all shrugged and headed for the door to the stairwell. On the landing we all stopped. There were presences in the gallery. We looked at each other. If we were bold we would have gone in and talked to them but none of us felt that bold. We scampered down the stairs as fast as we could. We just got to the door when there was another cry. It was so sad and so lost. Both chilling and heartrending at the same time. Tarik punched in the code and we opened the door and piled out.

The roar of the sea and the smell of salt hit our senses at once. There was a strong breeze and the moon shone brightly. We drifted out onto the driveway trying to get a sense of direction. Then suddenly the door opened behind us again. A figure in a black coat with a hood slipped out. For a moment the figure seemed to be mysterious, almost scary.

"Children!" called Mrs Jones.

She walked over to where we were.

"You heard the girl, I assume," she said.

We all said we had.

"Did she wake you up too, Mrs Jones?" Ashley asked.

"Yes Ashley, but I'm also worried. Something is wrong at the lighthouse I'm certain of it."

"What's the time?" I asked vaguely.

"One," Tarik replied, checking his watch. He was looking uneasily at the lighthouse too. "And me dad's over there. Somefing's wrong, I know it."

"Come on," Mrs Jones said starting to walk briskly up the road.

"We'll look to our own before we worry about the lass."
Tarik wasn't going to wait around. He ran on ahead and
everyone – even Mrs Jones – picked up the pace after him.
We ran crunching along the gravel in the moonlight, with the
wind in our ears and the sea crashing. Then we stopped. An
eerie darkness was spreading. We looked up and could see a
shadow falling over the moon. Slowly it was darkening. My hair
was rising. This was the vision Tawhiri-matea, god of storms,
had shown me in my dreams.

Everyone was breathing hard for we felt sure now that there had
been a disaster at the lighthouse. We began to run again and
were so busy hurrying that we were completely taken by surprise
when three dark figures loomed out of the dark in front of us.

"Thank God," called Dr Gursoy.

"Get help," grunted Dr Prosperov.

They were struggling along with Ken, who was bigger than
both of them, staggering between them. They stopped and Ken
slumped forward to his knees and they laid him on his back. His
eyes were open and glassy but he was breathing.

"What's the matter with him"?" asked Mrs Jones running
forward.

"Shock," Dr Prosperov gasped.

"Not bad ... but not good either," Dr Gursoy added quickly.

Mrs Jones looked round at us.

"Ashley and Sam. Go wake your mothers, quickly please."

"But." We were thinking of the ghosts.

"Now!"

We ran back up the road. We heard footsteps behind us and
Tarik was running too. He had to wake Gunter and Mariko.
We ran back towards the house when the girl screamed again. It

seemed to be more like a desperate call, than anything. A call for her mother. But we didn't have time to worry about girl ghosts when Khenbish might join her anytime soon.

We pounded back inside the house, and up the stairs. The presences seemed to want to know what was happening but we ran past them down the corridor. I burst into our flat. It would have been so much easier if I could turn the light on but everything was still dead. I pushed open my Aunt's door and ran up to her as she lay snoring away.

"Aunty Liz," I shouted, shaking her, "Aunty Liz get up! There's been an accident! Ken's hurt!"

She opened her eyes at once but it seemed to take a while for her thoughts to catch up. I shook her again.

"Ken's hurt! Mrs Jones wants you to come!"

And then she was awake.

"What's happened? What happened to Ken?" she asked sitting up and holding my hands to stop me shaking her again.

"Shock. Some kind of shock. He can't stand."

Aunty Liz swung out of bed, showing legs that were surprisingly lean for a woman who always seemed so old. She went to her closet and pulled on her old coat and grabbed her medical bag. She wiggled her feet into her boots and then she pulled a blanket off the bed.

"Where is he?" she asked.

I led the way out just in time to meet up with Mrs Robinson and Ashley. We bustled down the corridor. This time the presences were waiting on the landing. Corporal Higgins wanted to know what was happening but Ashley and I ran straight through him without answering him, and the women didn't see him. We thundered down the stairs and out into the bright night air.

We had barely started up the road when there was a roar from the garage. In a moment Mariko driving the Range Rover had caught us up, slowed long enough to let us swing into the seats and roared up the road to where Ken lay.

The small gathering of people on the road looked like guilty animals in the glare of the headlights. Mariko braked hard and we jumped out pushing past the cloud of dust that enveloped us in the headlamps. Aunty Liz and Patricia rushed to look at the big man on the ground, who stared vaguely at the sky. They checked his pulse and heart, checked his breathing and airway, and declared that he was stable but needed warmth and rest. The adults gathered together, Dr Prosperov looking most concerned, and they lifted him into the Range Rover. Mariko got into the driver's seat and reversed back the way she'd come at remarkable speed, leaving us kids alone in the middle of the road.

Nobody had even thought to question why we were all up at one in the morning.

"Ope 'e's OK," Tarik remarked.

"Shure was a strange kinda shock," Ashley added quietly, "all his signs looked normal."

"I thought ..." began Cam.

We all looked at her. She was usually so shy.

"I thought he had big fright."

We digested that for a moment, standing in the dark, halfway to the lighthouse. The moon was now half gone.

"Who wants to go to the lighthouse?" Tarik asked.

Cam and Scotty raised hands briefly.

"We all do," I said.

It wasn't bravery. It was more curiosity than anything.

271

So we turned and crunched our way up the slope to the lighthouse. As we got closer the breeze stiffened and the roar of the sea was much louder. The lighthouse loomed, a tall mysterious shape, dark against the night sky. We got to the door, pulled it open and stumbled inside in the dark, closing the door against the wind. Inside, the air was still and you got this powerful whiff like the smell of an old photocopier. The smell of oxygen ripped up by electric power. The accelerator glimmered slightly in the dark but the overall feeling you got was that everything that had happened here was over. The machinery was cooling down. The mystery had left the building.

Then as we wondered what to do, the cry came again. Much closer this time, and much clearer. Like a cry for a mother against the roar of the wind. Lost and desperate under the pitiless glow of the darkened moon and below the rush of the tide. We looked at each other. We knew only we and Mrs Jones could hear it. We knew, somehow, we must find who was making that cry and why.

"Are you guys ready?" Tarik asked

"Ready as we'll ever be," Ashley answered him nervously.

We all looked as sick as we felt, but we knew we had to do it. We wrestled the door open and walked back out into the wind. A sliver of moon reappeared and poured its light down on the sea which reflected back at us as we walked down towards the sea into the blast. We got to the rocks just before the cliff and stopped, buffeted constantly by the wind.

"Let's split up," Scotty yelled, "we'll cover more ground."

"Den we'll be alone iff'n we find her," Ashley shouted.

"Work teams of two," Tarik bellowed, "Me and Cam, Scott and Ashley, Sam and Tahira."

"Which way do we go?" Cam yelled.

Another soundless scream washed over us. We all looked north. That was the obvious direction.

We walked together north until we came to the path down to the beach. Tahira led me down the path while the others continued along the cliff.

We twisted down the narrow path among the rocks. It was easy to see because the moon was emerging from the shadow brightly and we soon came out on to the beach. The sand was wet and glistening and the waves were big and wild as they roared up the sand. Even the wind seemed to ease a bit and the beach felt wild and free as if it was kicking back and having fun when nobody was watching it.

Me and Tahira set out for the rocks on the other side of the beach, watching out for the sea which ran up the beach, like a playful giant trying to get our feet wet. We couldn't really see the others but we knew they were there, skirting along the track above us.

We were about two-thirds the way along the beach when Tahira stopped me and pointed at something on the sand. It was a set of footprints. Footprints left by a pair of bare feet our size, only slightly waterlogged. The discovery of footprints suddenly made me feel much better. I had dreaded the thought that somewhere out there was a ghost and some awful mangled body. But the feet were no bigger than ours. This was no ghost and if it was a girl she was no bigger than us. That, I could handle.

"Eez strange footsteps start 'ere," Tahira pointed out.

It was strange. They just started and went over towards the rocks as if the feet that made them had appeared on the spot. We walked along the beach towards the rocks and as we approached

273

them a new sense came over us. A silent sound of weeping and
fear. Whoever it was doing the screaming was really scared. Her
voice filled with dread and uncertainty.

We climbed onto the rocks, moving silently, and what noise we
did make was drowned out by the sea. We were drawn up from
the sea and away from the rocks toward the foot of the cliff.
There were bushes and pampas but I noticed a dark patch in
the cliff which seemed to stay permanently black no matter how
you looked at it and we felt drawn to it. Finally we came to the
mouth of a small cave. It was a slit in the rock no more than a
meter tall and barely wide enough to squeeze into. Something
told me Tahira should go first.

With more ability than I had expected, Tahira twisted herself
through the narrow entrance and crawled into the dark. Then I
heard her say "Salam," quietly, and then, "haalet, chetori?"

I followed her in. I was surprised to find there was a strange blue
glow in the cave.

"Sam djoo must stay outside!" Tahira shouted with sudden
force. The sea's crashing drowned even shouting.

"What!? Why?" I objected.

"Is not for boys!" she insisted.

Well, I wasn't going to take that! So I went in anyway. Tahira
turned to stop me.

"Should not come in!" she insisted, blocking me. She was
physically stopping me from seeing and I wanted to know why.
The white-blue glow was quite intense. I couldn't understand
what her problem was. I thought she was being selfish. But then
"No!" It wasn't words. It was an impression in our minds. Gentle
but still fearful.

"Let him in. I want to see him too," it continued.

The impression was so powerful that Tahira had no choice but to agree. Against her judgement she let me pass.

Now I could see the source of the blue-white light. It was a girl. She looked about the same age as us. Her pale, white skin was emitting a bright blue radiance lighting up the cave. She looked like she was a bit of the moon on Earth. There was a lot of light because she was completely naked. Her face had high cheekbones and big, slightly slanted, eyes which were electric blue. Her hair was black, long, and shiny and she had the beginnings of breasts on her chest. But the reason I knew at once she was not human were the pointed ears, the black mane down her back and the black feathered wings.

She was curled in a corner of the cave, her head to one side looking at us both from one to another. She didn't seem the slightest bit embarrassed about her nudity, although it clearly bothered Tahira and I didn't know where to look. But she was simply fascinated by us.

"*You, children, yes?*" The ideas were instantly in our heads. She made no sound.

We felt uncomfortable. We had no idea what she was, but we nodded.

She laughed delightedly – her first audible sound – at the combination of our moving our heads and thinking "yes".

I noticed her teeth were almost like ours but with longer, stronger fangs. More like a dogs, she also had short blunt black claws in place of nails. It all somehow seemed familiar if a bit unusual.

"*I, child, too,*" she told us silently in a flash of ideas.

I was surprised and not. I mean she looked like a girl rather than a woman but given the wings and it was hard to know what she was.

She smiled at our confusion.

I wondered how old she was.

"*Forty seven years,*" she replied instantly.

I realised at once she could read our thoughts whether we wanted her to or not.

"*Yes,*" she thought and nodded vigorously, making Tahira and me laugh. She laughed too. It was a girl's laugh and pretty.

"*How old are you?*"

No sooner had we remembered then she was already replying "*oh! in my world you would be babies in an egg!*"

The egg was a curious idea, like a natural egg, but artificial. It was for learning. We wondered where her world was: "Ahle kojayee? / where is your world?" we thought in our own languages. We only had to think it and her smile faded.

"*I don't know.*"

We wanted to know how she had come here.

"*I don't know. I was by the old monument. There was a bright light. I fell. I froze. And then I found myself here by the tall thing by the sea.*" She paused for moment.

"*This is the middle world, yes?*" she asked, slightly fearfully.

The concept of "middle world" implied surrounding worlds. But her use of it also implied something about a form of existence in contrast to something more complicated, and something far simpler which we didn't really understand.

For a moment she looked worried, lost in her own thoughts. I wondered if in her world her thoughts would be private. But Tahira had more down-to-earth questions.

"Esme tun chie?" she asked, and then seeing my confusion, "'Ow are you called?" she repeated.

It was strange hearing a voice again. So far everything had

passed between us silently. The girl-creature looked up, and tilted her head again. Then she swallowed slightly and spoke. "Tabika."

Her voice was almost a whisper, so she cleared her throat and said it again, practising something which she obviously hadn't done in a while.

Tahira smiled at her.

"Is it cold Tabika?"

"*No*," she smiled at Tahira as if it was a silly question. Tahira looked slightly embarrassed. I had the impression Tabika had 'said' something else to her that I wasn't meant to 'hear'.

"Would you like to come to our house?" I asked.

She looked at me intently with her bright blue eyes for a few seconds in silence. I realised she was reading my memories of the place.

"*No, I'm safer here*," her thought came back.

"But es not very comfortable," Tahira objected.

Tabika smiled at her.

"*You are kind*," she replied. "*But I am safe here.*"

"Safe from what?" I wanted to know.

"*Radiation*," The idea was filled with concepts I didn't understand but it came down to the fact she didn't like sunlight, radio waves, metals or electricity. But she also didn't trust adults and wouldn't say directly.

She didn't trust the house because of those things.

"But what will you eat?" Tahira wanted to know.

"*Animals, fish, birds, shellfish*," Tabika responded. "*It's what I eat at home.*"

Her ideas showed us she was used to hunting as a way of life.

"What if you are sick?" Tahira argued.

277

"*So kind,*" she smiled. But I could tell we were annoying her now, just as you can tell with a dog or a cat when the mood changes.

"We must tell the people at the house about you," I told her.

She looked me directly in the eyes. It was amazing the power she had in them.

"*Tell no-one,*" she instructed me.

"But they may be able to help you get back home," I told her.

"*No one,*" she insisted and I knew I would not be able to disobey her. The idea was burned into my brain like a fixation. "But what about the others?" I wanted to know.

"*What others?*" she asked.

"Our friends outside," Tahira said.

"*How many are you?*" she asked suddenly worried.

"Six," Tahira answered.

She looked at us for a moment in silence, considering this new information.

"*Go now. Tell them nothing. You may return later but make sure no-one sees you.*"

All this was communicated to us silently and instantly. We hesitated slightly. She must have thought us a bit slow or something because she "yelled" at us – which felt like a kind of psychic shock.

"*Go!*"

We scrambled outside and looked at each other. We walked on a bit aimlessly before Tahira spoke.

"What shall we tell them?"she whispered.

"Just say we didn't find anything," I said.

We walked on along the beach. The sea seemed almost angry with us in the moonlight. The eclipse was over. The sea was roaring and crashing onto the rocks sending spray flying and creating a fine salty mist in the air. The violence of the sea seemed to break some of the spell the strange girl had cast on us. We walked along skirting the waves as if they were a caged tiger. Then we heard a shout. It was Tarik with Cam coming the other way. We climbed up the path as they came down to meet us.

"She's stopped," Tarik said simply.

"Yeah," I agreed as if we'd heard nothing more either "and it's boring out here," I added.

"Did you see anything ?" Tarik asked.

It was a strange feeling, hard to describe, like a wall in your mind. I simply couldn't say anything about the girl to Tarik, "Nah," I gasped and shook my head.

Tahira did the same. We must have looked pretty odd to Tarik and Cam because they looked at us strangely so I tried to cover with a counter question.

"How about you guys?" I asked finding my voice strained.

They looked at each other briefly.

"Nah, we didn't see nuffin neiver," Tarik said.

"Well, I've had enough, I'm going back to bed," I said.

I led them up the path. Nobody said anything – partly because the sea was too loud, and partly because there just wasn't anything to say.

We found the others and everyone agreed that now there were no cries any more whatever it was that we had been looking for had gone elsewhere so we may as well get back home to bed. For some reason we all felt very tired now. The electric feeling in the air that had accompanied the cries had gone and the night just seemed spent. Now we wondered aloud how Ken was. He had certainly seemed pretty bad when Mariko had taken him away.

When we got back to the house there was still no power on. Ken was in the downstairs lounge lying under blankets on a couch lit by torches and firelight. Nergui had been roused and was sitting next to his son with his hand over his face. Everyone else was standing around looking worried.

The obvious problem was normally if anyone needed urgent medical attention Ken would fly them to hospital. Aunty Liz and Patricia Robinson however had doubts that a rescue helicopter would be sent unless they said Ken had had an electric shock but there was no sign that he had.

Ken had been sleeping outside in his van in a sleeping bag. Dr Prosperov and Dr Gursoy said that the machine had suddenly started malfunctioning drawing power at a colossal rate. The computers became unresponsive and then suddenly there was a massive burst of blue lightning up and down the central copper columns of the lighthouse and then everything went dead.

There was just a smell of slight burning but they couldn't see anything so they decided to give up until morning when they might be able to see what had happened. They had gone outside to find Ken staring like a dead man and the battery of his van completely flat.

The funny thing was Ken wasn't completely unresponsive. He'd grunt a bit if you tapped him and called his name but he kept on staring past you. It was more like he was sleepwalking and couldn't wake up.

Nergui took his hand off Ken's face. He looked concerned but not worried. He looked around at everyone, then put his hands together and inclined his head suggesting Ken was sleeping. Aunty Liz and Patricia agreed that he was probably all right but decided to watch over him just to make sure. So I went back to bed and Aunty Liz went downstairs to take first watch. I hoped the ghosts wouldn't disturb either of us and got back into my pajamas and bed.

I lay there for a while wondering about the girl in the cave. I couldn't help feeling worried for her. She was alone in a strange world and while she was obviously not defenseless I couldn't help thinking how much I would hate to be her. The cold light of the moon still spilled through the curtains. I wondered what I would do in her place. And with these thoughts I fell asleep.

•••

CHAPTER TWENTY FIVE: NIGHT ANGEL

So was she a dream?" Sue asks, frowning.
"No, she was real."
"Really real?"
"Oh yeah."
"Well, what was she? Where did she come from? How did she get there?"
"I'm coming to all that," I say.
And rubbing her chin and looking a bit tense Sue settles down, watching me closely.

•••

Khenbish woke the next morning with no memory of the day before. Not just the night, but the entire day. Otherwise he seemed completely normal. They went back to the lighthouse to check out the damage as soon as it was light and came back looking very grim. Every circuit in the entire building seemed to have been burned out.

Dr Prosperov had retrieved some data from the computers and was hoping that it might explain the unexpected surge. He explained over a cold breakfast that the programme had been set back at least four and possibly six weeks. Fortunately Renwick itself had been largely insulated from the surge but it appeared that a huge amount of current had been sucked into the

lighthouse from the national grid and the blackout was probably
at a nearby substation.

"Will require imaginative explanation," Dr Prosperov sighed.

We went to school as normal. It was the strangest feeling.
Knowing that somehow Dr Prosperov had yanked this girl
creature from somewhere – who knew where – to our world,
and I could not talk about it to anyone but Tahira. I found
myself often glancing at Tahira in class and she glanced at me.
Only Emma seemed to notice, and think about it.

Mr Wakefield had decided to expand on his medieval theme and
give us projects to do. These would be shown off to our parents
(he did say, "or guardians," looking at our table) at the end of
term school fair.

Group one had been given "knights and chivalry" so Marshall
and his gang were making swords and armour and calling each
other "Lord" and everyone else "peasant" in a way that seemed
to amuse only them and Mr Wakefield, who they called "my
liege" in a way that made the rest of us gag. Group two had been
given "food and agriculture", so Ella and Stacey were organising
a medieval feast – or rather their mothers were competing to
"help" them with one.

Group three had been given "buildings" and were making a
model castle with walls about a meter high out of concrete
blocks they got from Marshall's dad's hardware store. The boys
were making battlements and the girls were making "ladies
chambers" inside.

Perhaps Mr Wakefield had picked up on the spooky way we
knew what the others were thinking so he picked witchcraft for
us. Immediately we were teased with taunts of "burn them" and
nasty mutterings like, "A few warts might improve their looks"

which was obviously untrue because Tahira was the prettiest in the school let alone the class. All we knew about witches was from cartoons where they were always ugly, wore black, flew on brooms, said "double, double toil and trouble, fire burn and cauldron bubble" and cackled a lot while zapping people with green lightning. More modern witch and wizard stories, while making it cool, had nothing useful to say about medieval witchcraft.

Of course part of the problem was that for all of us the Middle Ages in Europe were completely foreign. The only European among us thought of African witches, not Middle Ages ones, and to him they were very real. He told us about some of the famous Sangoma from his area and we were impressed. Meanwhile our black American had more background on the European Middle Ages because she had "done 'em" as background to the Salem witch trials before.

But we all knew that if we were to dress in black with pointy hats and hand out apples while cackling it would almost certainly give Marshall's gang an excuse to bully us while playing at knights. It wasn't exactly going to be fun. We talked about it all the way home in the bus and as we started doing our homework in the cafe.

It turned out half the island had been blacked out but fortunately it was being put down to a lightning strike on the substation. When we got home not only was Ken in a good mood but the power had been restored and the first contractors were just leaving the lighthouse after a first look at it.

For the next few days work to rewire the lighthouse went quickly with electricians on the job twelve hours every day. After checking the computer data Dr Prosperov became excited.

As far as he could tell the experiment had been successful and he spoke constantly about an unaccounted 47.4 kilos which his calculations said had been transferred through the interdimensional gateway. He guessed it was some kind of gas which had overwhelmed Ken. He seemed to talk about this as if to reassure himself. He was obviously badly haunted by the deaths he had caused back in America.

Tahira's family had started the traditional Baha'i nineteen day fast. Technically Tahira was under age and didn't have to do it, but her mother was encouraging her to have less food during the day. Asal was considered too young but she was willing to try and match her older sister. The result was everyone was being careful around Tahira during the day. Tarik was surprisingly good, even though Tahira wasn't that nice to him. She was usually really hungry just when we were cleaning together before the sun went down when she could eat again. I found being nice was no use. She snapped anyway. I just had to back off and leave her to it. She was eating heaps at dinner and also pocketing food, she said, for later.

Both Tahira and me were really nervous about what would happen when Dr Prosperov ran his machine again. But Tabika was very pleased that Dr Prosperov wanted to repeat the experiment. She felt sure that if he did it again, her mother would be able to find her. She asked us constantly for more information about progress and it was hard to ask Dr Prosperov without raising suspicions.

Or I should say Dr Prosperov was easy to get information out of. It was his wife who we had to watch out for. Dr Morozov was naturally suspicious anyway, and we were sure she was watching us. Luckily her husband was giving her a lot of computing work to do as he checked his calculations so she couldn't follow us again.

The combination of knowing about Tabika and studying witchcraft was kind of scary. It didn't help when Mrs Jones stopped ignoring our homework. Normally she took no notice but when she heard we were doing witchcraft she suddenly became very interested in what we were saying, and what we thought about witches. In fact she became a bit intense about it.

"What rubbish!" she snapped when she heard us describe witches.

"Witches are ordinary women. They just have a different religion that's all. You all have different religions. Saying witches wear pointy hats and have warts is like saying all Muslims wear bomb belts and blow themselves up. It's prejudice. Wicca is just another religion."

"What's Wicca Ma'am?" Ashley asked interested.

Mrs Jones looked at our faces and saw we genuinely wanted know.

"Wicca is descended from the religion of old Europe. The people who built Stonehenge and all the stone leylines and circles found in Britain and Europe."

"You mean like the Celts?" Scotty suggested.

"No, from even before them Scotty. The Celts invaded Europe in recorded history. Their route took them past both the Greeks and the Romans three hundred years before Christ so they were much later. No, the old religion goes back four thousand years, well before recorded history. But like a Chinese whisper passed from generation to generation Wicca has changed and adapted itself to the times. It is probably nothing like the original which archaeologists investigate by digging in old bogs to find artefacts or bodies."

"Bodies?" asked Tarik a bit alarmed.

"Yes, archaeologists sometimes find the bodies of what they think are sacrificial victims, preserved like leather in the peat bogs. They are quite fascinating to look at. They think sometimes they have been sacrificed to the gods and sometimes executed depending on how they were killed and what they are dressed in. Of course modern Wiccans don't kill people any more than the Roman church burns witches."

There was a pause while that little nugget connected.

"So are you a ... witch?" Cam asked uncertainly.

"Yes dear, I'm a witch," she smiled.

There was an "Oohh" moment. That explained a lot.

"Negui is a Zaarin or chief shaman which is a bit like a wizard," she added, "and I expect Aunty Nea is ..."

"... a Kui-a," I interrupted.

Everyone looked at me.

"A wise woman," I explained.

"Exactly – which is all a witch really is," Mrs Jones said.

"You got a wand or somethin' ma'am?" Ashley asked.

"No Ashley," she laughed, "And I can't say Latin words backwards either."

"And I bet you don't 'av a broom neivver, right?" Tarik asked.

"No, for cleaning I have some Dysons and you, and for flying I prefer Qantas," she added.

We laughed.

"So what *do* witches have?" I asked.

"A lot of knowledge," she sighed. "Knowledge and wisdom. You get a lot of wisdom when you've lived as long as me. You see patterns. You see how Spirit works. That's how we make magic."

"Dad says there's no such thing as magic," Tarik said.

"I'd guess he thinks there no such thing as ghosts either?"

"Yeah," Tarik admitted quietly.

"But you see them because you can. Magic isn't technology. There's no lightning, no puffs of pink smoke. It isn't special effects like in movies. Real magic looks just like good luck or bad luck. It looks like something that should be completely random, but just isn't. Magic is what ordinary people call 'an extraordinary coincidence.'"

I suddenly got a funny feeling. A nagging suspicion. I caught Scotty's eye and he was thinking the same thing. All of us being at Renwick was an 'extraordinary coincidence'. We had talked about it for weeks.

"How does it work?" Tarik wanted to know.

"Well, not by saying funny words and waving a little stick. And not by cooking disgusting things in a cauldron either. Though we do cook some things we need but an ordinary stove will do. That's not magic though, that's just cooking. All magic comes from Spirit."

"'Ow do zhou mean, Spirit?" Tahira asked.

"To me Spirit is a feeling of purpose in life. Dr Prosperov calls spirit a dimension of our existence like up and down. He thinks most people have only limited ability to sense it. You children are especially sensitive. As sensitive as the most sensitive I have ever met in fact. A witch is a woman who works with Spirit to achieve her ends in the tangible world. To do this she needs a way to connect the spirit world and the physical world. The changes made in the spiritual world then happen in the physical world."

"How?" asked Tarik being slightly unbelieving.

"Well, that is the trick. It's not easy. But it starts with asking. You ask the Universe for something, you visualise it, you concentrate on it, and it can happen. But there is a lot more to it than that. You must understand balance. There is give and take. It takes a lot of practice."

"Are witches good or bad?" Scotty asked. He meant her kind of witch. He already had clear ideas about African ones who could be either.

"That depends on the witch, her spirit guide and the viewpoint of the person deciding. Back in seventeenth century Germany when the Roman Church burned girls as young as Rewa or Asal to death in front of everyone in the marketplace just because someone said they were a witch, you'd have to ask who was really evil."

I got a very strange feeling when Mrs Jones said this that she hadn't just read it in a book. You could feel the heat, the horror and almost hear the screams. It was like when Grandpop talked about the war. It wasn't a story to him. It was still happening somewhere in his soul. The same was true now of Mrs Jones.

"That's just horrible," Ashley said looking quite upset.

"Yes, and perhaps I shouldn't have spoken of it," Mrs Jones said regretfully.

"But if witches can do magic, 'ow come they was burned?" Tarik asked.

"Tarik, very few witches ever were burned. Mostly they burned girls who excited them. They associated sex with the Devil you see. If a girl made them think of sex, she must be an agent of the Devil, so they burned her to death."

That made me feel cold. The cruelty of it. The screaming in my ears.

"But couldn't you witches stop em?" Ashley asked appalled.

"No, because some of them had the same powers we had."

"What sort of powers?" Tarik asked.

"Powers like yours, but a lot more polished. Mind control. Moving things. Some could make fire. And kill."

"Can you do that, then," Tarik asked a bit awestruck.

"No. Could you?" she asked him directly.

We had to think about it. It was a sort of a test of character.

"Maybe. If I could save someone," Tarik answered,

Cam looked at him and nodded. They were both thinking of their mothers.

Mrs Jones seemed to understand.

"I thought so once too," she sighed.

"But for every action, there is a reaction. The more we fought with our powers, the more it proved there were witches and the more innocent girls were killed. To use Spirit for violence invites the violent spirits into one's life. And there are terrible, terrible costs in the ultimate balance that must be accounted for. You are children and seek immediate solutions, as I did too when I was young, but as you age you learn the deeper craft so conflict is prevented from the outset. Power correctly applied prevents resistance from ever forming."

"But 'ow do you learn thees witchcraft," Tahira wanted to know.

"Would you like to learn the craft?" Mrs Jones asked curiously. We all said "yes".

"I'm afraid I can only teach the boys so much. The craft is very different between male and female. I simply don't know how to be a druid."

That was a bit disappointing.

"But everyone starts the same way. The first step is to learn to pray or meditate. A witch must be able to separate her moods and desires from her spiritual side. Most people find it's easier to start if you focus on moving your body. We are physical beings and to understand ourselves being able to control our movements, our breathing, our heartrate and even our brains. There are exercises for all these things. Witches do some in their dances. Tai Chi captures a lot of them and Yoga all of them."

"You do dances?" Tarik asked.

"Yes dear, and sometimes we spin like the Dervishes in Turkey, and for the exact same reason. What I call 'the Universe', you call Allah, and others call God. It speaks to us," she smiled at him. Tarik was a bit confused by that, so Mrs Jones went on.

"What you are trying to do is find the seat-of-your being. You have to meditate to let your thoughts wander so that you can separate the seat-of-being from your life. From this you can learn to drive your brain and body rather than have them drive you. The seat-of-being or your life-purpose or your soul, whatever words you want to use, is what connects with the spiritual dimension."

"The next stage is to learn to ask Spirit for coincidences. Not by begging or threatening but simply by making a suggestion. You make a suggestion pleasantly to the Universe and simply go about your day keeping it in mind. After a while you will get an answer. Sometimes it is "yes" and other times it will be "no". As you practice this you will start to recognise the feeling of the Spirit who is responding to you and you will start to recognise your spirit guide."

"For the dances the circle we draw around us when we dance divides the inner world of consciousness and Spirit from the outer world of matter and energy. Sometimes there are two circles where the inner symbolises the wheel of life. The pentagram is the four elements and Spirit; the fifth element. This is the balance of time, place and spirit and our dance matches these elements and the requests we make."

"Sounds complicated," Ashley said.

"It is. It's as complicated as any of the other religions and just as diverse. Different teachers emphasise different things. Some have told me I have been too influenced by the East. I have borrowed from Sufis and Yogis and there is a lot of magic in central Asia. Nergui is our example of that."

"But if it's a religion does it have a God or lots of Gods or goddesses or what?" Tarik asked.

"The ideal person is a goddess for women and a god for men. Your Alevi ideal person is similar but different. Like you these ideals are ways-of-being not actual gods or goddesses. They are symbols. The stories about these gods are reminders of how certain values or ways of being can overcome other less desirable ways of being."

"But you don't have a real God?" Tarik suggested.

"We call God 'the universe' because the word "God" is male and suggests the pagan gods who were more like human chiefs or kings. Some kings, remember, insisted they were gods! Our religion – unlike most – is not male dominated, but, of course, the origin and the ending of all things is neither male nor female. What you call Allah or God as a Muslim and Alevi, Tarik, is the exact same self-aware infinite Universe we invoke. We believe, just as Sufi's believe, God is not separate from any part of the Universe (including us) and is conscious of every part of the Universe (including us) and our individual consciousness. Our task is to unite with that wider God or Universal

consciousness. That is how coincidences can happen.
I'm sure you recognise how this view is similar to Sufi teachings."

"and Alevi," Tarik nodded.

"But witches also see more layers than just us and God. We see many beings that are not symbols but true entities. In Spirit there are many, many entities. Some are like the ghosts here in this house. They have a strong identity but very limited location or consciousness. There are other spirits. Some are gods. They have limited consciousness, unlike God, but their consciousness can span time and places. They are like ways-of-being, ideals, ancestors or gods. The narrower their consciousness the more powerful they are right here and now. The broader it is the more powerful their unseen or magical influence over time. All together they are like broad strands in the cycle of life some cultures show as the rainbow snake consuming its own tail. You have probably encountered some of them already?"

I remembered the gods who had always haunted me and nodded in agreement. Scott and Cam did too.

"But what do witches do?" I asked thinking about the assignment.

"Well in the Middle Ages we made medicines because all the medicines had to be made from local herbs. The Church treated sickness as a sign of sin. We used medicines. We delivered babies, because it was so very dangerous for women, and so necessary for the next generation. We taught people about stars that signified times of the year for planting, and we made magic as we could."

It was just like our Maori elders and Tohunga – the Maori druids.

"But were there like, rituals or somethin' we could copy," Ashley asked.

"We danced and meditated in circles – skyclad," Mrs Jones continued.

"Skyclad?" Ashley asked.

"Naked."

We burst out with embarrassed laughter, looking around at each other. That was one thing we were certainly not going to do. But Mrs Jones ignored us.

"And we sang and chanted together. We had ordinary parties too of course."

Once again I was getting the weirdest feeling that Mrs Jones wasn't saying 'we' because the witches of the Middle Ages were similar to modern ones but because she was actually remembering it! There was also something else. Something she wasn't telling us about. Brilliant figures in the woods. A strange sense of lightness. Of flight. We had read about the Henbane – the drug – witches had used. Maybe that was what I was getting. Meanwhile Ashley boiled it down to what we needed.

"Well, Ma'am we gotta put on a show? What d'you tink we should do?" she asked getting down to business.

"Perhaps I could teach you a simple dance and a chant. They sound quite eerie when sung by children, and they can be powerful too, if you do them properly."

We looked at each other. We knew on the one hand it would confirm to everyone at the school we were a cult of whackos but if we could make it spooky enough the others might leave us alone.

Tarik shrugged, "I gotta ask dad if is OK," he said.

He wasn't the only one who was going to check. Tahira was

fascinated and didn't care what her mother thought, but she knew she had better ask. Religion mattered to her mother and Grandmother. Her father had died for it.

Luckily the parents couldn't see any religious significance in acting as long as Mrs Jones didn't put any in the show. So from then on we spent an hour after cleaning and homework on practising our circle. The only problem was it was taking up a lot of my time and we had to tend to Tabika.

At first we'd sort of tried to ignore her. We hoped that she might leave us alone and go away like some bad dream. But she didn't. She flew up to the house and 'yelled' at us to come out and talk to her. It was impossible to ignore, and though she seemed friendly enough her power over us was scary.

Typically we met up at about two in the morning. For some reason at this time the ghosts were also at their strongest. We tried to ignore them but they were curious as to why we were up and sneaking around. We didn't know whether Mrs Jones talked to them or not. So we pretended we were sneaking off together to pursue some secret romance – and for some reason they didn't interrupt us.

Tabika's main need was fruit and vegetables which she couldn't get from the land. She fished like an egret, flying beyond the breakers, then diving into the ocean like a small bolt of lightning. She seemed to be pretty good at fishing. She also killed sheep but I warned her about bodies so she disposed of the bits she didn't eat at sea. I knew if there was any sign that looked like dogs were killing sheep Tama Reeves and the farmers would be out with guns for sure. But Tabika wasn't complaining of hunger.

She drank from the springs and loved the rainwater. She liked fruit juices, milk and flavoured waters too. But she needed fresh fruit. She really liked oranges, apples, grapes, lettuces, kiwis and lemons but she didn't think much of bananas. She tried chocolate but didn't like it. Marmalade she did like. She loved potatoes, which she ate raw, but not bread or pastries. Her favourites though, were nuts and raisins, which she couldn't get enough of.

Food wasn't really her problem. Her main complaint was boredom, and loneliness. She wanted us to stay and talk to her about the world. She was interested in things like cars, televisions and computers as well as where food came from. Often we didn't know the answers to the questions she asked so we had to look them up on Wikipedia. She was also interested in the wider island – but she was too nervous of adults to explore too close to where people lived. She complained our world was very polluted and was appalled when we told her this was one of the cleaner parts of it.

At night she flew around the lighthouse and even Renwick House itself. Often she would wake us, while flitting about outside. We were constantly worried someone would see her – but she told us that was impossible – which made us worry that either she was wrong, or that we were going mad.

Tahira especially didn't feel comfortable with Tabika's nudity and gave some of her clothes. Sometimes she wore the blue skirt but her attitude to clothing was that it was purely for decoration. She was like a little child from some jungle tribe with simply no sense of modesty about covering up. She said her people had stopped wearing clothes thousands of years ago because they had no purpose. It was kind of embarrassing. But she couldn't understand why it made us uncomfortable and suggested we get undressed too. Maybe that was to tease Tahira. But there was no way we were going to strip – our shyness aside – it was freezing! Tabika herself didn't seem to feel the cold at all. Somehow the power that allowed her to fly or move things kept her warm as well. She did like softness though. She appreciated the Persian carpet, sheepskin and cushions we sneaked her. She loved candles too – even tea lights – but especially scented ones. She could light them, or put them out, just by looking at them. She liked decorations, and even squeaked with pleasure when we gave her something shiny to put in her cave. She also had an amazing way with plants. They seemed to grow at her command, and flower regardless of the cool of autumn. Her little cave was now overgrown with a white flowered creeper.

We asked her questions about her world. She was quite happy to talk about her home and family. It seemed to make her feel better and hopeful that she wouldn't have to stay in our world forever. She said she lived in a world of trees, meadows, flowers, rivers and streams. The sun was different, she said, with less violet light. There were animals of various sizes, shapes and colours too. She mentioned sheep-like animals, fish and birds. We also got flashes of horses, monkeys, bears and dolphins. Some of them could talk and play with her people. They played at changing the animals and themselves – Tabika was very pleased with her wings, which she said were very fashionable. I got the feeling her mum didn't like her mane so much. She said they learned what she called "weaving","shaping" and "dancing" but we couldn't understand exactly what she meant by this. Shaping seemed to involve growing things large and small. But we could understand when she talked about people in her family.

Her mother was called Morganne but she said she had not one,
but two fathers, Dayan and Merin, and a brother, Pike. She
spoke of her friends Freya, Rose and Niku, and her talking pets
Sky, Dandelion, and Moon and wondered what they would be
doing while she was here.

Sometimes we wondered if we were her new talking pets.

We should have realised that after a while, nearly everyone
noticed that me and Tahira were always tired in the morning.
But, of course, we were too tired to notice that we were noticed.
It was not so much at home, where everyone was distracted
by the work at the lighthouse or our Witchcraft project, but
at school. Mr Wakefield took me aside one day and asked me
straight-up why I was tired.

Of course, even if I'd wanted to, I couldn't have told him.
Tabika's spell over us meant we simply couldn't talk about it.
That meant I had to make something up. But when you are tired,
you aren't very good at making things up. So I told him we were
busy at home. His obvious question was why was I tired but
Tarik, Scotty, Cam, and Ashley weren't? I said I didn't know,
which of course made him suspicious.

He asked Tahira the same question when I wasn't around. She
just said the sea kept her awake – a believable enough lie seeing
she had never lived near the sea before. Still I don't think he
believed her either, because I noticed he took to watching us at
lunchtimes. He suspected we were sneaking off at night for sex.
It was stupid, but that was him all over.

Unfortunately he wasn't the only one. Emma was getting real
antsy with me these days. She didn't say anything, but her
annoyance with Tahira was easy to understand, and I was just
too busy to spend any time with her. I tried to tell her I wasn't

into Tahira but our secretive glances and obvious lack of sleep made Emma very sarcastic. That didn't help things much either. Meanwhile at home Tahira's mum Mitra, and grandmother Soraya had nearly caught her slipping out lately and they seemed to be on watch. Aunty Liz too, was also starting to keep a closer eye on me. One night when we hadn't been to see her for a few days Tabika came to get us. She "yelled" at us to wake up and made us come out to her. She was very grumpy and accused us of abandoning her.

We tried to explain that it was hard to get away because our parents were watching us and unlike her we couldn't make them sleep. For quite a while she wouldn't listen and just cried about why we had to help her. Finally Tahira got her to think more clearly and we changed our arrangement so that Tabika would come and get us on alternate nights. That meant we wouldn't both be tired on the same night.

That was a huge relief! It meant we got a chance to catch up on sleep and it also threw the adults off our trail. Whatever Tabika did to make everyone sleep worked very well and the only problem came when it rained and she got lonely because we couldn't come out and get wet because we could never explain our wet clothes. Then one week it rained for five days straight and we didn't go out.

Finally she came for me when it was absolutely bucketing down. I pointed out that if I got wet everyone would know I'd been somewhere. She simply said if I didn't wear clothes I wouldn't have a problem. I said it was far too cold not to wear clothes (and there was something creepy in her suggestion I didn't like). We argued for a bit and it was interesting that she didn't try and command me. She had power but she was up against some rule she knew she had to observe. I was pretty sure that somehow I had the upper hand.

Finally I agreed that if she could keep me warm, I would come out in a towel. I thought about wearing underpants or swimming trunks but I couldn't think of any reason that would convince Aunty Liz why they would be wet either. One more or less wet towel on the heated towel-rack wouldn't surprise anyone.

It was about two in the morning when I came out of the door clutching my towel and a bag of oranges nicked from the kitchen. I felt a bit silly and vulnerable but she needed company. I had to come outside because she was scared of the iron in the door. She didn't like iron or any metal. She said it depleted her powers.

So I stepped out into the freezing rainswept night wrapped in a towel to meet a naked glowing moon girl with black, feathery wings. As always it made me feel nervous and sick in my stomach. Immediately the water was in my eyes and my skin was goosebumped and shivering uncontrollably. I was already determined that if she didn't somehow make me warm very soon I was going back inside. She landed and walked up to me. I was vaguely aware of her glowing body approaching me but could hardly see because of the rain in my eyes. She put her hands on my shoulders. It was the first time I had touched her skin and I was surprised how thick it felt – like leather. I thought "no wonder she doesn't feel the cold".

Then a strange feeling surged through me down from my shoulders into my arms, through my chest and spread through my whole body. It was this most amazing glow that warmed through me making the freezing rain feel like a warm shower. The tensing in my muscles and skin lifted and suddenly it felt quite nice to be outdoors – even on a night like this one.

I looked into her smiling face and her big eyes.

I thought, *"no wonder you don't mind running about nude."*

She tilted her head, smiled and silently replied, *"yes."*

I thought of the long walk to the cave.

"I don't suppose you can make me fly as well," I asked.

"Of course," she replied. Then she added, *"Are you sure you want that ugly wet cloth around your lovely soft body?"*

I was tempted. It was a pain holding a sodden towel flapping around me now that the rain was warm. Like wearing a towel in the shower. But I was also suspicious. I could sense she was a bit excited by the idea of getting me naked, close to her, alone and there was something a bit dangerous about an excited, powerful, alien creature with a mouth full of sharp fangs I wasn't sure about. For all I knew about her she might try to eat me. Ugly and uncomfortable as my towel might be it meant she had to deal with me as a person rather than a body. She probably read my mind because her sense of excitement passed like a cloud over the face of the moon.

She came around behind me put her hands under my arms and lifted me into the air. It was almost as if gravity had sort of decided to look the other way and give us a break. We rose lightly, up, up, and out over the bay. I looked down at the angry, black sea and hoped she didn't drop me. I knew at once she had registered my thought and discounted it as simple animal fear. Tabika powered our way through the wind gusts and lowered us down by the mouth of her cave. As we landed it seemed gravity had remembered us again and I felt heavy, like you do getting out of the swimming pool. Tabika led the way into her cave, the candles lighting by themselves as she entered. She sat back on the cushions, and I tossed her an orange from my bag which she caught easily, then I put the bag between us, sat down and took one for myself.

Tabika was odd about fruit. She liked citrus skin, apple cores and kiwi skins too – which seemed a bit rugged on the stomach to me. She started biting into her orange with her sharp, pointed teeth. As she did so she started "talking" to me telepathically.

"I've been thinking about some of the stories my mum used to tell me about when she was younger. She's pretty old now, about eight hundred or so ..."

"Your mother is eight hundred years old!" I interrupted, aghast. She must have glimpsed my mental image of an ancient, toothless woman, because she objected at once.

"Eight hundred isn't that old. Grandmother Durga, is over four thousand and she's still very beautiful."

"Oh, OK," I shrugged. Obviously these beings had a very different idea of "old" to us.

"Anyway, my mum used to tell me stories about her travels through the worlds, and one of the places they used to visit was this world."

"Your mum used to come here? To Earth?"

"Yes, it used to be very popular with our people. My mum said they used to have a lot of fun here."

"Doing what?"

"Playing with you people."

The idea of play she used was one of "harmless fun" but it occurred to me her viewpoint was that of her people, not ours. I wondered if we humans had enjoyed this "play" as much.

"What sort of play?" I wanted to know.

"Love play," she said biting the orange and tearing it to bits with

her fangs. The juice squirted on her chin and she wiped it off with her arm. The idea included light-hearted romance and sex. I felt uncomfortable.

"What did our people think of that?" I asked her.

"*Well ...*"

It was obvious she had no idea. All she knew was what her mum had told her.

"*I think they liked it,*" she said uncertainly, finishing the orange.

"Why do you think that?" I pushed her.

"*Wouldn't you?*" she asked, smiling and shrugging cutely.

It was a pretty crass appeal. It wasn't that she didn't turn me on; she was pretty enough; but she was just too bossy – and the claws, fangs and wings didn't help. She scared me.

"*No,*" I thought immediately.

She was a bit pissed off by that.

"*But you like looking at me,*" she smiled, stretching out slowly and showing herself off.

"*I like looking at you too,*" she said turning those big blue eyes on me. I had to look away. I could drown in those eyes.

"That's true, I do like looking at you," I admitted shyly, "but looking and touching are different."

"*Why?*" she challenged me, running her hands over herself, still trying to turn me on.

I couldn't get my thoughts together. Part of the problem was she was right. She did turn me on a lot. Even just thinking about her. But at the same time I was still scared.

"*It's just ... just too scary,*" I thought more than said.

"*Don't be frightened,*" she murmured to reassure me, moving closer and thinking of my fear of the flight over.

"No, no, you don't understand!" I said at once, backing away and stopping her in place.

"This isn't like being scared of heights. I'm not scared of you hurting me. I'm scared of ... I'm scared of you using me. It's about you wanting to do it with me, because of what your mum did, and I'm just ... well I'm just there."

She hesitated confused.

"*But you like me?*"

"Yes, but not ... I don't want to do *that* with you Tabika."

She looked confused.

My brain finally seized on what it was that I felt.

"It's not fair Tabika. You have powers which are just too much for me, and I'm not a toy for you to play with."

"*But I'm not going to ...*" she began, but I interrupted.

"You said we were babies and compared to you we are. I'm just twelve. I don't want to be played with the way you think your mother played with adult humans long ago. I don't think ... it's not .... Let's just be friends and not something I know I'm not ready for and which honestly I don't really think you are all that sure about either."

Tabika had been showing herself off, knowing it excited us both. But now when she had offered to do something about it and I had backed away she was confused. It was very awkward and uncomfortable. I hoped she wouldn't get pissed off. It would be a long, cold, walk home. She hugged her knees up under her chin thoughtfully. She sat there thinking and "said" nothing to me for quite a while. Finally she "spoke" and it was strong because her heart was in it.

"*Mum once said that our people are about a ten thousand years more advanced than yours. But we come because we keep learning from you. And it's true. You want respect. And me*

treating you like a sex toy isn't respect. That's why it's wrong."
She *had* understood. It made me feel much better. Less nervous of her. I let out a big nervous sigh. She had decided to not do something even though she could, because it wasn't right. It made me trust her much more.

But then as she sat there lost in her own thoughts I realised this was new. It was obviously connected to her mother.

"Why do you want to be like your mother anyway?" I asked into the silence.

She raised her head and looked at me.

"What do you mean?"

"You wanted to do what she had done," I pointed out.

"No, not really!" she denied it.

"Yes, you did," I insisted.

She was about to get angry and deny it again, when a look of realisation crossed her face and she realised I wasn't wrong. She let out a huge sigh, and threw herself back among her cushions, holding her head.

"Oh I don't know! She's just so amazing and famous, and I just wanted to feel like I could do something that she did," she admitted.

"Is she really something special where you come from?"

"Oh yeah, leader of her generation and all that. Everyone thinks Morganne's ah-mazing."

I found it strange and yet comforting to find her emotions so easy to understand. I didn't always.

"Is that not so good for you?"

"It's ... Well ... everything ends up being about her. *People only look at what I do as it reflects on her. She'll probably make a huge deal of finding me again. It will be about Morganne's lost*

daughter, not what Tabika went through."

"That sounds a bit worrying," I thought, wondering if Morganne would punish us.

She looked at me as if for the first time.

"Oh she'd never harm you," she assured me seriously.

"What about my friends?" I asked, thinking of Dr Prosperov as the cause for her being there.

"She won't punish ignorance, but she will scare them, all right."

We fell silent, both thinking about that from our own perspectives.

"How does your brother cope with your mother?" I asked.

"He keeps as far away as he can."

"And your fathers?"

"Oh they're just good little husbands who keep the family running."

I almost laughed. I doubted she was being fair because she was so fixated on her mother. But I was still interested in the situation she was in.

"So this ... accident ... you being here ... it's ....well ... it has potential for you to change things a bit doesn't it?"

"That's why I thought of you," she admitted wriggling uncomfortably, and curling in a ball. She wasn't showing her body off at all now. *"I thought it would give mum something to think about."*

"Bit sad," I thought. The problem with telepathy is thoughts like that slip out before you can stop them.

"Yeah," she admitted, *"it is."*

"You know what? I think you should meet Dr Prosperov and Mrs Jones."

I enthused for a while about them.

She didn't look very interested.

"I don't trust your adults. Mum told us they sometimes killed our kind in the old days. I don't see any point in testing it. Too much risk, no reward."

There was another pause.

*"You said your people came here. But how?"*I wondered.

"Bending," she answered, distractedly, thinking about her family.

The idea was joining two places by bending them together – it didn't make any sense to me, but it did seem to suggest there wasn't any kind of spaceship was involved.

"Why did they stop coming?" I asked.

She looked at me, surprised.

"We didn't. We still come sometimes. But we have to be careful of the others. They are very strong here now."

"The 'others' ?"

"The galactic government."

The idea was of a large organisation which regulated things throughout the galaxy.

"What galactic government?" I asked, mystified.

"Well, they won't incorporate your world yet because you're not advanced enough, but they are here, watching you. They even have a special race called 'the watchers' to live among you."

"And that's why your people don't come here so much?"

"Yeah, they don't like us."

"Why not?"

"Because we don't need them, and we won't harmonise with them."

"Oh."

I must have looked pretty clueless so she went on to explain.

"*Look, you've got a little sister, right?*"

"Yeah," I replied wondering what Rewa could have to do with it.

"*OK, imagine your little sister has a lot of other little girls around to play.*"

"OK."

"*So you don't mind that, right?*"

"No, why should I?"

"*OK, imagine they tell you, you have to play their games.*"

"OK," I shrugged.

"*Then they say you have to play their way.*"

"Mmm," I could imagine that would be annoying.

"*Then you have to do what they do – and I mean, do everything the way they do it.*"

"It'd get pretty boring," I admitted.

"*Exactly. So we don't want any part of their system.*"

"Fair enough," I agreed.

"*But they don't think so. They consider it a crime not to join them.*"

"Why?" I asked, astonished at such a dumb attitude.

"*Because they're machines and they have a problem with freedom. Even the very clever ones.*"

"Oh."

She smiled at me the way people smile at dogs when they don't understand.

"*That's what we find valuable about you, you see. You are free. And sometimes even very advanced people like us, can learn from free, primitive people like you.*"

"Primitive?" I was a bit shocked by her honesty.

"*Yes,*" she said honestly, "*Well, you are. You've told me as much.*

You can't re-shape energy at will and you are all determined by your genetics rather than determining them. You are ruining your world with all this pollution because you are so primitive and your morals are full of contradictions. So yes, you are primitive. But at the same time you are free and despite the failings of your world you are still good people. You've still taught me a few lessons. About respect ... and kindness."

"Does that make us good pets?" I asked.

It was an honest question. Tahira and me had talked about it.

"*Pets!*" She actually laughed. It was a pretty sound. Then she realised I was serious.

"*No! No! Pets are dependent ... I'm the dependent one. Maybe I'm your pet!*" she smiled.

"You are way too scary for a pet," I assured her.

"*Are you really scared of me?*" she asked, surprised.

"Of course we are! Look at yourself from our point of view. You're strange and have powers against which we have no defences at all."

She was quite taken with that.

"*Wow! And I just feel scared of the center or the watchers finding me; lonely, and wishing I could get home.*"

I had to admit I hadn't thought of her that way either.

"What would these others do if they found you?"

"*Use me as bait. They would probably put controls in my brain and a tracker in my stomach. They want to find our world and kill us all.*"

"That's horrible."

"*Yes. Now you can see why I want to hide as much as I can. But I never thought I was frightening. I knew you were scared but I thought it was because I was so different. Realising that I seem*

309

*dangerous just makes me appreciate you two more. I thought
you just felt sorry for me."*

"Well we do, but I think it's because we just think you being
forced to be here, isn't fair. We wouldn't want it to happen to us.
So we just want to help."

*"I like the way you talk about 'fair' Sam. You've said it twice
tonight. It's a source of great strength in you. And you are
helping me. I don't know what I'd do if you and Tahira weren't
here to help me. Thank you."*

"Maybe you wouldn't be here in the first place," I pointed out.

*"Actually, my weaving teacher would say I'm here
because you're here, and vice versa."*

"How does he work that out?"

*"That's what weaving is, it's about time and destiny. It's very
complicated. I'm just a novice."*

"That is a pretty amazing idea Tabika." I admitted, thinking of
what Mrs Jones had said about magic.

The idea that she had been pulled by who knew what means to
meet us was strange and fascinating but I knew I couldn't get
my head around it all at once. I was too tired. The conversation
seemed to be at an end. I looked for the exit.

"Shall I fly you home?" Tabika offered, getting up.

"Yes please," I accepted quickly, thinking of the weather outside.
We made our way out of her cave into the blast of rain, which
was thankfully still warm. It was still dark – and I mean very
dark. The only source of light was Tabika's own pale blue glow.
The seas seemed, if anything, even bigger than when we'd gone
inside. They were impressively violent. But Tabika moved very
confidently behind me gripped me under the arms again and
once again gravity seemed to forget about us. We rose quickly,

Tabika seemed to be using the fierce winds expertly and we
zoomed over the sea at enormous speed. It was fantastic fun!
We landed in front of Renwick, the wind still blasting us. I
turned to face her.

"Thanks for talking to me – even if I am scary," she smiled,
showing her fangs a little.

But I wasn't as nervous of her now that I understood her better.
"I liked getting to know you better. It made you seem more ...
like us, I guess," I said.

*"We are more alike, than not – at heart anyway. And that's the
main thing."*

It seemed true, and all the more pleasing given she was a
glowing angel-like, girl-creature with sharp teeth.

*"I'd better take the energy link off before you go through those
iron doors or we will be burned."*

She put her hands on my shoulders again, but this time her arms
were bent and she stood closer than she had when she had done
it the first time. And this time I was more aware of her body
because we were looking each other in the eye. She felt very
warm and nice.

"It's going to be really cold," she warned softly. "Let me distract
you."

And then she kissed me. It was just a quick kiss – more than a
peck like I might get from Aunty Liz at bedtime, but not a long,
drawn out movie snog either – just an warm smack, eye-to-eye.
She pulled away, smiling, half-shrugging, half-embarrassed. I
was so surprised the shock of the cold didn't hit me, even as she
stepped back, gave me a small wave, glowed brighter, flapped
her wings and rose into the blast. She let the wind take her for a
moment and then began to control her flight round in a large arc

heading back to her cave.

I don't know if it was because it was my first kiss from any girl, quite apart from an alien one, but the effect on me was huge. I felt fantastic. Like a huge warm bomb had gone off inside me. The sad thing was how short it had lasted. I watched Tabika disappear into the distance before even I had to admit standing outside in a rainstorm wearing nothing but a wet towel is really cold. But as I turned back to Renwick I noticed something above me in the galleries. I looked up and saw the gray shadow of Corporal Higgins looking down at me. He had seen the whole thing. What if he talked to Mrs Jones? Now my insides were joining my outsides in turning to ice.

I ran inside, shivering, up the stairs two at a time, trying to get to our apartment. But even as I got to the lounge door I could "hear" Corporal Higgins behind me.

"Who's ya girlfriend son?"

I wasn't going to stand around "talking" to him about it, and kept running through the darkness. He followed, calling after me

"Not exactly from around 'ere is she?"

I wondered who he would wake up. My plan was simple: get dry; get dressed; get in bed. If I could at least get that far I could work out the rest later. I ran down the corridor, quietly opened our door and slipped inside.

There is something very still about a place full of sleeping people. Their bodies are there, snoring softly, but their minds are somewhere else. I slipped into the bathroom, took off my sodden towel, squeezed it out over the bath, then put it on the towel rack to dry. Then I dried myself, snuck (naked) into my room, put on my pyjamas and got into bed. My feet felt dirty but

I didn't want to risk waking everyone with the sound of running water.

I lay there thinking about what had just happened. Did that mean Tabika liked me, or was she just "playing"? I was glad she hadn't kissed me at the beginning. I could be even more confused than I was now. She could have talked me into anything. I thought about talking to her and realised how lonely and friendless she must feel. I still couldn't really get my head around her world completely. It was probably like trying to explain a computer game to a caveman.

But there was still something awfully basic about things between people, regardless of the technology they may have to hand. I fell asleep thinking about stars and Tabika.

CHAPTER TWENTY SIX: PATUPAIAREHE

In the morning I was, typically, hard to rouse, but nobody said anything. I was watching like a hawk for some sign Corporal Higgins had said something, but he obviously hadn't – yet anyway. It was strange going to school feeling the world had changed in the night, but absolutely nobody knew.

If you'd asked me what exactly had changed, I would have had a hard time telling you. Tahira went out with Tabika the next night, as normal, and I caught up on sleep. But something had changed. It was a special relationship now. I felt closer to Tabika since she had told me about her family. It wasn't just an embarrassing secret, but a relationship based on honesty and affection.

It wasn't raining the next night I was due to go out to see her. I also had good news. Dr Prosperov had announced that night the re-wiring was now complete and they would now start two weeks of system tests and lightning capture. He told us we would have some new guests for the startup of the rebuilt system, including Aunty Nea, Professor Lana Vilenskaya, and Professor Dubrov. He seemed very excited by the prospect. I hoped I didn't look quite as obviously worried as Tahira did.

I set out early for Tabika's cave. The house had only just gone to bed and I had hoped that way I could avoid Corporal Higgins.

That part of my plan worked well. There were no interruptions and I got to the cave without anything going wrong. The only problem was Tabika wasn't there.

I waited and waited outside but it was wet with seaspray so I snuck inside. It seemed strange to go inside her lair when she wasn't there. I took my jacket off and lay down under it and rested, listening to the sea just fifty meters away. I must have drifted off for a while, but then I woke up feeling stiff and sore. I was just about to give up and go back to bed when the candles lit by themselves and in walked Tabika. In her hand was the haunch of gray furry meat of what looked like a rabbit, and around her face a lot of blood. Without meaning to I made a noise of shock.

I must have surprised her because she screamed briefly, dropping her catch, the lights went out, and she suddenly lit up the cave with red light. Her face, usually pretty, was a terrifying snarl of sharp teeth and flattened pointed ears. Her eyes, usually big and blue, shone with a brilliant red light. It was the most terrifying thing I had ever seen in my life. Even more frightening than my murderous father who for all his rage and insanity was still only a man. This creature who had replaced Tabika seemed supernaturally evil. I screamed with a voice I didn't know I had, deep and animal-like.

In the blink of an eye the candles had returned and Tabika, still bloodstained, was back to her usual cute self again. But I was shaking uncontrollably, heart pounding, curled up in terror. She was "talking" to me like a spooked horse, she came up and held me, her wings wrapping around me all soft and feathery.

"Sam, Sam, It's OK, it's only me, I won't hurt you. You're OK."

Her touch was warming through me, as her thoughts reached

315

out to calm my shocked mind.

"Wow, that was something," I told her, and while I wanted to be calm, I was still shaking uncontrollably. My mind was still reeling and my heart was still beating like I had been running for my life.

"*I'm sorry I frightened you Sam. I thought I was being ambushed.*"

She was holding me very tight. I moved so I could hold her but I couldn't reach around her back because her wings got in the way.

"I'd been waiting for you."

"*How sweet.*"

"Were you hunting?"

"*Yes, I got this little creature. Not great eating really.*"

I let myself calm down in her arms before asking my next question.

"Why do you eat raw animals? If you are so advanced why do you act so primitive?"

She smiled.

"*We need blood. Blood and bone to help us regenerate. It's how we live so long. And we learn to understand nature by being part of it. Part of our being is animal, so we keep in touch with that animal nature and learn to hunt like animals. Like so many things our people only came to understand it's importance when we almost lost it. It's another thing that separates us from the machines, I suppose.*"

She held me for quite a long time. Then she said, "*Your mother is here.*"

I already knew that. She had been watching over us ever since I screamed. I had noticed Tabika notice, and try to identify her.

"*She loves you, but she's scared of me,*" Tabika summarised.

"I know."

She let me go and sat back. I sat up.

"*Why is she over there?*"

Tabika referred to death as a view on our world – like standing at right angles to a place and time out of sight.

I explained my story as quickly as I could. Tabika went over to her bed and listened, absolutely fascinated.

"*And I thought I had family problems. I'm spoilt compared to you,*" she said. I found myself warily comparing angel Tabika and my memory of demon Tabika.

I explained that while my story was unusual, it was normal at Renwick and briefly told her the others stories. Finally I finished with Cam.

"*You are all so brave,*" she wondered. "*No real power but you deal with your out-of-control world accepting huge risks. You make me feel boring. This is another reason we still visit you. We remember the power of things like courage and love when you have so little else.*"

She really meant it too. But I had to point out we were a very unusual collection of kids.

"Most humans aren't psychic. Most people don't even believe in psychic stuff, so to get seven psychics in one place is very unusual."

"*You're right,*" she agreed quietly.

"*There's definitely something strange happening here,*" she added.

She stood up to think, folding her arms in front of her.

"That's what we think," I put in.

"*No, it's bigger than you think,*" she said certainly, "*because I'm part of it now too. And for that to be true means this is weaving far beyond your wise ones. You said yourself this ... elder ... what was the name of the one who brought me here?"*

"Prosperov."

"Yes ... he has no idea of my presence?"

"None," I confirmed.

"Then your Prosperov has no idea what he is doing," she decided and resumed pacing.

Then she added something that chilled me.

"But someone ... or something ... definitely does. And that worries me."

"What do you mean?" I wanted to know.

"Prosperov is being influenced. There is no other way he could be bringing together all these people. It couldn't happen by chance. Someone wants our worlds to collide ... and they've abducted me to get at mum," she concluded.

Suddenly Dr Prosperov's lighthouse was beginning to look less like a rich man's science hobby and more like something much more sinister.

"Your mum isn't going to be pleased with whoever took you, is she?" I asked Tabika, thinking of how scary she had been and wondering what her mum would be like.

"No," Tabika confirmed quietly in a way that suggested 'annoyed', was going to be a massive understatement.

We sat there thinking about what might soon happen. Then I realised I hadn't told Tabika what Dr Prosperov had told us.

"So he will run his machine in fifteen to twenty days?" Tabika summarised.

I nodded.

"What can we do?" I asked.

Tabika sat down.

"*Nothing,*" she replied grimly.

"Should we tell Prosperov?"

"*No! I want to go home!*" she said.

"But what about 'world's colliding'?" I objected

"*They must collide,*" she said grimly. "*They have already collided,*" she added waving at the cave.

"*We'll just have to see what comes of it,*" she finished.

I must have looked worried.

"*Don't be frightened Sam. Yes, we are dangerous – especially if we think we are cornered. But we aren't evil even if you think I looked it. My mother will be angry – what mother wouldn't be? – but she won't kill anyone. Your Prosperov will just have to face her anger and apologise. What else can he do?*"

I thought about that for a moment, and had to agree that as we were in no position to do anything else, Tabika was right.

"*OK, but what about the secret instigator behind this,*" I checked.

The nice thing about telepathy is you talk in ideas, so you can say things you don't know the right words for – 'instigator' is a word I had to look up later.

"*Whatever it is, it is bigger than us. It's game is long and strong. We will have no idea until our weavers can look at it.*"

I had to admit I had no idea what she was talking about so I was hardly in a position to suggest anything else. Once again there was nothing left to say.

"*Shall I fly you back?*" she asked.

"I'd love it, but Corporal Higgins saw you last time."

Tabika was concerned about that.

"*That house is full of links to the dead realm … It's possible the* '*secret instigator' is a ghost. Maybe I should keep my distance more,*" she mused.

I had no idea.

"*But then how would I meet my friends?*" by which she meant me and Tahira. She got up, I picked up my jacket and put it on. Then we went outside into the night. There was a slight breeze but no clouds. The stars twinkled down on us.

I was pleased she called us friends. But I also got the clear impression that her relationship with Tahira had deepened too – probably because Tahira would relax without a boy around.

"*I know! I'll fly you up the hill behind the house, and you can walk down the road.*"

"OK," I agreed

She went behind me and held me around the chest. I could tell she disliked the feeling of my jacket.

"*It would be much nicer if you weren't wearing clothes again,*" she smiled. "*Tahira doesn't.*"

I was shocked.

"Tahira sneaks out to you naked!?"

"*She hides them outside. She's not dumb enough to be caught sneaking back in without clothes. Her mother would never cope.*"

"So you two go about at night in the nick?"

"*Of course ... it's what witches have always done with us.*"

"Witches!"

"*Of course witches. What else is a psychic girl called?*"

I thought for a moment about that.

"Were all those witches in the middle ages girls like Tahira?"

"*They were my mother's friends. She visited your kind many centuries ago in an island they called the land of the* Angles."

It was the first time she used an idea of a sound to say something.

"Really? Weird name," I said imagining a place full of triangles, rectangles.

Tabika burst out laughing. She tried to stop, looked at me and started again. I didn't get it. She took a while to calm down.

"*They were* people S*am. Their tribe was called* 'Angles'. *I didn't mean angles.*"

The distinction was clear in thought.

"Oh," I felt stupid.

"*I'm sorry, I confused you by using words. We don't use them for that reason. I shouldn't laugh. But your idea of my mother with all these shapes was so funny.*"

She giggled again.

I liked her laugh. It was one of the few things she did that made me feel completely at ease with her. It was something familiar. Like a human girl. The moment passed.

"*Anyway, let's go?*" she asked.

"Yeah."

She picked me up and soon we were zooming over the bay, under a sickle moon. It felt fast at the time. And nice in Tabika's arms.It wasn't a long flight. She set me down by the tiny church at the top of the hill. But she wasn't in any hurry to go and I had no reason to hurry either.

"*I like this house, there's something nice about it,*" she said of the church, curving her wings about her.

She was right, it had a friendly feeling, like a relative who you like visiting.

"It's a 'house of God'," I said sitting on a bench outside. Tabika stayed standing.

"Tahira said it was a house of Jesus."

"Oh ... well that's true ... but Jesus is the son of God."

"There are many sons and daughters of God," she said and then sat next to me on the bench hugging her knees.

"Do your people believe in God?" I asked uncertain if this was something aliens thought about.

Tabika sat down and smiled at me like I was a dog talking about the moon.

"God is not a person, Sam." she said certainly.

"I never could believe that," I conceded. "... so what is God to you?"

Tabika laughed at my question. Her feet hit the ground.

"Everything!" she said.

"God is everything?"

She stood up, and spread her arms and wings.

"Everything!"

She said it in a way that went beyond just belief that everything was God. It also implied 'everything to me'.

"How so?"

"God is the source of our power."

Her idea of God was really complicated. Impossibly more complicated than mine or even Mrs Jones's. It meant all the possibilities of the universe, the balance of giving and taking, and all the stories of all the creatures. It was science, morals, and ideas of beauty all mixed together. I really was a dog talking about the moon compared to her.

She smiled down at me.

"It's also about what we do, Sam. Even a dog can act in a way that is closer to God than either of us. Knowledge and ability are not fair, but in action we are all equal. And as I said before,

that is why we come here."

"But you'd rather be home."

She sighed and sat down again.

"Yes ... It's been an adventure but I am slowly getting weaker. If I stay too long my powers would be gone."

"Would you die?"

"Eventually. To live here I would need to transform into one of you first. Otherwise the radiation pollution would kill me quite quickly."

"Can you do that?"

"Yes, some of us marry your people and change. Of course they can never change back."

"Why not?"

"Radiation damage. To withstand your sun we need to stabilise our bodies but once you do that you can't tap the universal zero point energy, nor can you transform back."

"So you become like us?"

"Not even that. You are strong here. We become sick and weak. There are many sad stories of our people falling in love with yours and transforming only for the earthling to die, or discover he only loved our power not our soul. My friend's aunt, Lana, lost her love a hundred years ago like that."

"That would be sad," I told her, "I wouldn't ever want to see you become one of us. It pleases me to know that you are as you are. I like you for being different and exciting."

One of the limitations of telepathy is you can't be indirect. You have to say what you think. Communication is by idea, not words, and it's a lot faster than talking. Ideas just fly back and forth.

"I'm glad you see me that way, Sam. I hope I'll be able to come

back and see you after mum finds me again."

"You could meet the others too."

"Yes."

"Why don't you meet them now?"

"Crowds can't keep secrets."

I accepted that as only sensible.

"Fair enough."

"You better go sleep. Tahira says others are noticing you are tired a lot."

"Are they? I try to hide it, but it's hard. I wish there was a way to not be tired."

"It can be done, but you'd need to grow extra brain tissue."

"Ewwww," it sounded gross.

"It's simple. If you need extra abilities, you just grow them. You just aren't used to it because your people aren't up to that stage yet. Our people passed it ages ago. Now I can grow anything I want. If I wanted horns like Daya I could grow them, or silver hair like Merin. We change our bodies like you change your clothes."

"Is it that fast?"

"Well no, not that fast. My wings took a year from design to completion. Cell division can't be rushed or you get problems later."

"But your people can change our people?"

"Of course. Our people have often adopted earthling orphans and children in danger and changed them so they can live better in our world. We used to leave the parents with biological robots in their place."

"What are biological robots?"

"They are copies, but their purpose is given to them. They have

*no souls as we do. These ones lived to deceive and that was all.
The galactic government is overrun with biobots. The Others
used to think they were in charge but now the biobots rule
them."*

"That doesn't sound so good."

*"The Others have made many mistakes. Some have tried to
adapt their bodies and become infected. Our technology is
very good, but very subtle. That's why we live so long without
disease."*

"I wish we could do that."

*"Mum has changed some earthling friends. She can even extend
your lives. Not as long as us of course but your bodies don't
need to age as quickly as they do. It's not something we do
often but we can."*

"Can you?"

*"No, I still haven't learned it. That's one thing I have learned
from being here. All that stuff they want to teach me is useful."*

"I wish what we learned was useful. All we get is old history."

"Tahira said the same thing."

I thought for a moment about school.

"I'd better go," I said.

She got up and hugged me. I felt like kissing her but she turned
away.

"We shouldn't do that," she said.

"But you wanted to before," I pointed out.

She let me go and stepped back stretching out her wings.

"Yes, before I realised how incredibly exciting it is," she
confessed, *"I think that's why our people and your people
get a bit crazy around each other. It's like two different but
powerfully attractive energies. I could understand Sister Lana*

*for the first time after we kissed. I was so excited I couldn't
sleep! But I don't want to get crazy now, I need to be able
to think calmly about something other than you. I think it's
getting too dangerous for that."*

"I know what you mean."

It was good to know she felt the same attraction. She glowed
brighter.

"See you in two days," she said.

Her wings swept her into the air and she was up and gone, a
blue light heading over the hill.

I was alone on the top of the hill by the church and the
graveyard. It was a pleasant night and the air felt still and warm.
I had just begun to crunch down the gravel road and there was a
slight change in the atmosphere. It was like that moment when
everyone is looking at something behind you, wondering when
you'll notice it – except there was no one there. Still, I knew the
feeling well. A presence was behind me.

I turned to find a big Maori soldier standing behind me smoking
a pipe. I could see from the stripes on his World War One
uniform that he was a sergeant and he was wearing a greatcoat,
helmet on his head and pack on his back. The smell of his
pipe was pleasant, as was his manner. I guessed he was in his
twenties but he seemed older. More confident than his years. He
spoke to me in Maori but I understood his thoughts clearly. He
walked beside me into the dark pines that surrounded the road.

"Hey boy, you're out pretty late. You should be home in bed."

He wasn't grumpy, just concerned.

"I know. I'm going now. Where are you going?"

*"Aw see, I gotta report to this Renwick House eh? Somethin'
to do with this 'flu we've been getting. They say we'll get some*

kind of special medicine there or something."

"That's where I'm going. I live there," I told him.

"You live there? I heard it's a hospital."

"It's a convalescent home. My aunty is a nurse. I live with her there."

"A nurse eh? Is she pretty?" and he giggled briefly at his own cheek.

"Nah, just jokin' eh? Me, I got a missus at home. And a baby. Where are you from son?"

"Northland, Nga Puhi."

I gave him my tribe because I knew that was what he wanted to know.

"Arawa, me."

That meant he came from big Bay of Plenty, south of here.

It was incredibly dark under the pines. Fortunately my companion was leading the way at a confident march, so I kept pace beside him.

"So you're a sergeant aren't you?"

"Yup. Field promotion after Paschendale. Easy choice for them. I was the only one from my platoon not wounded!" He sort of giggled. But then he became serious. *"But it was bad news. Lot of my mates died, eh?"*

"But not you."

"No fear. I was too quick for 'em. Too quick, and too damn lucky. Lucky's the most important. S'all just luck. Lot's of good men died eh? I didn't deserve to live more'n them. But I was just lucky."

He kept talking about the importance of being lucky. About his Hei Tiki, his rabbit's foot, his four leaf clover. It was sort of weird, like a dream which goes on and on about something and you know it's really about something else.

Finally, when I got a word in, I asked him his name.

"Wiremu ... Wiremu Apirana Aroha ... or Bill Love, to the Pommies, eh."

Slowly Renwick House was emerging through the trees. He asked me my name.

"You know Sam I couldn't help seeing that Patu-pai-a-re-he you were talking too. You got to be careful of them. They take kids away and they never come back. You ask the old people. There's lots of stories about it ... You need to be careful, eh."

We came to the end of the road.

"Well I'd better report to the guard house. You go on in to your Aunty and I'll see you later."

"Thanks for guiding me Wiremu," I replied.

"Remember what I said about the Patu-pai-a-re-he. See you later Sam."

And he just sort of faded, like a memory. He had guided me in total darkness down the road and given me an interesting bunch of things to think about on the way. A good shepherd ghost – the best kind.

I looked up at Renwick. Now I just had to get past the petty, mean kind, and get to bed. I had a cunning idea to avoid Corporal Higgins and his friends. Instead of coming in the front door, I'd try the back that way I could get to bed quicker.

But when I got there I was surprised to find the lights blazing. I snuck in. The kitchen was brightly lit, and through the window in the door I could see Cam's dad making pastry. Suddenly he looked up and saw me. For an instant he looked worried, then he recognised me. He smiled and waved. I waved back realising there was no way I could avoid questions now.

I raced up the stairs and stole into our apartment. I was in my
PJs and bed in no time. Nguyen had only seen my top. My story
would be I was just raiding the kitchen. I decided I'd better not
visit Tabika as usual. I'd tell Tahira to pass on the message.
And suddenly it was morning and Rewa was waking me. As
usual my head was pounding and I was late.

That lunchtime I caught up with Tahira. She was a bit alarmed
by my description of demon Tabika and rather embarrassed
when I let on I knew of her night time nudity. But I didn't tease.
Who knew what Tabika said about me? Even so Tahira and
I now had a relationship based on trust and that made for a
certain degree of familiarity.

Of course Mr Wakefield had to show up and get completely
the wrong idea. He pounced on us and put us on litter duty for
no good reason at all. That pissed me off because what I really
wanted to do was go to the library and look up Patu-pai-a-re-he.
Unfortunately I didn't get a chance all day.

CHAPTER TWENTY SEVEN: CONTACT

It was exactly four weeks after the explosion at the lighthouse that Dr Prosperov came down to the lounge and announced there was a good chance of a lightning storm that evening. Only lightning strikes could provide enough instant power to open the dimensional portal. Once it was opened just a fraction of an atom's width the system could sustain a data link with the other side.

The technical team consisting of Dr Prosperov, Dr Gursoy, and Dr Morozov, observed by Professor Dubrov would be very busy today checking and preparing the set-up. Our instructions were basically to help out where we could, but mostly to keep out of the way.

The others, of course had no idea what would happen if the experiment was successful. That was partly why Dr Prosperov had assembled his psychics. Mrs Jones, Aunty Nea, Khenbish's dad Nergui. He wasn't sure what he would be dealing with but he was sure it would involve psychic influence.

Strangely, the other kids were more scared than Tahira or me. Tarik and Ashley's wild speculations ranged from unleashing the hounds of hell to creating a black hole. Tahira and me knew that what was coming was going to be difficult, but at least we knew we had done our best with Tabika. Whatever form her mother's anger took, at least it would be better than hordes of demons, or being ripped to atoms by cosmic forces beyond human powers of control.

The day was wet and stormy. The sea crashed through the narrow inlet and pounded the beach misting it with spray drift. The trees were thrashing around like demented things while inside the house the sense of tension was mounting.

Everyone was quiet and stayed out of the way in the lounge upstairs or in our rooms. Even the housework was suspended while the men got ready.

Professor Dubrov had rigged up a set of cameras at the lighthouse to a recording desk in the front lounge and moved some of the big TVs down so we could watch as well. There were also a set of recording computers and an emergency system for killing everything if it seemed to Dubrov and Morozov that the lighthouse crew (which would consist of just Dr Prosperov and Dr Gursoy) had lost control. Dr Prosperov had warned Dr Gursoy that they did face a risk that the system would become unstable and kill them and asked if he really wanted to be in the lighthouse.

Dr Gursoy was staunch. He said this was the most important physical test since Oppenheimer's atom bomb test in New Mexico in 1945 and he was proud to be associated with it.

Dr Prosperov thanked him because, "is practically impossible without you."

But as the build-up continued he was clearly quite nervous and fussy. More than once Morozov gave him a blast in Russian and you could see him struggle to contain himself. Dr Gursoy was already over at the lighthouse steadily calling out actions as he did them. Finally, they were almost ready and it was time for

Khenbish to drive Dr Prosperov over to the lighthouse, and raise the lightning conductor. Outside we had already seen the first flashes of lightning out to sea and the drum roll of thunder was getting louder and more frequent. Dr Prosperov kissed his wife quickly for luck and ran hunched against the rain to the waiting Range Rover. We watched the car drive off around the bay, its lights twin cones in the spray-misted gloom.

Now we went down on the lounge where Dr Morozov was talking with Dr Gursoy. We took our places behind her watching the screens. Then a few people went into the kitchen to make snacks. The atmosphere was kind of surreal. Sort of like watching your uncle getting ready to launch his first moon rocket from the lounge, or something.

As Dr Prosperov arrived at the lighthouse a big flash briefly lit the room followed a few seconds later by the loudest thunder yet. There was no doubt the storm was closing with us and the experiment could begin. Dr Prosperov checked that everyone was ready and flicked the switch to raise the conductor. The outside camera showed the mast smoothly sliding up the centre of the lighthouse. The inside cameras showed the control room.

"Plasma charging," Dr Gursoy called out.

The column of gas inside the copper coils below the mast began to glow a dim orange. It was really like a huge neon tube as tall as the lighthouse but when the lightning crashed through it, the light would be blinding.

"Blast shields down," Dr Prosperov ordered.

Heavy darkened welding glass plate slid down over the control room. It was just in time.

"Ionisation levels rising," Dr Gursoy called.

This meant the mast was beginning to react with the clouds

above. Dr Prosperov had already explained to us the channel for lightning starts at the high point on the ground the lightning finally strikes. As the air becomes charged it creates a pathway for the opposite charged lightning in the sky to pour down.

There was another flash outside and two seconds later a mighty roar that made you want to duck.

"Rising," Dr Gursoy called again calmly.

That bolt had been close, but not directed at the lighthouse. But it felt like the electric tension outside was being mirrored in the lounge. Morozov had magnified the computerised dial showing the voltages on the mast on one of the screens. It was climbing slowly, but steadily, towards the red line.

You could see the sick tension on Dr Prosperov's face. Any time now all his theories would be proved either completely wrong or completely right.

"System status?" he called to Morozov.

But she never got to answer. A flickering of light outside confirmed the picture on our screens. A vision of a lightning bolt dancing and twisting from the lighthouse mast up into the clouds above like an electric tornado held us mesmerised. It had been one thing to catch the lightning but now the system Dr Prosperov had designed, and Drs Morozov and Gursoy had built, was hauling power out of the sky at enormous rates.

The camera in the lighthouse control room had gone a bit fuzzy but still showed the two men concentrating on the screens in front of them while light flashed and flickered around them. Suddenly the lightning stopped.

"Phase two started successfully. Supercapacitors holding, rings fully charged," Dr Gursoy commented on the screen. We could also see the mast, visibly smoking, retracting.

"Blast shield up. Cameras three and four online," Dr Prosperov said, flicking switches.

A new view came up on the screen. It showed a big round table as if someone had sliced a metal ball in half. In the middle was a round depression as if it was made to hold a ball while overhead were a whole bunch of tubes all pointing at the centre of the depression.

"Vortex seeding started successfully," Dr Gursoy said.

At first nothing happened. Then slowly we began to notice tiny dancing violet lights that flickered around the boundaries of the invisible globe in the depression. Then in the middle a tiny but absolutely brilliant light began to shine. For a moment nobody said anything. We just stared at the light which gave us this wonderful feeling, as if we were looking at the very first light of creation.

"Bozhe Moy!" Dubrov gasped, sitting down in amazement.

"Vortex steady at zero point six four nanometers," Dr Gursoy said.

"Bandwidth?" Prosperov asked.

"Two to the sixteenth power," Morozov replied.

"Transmitting."

I didn't know about this part but Tarik asked the question for me. Morozov's eyes flicked up, then she made a few movements with her mouse and some classical music came out of the speakers.

"Bach!" smiled Dubrov.

"I thought if to transmit anything to other world. Mathematical progressions in Bach's fugue both recognisable and pleasing," Prosperov told us over the video link.

The music was old-fashioned and complicated. It made me think

of old clocks and music boxes with ballerinas that Rewa loved.
Suddenly the light in the depression flickered for a moment.

"Vortex energy density climbing," Dr Gursoy warned.

"Reading?" Dr Prosperov demanded.

"Two point six electron petavolts," Dr Gursoy called.

The light began to grow and intensify.

There was a flash of lightning outside and for a second the
picture distorted and then cut out before recovering again.

"One nine two electron petavolts," Dr Gursoy read

"Origin? Origin of power surge?" Dr Prosperov called urgently.

"Our side is steady Gennady," Dr Gursoy grinned.

Professor Dubrov let out an "Oorah!" and started dancing
around the room.

Dr Morozov looked amazed.

"What's happening?" Mrs Jones asked for us all.

"Someone picked up phone," Dr Morozov said looking
concerned at her screens. Dr Prosperov asked her something
in Russian and she replied while frowning – a picture of
concentration. The light on the screen was so strong Dubrov had
to zoom the camera out.

Then suddenly it went out. The screen seemed suddenly dark
and empty.

"What happened?" Dr Prosperov demanded immediately.

"It's ah ... I can't," Dr Gursoy was looking at the screen trying to
decipher the information.

Then Morozov said something in shocked surprise in Russian.
Dubrov quickly zoomed the camera back on the depression
where the light had been. In its place was a perfectly round pale
red glass ball about the size of a marble. And in the middle of the
ball was an intense red light as if a laser beam had been frozen

and encased in a sphere of pale red glass.

"One hundred grams," Dr Prosperov breathed.

Professor Dubrov made a short speech in Russian and then started in English.

"This epoch making moment. Not only has Prosperov achieved matter transference he has achieved simultaneously communication with non-terrestrial civilisation. This is beyond calculation!"

Suddenly the light inside the glass ball began to pulse.

"Unless they've sent us a bleedin bomb init?" Tarik whispered to me under his breath.

We all watched, mesmerised as the light in the ball pulsed like a slow heartbeat. Dr Gursoy sat back and looked confused.

"What do we do now?" he asked, but he never got an answer. There was another flash outside and the picture went snowy followed by an enormous roll of thunder.

"*GIVE ME MY DAUGHTER BACK!*"

The power of the impression hit us like a truck coming through the side of the house. All the psychics looked white-faced and even Aunty Liz seemed to have felt something. The view of the lighthouse had come back.

A questioning look had appeared on Dr Prosperov's face as he looked around.

"Oh mah God!" screamed Ashley looking out the window.

She looked frozen by fear. Everyone ran to the window and looked up. The clouds had been dark and low in the sky split occasionally by brilliant flashes of lightning. But now everyone who looked up was seized by terror. Professor Dubrov was so overcome he simply fainted. We all fought back a desire to run like mice into any available dark corner abandoning any dignity.

For the black and boiling clouds had formed themselves into a woman's face. Her hair streams of cloud twisting like snakes. Her eyes blazing balls of white-blue lightning. And she looked terrifyingly angry.

Time seemed to slow down.

Every heartbeat seemed to be a lifetime.

The wind dropped to an eerie stillness.

It was like a dream where you can't run any more.

And then in the blink of an eye

they were right outside.

There were four of them – I guessed Tabika's fathers, brother and mother.

As with the daughter there was no mystery as to what sex they were. But while they were all two legged with arms and a head that was about as far as family resemblance went.

In the centre stood Morganne. Like Tabika she was pale white, but shining so brightly now she was almost as white as snow and the blue tinge of her radiance was only visible in the shadows she cast. Her long red hair fell down behind her shapely figure which was clad in a long black web like dress which covered her lower body more than her upper. Out from her back behind her rose four large oval insect-like black and transparent wings. Her face was perfectly beautiful but right now her eyes were red, in her hands was a brilliant white sceptre and she was obviously in no mood for argument.

The father to her left seemed like a cross between a faun and a devil. He was dark, not like Ashley who was browner than black. The skin of his human torso was sort of black-gray. Below this his legs were covered in long brownish fur ending in hooves and there was no doubt he was a billy goat. Out of his head protruded two curly rams horns between which black curly hair fell and appeared to grow down his back. Only his brown eyes looked human rather than goat-like. More thoughtful and pained than angry. Nevertheless he held a huge twisted wooded staff in his hand at the top of which was a violet jewel which shone brightly.

The father to her right was better looking. Not quite as big as his opposite number but he was still not small. He was muscular and his skin was deep tan but shone as if wet. Over his shoulders he wore a long cape which hung down to his calf. It was the most fascinating brilliant green colour with patterns that shifted and changed continuously. He had long braided white-silver hair with a neat moustache under a hooked nose and a long fine beard. On his head he wore a silver crown and in his hand a thin silver staff topped with a green jewel which shone as brightly as the violet one.

Behind him and to the right was a boy version of Tabika except his feathery wings were white and he had white hair on his head and body. His eyes blazed blue. He too carried a glowing sceptre. He looked like an angel – an upset and angry angel.

"Patupaiarehe," smiled Aunty Nea.

"Vila," whispered Morozov to herself.

"Peri," Mitra muttered to her daughter and granddaughter.

"Kitsune," Mariko whispered to Gunter clutching him.

"Hollda," Gunter replied holding her.

"Tuatha de Danaan," said Mrs Jones calmly.

"Is that lady a real fairy Aunty Liz?' Rewa asked slowly as if mesmerised.

I noticed the video link to the lighthouse was dead.

"*COME OUT OF YOUR HOUSE OF IRON OR DIE BURNING IN IT*," Morganne commanded.

There was no sound. Only command and a very real threat. When a crowd like this appears and gives you orders that hit your brain like a bolt of lightning resistance simply doesn't even occur to you. You do like the winged lady says – and quickly too. The psychics didn't explain, we just went to the door with some of the adults pushing ahead and some hanging back.

We poured out of that house like it was already on fire and crowded together, children at the back. We felt like a mob of spooked sheep.

"*WHO SPEAKS FOR YOU,*" Morganne demanded silently. She looked like she was ready to melt us with her glare.

"I do, Morganne, Queen of Fae," came a familiar lilt from the back of the crowd.

It was Mrs Jones who stepped out from the crowd and dropped on one knee.

The red light in Morganne's eyes went out, replaced by a fabulous blue. Her head tilted in astonishment.

"Dee Dee?"

To my surprise Morganne spoke these words. Mrs Jones looked up smiling like a naughty imp. She suddenly looked five years old. Morganne's eyes were wide with astonishment.

"Dee Dee!" Morganne cried out again and flew to her on an invisible wind, her wings motionless. Mrs Jones stood and they looked at each other for about five seconds. It was interesting that while Morganne seemed huge in comparison with Mrs Jones, she was actually small – the same size as the little Welshwoman. Suddenly Morganne swept the dumpy old woman in her arms. They hugged for a minute.

The two fathers looked at each other and shrugged. The fire in their eyes was replaced with faint annoyance. But the two women wouldn't be rushed. Finally they released each other. A glance from the silver haired father I guessed was the one Tabika had called Merin and Morganne was serious again. She said no words but she was obviously asking her friend a question.

"I don't know anything about your daughter Morganne," Mrs Jones replied looking nervous.

That wasn't the right answer.

"*Dee, she is HERE*!" was the impression we all got.

Morganne really did stamp her foot.

The whole situation was just too weird. Like sending a spaceship to Mars then being stopped by an angry martian policeman for speeding who turned out to know your aunty.

"We do not have her Queen Morganne."

Now it was Lana Vilenskaya who spoke. She slid out from the back totally fearlessly and it was clear that not only Morganne, but also the fathers, knew her too.

They looked at her with obvious pity in their hearts. And suddenly I realised that our Lana was the one Tabika had spoken of. Her friend's Aunty Lana. The one who had transformed for love only to lose both her love and her former life.

"These people don't know where your daughter is," she said.

Morganne might have felt sorry for Lana, and perhaps a hint of revulsion too, but she was still a mother with a missing daughter and she was not going to give in. For a second the two women eye-balled each other. I could see the anger and frustration building up in Morganne and it didn't look healthy. I glanced at Tahira who looked away and I realised she didn't want her mother to know what she'd been up to. It was up to me. If I did nothing Morganne might do something we would all regret. I ran forward hoping Tabika's spell had finished.

"Queen Morganne ... Tabika ... she's living in a cave near here. She's been hiding and wouldn't let ... me ... tell."

Suddenly everyone was looking at me.

I was between the humans and the aliens and I felt suddenly rather alone.

Queen Morganne looked at me rather like someone might look at a talking beetle.

"*If she's free why has she not come*?" The horned father silently asked me. I turned to look at him. For such a big, scary looking dude I was surprised at the gentleness of his thought.

"I think she's proud of her cave," I said.

Morganne looked annoyed – not with me, she believed me – but with her absent daughter.

"She wants you to see," I added quietly, locating the cave exactly in my thoughts to them.

The horned father smiled. Pike, Tabika's brother, leapt into the air blazing brightly under the dark gray clouds and flew swiftly in the direction of the cave.

I sidled back to the Renwick huddle and found myself next to Dr Morozov.

"Daughter weighs 47.5 kilos, yes?" she asked quietly out the side of her mouth.

I nodded.

Aunty Liz came through the crowd and turned me around.

"Sam why didn't you say anything?" she scolded.

"I couldn't Aunty Liz! That girl did something to me! These people have powers!"

Aunty Liz glanced at Morganne who simply looked so full of

power there was no question about what I said.

Suddenly all the visitors looked in the direction Pike had gone. Then looked at each other. The horned dad stepped back slightly then seemed to vanish into a blackness that lasted for barely the blink of an eye.

The Range Rover was driving the road from the lighthouse to where we stood outside Renwick.

"Dr Prosperov didn't mean to abduct Tabika. He didn't even know he had abducted Tabika," I began to explain to Morganne. Morganne said nothing in a way that made me uneasy. She looked like an annoyed cat who is ready to claw someone.

A flurry of violet spots of light appeared condensed into a brilliant point of light which expanded so that we all had to shield our eyes and the horned dad and his two winged children once again stood among us. Tabika dashed to her mum and gave her a big hug which was returned uncomfortably. Then apparently proudly explaining to her parents how she had survived, Tabika bounced over to me, took me by the arm and turned back to her parents. Their conversation was short and Morganne while clearly relieved to see her, seemed annoyed as well.

Tabika ruffed my hair, hugged me, and then spotted Tahira who was trying to hide behind Soraya. Soraya looked appalled at Tabika's lack of clothes. Tabika skipped into the crowd and put her arm around Tahira too, kissed her cheek – which went brilliant red – and then pranced back to her parents. I looked around and saw everyone looking at me accusingly, thinking the worst. I couldn't help it. I went bright red too.

"What?" I demanded.

"Sam!" Aunty Liz did not look impressed.

"She just doesn't wear clothes!" I said hotly, "Look at them. None of them do! Tahira tried her best to get her to cover up." Tahira's mum and grandmother began rapidly questioning Tahira in Persian. She was as defensive as I was.

But this was interrupted by the arrival of the Range Rover. There was a brief pause as the visitors turned to regard the newly arrived vehicle. I could see Khenbish at the wheel looked shocked. Dr Gursoy was bewildered. Only Dr Prosperov looked unsurprised and businesslike.

He got out putting his walking stick down first and then calmly got out of the car and walked towards the visitors, the others following behind. There was an ominous silence as Morganne clearly gave him a blast.

And then a curious thing happened. Dr Prosperov almost fainted. Dr Morozov gave a short scream as his eyes rolled up in his head and he staggered and then he caught himself. Dr Gursoy and Ken rushed forward to catch him but stopped – repelled.

For it was the creepiest thing I have ever seen – and believe me I've seen some creepy stuff. Dr Prosperov smiled in a cunning way his eyes flashing as he looked around and began to chuckle and I knew – I think we all knew – this was no longer Dr Prosperov. He was possessed.

CHAP+ER TWEN+Y EIGH+: LUCKY

I must apologise fair Queen Morganne to you, your daughter and family for my deviousness in assembling you here in these circumstances. I must admit however, that rack my brains as I may, I could think of no other means to compel you and these most promising earthlings to intersect."

He both spoke and projected these thoughts and the combined effect had everyone's attention, even though it was not as forceful as Queen Morganne's projections. His voice was Dr Prosperov's but the tone and intonation were not. The Russian accent was completely gone and there was something oily about this Spirit's manner.

"Who are you?" asked Merin, who was standing in front of his family. Evidently the more skilled in these circumstances.

"My host calls me 'Lucky' mighty Merin, and lucky I am and luck I have brought him and all these earthling folk. I am lucky that he had the intelligence and the talent equipped with such base tools as these primitive people command, to probe Yggdrasil – the tree of worlds in which I had been imprisoned all these centuries. I am lucky too that when he realised my presence he did not at once have me cast out, for in my weakened state, without a host, my existence and indeed my purpose would be at an end. And I am lucky too that the only being to probe

Yggdrasil in ten centuries allied with my purpose as soon as I explained it."

"What is your purpose, Lucky?" Mrs Jones asked. She too seemed used to possessions.

"Mistress Dee, oldest, last, and may I say greatest, of the immortal Earth witches. I am but the meanest vagrant, bereft of all but my wisdom and this borrowed tongue. And yet my purpose is immodest. It is to bring about, in centuries hence, the final defeat of the rulers of the galaxy by those they have despised, oppressed and persecuted for millennia. But for that purpose to be achieved there is a more pressing matter involving this world. For it is clear that unless we (and by 'we' I mean all here) intervene this world will not survive to play its central role in that downfall."

"Frozen in the smallest unit of space but liberated across the higher dimensions I have been afforded a unique opportunity to traverse the potentialities of the future that may become the Universe past. For centuries I traversed the sweep of time and perused the Universes-that-may-be of unresolved potentialities. And for all my efforts in seeking this way to escape my unjust imprisonment I learned but two things of direct consequence to my circumstance."

"These were: that the only physical way out of this trap was the way I had gone in; and that no matter how the future resolved this world, this Earth, is crucial to the fate of the nine civilisations in this galaxy joined by the ancient tree of the ten dimensions – Yggdrasil."

"More immediately I also foresaw this world faces its greatest crisis in a mere fifty years and were I not released before then, all hope of change in the galaxy would be extinguished as this world died about me."

"My only hope lay in the minds of men for only there did the ember of my influence still glow. But, alas, mine was not the only voice to disturb the slumbering populace. I could but whisper through the cracks between the worlds of my prison to those whose imaginations passed nearest. Far louder voices, including the demands of those who so cruelly inured me, stirred the baser passions of these primitive minds to fervour, outrage and war."

"Miraculously a century ago I found a young man whose open mind and innate talent needed little guidance to find his way to the threshold of my prison. I whispered secrets in his dreams which in his hands became the substance of my plans for escape. Doggedly, I educated him from Serbia to America as he strove to realise the insights I furnished. Alas, he passed before I could show him the keys to the Tree and my own release. Imagine then my despair when but a century remained until the bars of my cage would close forever and he departed leaving his papers to be removed by agents of my enemies."

"And yet even as the decade of my doom drew ever closer, year by year the gate of potentiality which allowed for my release did not shut. Miraculously the superplex of unresolved potentialities rushing for the temporal event horizon that borders future and past still did not rule out my release. I saw in this an act of providence beyond my powers to predict."

"Certainly were it true I would claim I guided good Professor Dubrov and his remarkable protegé to release me. Yet, I did not! I was only roused from despair when I recognised how close Dr Prosperov already was, as his group of Zaarin increased the power of their probe. The credit for these discoveries lies with

Gennady Prosperov alone. And so it was twelve years ago that he released me from my prison by accident."

"I regret my release prematurely but temporarily released six old souls from this world. But over a dozen years I have worked to help Dr Prosperov to reunite them. I have woven as expertly as I can the luck, the coincidences, and the joins between all present to achieve but one end. To secure the future of twelve future leaders of this middle world who stand a chance of guiding its people and civilisation into the future where Earth may play a role in securing the freedom of all races of the galaxy."

"Tenuous as it may sound only these twelve can make choices that will lead Earth from self-destruction to survival. And those choices will not be easy, or obvious. Already the Earthlings have deceived themselves through decades of distractions from truths they do not want to face. Already they overburden their world and ignore the consequences of their greed. As sure as God is the source of all possibilities without the right leaders this world will collapse in war, starvation and plague in less than the lifetimes of the earthling children here today."

"But Earth is not alone. To the visitors from Fae, I say this. Your world is not the safe haven you imagine either. Your world will be threatened in the lifetimes of Pike and Tabika. This half-forgotten playground, Earth is now, as it ever was in your youth, Morganne the fair, Merin the wise, Daya the compassionate, the thread through which all your weaving runs."

"Abandon Earth and all your weaving unravels. Abandon Earth and your enemy's enemies triumph here and you know Morganne of Fae, your enemy's enemies are not your friends. Abandon Earth and your grandchildren, great Daya and Merin, will be pursued so that there are no longer any worlds left to

abandon. The defence of Fae then, starts or ends here on Earth."
He stopped to gather his argument.

"The dead see much hidden from the living. Neither dead nor
alive I have seen much that you cannot and much you can
perceive. This then is my craft: the threads of all your races'
fates pass through this world. You will share a common hope or
a common doom – not immediately to be sure. The survivors
may see out another millennia. But elders of Fae, for want of but
a little compassion your children," and he glanced at Tabika and
Pike, "too will face a meaner inheritance than they have yet been
promised."

He stopped again, sighed, and looked around. He almost seemed
to be in tears.

"Over twelve years I have laid my plans and guided my host
and you all as much as was in my limited power to do so –
individually – to this point. I have done all I can. I have put my
case as briefly as I can. I can do no more."

And with that he dropped his head.

There was a very long silence.

A long, black, squall was approaching. The wind picked up.
It was cold. You could smell sweet rain over the kelp and salt
stones of the sea. At some unheard request the two children
walked to a father each and held his staff.

"I'll see you again soon, Tahira and Sam," Tabika 'whispered' to
us.

"Thank you."

Then, as if they'd been a picture projected through a tiny black
hole, they vanished into a darkness. Half a minute later the
rain came pelting down. Morganne went over to Dr Prosperov.
At first we waited but it was just too wet and we all ran inside.

Lucky and Morganne 'talked' for about five minutes, rain pouring down on them the whole time. Then Morganne also vanished into nothingness, and Dr Prosperov collapsed. Ken and Gunter helped carry him inside. Everyone gathered around in the hallway as he entered. He had woken up but wet and muddy, he looked drained and disoriented.

"Please to forgive me. Am … am too tired to answer," he said to everyone. They took him upstairs guided by Dr Morozov. We watched as they climbed the stairs almost too numb to do anything else. For a moment there was silence as he disappeared from view.

"WOOOOHOOOO!!!" exploded Mariko as loud as she could, completely shattering the quiet.

"HOW INCLEDIBLE WAS THAT? WE JUST HAD A WHOLE BUNCH OF F_____N FREAKY ALIEN FAIRIES VISIT US!!"
Even shouting it didn't seem to break through the shock. The whole idea just seemed too strange to believe it had really just happened. But Mariko (who like everyone, was wet through) had the answer.

"I say we do serlious HARD drinking!"
That got a laugh.

"And eating also," Gunter put in, coming down the stairs, followed by Ken. Seeing it was dinner time that suggestion got more approval. We all started to move toward the kitchen Mr Trân leading the way.

At first nobody talked about what had just happened in front of them. I was impressed at how quickly the adults could organise dinner and finally when we all had some burgers and chips whipped up we gathered around to talk about it all. Everyone had been a bit sus about Mrs Jones and Lana Vilenskaya, so it wasn't surprising that Mrs Jones stood to speak.

"I imagine seeing Morganne and her family appear like that was probably quite a shock to you all. My acquaintance with her too, must have seemed simply bewildering. I feel I owe you all an explanation."

She sighed looking around at our slightly worried faces.

"I am indeed human like you but I am very, very, very old. I met Morganne eight hundred years ago when I was younger and much prettier. My name was not always Jones. My names have changed many, many times as I have moved and married, but the name of my father was Dee."

"My father and mother followed the old religion and practiced the Craft. In those days Morganne's people visited our glades and clearings often and both peoples enjoyed nights in each other's company. From my youngest days I grew in the knowledge of our secret night time visitors."

"I met Morganne when she was Tabika's age, and I Tahira's. We became the closest friends and loved each other very deeply. As I grew into womanhood our secret friendship sustained me until I was in my mid-twenties, but then, as it will, questions of marriage and my future arose. Morganne could not bear to see me marry and bear children now, but I explained that at twenty-five I was already considered an old maid and if I were to have any children to care for me, as I cared for my parents, I needed to find a husband. I would not go with her so instead I allowed her to change me. She delayed my aging so that our love could continue without the need for husbands and children."

"My parents died soon after each other when I was sixty, and yet it seemed I had not aged a day. But I could not remain. I was an outcast, regarded with suspicion in our district and there were

men-at-arms who I knew thought to capture me for their own.
I began to move. I became a wandering healer and I travelled
throughout Britain and later Europe. My adventures would
fill many volumes, but as I travelled the innocence which had
so delighted Morganne fell away. She too was changing. We
quarrelled and finally parted."

"I have loved many fine men and women in my long, long life.
But I never forgot the love of Morganne and have ever prayed
for her. To be re-united with her again even now in the autumn
of my years still warms my soul as it did when we were young.
And yet even as I delight in this unexpected reunion I must say
I am as bewildered by this entity 'Lucky' as any of you. How he
has contrived this meeting is a mystery even I cannot fathom.
Dr Prosperov drew me here on the understanding this was to be
a school for young psychics and his deception has left me with
many questions."

She seemed to run out of steam and then looked to Lana and sat
down. Lana looked slightly guilty, but took over.

"I too am human now, but I wasn't always. I was a Fae and knew
Morganne and her family distantly on our world. Like Morganne
I found love on your world, a love greater than any I had ever
considered possible."

She paused for a moment.

"His name was Andrei Klyvev and he lived near Tomsk in
Siberia. He was a hunter by trade but a poet too, with a mind I
thought the most beautiful thing in the galaxy. We met before
the revolution and fell deeply in love. So much so, I gave up my
powers and ten thousand years of potential life for him."

I simply couldn't imagine why anyone would do that! All the
adults were looking at Lana with nothing short of awe.

"Then the Revolution came. At first it was difficult but increasingly the Reds made our lives impossible. Our son died. I had made a terrible mistake in the stabilisation process and it was that which killed my baby. Even though Andrei's poetry was at first accepted by the Party as socialist and nationalist; idealism, paranoia and politics soon saw him being criticised. Instead of remaining silent as I begged him, he exposed the contradictions of his critics, not realising that the Soviet system was itself a contradiction: a mythology of revolution wrapped around the apparatus of the most sensitive, paranoid and oppressive of Tsars. He was denounced, sent to the Gulag and finally shot."

"It was I who introduced Gennady to Nergui and his brother Zaarin or great shamans when he was younger. Nergui and the others had long known us, just as Deirdre's people had. I knew it shattered Gennady's Soviet mindset, and, of course, ultimately in turn led him to help me escape the Soviet Union, but also finally led to the deaths of the six great souls who were working with him in Chicago, and the release of that entity we all saw possess him. Like Sister Dee I was as surprised as any of you when Lucky revealled himself."

"Dat really creeped me out!" Ashley blurted out to herself.

A lot of people agreed with that, but they all wanted Mrs Jones to explain what it meant.

"Possession comes in many forms. Some people are simply possessed by an idea or an ideal. Some people possess multiple consciousnesses. When we say someone is possessed by a spirit we don't necessarily mean being possessed by an actual entity. But that can be one of the possibilities. Such entities do exist and their influence on the world can be greater than we

PART TWO: THE WEAVING

imagine. Sometimes they possess many people simultaneously – normally, as in this case, willingly. But it is very rare for them to be so … well quite so forthright about their outlook. In fact I have never encountered anything like this entity Lucky in all my years of working with the Craft."

"There was mention of a world tree? Yigg something? What was that," Bernard asked.

"Yggdrasil iz der Vorld Tree in der Nordic Sagas," said Gunter. "It connects the nine worlds including Asgard vere zer Gods come from and Midgard vich is ze old Nordic name for our vorld."

"That, of course, is a primitive interpretation of what your people understood, when they asked their gods where they came from," Lana interrupted.

"The tree is an informational structure at the very core of the Universe, but exactly how this entity could be entangled in it and remain conscious of the future is not something even I, with my advanced understanding of such matters, can begin to explain. We have long suspected there exist dimensions where pure consciousnesses persist but they are beyond our reach. They approach we material beings but we cannot approach them. This entity Lucky is certainly one of the most unusually … direct, I have ever heard of. But perhaps the passage of time has made him desperate. Even so the weaving he has wrought to bring us all together shows that he is indeed a focussed and formidable power."

"And yet …" interrupted Mrs Jones. Lana looked at her.

"Yes Sister Dee?" she asked.

"It was you that brought Gennady and the six Zaarin together. At the time even this Lucky said he despaired at ever finding a way out of his prison. As even he said, the door was closing, but did not shut. Lucky has certainly woven much since his release, but there is more to this, as I think even he realises. You were already a part when you met your love."

"Yes, you are right Sister. There may indeed be a greater providence than even we imagine," Lana agreed.

"Waal dis is all very interestin' but what de hell does it mean fer us?" Patricia asked. "Ah mean to say, ah signed on to work in a house, an here we are talkin to aliens and it tuirns out da boss is possessed by God knows what? Ah mean ah wanna know what ahm doin here, and whether ah really wanna be a part of all dis?"

Auntie Liz, the Khadem's and Zoe Khumalo agreed. Mariko, Gunter and Mr Trân were quieter – just thinking about it.

"If I may venture a point of view?" Dr Gursoy put in.

Everyone was quite interested in what Dr Gursoy had to say because he had been closest to Dr Prosperov's experiment.

"It seems to me we have all had ... well, I know I have had ... the biggest shock of my life. When today began, I thought I was about to be involved in the proof one of the most remarkable breakthroughs conceived by a human mind. That succeeding was itself a momentous occasion – as I'm sure Professor Dubrov will attest when he comes to. But on top of that we made contact with an unknown civilisation! A scientific breakthrough itself beyond calculation. As a scientist and engineer I am still astounded at what Dr Prosperov (and to a lesser extent those of us who have helped him) have achieved. I think we all need to recognise that with very little resource this team here has progressed human science by two or three centuries, or to put it another way, we are two or three centuries ahead of the rest of science on this planet."

He stopped and let us consider that.

"But I am not just a man of science. I am also a man of faith – a man of God. I must admit my religion does not provide me with the confidence Mrs Jones or Professor Vilenskaya show in responding to whatever this being Lucky actually is. I admit to being highly uneasy with almost everything about it. Some might say painting the world in black and white, good and evil, does not allow for the breadth and scope of God's design, and yet I am drawn inevitably back to this question: Is this Lucky a being I can trust with not only our physical lives but also our spiritual wellbeing as well? It is a question which, frankly, troubles me, and I think troubles us all."

There was a lot of nodding and agreement around the room. Even Mrs Jones and Lana agreed with him.

"In my faith (and I suspect in most of yours) we look for the divine in the world, knowing that, though there is indeed evil, the good is greater. I do not pretend to understand everything that Gennady does or why he does it. I do not pretend to understand everything that Mrs Jones or Professor Vilenskaya have spoken of. But what I do understand is that I have never before met a group of people who give me as much hope for our world as all of you gathered here and now. Whether this Lucky is an angel or a demon or something else besides, the only thing – the only thing – that makes me tend to believe what it has said, is that the means by which it will accomplish its aims is through us."

He looked around at us all. It was a comforting thought.

"So what I am trying to say is that it is my faith in your goodness, your decency and your humanity – Professor

Vilenskaya included – which illuminates for me the hand of God in this ... absolutely incredible adventure, because without us, as this being Lucky has admitted, he really is nothing. It's the only thing that comforts me."

There was a long awkward silence. Then Mr Trân, who had been nervously nodding also spoke.

"I agree Dr Gursoy. When we must choose path we look at who choose what path before us. We see this is path of rich greedy man. This is path of mean lonely lady. But path of good man or good woman easy see. Can be hard walk but always easy see. I think Dr Prosperov walk on right path. I not scare of Lucky. He try hard. He care for people."

Face blazing red, Mr Trân stepped back.

"Yeah ..." Ken agreed slowly, "I think Nguyen said it for me too. I dunno what exactly we're getting ourselves into but nothing about it seems wrong to me."

Nergui interrupted him quietly and he bent to listen to his father.

 "What do you think Aunty Nea?" Lana asked.

"I met the Patupaiarehe as a girl and among them my greatest love, but I was shy and would not go with him. I met Lucky after I met Dr Prosperov in my dreams long ago, Lana. No-one should fear him. He is good, not evil. I believe it would be worse to ignore him than listen, but I will not live to see the disasters he fears or the world he hopes for. You must make your decisions for yourselves," she said. I was struck by her common sense and courage, knowing she must soon die.

Ken spoke for Nergui.

"My father says Lucky arose from the tree of life to bring forth the rainbow world serpent who eats his own tail and protects the

Earth. We should celebrate his release not fear him,"
Not even Ken seemed to understand what the old guy was
talking about but it seemed to be a vote in Lucky's favour.
Focused discussion broke down into different groups after that.
Everyone seemed to just want to talk about what they had seen.
Even Rewa and Asal.

"Sam how did you meet that nude girl?" Rewa asked.
I told them all about meeting her and what we'd been up to.
They were fascinated by her flying and lighting candles by
willpower and her scary side. But they weren't so into her nudity
or eating small animals raw. They wanted to know what she was
like. I said she was fun but also a bit scary because you never
knew what she would do or think. This didn't seem too worrying
to them. I think because they felt that way about so many adult
things anyway, that they were used to it. I found that so trusting
and cute but then I realised that might be how Tabika thought
about me and Tahira.

Aunty Liz was looking at me like she wasn't sure whether she
trusted me or not. She had been shocked when I had gone
forward to Morganne and even more shocked when Tabika had
taken me by the arm. I had the strong feeling I had only avoided
a telling-off because she was trying to keep up with everyone
else.

You could tell the others who had been out that night were
pissed off with me and Tahira for keeping Tabika secret. They
circled around us pressing us both for details. I could tell Tahira
was terrified I was going to spill the beans on her and Tabika
but I thought she should be more worried that Tabika might
come back and blab. The talking went on for a long time but by
ten I was exhausted. I finally followed Aunty Liz upstairs, had

a shower, and went to bed. She came in to see me before lights out.

"Sam, Aunty Nea told me that when she met those Patupaiarehe when she was young those fairy girls were pretty frisky with the boys."

She let that just hang there a moment.

"Is there anything you want to tell me about?"

I felt a bit shy but I knew I had to tell Aunty Liz everything. It was hard but it made me feel much better. When I finished she hugged me.

"I'm proud of you Sam. A lot of boys your age would have been much dumber than that. It's easy for a boy to fall for a pretty girl who makes it look easy. Believe me there is nothing easy about love. But you didn't let her use you, or push you around. Not too many boys your age would have done that," she told me.

But then she added grimly, "of course if I hear different from anyone else, you might be safer with your father eh."

I smiled. I knew it was an empty threat.

"No fear, Aunty Liz," I told her and went to sleep.

CHAPTER TWENTY NINE: TRIAL

April was a dreary month. It seemed to get wetter and darker every day. Dr Prosperov had emerged to answer our questions, but he seemed depressed.

Yes, Lucky had told him we were psychic. Yes, the plan was to involve us in the scheme to find and assist the future leaders because he was sure these kids wouldn't listen to adults. Yes, he hoped our parents would cooperate because he already knew of their own experiences. Yes, Lucky said we were the reincarnations of his six Zaarin.

But the whole plan had turned on Morganne of Fae and ever since she had vanished that evening in March there had been no sign of her, or her family. He continued with his business but it was plain his heart wasn't in it.

If Dr P was down, for us kids the best part about living at Renwick was Mr Trân's food. We got hot chocolate for breakfast with pastries followed with eggs benedict or pancakes or waffles. Dinner was always restaurant quality although Mr Trân was experimenting with food from around the world so you never knew what it would be. One night it'd be Greek lamb, another it would be French stew, the next Szechwan duck, then gumbo from the Caribbean. He gave us little printouts about the places as well so it was quite interesting really. Certainly more interesting than social studies at school.

And now that I was no longer distracted from Mr Wakefield's stuck-up snottiness by Tabika I could rejoin the others in experiencing it in high definition. The greasing he encouraged from Marshall McLachlan and his mates made me want to puke. His jokes were just nasty, and usually a bit racist, while his attitude to us was that we were subnormal and therefore anything we might ask, or say, was automatically something for the whole class to laugh at.

We suffered in two ways. One was that in some things we were too good. Tarik was better at maths than Mr Wakefield who didn't like that. We also knew more about the world than he did, and he didn't like that either. When Tahira assumed Mr Wakefield spoke French (because he used a French phrase) and responded with a two minute torrent in the language Mr Wakefield was left with his mouth open, looking like a dork. He didn't like that either.

But what none of us were any good at was writing. Some like Cam, Tahira and Tarik had the excuse that English was not their native language. But truth be told none of us were any good at even forming letters right. And forget about spelling. That meant Mr Wakefield could cover our written work in red pen marks and sarcastic comments. He sometimes liked to read our mistakes out to the class for a laugh. He didn't say who had written what, but he didn't make it hard to guess.

There was no escape. The rain meant lunch and break had to be inside. And while our leftover based lunches at least gave us a slight lift it wasn't enough. The hours in class seemed to drag by. We were doing fractions – which I hate – book reviews – which I also hate – and the environment – which could have been interesting except it seemed to be mostly about paper and paper recycling which I found pointless because the paper we made was thick, fell to pieces, and really lame.

I wasn't alone. The others slept, doodled or stared out the window just like me, while Mr Wakefield snickered over the fresh greasing from Table A. We started racing pet woodlice out of sheer boredom.

But we did read everything we could find on fairies. Fairies, Patupaiarehe, Tuatha de Danaan, Vila, Peri, and Kitsune. The interesting thing was the stories all described pretty much the same thing. Fairies were small, pale and had red hair. Some had tails, and some could change their appearance. They were associated with caves and only came out at night. They did not like iron because it drained their powers. They had romances with people and sometimes changed to live as humans. They taught people things like weaving or fish traps. And there was mention of how they stole children and left "Changelings" – fake children in their place. Nobody mentioned the real children were in danger from parents or stepparents as Tabika had said. Maybe they were. Maybe they weren't. Who would know?

Of course we never talked about Renwick stuff when other kids were around. We knew they would be dorks about the ghosts and any mention of fairies was asking to be laughed out of school. But when we were safely on the Betty with Mariko loudly playing whatever 80s tracks she had adopted for the day, we would talk about ghosts, fairies, other supernatural creatures and, of course the kids at school.

Almost always the stories we told each other involved Mr Wakefield and Table A wetting themselves with terror and us laughing about it. But really the only bright spot on the horizon was Easter and the prospect of a four-day weekend full of chocolate eggs and hot cross buns.

Mariko had decided she was going to organise an egg hunt, but being a designer she couldn't just buy a bunch of chocolate eggs from the supermarket. Instead she got us making chocolate using cocoa beans from Samoa, sugar from Fiji and cream from New Zealand. We experimented making chocolate for about a week. Then she bought eight unfertilised emu eggs from a farm in Clevedon. The night before Easter Friday we blew the emu eggs out. Man, that was a lot of work! Aunty Liz and Mitra had to blow Rewa and Asal's eggs. Then we made our chocolate and carefully filled our eggs in layers so that it coated the inside of the shell.

Mariko told us on Easter Sunday our eggs would be a particular colours and we would have an Easter egg hunt. She had us choose our colours from a range of red, blue, green, silver, gold, or violet. I wanted red. The two little girls wanted pink but got gold. Then we went to bed. We had almost forgotten about the Fae.

But at that stage I didn't know two important things. The first is that Easter is a festival older than Christ. That wasn't important in itself but it explains why it's not on the same day each year like Christmas. It always falls on a full moon. The second, and more important thing our library reading had not picked up is that the fairies only appear on the full moon – just as they had when Morganne had last appeared.

For some reason everyone seemed restless that night. Rewa and Asal took ages to go to sleep and the ghosts were wandering through our apartments, chilling us – something they rarely did. The clouds poured through the sky all ragged and broken letting the bright moon shine through. The sea seemed especially loud and I remember lying in my bed watching the moon burst through and then get swallowed up again while the sea roared up onto the beach.

The sound that woke me from an almost-sleep was like the biggest, longest, deepest conch shell you ever heard. It was like the sound vibrated inside you, like you were a part of the sound. The silence that followed it was like the universe drawing breath. I dashed to the window. Outside there was a huge ring of fire on the beach. A ring of fiery torches held up by creatures of all shapes and sizes. There were bright fairies both naked and not, satyrs like Tabika's father, centaurs and sphinxes together with wolves, and monkeys, bear and panther-like creatures all milling about but very clearly holding this ring shape.

A flash of blue whizzed right by my window followed by another and another.

"Oh my God what's happening?" I heard Aunt Liz say from the lounge next door. I could guess already. But then a bright white girl appeared at my window. I opened it at once. The air outside was hot like we were somewhere else and autumn forgotten.

"Sam isn't that...?" Aunty Liz seemed to be muted out.

"*Sam! Come out and see!*" Tabika called excitedly. "*It's the Council. The whole Council is convening here to hear Lucky!*" Another girl and a boy appeared next to Tabika. The girl had fluro blue insect wings which I thought looked really cool. The boy had feathered wings like Tabika. They were all brilliantly bright.

"*This is Sheba and Ikarion.*"

The weird thing was they seemed to find me as exotic and strange as I found them.

363

"Come on out," Tabika called. *"The second horn is about to sound. Daya's calling!"*

I could see in the distance the goat-man put his mouth to the horn and then another long amazing wave of sound vibrated through the night as if stopping every atom in motion and making it reconsider its flight.

I pulled on some jeans and a shirt and went out into the living room. Aunty Liz looked shocked to see me getting dressed.

"Sam what are you doing? What's going on? What do they want?"

I didn't give her time to try and stop me. I just called out over my shoulder.

"They've come to talk to Lucky. It's their government! This is really big!"

And then I ran out and along the corridor which was filling with everyone else. I shouted what I had told Aunty Liz back over my shoulder but I kept running. I ran down the stairs passing Tahira and her mum on the way and slid down the rail leapt off at the bottom and ran outside.

It was just amazing outside. The air was unnaturally hot instead of cold and damp. It felt exciting. All around the place the younger Fae were whizzing about at enormous speed apparently loving the sense of occasion and the feel of new air under their wings. There was a kind of buzzing as with a crowd when everyone is talking except it was purely psychic so all you got was this feeling of buzz without any noise except the sea pounding the beach.

I ran up toward the circle and noticed that gravity seemed to change a bit. I felt a bit lighter and bounced higher as I ran. As I got closer to the circle I saw creatures, still apparently 'talking' turn to watch me. A tall, dark blue woman with fluro blue and orange wings smiled at me.

"*Hello, Earthchild who are you seeking?*" she asked. She seemed very friendly and relaxed and I liked her immediately.

"Tabika."

"*She's showing her friends her cave. She'll be back in a minute.*"

"What's going to happen?"

"*We're going to question the Spirit and decide what to do. Look here's Tabika coming.*"

The five blue lights grew quickly as they flew toward me. Then they landed around me. Tabika gave me a hug and then she introduced the rest of her friends.

"*Daya will make the last call soon and then we'll all have to be quiet,*" Tabika told me. "*You should go back and tell your people what's happening. They'll be anxious.*"

"OK."

So I ran back to Renwick where everyone had formed a crowd in front of the house.

"It's their government," I told them." They've come to talk to Dr Prosperov."

"Tabika says when the third call is made everyone has to settle down and pay attention."

Then just as I finished speaking the third blast on the conch sounded this long, long, long sound which sorta went Ooooooooooooooooommmmmmmmmmmmm."

It went through everything and made your spine tingle like a ghost. It made all the Fae stop what they were doing and settle down. In a few seconds there was complete silence – just the surf and the wind and the dancing flames. It was eerie.

An older Fae walked into the ring. He looked like Merin, but his

365

long cloak was blue and his hair and beard were gray. He wore a crown of green glowing leaves and carried a heavy staff of wood with a green glowing jewel in it. Then from the opposite side an older female who looked like Morganne but older stepped into the ring. She was dressed in a similar cloak to the man but her crown was violet as was the jewel in her staff.

It was the strangest feeling, it was like there was a click, and a click, and some sort of decision had been made. The clicks flew. It was amazing the way they discussed stuff. So fast. It was like someone talking as fast as ideas occur.

There was a stir behind us. Dr Prosperov had come out. He was wearing a black coat and carrying his stick. He looked tense, like he was going to go out to face some terrible opponent. Dr Morozov was looking very pale. She really didn't look like she wanted him to go at all. Mrs Jones was advising him quietly.

"Just relax and be open. A ring is not a trial but it is a test. You'll know how it's going, they don't hold back."

I don't know if Dr Prosperov heard anything she said. His eyes were everywhere and I wasn't even sure who he was. Suddenly there was a huge drum boom. The ring at our end parted and everyone was looking our way.

"You're on," Mrs Jones told him.

I will always remember that sight. Dr Prosperov walking alone, with his stick, toward the flames and the strange creatures before him. He walked slowly into the middle of the ring which closed around him.

Sam's history of the Changels' origins recalls their early training by Mike, Sam's ex-SAS grandfather. But Sue's attention is wandering as she seeks comfort in simple domestic routines from Sam's strange tale. Meanwhile Sam discovers that while he has been resting, his enemies have been closing, and very soon he may have to flee.

To get your copy visit the website: www.changels.info

FACT OR FICTION?

The Kurdish struggle for independence has brought Kurds into conflict with four governments. The conflict continues as at 2017.

Ergenekon has been an underground political-economic grouping within the Turkish military-political complex for decades. In April 2011 over 300 members were arrested. While Tarik's personal story is fictional most elements are not. The GAP scheme and the Ataturk dam are indeed real. The Sursuluk scandal (involving a politician, police chief, wanted criminal and former beauty star killed in a car with guns and drugs in the trunk) is a historical fact, as are the deaths and power struggles within Turkey during Tarik's nominal life-time. The character of General Cem Erkender is a fictional amalgam of actual people. I am indebted to the anonymous Hadia (Iraqigirl. blogspot.com) for her description of life in Mosul, Iraq during the US occupation.

For information on Hwange wildlife park and its elephants I (again) recommend the works of Sharon Pincott (Sharonpincott.com). Joyce Mujuru's rise to Vice President of Zimbabwe did follow a change in the Zanu-PF constitution at a meeting in Bulawayo in 2004 where Emmerson Mnangagwa lost sway. Diamonds were discovered in Tsholotsho in 2008 and announced by the Zimbabwean Government in 2009. The stories of veterans taking over farms, the establishment of game parks and escape across the Limpopo at Breitbridge (including the guide lady) are amalgams of many true stories. The character of Bisani is completely imaginary.

The Hispanic street gang MS-13 was not active in New Orleans before Hurricane Katrina. Connections between the Mexican Sinaloa cartel and MS-13 have been drawn by law enforcement authorities but remain speculation. The use of gift cards by cartels to repatriate funds to Mexico is noted by the US Drug Enforcement Agency on their website. It is true that if the Robinson's stole six million dollars it would be one of the largest thefts recorded.

Dr Prosperov's theories rely on artistic licence with passing reference to Shannon Entropy, String Theory and the Holographic principal.

I do not pretend to be a physicist as any physicist will quickly see. However we are clearly entering a period of paradigm tension between the standard model which has come to rely on dark energy (97% of all energy in the universe) but which we can't detect, and dark matter (84.5% of all matter) which we also can't detect either. The standard model may be correct or physicists are inventing things because their gravity formulas are wrong.

As Thomas Kuhn hypothesised in "The Structure of Scientific Revolutions" scientific world views accumulate more and more inconsistencies until they are replaced by a better world view which explains more. More than three dimensions (and time) seems to be essential to the new world view and has been helpful to theories starting with Theodor Kaluza who formulated general relativity in five dimensions in 1919. Five, ten or eleven dimensional models of the Universe are speculations proposed by modern String theory and its many derivatives. Unfortunately few of these mathematical speculations constitute science because they do not generally offer experimentally falsifiable predictions needed for proof.

To understand these theories the author recommends "Warped Passages" by Professor Lisa Randall. Other texts of note include "Flatland: A Romance of Many Dimensions" (1884) by Edwin Abbott Abbott and the notional sequel "Flatterland: Like Flatland only more so" (2001) by Ian Stewart. String theory and time is extremely complicated and somewhat sketchy so I've mostly made this up to suit my narrative needs.

The superyacht Le Grande Bleu visited Auckland over the Christmas of 2006/7. The fictional yacht Le Monde Bleu in the story is obviously based on this occurrence at roughly the same time. No inference should be drawn between the real yacht and its owners and the imaginary one and its interaction with the imaginary character of Dr Prosperov.

Soviet research into parapsychology was centred at Leningrad State University under the term Psychoenergetics. Aleksandr Petrovich Dubrov is a co-author of "Parapsychology and contemporary science." The fictional Professor Dubrov in my story is obviously not the same person.

The character Lana Vilenskaya is based on the real person Larissa Vilenskaya, a Russian psychic researcher who left the USSR during the height of the Cold War but died in an unusual train accident in Menlo Park, California on June 13, 2001. The name Vilenskaya is curious because Vila are a form of Slavic fairy, while the feminine suffix –skaya means "from the region of". The author wishes to honour Larissa's extraordinary life by naming this fictional character after her. Other than their names there are no similarities between real person and fictional character.

Sam's putative ancestors Papahurihia and Te Wharete are genuine Nga Puhi ancestors and their legendary powers of teleportation and invisibility are in accordance with tradition.

All the Maori Atua (gods) mentioned in Sam's vision are traditional. The lunar eclipse of March 3, 2007 depicted in the story on the night of Tabika's arrival was widely visible all over the world but was not visible at all from New Zealand.

Fairies, Tuatha, Phae, Vila, Pari, Kitsune, Patupaiarehe are all names of elusive magical people who interact with humans in popular myths from cultures as far apart as Ireland, Germany, Russia, Persia, Japan and New Zealand. Most of these mythical people are associated with caves and red hair. They may be mythic memories of Neanderthals who are thought to have been red-haired.

Andrei Klyvev is a fictional Russian poet modelled very loosely on Nikolai Klyuev, a homosexual modernist poet executed by the Bolsheviks.

NOTES ON LANGUAGE

Tarik Gursoy is nominally a member of the Hýdýsor clan of Kurds from Adiyaman province in Turkey. His mother tongue is Iraqi Kurdish (Soranji) but Tarik's father's dialect is Turkish Kurdish (Kurmanji). The two are mutually intelligible but are very different to Turkish, the sole official language of Turkey. Tarik learns street English in North London. It is typical of Kurds in London (and indeed all language learners) to use many repeated phrases to avoid the problem of dealing with the complexities of the underlying English grammar. In this situation Tarik uses a form of mock cockney (mockney) and over-uses the confirmatory questions "you know what I mean?" and "yeah?" and "innit?" common to North London due to anxiety about the underlying language. Youtube video by Kurds in London has been my main direct source for this rendering.

Scott Highborough/Khumalo's language is centred on Tshlotsho near Hwange national park in Zimbabwe. He has inherited a great many South African terms from his father and uses Zimbabwean turns of phrase. I am indebted to Sharon Pincott for her blog posts on language encountered at Hwange.

The Gaelic prayer quoted by Mrs Jones in Chapter Twenty is Fois Anama / Soul Peace translated as follows.

O 'S tus a Chriosd a cheannaich an t-anam
(SINCE Thou Christ it was who didst buy the soul-)
Ri linn dioladh na beatha, (At the time of yielding the life,)
Ri linn bruchdadh na falluis, (At the time of pouring the sweat,)
Ri linn iobar na creadha, (At the time of offering the clay,)
Ri linn dortadh na fala, (At the time of shedding the blood,)
Ri linn cothrom na meidhe, (At the time of balancing the beam,)
Ri linn sgathadh na h-anal, (At the time of severing the breath,)
Ri linn tabhar na breithe, (At the time of delivering the judgment,)
Biodh a shith air do theannal fein; (Be its peace upon Thine own in gathering;)
Iosa Criosda Mhic Moire mine, (Jesus Christ Son of gentle Mary,)
Biodh a shith air do theannal fein, (Be its peace upon Thine own in gathering,)
O Ios! air do theannal fein. (O Jesus! upon Thine own in gathering.)
Is bitheadh Micheal geal caomh, (And may Michael white kindly,)
Ard righ nan aingeal naomh,(High king of the holy angels,)
An cinnseal an anama ghaoil, (Take possession of the beloved soul,)
Ga dhion dh'an Triu barra-chaon, (And shield it home to the Three of surpassing love,)
O! dh'an Triu barra-chaon. (Oh! to the Three of surpassing love.)

From Carmina Gadelica Hymns and Incantations Ortha Nan Gaidheal 1900 volume I of Alexander Carmichael's field translations.

Dr Prosperov recites the kabbalist Chanukkah candle prayer

"Baruch Atah Adonai, Barucha At Shekhinah,
Eloheinu Melech Ha-Olam;
Baruch Atah Elohim,
Eloheinu Melech Ha-Olam -
asher kidishanu b'mitz'votav v'tzivanu l'had'lik neir shel Chanukah.
Amein."

Translated

"Blessed are You Lord, and Blessed is Your Shekhinah,
Ruler of Time and Space;
Praise to You, Elohim,
Sovereign of the Universe -
Who has sanctified us with the commandments
and commanded us to light the lights of Hanukkah.
Amen."

Please consider reviewing this book

www.ingramcontent.com/pod-product-compliance
Lightning Source LLC
Chambersburg PA
CBHW050907250626
47155CB00001B/141